TO THE STARS
AND BACK

TO THE STARS AND BACK

STORIES IN HONOUR OF
ERIC BROWN

Edited by Ian Whates

NEWCON PRESS

NewCon Press
England

First edition, published in the UK May 2024
by NewCon Press
41 Wheatsheaf Road, Alconbury Weston, Cambs, PE28 4LF

NCP 330 (hardback)
NCP 331 (softback)

10 9 8 7 6 5 4 3 2 1

ISBN: 978-1-914953-79-8 (hardback)
978-1-914953-80-4 (softback)

Editing and typesetting by Ian Whates
Cover art by Jim Burns, cover layout by Ian Whates

CONTENTS

For Finn, and for Freya

In Honour of Eric Brown
*Who I like to think would have
been proud of this book*

INTRODUCTION
BY IAN WHATES

I first met Eric at an SF convention in the West Midlands (Novacon) in 2007. We hit it off straight away – as most people tended to with Eric. I recall, as a group of us bundled into taxis and were ferried to a curry house in Walsall, Eric enthusiastically speaking of his love for the novels of Barrington J. Bayley – a writer whose work had escaped me until that point but whom I would subsequently come to discover and appreciate on the strength of that endorsement.

The following day, Eric was due to be on a panel and confessed to being terrified as he had never appeared on a panel at a convention before (a fact that astonished me).

"What if I can't think of anything to say?" he asked.

"Who are you on with?"

"Ian Watson and Charlie Stross."

"Don't worry," I assured him, "you'll be fine."

And so he was, holding his own in the presence of these two erudite and forceful personalities.

Shortly after this, Eric and his family moved from their home in Yorkshire to a Cambridgeshire village not far from us, and we became firm friends. The two of us would frequently venture out to local pubs and Indian restaurants (the latter being a great passion of Eric's after he had spent a year travelling around India in younger days). Soon after the move, Eric told me he'd arranged to meet mutual friend Chris Beckett for a drink in Cambridge, asking if I fancied coming along. Thus began the

Pickerel Irregulars – a group of SF writers and readers from the Cambridge area who would get together every six weeks or so, almost invariably at the Pickerel in Magdalene Street. Initially with a core membership of myself, Eric, Chris, Una McCormack, Ian Watson, Rebecca Payne, Phillip Vine, and Sarah Brown, these gatherings became a real highlight. We were joined on occasion by friends such as Kari Sperring, Keith Brooke, Philip Palmer, and on one notable evening by visiting US author David Brin, but the core attendees remained pretty constant; until that is, Ian Watson left on the feeble excuse that he was moving to Spain, followed soon after by Phillip Vine who likewise moved away to escape us (though not so far), while our numbers were bolstered by the welcome addition of Beck's husband, scientist Eeson Rajendra.

Eric and I shared a lot of passions: books, science fiction, football (okay, he was a Leeds Utd fan, but nobody's perfect), food – I still recall the excellent vegan curry he cooked for Helen and myself when we visited him in Cockburnspath… And beer. In particular, Eric was a passionate advocate of Timothy Taylor's Landlord, a fine Yorkshire pint which I also greatly appreciate, though perhaps not with Eric's fervour; more than once I heard him refer to it as, "Nectar of the Gods." Rick Stein's endorsement of Landlord as one of the finest beers in Britain and a particular favourite of his (during an episode of his Food Stories broadcast in late February 2024) would have pleased Eric no end.

One area in which we differed, however, was music, which has always meant a great deal to me. Eric once told me, as we queued one summer evening to enter the Cambridge Beer Festival, "I don't get music. I mean, I can hear a song and like it, but music doesn't move me, doesn't reach me the way that a great piece of writing will. I know I'm missing out…"

At least, I didn't *think* we had a love of music in common. Except that some years later, long after the family had relocated from Cambridgeshire to the borderlands of Berwickshire, Eric,

Finn, Freya and Uther (prince among dogs) came to stay with us for a few days. We spent one memorable evening with youtube up on the TV, choosing songs and artists we thought the others would appreciate (there may have been alcohol involved). Eric surprised me, enthusiastically taking the lead in selecting some very obscure pieces, which suggested that perhaps he wasn't as disassociated from music as he'd claimed.

You may note that so far this introduction has focused on Eric as a person and my recollections of him, but I've made no mention of his writing; of the warmth, the imagination, the emotional intelligence that permeates pretty much everything Eric wrote. Such qualities are, of course, a reflection of the person who wrote them.

When it came to contributing a story for this volume, I was tempted to write something that touched upon or gave a nod to his own work; his wonderful Kéthani stories in particular offer plenty of scope in that regard, or the 'Starship' novellas featuring David Conway, the Bengal Station novels, or his 'Salvageman Ed' stories, not forgetting *The Kings of Eternity* (a novel I'm especially fond of)... Eric created so many memorable characters and settings, but the best way, the *only* way, to discover these is to read them for yourself.

In the end I shied away from writing a direct tribute to any of Eric's oeuvre, hoping that others would cover that particular base for me. Eric has read a number of my stories over the years and has always been complimentary. So I decided to include a story with a pacey opening and featuring enigmatic aliens that I'm confident Eric would have appreciated.

One final thing we had in common, which I've shied away from referring to until this juncture, was cancer, and I can't pretend that our frequent telephone conversations in recent years didn't cover the subject.

I last spoke to Eric in February 2023. He was in good spirits, and was due to be going into hospital a couple of days later for a consultation, to discuss the results of recent treatment. "I'll phone you to let you know how I get on," he said.

Two or three weeks passed and I realised I hadn't heard from him, so phoned to check on how he was.

Finn answered. "Oh, Ian…"

Eric passed away a few days later.

It's difficult to articulate how that felt; my hurt at the death of a dear friend, the shock because he had sounded so well when last we spoke, my guilt at not having made the effort to travel up to see him more recently (yes, there were reasons, but…) my concerns for Finn and Freya and how they would cope with such a loss.

I wanted to do something, however slight, and my thoughts turned to a book. My desire with *To the Stars and Back* is to honour someone who mattered, in the belief that he would have been quietly chuffed by the result. I approached authors who had known Eric and whom I knew to have valued him both personally and professionally. When asked, each and every one of them said, "Yes."

Eric Brown was a fine writer. His work won him awards, his storytelling won him readers; more than that, though, he was a special person, and that won him many friends.

– Ian Whates
Cambridgeshire
March 2024

RODEO DAY

Philip Palmer

The sludge is blacker here. Thinner. Fact is, it's more slime than sludge. The wind blows from the east and also from the west, creating maelstroms like you wouldn't believe. But Gus has seen worse. He's seen tornadoes so high they burst through the clouds and touch the very boundaries of space.

Or so he says. But fact is, Gus is a something of a tall tale teller. Swallow that crap with a handful of salt, as my grandma used to say.

Gus is flying now, near enough. His heels are shooting compressed air into the ground, carving out deep holes in the sludge which fill up almost instantly. But the recoil keeps him aloft.

Big Gus is a giant, forty metres from his tin head to his metal heels, four times the size of an average-sized house in Capricorn, Gus's base camp. Big Gus's head is silver, and bears a clown grin on his painted-on mouth. His eyes are round and large, but those are just for effect. His real eyes are embedded in a thick receptor band which stretches all the way around his head to give him 360o vision in every frequency of the electromagnetic spectrum.

And he's ready for bear. 'Cause Big Gus has cannons fore and aft on his chest and back and four hollow arms all of them loaded with missiles that can be fired out of his palms. Apart from his outer core his entire body is a missile carrier. He packs a harpoon gun too, and the quiver on his back holds the spare harpoons that he will need if he sees a flock of Stinging Stars.

Gus, the real Gus, the flesh and blood Gus, well, he sits loosely in his harness, muscles like jelly. He is encased in a VR suit with sensors connected to every body part except his penis and his tongue and with a needle in his brain that connects to his exo's control systems. He can feel the wind on his floating giant body,

11

beating against his metal hide. He can see larvae flying in the air like cannonballs, and seedpuffs, and sparkle-balls, and sludge-storms spitting and whirling. With a blink of his eyes to allow him to change focus, he can see microscopic viruses swarming, hunting for their prey. With another blink he can see a flying Black Blimp a thousand kilometres away.

The air around him is viciously toxic. The winds are so savage they would flay the hide off an Earth-born animal in moments, if it could breathe the toxic air long enough to stand upright, which it couldn't. And yet the closer to the sludge you get, the more habitable this planet is. 'Cause there is heat emanating from the sludge that allows life to flourish, above and beneath the surface.

But the above-sludgers are Gus's goal. Ugly-as-fuck- creatures that are hardy enough to survive the whipping of the winds, and that are well insulated enough to endure the below-zero-Kelvin air.

Creatures that suck up nourishing sludge through their anus and spit out arid waste from the mouths and ears and gills.

Creatures that can fly, buffeted by winds but still able to tack from here to there.

Creatures that can hop on the sludge like flies dancing on shit.

And huge swollen creatures that can hover like hot air balloons on what is generally considered to be the most appalling planet occupied by humankind.

And he is in his element here. He is a giant with rockets in his heels and missiles in his arms. He is Gus, and he is the hellion who rides Big Gus! Nothing can hurt him, or so he believes. He is the lord of all he surveys. Or so he will tell you, if you are slow-moving enough and polite enough to get trapped into listening to one of his endless anecdotes.

And now Big Gus sees a Black Blimp sixty kilometres away and he powers up. He shoots up into the air and flies like a missile, two of his arms outstretched and holding a harpoon between each of those palms. At full acceleration, this metal motherfucka is faster than the fastest Stinging Star.

The Black Blimp sees him ten minutes too late.

Like an angry fox chasing a dinosaur, the ruthless exo-skeletal hunter hurtles after the vast, ghastly Black Blimp. The alien monster is ten times the size of the largest whale on earth, and it is jet-propelled by gases venting from holes in its globular body. And when he is close enough, Gus fires a smart harpoon which kinks and veers until it hits its target. Thunk.

The arrow-tip burrows its way into the creature's hide.

Electric bolts pour out of the harpoon into the creature's body.

The Blimp twitches and flails as a barrage of electric shocks assail its flesh and organs.

The creature's brain dies almost instantly, but its insensate body is still pulsing twenty hours later, when the dissectors butcher it into ten million shards of flesh.

The General is running the book on Rodeo Day. Gus is odds-on favourite: he's had the best average for nine of the last ten years. Last year had been his downfall, though, when Luke came surging through as King of the Rodeo. Though many considered that to be an aberration. There was a theory circulating, whispered in corners, barely said out loud, that Gus had gone soft. That he'd chosen to let his son win.

Martella bets two million credits on herself. She is an optimist, and a fool. Her skill is hunting; everyone on this godforsaken planet admits there is no better hunter. For Martella never gives up. She never gets tired. She once hunted a herd of Freaks for six weeks straight, eating from a tube and pissing into a catheter, until they fled into a network of caves inside the high mountains where their vile, asymmetrical, pustulently Freakish bodies could safely hide.

And then she'd blown each and every mountaintop away until the cowering pathetic creatures crawled from the rubble, and then she'd scooped them up in her giant gaping mouth. A mountain range fifty times the size of the Alps had been lost, but the company earned ten billion credits from the flesh they'd acquired that day.

But this is the Rodeo. And the Rodeo ain't about hunting. It's about being totally fucking tip-top at a broad range of skills. It's about looping the loop in your exo-body and spinning a cartwheel like a circus clown, before corralling a herd of Car-Crashes into an armoured pen the size of Paris. It's about flying a giant robot body through air as thick as molasses while being attacked by armies of monsters more hideous than any child's nightmare.

And it's about butchering a two-headed three-torsoed Mastodon in an exo-body that is armed only with a hardmetal sword. And raining chunks of pustulent alien flesh on the space-suited crowd below you in an aerial display of virtuoso slaughter.

Martella does one thing well and only one thing; she is undeterrable. The Rodeo is, therefore, not for her.

But no one tells her that. The feeling is she's rich enough she can afford to lose a couple of million credits.

As the saying goes: who gives a fuck?

Not me, and that's for sure.

"You might want to hedge that bet?" suggests the General kindly, but she shakes her head.

"Two for the Ten, to win," she says, and the General takes her cardswipe with a shrug.

The Ten means:

the lassoing of a giant Gogol;

the Mastodon butchering;

the harpooning of Stinging Stars;

the Car-Crash Wrangling;

the Minotaur wrestling;

the sharp-shooting of a flock of Freaks;

the corralling of a swarm of Shanks;

the barrel racing;

the three spear & harpoon contests with a random selection of local monsters;

and finally, the bareback riding of a Black Blimp.

Those are the ten events of Rodeo Day. Each event has its own cash prizes payable, and there is also a prize for the best average over all ten events, plus free meals and free booze for a year. Plus, of course, though this is never publicised, unlimited free access to the gorgeous multi-gendered whores who own and run the colony's licensed brothel on Tooley Corner.

Gus usually wins, which means he's rich; but he drinks only in moderation, lives frugally, and has never been observed going to Tooley Corner. He is known by his fellow wranglers as the Monk.

Some believe he has never had sex, which is why he chose to have a clone for a son. In fact Gus has a girl in Pueblo Alley, but he keeps quiet about that.

"Gus?" says the General.

Gus gives the General a scornful glare. That's as close as he gets to friendship.

"I'll put a hundred thousand credits on Luke. To encourage the goddamn useless fuckwit," Gus says.

The General shrugs. He looks at Luke, Gus's son. Luke is in all respects a chip off the old block. Mean. Selfish. Ruthless. And the spitting image of his dad, except for the lack of grey whiskers, and the abundant hair on his head.

"Luke?" the General asks.

"I'm betting on myself,' Luke says sullenly.

"Thanks for fucking nothing, son,' Gus snipes.

"Go fuck your asshole with a rusty spike, Dad,' Luke says.

"Doctor said I shouldn't do that more'n twice a day," Gus explains, in his best forlorn tones, and everyone grins.

"Kali?" asks the General.

"A million on myself,' Kali says.

"Goofy?'

"Swipe the card. A mill,' says Goofy.

"On yourself?' says the General.

"Who else, brother?' Goofy says.

"I'm betting on Gus," says the General. "Who is gonna wipe the floor with the rest of you motherlovers this year, ain't you, old-timer?"

"We'll see what we see. When we sees it," Gus intones.

"Don't let this whippersnapping youngster beat ya again,' the General reproves.

"I never would do a gutless thing like that," Gus says angrily.

"No one *let* me win," Luke says sulkily.

"Hell, I did let you win," Gus says, cackling. "I knew you'd cry like a baby otherwise!"

"Go fellate a Car-Crash, old man!' says Luke.

"I did, I just ain't swallowed yet," Gus replies, quick as a flash.

The General makes a face: *Gross.*

15

Car-Crashes are without doubt the most monstrous and ugly creatures you could dread to encounter, on a planet full of ugly and monstrous creatures.

"You got no goddman chance, old man," says Luke.

Gus shrugs.

Every part of him wants to be gracious. And yet, he can't be.

The fact of it was, the real truth of it: last year his son Luke'd beaten him fair and square. The boy had better technique. More speed. Superior reflexes. What's more, Gus had foolishly taught him all he knew, every sneaky trick. The cocky young pupil outstrips the ageing master. Which was good, weren't it? After all, Luke was flesh of his flesh. Literally.

Gus knew he oughta feel proud. Not jealous. Jealous was just plain wrong. A father shouldn't ever be jealous of his own son. That was against nature.

He fucking well was, though. Jealous, that is. It ate him up.

"I've changed my mind, take off the money I had on Luke, I'm betting everything on me," says Gus, spitefully. "Fifty million credits off my tab, and you only pay the pot if I get the highest average, and get clear wins in nine of the events."

"You got money to burn, old man?" asks the General.

"I guess I have," says Gus, darkly.

Cause this is my last rodeo, and I ain't ever going home.

"You want to grab a beer tonight, Gus?" asks Luke.

Gus rebuffs him, instinctively. "Shit no. Not tonight. Jeez. You'd go drinking before a rodeo?"

"Suit yourself, old man," says Luke.

Gus had been handsome once; he could see that in his son. But five rejuves down Gus had skin like sun-hardened leather, and a paunch as taut as a horse saddle. Whereas Luke was, well. Clear skinned and slim and pretty as a fucking girl.

Goddamn him to hell.

"Nah, you go out, have some drinks, enjoy yourself," Gus says, sharply. "Pick up a girl somewhere. Or a boy. I used to like me a nice young boy, in the days before I had lizard skin."

"I thought we'd hang out," Luke says, shyly.

"I ain't got time for hanging out," Gus tells him.

"What's going on in that sly old head of yours, Gus?" Luke asks.

The boy is quick on the uptake. Gus has to give him that.

"Just not in the mood for a beer," Gus lies.

There is no dark or light as such on this terrible planet; no way to tell ghastly day from dismal night. But this, well, this feels even gloomier than usual. There are six moons, but no moonlight. No stars are shining in the sky. The only illumination comes from Glowfish spurting out of the sludge and mating in mid-air. Like those angry flashes you get when you rub your eyes too hard.

Even so, Big Gus is able to perceive the world through a range of senses that includes sonar and X-rays and infra-red. He don't need light.

And now Big Gus is stalking a Black Blimp. It has sunk deep into the sludge and Big Gus has spent half an hour watching it go down. He tracked its progress with his electro-magnetic eyes as it descended to its anchor point. And then, thanks to a barrage of sonar bleeps, Big Gus can see the shoals of Cuttles and Spikes that flock around it, eating its flesh as it floats in toxic sludge. Gus knows this is a creature with no pain reflex and a regenerative body mass. So as the sea monsters eat it, its flesh grows back, faster than they can chew.

Gus don't dare allow Big Gus to go into the deep sub-sludge, the pressures are too great. So he bides his time until the Black Blimp has drunk its fill of sludge. Eating as it is eaten. Bloating back up to its original girth and greater.

Finally the great beast drifts back up and breaks surface. Gus sees it and his body leaps; his body-jets flare. And Big Gus flies.

Big Gus lands on the Black Blimp's back and buries pinions six metres deep into the creature's flesh and holds on tight.

The Black Blimp fires itself into the air like a rocket, with Big Gus clamped aboard its hide. The Black Blimp don't know, don't fucking care, who or what this is. But the antibodies that live on its skin – big as rats some of 'em – they go on the attack. Biting Big Gus's metal skin, tugging at the pinions to try and rip them out, slashing him with claws sharper that diamonds. Swarming up his

17

body and over his head. Big Gus fires his small guns to scatter the clotted swarms of viral defenders. He slaps and kicks and sweeps aside the hordes that attack him. With two of his arms, Big Gus continues to grip the pinions that impale the Black Blimp. Gus knows that this high up in the planet's atmosphere, where the winds wrack harder, he will have little or no power of flight. If the Black Blimp shakes him off, he won't stand a chance.

The Black Blimp soars higher, maybe hoping the thinner air will asphyxiate his attacker. When that doesn't work it changes direction and plummets downwards a thousand klicks and dives into the sludge; and then out again, brown with filth. But Big Gus clings on.

The Blimp flies upwards again; the air is its natural habitat. It loops the loop, shrugging its blubber until its flesh is like a whirlpool. Big Gus clings on. It crashes into crags of solidified sludge in the hope of crushing the metal monkey on its back. But no dice. Big Gus slips and slithers wildly around the body of the beast, but he doesn't fall off.

Eventually the Black Blimp seeks out a fellow Black Blimp and the two monsters smash against each other, again and again, their antibodies merging into a unitary army to attack the interloper.

Big Gus holds fast.

After six hours he de-pinions and flies back to base. Six hours Black Blimp riding. A base record. Unverified because there is no independent witness. But it's all logged on the black box. Gus knows he is at the top of his game.

And that's imperative, because he knows he has to win this Rodeo. It will be his last ever. *The* last ever. Because once the rodeo is over, Gus is going to end it all. His world will be swept away. All his people will die. He will die.

Only Luke will survive. He might be an ornery and annoying little tyke, but Gus owes him that much. Luke will live – if, and only if, Gus can get him off-planet before he begins his revolution.

The Freaks.

He has always hated those vicious little bastards. But like it or not, they are a part of him now.

One day, acting on a strange compulsion (*Leave the base, fly far away, swim, then drink*), Gus had flown Big Gus far from the base and he had sunk its robot chassis down into the sludge. Once underneath the sludge, though still close to the surface, he'd opened his mouth (*That's it, drink!*) and he had allowed hundreds of gallons of toxic sludge to seep into his outer core. Then he'd surfaced and hovered and waited (*Wait a while, Gus!*) until a flock of Freaks alighted upon the sludge below him. And instead of killing them (*Do not kill them, Gus, these critters are your friends!*), he'd allowed them to clamber up his metal body and stand inside his mouth. And then, using steel cables in Big Gus's throat to generate a swallow reflex, he'd swallowed them all.

Each of the alien beasts was sucked inwards, down the empty shaft of Big Gus's throat. Into the microhabitat of Big Gus's torso: in other words, the outer core.

The sludge in which the Freaks now swam reached from Big Gus's knees as far as Big Gus's stomach. If he'd had a stomach. And above that was air, sucked in by a series of metal belches. And so the Freaks could dance on the surface of the sludge, and feed on the sludge microbes beneath them. And when their buoyancy tanks were full they could float like giant pollen balls inside the vast expanse of Big Gus's upper torso.

It is the perfect hiding place. Like all the wranglers Gus has crews of technicians whose job is to purge his exo-body of alien lifeforms. But they have no reason to venture *inside* the metal frame of his Big. And no reason to suspect that the giant exo-body has become a walking, flying, hovering alien habitat.

The Freaks are safe inside Big Gus. It's a haven for them. The Black Blimps can't piss acid on them. The Stinging Stars can't eat them. The Car-Crashes can't catch them and torture them in order to savour their pain. And there are no human hunters inside Big Gus. No one to slay them and put their flesh and brains into a liquidiser to sell for protein, and for their all-precious DNA.

DNA: the double helix of life; that is the treasure at the heart of it all. DNA is why the Freaks are so valuable: ten thousand times more valuable than a Black Blimp, per gram of body weight. There are a myriad uses in the gene factories of Earth and its colonies for

Freak DNA. It can be used to heal cancers and motor neurone conditions and dementia. It can restore memory cells, making childhood recollections return in a vivid rush of colour and smell and feelings. And it is a key ingredient in one of the richest blends of regenerative juice.

So while the Black Blimps are harvested for their edible flesh and their immune systems and the Stinging Stars are hunted for their neurons and their internal organs, the Freaks are – together with one hundred and ninety-four other species across Human-Occupied Space – harvested in order to allow human beings to live longer and healthier lives.

For this to be legally possible, however, the Freaks have to be registered as non-sentient. And thus, they are so registered. The official taxonomy audits them as less intelligent than algae or plankton. 'Animals' in name only, no better than motile plants.

But Gus knows that is just a sham. He knows that these creatures are as clever as humans – in fact, to be candid about this, they are very much cleverer. They have language, they have poetry, they entertain abstract concepts: they are smart.

Very smart indeed, in fact, as Gus has learned in recent days. The solitary Freak which had first crawled up Big Gus's nostril into his skull and connected with Gus's mind had learned English within twenty four hours. It had excavated the language directly from Gus's brain. Two days after that, the Freak had learned human mathematics too.

Now, all the Freaks inside Big Gus can read and converse in all but a few of the Earth-human languages. And they have absorbed vast amounts of data about human history, culture, and technology. Whatever Gus reads, they can read. In his leisure hours, he is blitzing his way through the collected works of literature of the human race. It will take a while but Gus is confident that eventually the Freaks will know everything that there is to know since man began to count the stars. For their memories are infallible, and their minds astonishingly fast.

Yes, they are smart all right.

So how come humans beings think it is morally acceptable to hunt and kill members of a species as hyper-intelligent as this? Gus often asks himself.

And: *Don't these poor creatures have the right to take back control of their own planet?*

Gus, in his distant ancestry, is a Cherokee. It is his fond fantasy that he is a Native American throwback, though he has never been to Earth. Perhaps that is why he has agreed to do what the Freaks have asked him to do. Because they are kindred spirits?

Or perhaps, Gus sometimes wonders, maybe the Freaks are *really* smart. Maybe despite their lack of tools or technology, they have other weapons that allow them to stay alive.

Maybe they can *control minds.*

That thought often worries Gus. But never for long. Every time the thought enters his mind, he feels a deep bliss settle upon him. And the thought quietly slips away. And Gus basks in contentment.

These are my children, I love them, Gus thinks, after such moments of transitory doubt.

What monsters we human beings are, to murder these intelligent and kind beings for the sake of their flesh and their genes. It's like stealing their souls. So that's why the Freaks deserve to live, and why we humans deserve to die!

Part of Gus knows what is happening to him. That's what makes it so terrible.

In his dreams, he understands it clearly. When he dreams, the voice in his head vanishes and he becomes aware that he is a puppet being manipulated by an evil alien race. Mind-controlled by creatures with bodies like squashed toads and tendrils instead of eyes, who are bent on destroying all his friends, and who are clearly possessed of psychic – psychic – psychic –

Then Gus wakes from his terrible dream, and he thinks: *The poor creatures – they're so lovely and so darn cute – they truly deserve their chance at freedom!*

"Down the hatch.'

Rotgut whisky, the best remedy for trembly belly on Rodeo Day. Gus drains a glass and Martella refills it. Luke slams his down. The General takes a sip. Kali, Linda, Goofy, the General and Captain Munchkin all drain their drinks in sequence, like dominos falling.

"Are you okay, Gus?" Kali asks quietly. The whites of her eyes are bloodshot, with dark brown irises around her black pupils. Her

21

metallic face is cybernetically engineered to register emotion just like a normal face. Gus can tell she is anxious.

"I'm good," Gus says.

"You've doubled up your bets outside this book," Kali says, reproving.

Gus has bet his entire retirement fund on the rodeo. If he loses he'll have nothing left. If he wins –

"That's how confident I am," Gus says.

"Leave the old man alone," says Linda. Linda is a shortass; on her tippy-toes she is no taller than Gus's belt buckle. And she has Polynesian ancestors and a tiki tattoo over most of her face. Apart from Gus, she's been on this planet the longest.

"I hear, uh, you've booked a place to the Colonies," Goofy observes. He is a scientist as well as a wrangler; he doesn't need to do this shit, he could make his living in the lab. But he chooses to be here.

"I've reserved a place. Just on the off-chance I win and become a trillionaire," says Gus.

"Where to?' Goofy asks.

Gus barely hesitates.

"Somewhere nice," Gus says. "Somewhere where a man can breathe the air, and eat beef every Sunday. One of the good places. The kind of place a man can call home.'

Somewhere where my son can live in safety, and curse me every day.

"When did you last sleep?" Linda asks. Gus shrugs. She lets it be.

"Okay then. We all know the rules," announces the General sternly.

Murmurs of assent: of course they all know the goddamn rules.

Eighty-three wranglers from across all the planet's twelve biodomes will compete. There are always sidebets on which city's crew gets the most points, but the only success that matters at the rodeo is to be the one wrangler who wins most or all of the Ten events. All or nothing. Kali lost her entire body one year, when a Black Blimp ate Big Kali up and crunched her and spat the skull out with Kali inside, screaming as colloidal sludge flayed her. But she was back the following year, wearing a body and face of metal and lab-grown plastic.

"Dad," Luke says softly.

"What?" Gus snaps.

"Are you, like," says Luke, softly, "okay?"

Gus stares. He realises: he must look like a madman.

And indeed he does. This old man hasn't slept or depilated or moisturised or rejuved in months. His white beard is bushy and unkempt. His hair is dry as a bone and it has grown down to shoulder length. His skin is even more wrinkled and rough than usual. His eyes are crows-footed and narrowed like a man who's been staring at the sun too long. Gus had seen himself in the mirror this morning, and had been appalled. He'd even thought of going in a cosmetic rejuve joint, for the sake of appearances.

But then a thought has passed across his mind, like a cloud on as sunny day:

No! Don't do that! What's the point? You'll be dead by the end of today, and so will the rest of your evil kind, you sonofabitch! his inner voice had told him.

"Let's go rodeo," says Gus.

Before I tell you the rest of this tale, I guess there's something you ought to know, about Gus and Luke.

About why this man gave birth to a clone generated from his body's own cells, rather than creating an embryo by any of the more conventional means.

It was not vanity, as the spiteful people like to say. That's not it, it's really not.

What Gus will never tell you, and what I am not about to tell you either, is anything truthful about the great love of Gus's life. Let's call her 'Clara', though that wasn't her name, and she wasn't a 'she', in any meaningful sense.

Gus and 'Clara' met on a mining planet half a light year from this planet. It was the classic Boy Meets Girl/Boy Pursues a Forbidden Love for Girl Scenario; except, Gus was an old man by then, and as I say, she weren't no girl.

How can I describe Clara? Clever, funny, two eyes, two legs, two arms, skin rather than scales or feathers; other then that, visibly not human in any way. How they consummated their forbidden love is none of your business. But love is love. So when she suggested they should share a child, they pooled their savings and found a way. But remember, this was back in the day, in the darkest days of the Galactic Corporation. That meant miscegenation between species was illegal, a capital offence.

But no one found out. As it happens, Clara's downfall was unconnected to the birth of Luke.

Boy meets Girl; Girl Gets Executed by Bigots. That's the long and the short of it.

You see, Clara was caught up in a galaxy wide sweep of non-human Corporation vassals in what can fairly be considered to be the largest and most unforgivable act of genocide in human history. Look it up. You'll find nothing about it. Another gap in the history books; there are lots of them.

And all this is what you need to know in order to understand Gus's relationship with his son. For twenty-six years, the old guy has schlepped his motherless baby around with him from planet to planet, as the baby became a child, and the child became a man; ending up on this godforsaken shithole. All the while never talking to his son about who Luke's mother was or how she died. Living a day at a time; an hour at a time; a second at a time. As most folks had to do back then, in the days of the goddamned Galactic Corporation.

So this much you now know. I'm telling you no more.

"Check forty-one. Check forty-two. Check forty-three. Check forty-four. All checked, wrangler. You're good to go. Give 'em hell, eh, Gus?" The Tech grins enthusiastically. She is real-young and blonde and probably dreams of being a wrangler one day. Gus pities her and envies her in equal measure.

"I'll give 'em hell," Gus reassures her. He swallows, moistening his mouth and throat. His body is relaxed, his helmet unfastened. His VR suit is sturdy enough to survive vacuum or acid rain and can keep him alive up to three minutes if Big Gus is ruptured and sludge flows through the cracks.

The Tech connects the neural jack to Gus's skull needle. The needle is nano-technology at its finest: eight centimetres of pin-slender metal honeycombed with datachips and processing power that is drilled deep into his cerebrum. A condensed miracle of engineering that is not just an internet router and a hard drive, but is also Gus's machine interface.

The 'snick' of jack into needle socket is better than orgasm. It is a spiritual moment for all wranglers. It is the moment when a wrangler's mind becomes as one with a wrangler's Big.

Gus closes his eyes and blinks, and when he opens his eyes again he is Big Gus.

Eighty-three exo-wranglers in their giant robot bodies hover high above the swirling horror of the Whirlpool. Trucks the size of a small town hover too, loaded with alien game. Big Gus's visualiser renders the scene with a pale pink hue, like early dawn. The exo-skeleton Bigs look like Titans from before the birthing of the Greek Gods. Flocks of tiny Hens' Teeth float calmly amongst them, their gossamer wings supporting bodies of bony armour, too stupid to know there is about to be carnage.

One of the trucks opens up and a swarm of Stinging Stars erupts out of it. They are fast and vicious. They immediately target the exos in a bold and savage attack. They must have language because each new batch is smarter than before. They no longer try to run away, as they did in the early days; instead they attack in unison at great speed, their spiky beaks upraised, and in wave after wave they charge in an attempt to peck holes through the metal skulls of the Bigs.

But the Bigs are ready for that. Harpoons hurtle towards the soaring Stars. Each harpoon is tagged with the name and colour of the wrangler who fired it. Hundreds of harpoons hit their target. But a wrangler from Icelandia screams as his metal skull is breached by a flock of Stars and oxygen billows out of the hole and his exo plummets down and falls into the sludge.

As the exo-body starts to sink, dozens of Stinging Stars fly out of the ruptured head and a hail of harpoons impales each of them bar one. A solitary survivor. But it can see that it's trapped, with no

25

way of escaping through the barrier of Bigs. So it flaps its seven wings then pitches downwards and drowns in sludge.

Gus registers three hundred and forty-two hits/kills in less than two minutes. Each harpoon injects a buoyancy ball into its victim to keep the dead Stinging Stars aloft until they can be harvested. There must be, Gus guesses, more than two thousand floating dead creatures in the air, a seventh of them slain by Gus.

Luke hasn't fired a single harpoon. That registers alarm bells in Gus's head. What is he playing at?

Gus wins the event by a country mile. He wins the Black Blimp riding too. His long nights of training are paying off. He clings on for forty minutes longer on his beast than the next best rider, a Celtic woman from David City.

The Car-Crash Wrangling is easy – all you have to do is herd a couple of hundred Car-Crashes into a containment tank, whilst being attacked by hosts of screeching flying monsters from Hell. Gus aces it; he's the oldest wrangler there, and in his youth he'd trained on Mark 1 exos, which could only be controlled with joysticks and pedals and eye-blinks. The old skills have never faded for him.

Then comes the barrel racing.

The 'barrels' are dirigibles, helium balloons with robo-guns festooned across the sky, spanning an area the size of a capital city. The cannons fire blanks but any exo who is hit has to retire from the race. Exos are allowed to collide against each other strategically, like dodgem cars. The dirigibles move, to make things harder still. And the object is for each exo to weave a cloverleaf path through the dirigibles without ever being struck by a missile, or thrown off course by a rival exo's shoulder charge.

All this takes place with exos racing at an average six kilometres a second, a touch below escape velocity for an oxygen-atmosphere planet.

Big Gus takes off fast, loops the loop, and creams the first three Bigs behind him with a leg swipe that cannons them into each other, losing them vital seconds.

That puts Big Gus a tad behind, though. Big Larry and Big Kiah are ahead of him, shooting their rocket jets in his face. But Big Gus opens up his boot jets and soars above them and pisses oil from a jerry-rigged tube in his groin downwards upon their hot metal bodies. As it hits their hulls the oil burns, creating billowing clouds of fumes, throwing Larry and Kiah off focus. And now Big Gus is ahead.

Then he flips over, reversing his vector in an instant after glimpsing a rocket flash on dirigible One, the token of a direction change. Gus then swoops and loops around One and arcs around to Two, and is past them both, looping around until he is close to Three.

Then he flips and lets Big General hurtle past him, in a failed kamikaze cannonball. Gus doesn't bother reproving his old friend, he is too busy focusing on the field of players. He back flips and hovers above the backs of Big Martha and Big Boy, and fires paint shells at their exo-bodies, staining their hulls purple, taking them out of the game.

Paintballing for giant robots; what greater sport is there?

Shoals of paint-missiles fired by his rivals fly at him like swarms of coloured hornets, and Big Gus dodges them and chaffs them with effortless ease.

Inside his exo, Gus in his gimballed chair whirls around to the point of nausea but keeps his mind and hands and heartbeat in the body of Big Gus.

Soon he will take Big Luke out of the game.

And after that, the actual Luke will be escorted to the space port by freelance security consultants with space navy training, hired at great expense by Gus; before being bundled on a one way trip to another planet.

And then, once Gus has won the rodeo, and the result has been declared, and once all his winnings have been transferred to Luke's off-planet tab, the revolution will begin. And Gus will start to destroy all his old friends in order to return this planet to its native population.

By then Luke will be far away. And safe.

At least that was the plan.

But none of this ever happens.

Gus is half way through a cloverleaf turn when a whisper enters his mind via his skull needle. It is Luke's voice, his son's voice, and it is quiet, and confiding, and anxious. "They're coming for you," Luke whispers. "You have to get the hell out of there, Dad!'

"Luke?" Gus vocalises back.

"I've heard them talking. They think you're a traitor. Dad – you're not – are you –?"

Gus figures it all out very quickly.

The conspiracy to steal this planet back has been uncovered before it has even begun.His betrayal has been betrayed.

Three giant exo-bodies with POLICE logos on their hulls come hurtling at him, their body cannons firing. Explosive shells are being shot at him, and these are the real McCoy – Gus can read the heat trails and feel the mass. His robot body ducks and dives and he thinks about returning fire with his own high ordnance weaponry but he can't bring himself to do it.

Instead Big Gus shits out a thermobaric; and takes off. Behind him Gus can feel the shock waves as the bomb explodes in mid-air, scattering the cops and the barrel-racers. Close up, this bomb would rip an exo to pieces, but Gus has judged it well. The shock waves will send the exos spiralling off course but are unlikely to create any fatalities.

After all, Gus isn't about to start killing his own kind. Is he?

Is he?

Evil slime humans kill them all kill them all kill them –

Gus snatches his own mind back. This is wrong. Wrong!

Killthehumanskillthehumanskillthe

Ugly. Dark. Hate. All the dark memories. All the times those bastards – those bastards –

Big Gus fires a missile, a real missile, and Big Kiah explodes. A direct skull-strike. Kiah is dead. Then Big Gus spins and –

In a moment of clarity Gus realises he has just murdered a friend, and is about to massacre all his other friends. His mind races. Then it slows down. He thinks about it. He finally figures it out.

Telepathy. Between an alien and a human? How can that be possible? How can –

Kill them Gus, you're ours now. Kill!

Gus is a rationalist. He doesn't believe in the supernatural. Telepathy! That's just pseudo-science! How the hell can —

It hits him.

These days everyone is telepathic, he realises. You just need to think a thought and a search engine provides an answer to your question. You say a silent *hi* to a friend with your internet switched on, and they say *hi* back. You don't need to Skype or phone or text, or use any of those anachronistic technologies; you just think the sub-voc thought, and hear the sub-voc thought that comes back at you.

Abruptly Gus rips out his neural link, disconnecting jack and needle, with an agonising wrench.

Then he reaches his hand to the back of his head and holds the tip of the cerebral needle in his fingers. This is his state-of-the-art bluetooth brainchip; ungraded at company expense on a yearly basis which is why it's made to be detachable. There's a loop, which no one ever uses except during the upgrade; he tucks one finger inside it.

And he yanks the needle out. Slowly, carefully. Like pulling a dagger out of a corpse's brain. Except, it's his brain, and he's still alive.

And then, finally, it's out. He drops the nano-needle on the floor, and looks for it, but it's so thin he can't see it any more. He can feel blood dripping from the back of his skull. His head starts to thump. He has lost his internet connection, and the absence shocks him. He has no search engines at his disposal. He cannot track or post to his Friends. He can't access weather data or news feeds or watch TV shows with a single sub-voc command, as he has always done. His brain is alone now, for the first time in two hundred and more years. Since he was a teenager, with a virgin brain.

But at least the whispering voices have ebbed away now, to nothing.

Which means: He's done it!

He's free.

Gus is now riding Big Gus old-school; with no neural link to Big Gus's body and no internet connection either. He has to navigate entirely via the instruments on the console in front of him; a bewildering display comprised of scores of dials and screens and flashing lights. He can hear the roar of the wind through the earphones he finds in the box beneath the 'windscreen' of Big Gus's eyes. He reads the sonar and the X-Ray data via the graphical displays, as a blind man reads a tapping cane. He has to calibrate the changing wind speed and his vector and velocity and height in a single glance at eleven different monitors.

"SOS," Gus says over the radio. "I need some help here. I've lost control of –"

Oh Gus, says a voice in his head, faintly. *Why did you forsake us?*

He is shocked. Are the Freaks really still there? Inside his brain? He'd thought the nano-needle link was the only way it could –

Then the voice becomes silent.

The ghostly alien remnant in his brain has gone.

Then Gus sees the giant robot bodies of Big General and Big Linda and Big Kali approaching him, looping the loop with a sharpness that would shatter any lesser metal. They pause and face him. Three behemoths with staring eyes and painted-on mouths. Big General's hull is a *trompe l'oeil* Confederate uniform, and his painted-on mouth is a wolf's snarl. Big Linda's body is jet-black and has broad shoulders and conical metal breasts and is twice the size of any of the men. Big Kali is sleek and silver, shaped like Kali herself, with a slender frame and long legs; she has double cannons on her front torso.

"Let me explain," says Gus over the radio link.

Too late. His three friends fire their weapons. He blocks them with chaff that detonates their shells in mid-air. His own missiles hurtle out of Big Gus's palms, though they are paint missiles not real ordnance; then with spurts of air from his boot-jets he moves rapidly away from their counter-counter-attack. Their bullets bounce off him, like hail on a tin roof.

He wonders: *How did the cops know I was planning to betray them? I hadn't done anything yet! I wasn't planning to do anything for another few –*

He registers, five klicks away, a series of explosions. His instruments tell him the nearest biodome has blown up. He is also aware of a pair of rogue exos firing live explosive shells at the barrel racers, blowing them out of the toxic air. He zooms with one of his twenty mechanical eyes and recognises Big Carl from Samuel City on a killing spree, blowing up his fellow Bigs.

His other eyes stay focused on his three immediate adversaries. Big Kali is bright pink now; Big General is splashed with scarlet.

Big General speaks, in cold and alien tones: "You were supposed to be one of us, why have you forsaken us?"

Gus feels a chill.

He pans with his dorsal eyes and gets an overview of a battlefield that spans fifty kilometres or more. All around him, exos are fighting exos. Bitter dogfights are being waged between giant Bigs in an atmosphere like burning tar. Missiles in flight flip and veer as their fire-and-forget sensors stalk their prey. Arm cannons spit their shells on to metal bodies.

And missile flares blaze bright.

And exo-bodies explode like stars turning nova.

It is the battle to end all battles; an aerial combat between rival armies of giant robot bodies, waged above oceans of black poison!

By now Gus fears the worst, but he tries anyway. He speaks not subvocally but into his radio:

"Guys listen I'm on your side. This is an alien assault, you're right about that but I'm on your side. I've disabled my alien mind control. These bastards are telepaths and worse. We have to join forces —"

"We know what we are," says the General's voice, flatly.

"We know you have betrayed us by cutting off our access to your mind," said Linda, without intonation.

"We know," says Kali. And her voice is cold as the air outside.

"Dad, what the fuck is going on? This is civil war!" screams Luke, whose robot body has been badly damaged by rogue exos and which is veering on a path towards his father, getting closer by the moment.

Gus understands it all now. He isn't the only one. The Freaks are too smart for that.

The General, Linda, Kali: All of them are now alien puppets. Just like he had been.

"How many of you?" he asked.

"Nineteen. Out of eighty-four," the General's flat tones tell him.

"You can't win," Gus tells them.

Big Kali fires a rocket from one of her chest cannons. Gus's instruments follow it and they register the moment when Big Luke explodes. His son's death appears as a yellow and scarlet flash on one of his monitor screens. Luke's demise would, Gus realises, have been instantaneous.

The yellow flare lingers a heartbeat then that too is gone.

I guess, being a sensitive soul, as I'm sure you are, you can imagine how Gus felt then. At the moment his son died in front of his eyes. You can imagine, I'm sure you can. So go ahead. Imagine it!

But you're wrong. Whatever you're thinking, you're wrong. Gus felt nothing at all. He just carried on living, as he had always done, hour by hour, minute by minute, second by second, millisecond by millisecond. For that's what's people did back then. To get through all the shit of it all.

"Go fuck yourself!" Gus screams at his son's murderers, as a hail of shells and bullets come hurtling towards him.

Big Gus is up and flying. He fires his four arm-cannons at Big Linda and uses the recoil to thrust himself upwards, and kinks a path around Big Kali and Big General. He head butts Big General and dents his torso. His smart shells miss their mark, but arc around and return to try again. And the three alien-controlled exos weave and dodge to avoid the missiles; but run into a concentrated blast from the rockets in his boots.

Then Big Gus grabs Big Kali with his metal fist and rips her head off. His sensor-eyes register Kali herself dying in the unforgiving cold winds. He hears her scream at him through the radio link:

"Thank you, Gus! At least one of us managed to beat those –"
And then Kali, the real Kali, is silent.

Big General is the next to die; a rapid fire series of shells cracks his carapace and the wind does the rest and rips him apart.

But by now Gus is surrounded. Four more alien-controlled exos arrive. Big Linda is still in the fray, and her guns are the largest ever built on this planet. It's five exos against one. He has no chance of defeating them.

Big Gus barrel-races a path through his enemies, dropping thermobarics as he goes. It is a stunning manoeuvre, performed without a neural link. Gus wishes that Luke had been there to see it and marvel.

Then Big Gus flees.

Behind him, the battle continues.

It surely was the Rodeo to end all Rodeos. Gus watches it all later, on the 'computer screen' that he found in a storage cupboard in Big Gus's skull. That, in case you were wondering, is a brain-computer interface without any neural wiring.

Gus realises by now that the authorities must have got wise to the rebellion, and that's why he was attacked by the police exos. Their surveillance had identified Gus as a potential rebel along with two others, and a plan was put into motion to eliminate them.

But in fact there were twenty alien-controlled exos there that day, including Big General, Big Kali, Big Kiah, and Big Linda.

And so the counter-attack was swept away, with terrifying ease.

And on that day, that epic Rodeo Day, the alien-exo bodies fought against the best exos ever to be ridden by human wranglers, in a battle for control of the entire planet. It was a war such as the universe has never before seen. All recorded by space cameras in 3D with vivid close ups and in exhilarating mid and wide shots.

It was brutal. The battle left the toxic air boiling for minutes after it was all over. There were no survivors.

Except of course, for the goddamned aliens. Almost all the Freaks survived, even when their exos ruptured and were exposed to toxic air and sludge. For this planet is their habitat. It is, in fairness, their home.

All Gus's wrangler friends died in that combat. The admin and scientific staff of the twelve biodomes were slain later, during the final clear-up. But the death that hurts Gus the most is that of his son, Luke.

I miss the sonofabitch, Gus sometimes thinks, in one of his rare, brief moments of introspection.

Gus is in hiding now. He flew from the battlefield, anticipating the defeat that was to come, and now his Big Gus is buried deep in sludge. Biding his time.

Gus is not a coward, in case you were wondering. He never was a coward. But he's old, and sly. And he has some of that Native American blood in him somewhere, and I guess that means he knows there's a time to fight; but also, there's a time to lie low and prepare your ambush.

I loved you, Luke, you musta known that, but I guess I never said so. Not ever. Not once. Too late now.

There Big Gus dwells, sub-sludge, for year upon year, just below the meniscus. And for all that time Gus is bored, claustrophobic, but safe.

So how do I make it right?

Big Gus shares his exterior habitat with the Belly Whales and the Fang Fish and the Car-Crashes and a host of other malign creatures. Sometimes they try to eat him but nothing much short of a nuclear missile can break through Big Gus's hide. So his body stains and warps, his hull becomes green and black and purple, and lifeforms bloom upon his metal skin. But inside, Gus is safe.

How do I honour your memory, you arrogant father-patronising asshole best son I ever had?

Gus has programmed Big Gus to synthesise sludge and turn it into water and nutrients, to sustain the life of his tiny human body living inside the giant robot chassis. Big Gus drinks flame every day to burn out the rest of the Freaks in his body. But they have no power over Gus now. He has no internet connection, and he knows that he can never access the galactic web again. He controls this huge metal body with his hands, and his eyes, and his ears. The Freaks are just the bacteria in his gut, and day by day he burns away more of them and vows that one day he will be clean.

By doing this. That's how I will honour you. By fighting this war, alone, without mercy, without despair. Till I win. Till I take this planet back. For humanity. And for you. And, frankly, for the hell of it.

All this happened more than four hundred years ago.

If you had known Gus back then, in the heyday of his robot wrangling exploits, you would not have liked him, in my opinion. He was a crude man, an ignorant and an uncultured and a cruel man; and I should know.

Today a statue stands in the main square of a giant megalopois now known as Rodeo City. A solid steel statue of Big Gus, and beside it Gus, dwarfed by his robot body, and Luke. His son, Luke. The spitting image of his dad, except with much smoother skin, and no grey whiskers.

The stories of Gus's victories against the aliens known as 'Freaks' are legion. Many of them are true. Four centuries of war, one man against an entire planet, who would have thought it? Who would have thought that Gus could actually *win?*

But he did. In the process, he lost most of his body parts including his penis and his legs and most of his sensory organs. He built himself new body parts out of metal and organic plastic when he needed them and he fed himself through a nasal drip, and he made his pilot's seat into a self-flushing commode. He rebuilt Big Gus so many times that not a single part of the giant metal beast has not been soldered or replaced or regrown.

And finally, after centuries of guerrilla warfare, one man against a world, a peace was brokered. A grudging but genuine truce between the natives and the invaders.

The Freaks are now to be called Mami Watas, after the South African water deities, which is felt to be a more flattering term. Their ownership of 90% of this watery planet is undisputed; in return, humans occupy and control the solitary land mass, and pay them taxes.

And so, on that basis, human beings were summoned to return to this planet. A few at first; then a few thousand. Then many more. The civilisation known as Lukeworld is now one million strong and it is the busiest trading port in this quadrant. Still a terrible place to live, but the flesh-miners who dwell on this planet are free, not slaves. There is no Corporation to control them. Genocide has become a crime, and the demonstration of discriminatory behaviour towards citizens of a different species is punishable by massive fines. And all these DNA-miners will, eventually, be rich enough to buy land on a human-compatible planet, and retire.

Don't whisper it too loudly but some say Gus himself is still alive. Three decades after his final victory he is still out there in the waste swamps of this awful, cruel yet endlessly fecund planet. His body has rotted away to nothing, his eyes and ears and skin have been replaced by artificial counterparts, his brain has merged inextricably with the neuronic interface with Big Gus.

And the colony he enabled thrives. The planet supports humankind once more. The non-sentient alien monsters are farmed once more, for their molecules and ribosomes that allow humans to live exceptionally long and healthy lives.

Gus is oblivious to this. He is entirely Big Gus now and Big Gus is him.

Big Gus, the robot giant with rockets for arms, will live forever, one day at a time. One hour at a time. One second at a time.

One millisecond at a time.

Don't look back. Don't think on what has been. Never regret.

Sometimes, despite himself, Gus remembers the past. But not often.

Sometimes he thinks about how his story has been told by gifted tale-tellers who celebrate what they call his 'heroism'. But that thought gives him no pleasure.

Let me admit it now. The truth of it all. You may have guessed already, I'm sure that you have.

I am Gus. I am the terrible father of the child born of my flesh; the child who never knew his alien mother. I am the giant metal machine who may live forever, never looking back, day by day, second by second, millisecond by millisecond. And having told you my tale, I say to you now – Do not seek me out. Do not try to find me. Do not try to make me rejoin the human race for I no longer belong to it.

Please, I've done all I can for you. Now leave me be.

LAST ORDERS

Una McCormack

The pub was dark when she arrived. Across the road, a couple of windows in Magdalene were yellow behind drawn curtains. She pushed open the door (it was not locked), and turned on the light.

She performed the usual ceremonies. Turned on the heating, then the music system. Wondered what to play and settled, tonight, on something that Martin would have liked. Fairport sung 'Meet on the Ledge' as she got herself a pint of lemonade. When Sandy started on 'Farewell, Farewell', she decided she needed something else. Hits from the 90s. Songs from a different age, before the world turned upside-down. She kept the music low. Enough to populate the space; not enough to overcrowd her.

Their usual table was the big round one at the back of the pub, underneath the television (not even repeats, these days), and within striking distance of the toilets. A while now since the table had been fully populated, but old habits were hard to break and there was comfort in ritual. She sat in her seat, placing her lemonade on her right side, her book in front of her. She took out her phone, played a couple of games of Sudoku, and put the phone back down. Amazing to think that she used to spend hours staring down into this dim little portal. There wasn't much worth reading there any more. She had been thinking recently of those early days online – mailing lists and web rings. Do-it-yourself sites, coded by hand, buried eventually under the tsunami of social media which was itself now nothing more than a trickle. She'd looked up one of those mailing lists a few weeks back. A site that hadn't been updated in twenty-four years. Dead links. Names of members (the pictures were long since lost), most of whom she had forgotten completely, but in whose distant lives she had once been intensely entangled, albeit at range. She did a few sums to work out who was likely to be alive, who was likely to have gone. Perhaps they were all gone. Perhaps they had all decided to leave. It was the popular choice.

She reached for her book. She read more and more these days, paper rather than screens, but hadn't she always wanted the time to read? The door opened, and an elderly couple came in – regulars, like her, although they never exchanged more than nods – and their old border collie. The man went to the bar and made a couple of G&Ts. The woman changed the music to some quiet jazz. They sat at their own table, right by the door. The dog slumped down by their feet, and slept. They would stay an hour or two, talking quietly to each other, and then wash their glasses, nod goodbye, and head for home. Tonight she found herself looking at them over the top of her book, wondering idly what kept them here on this emptied world. Children? Grandchildren? The dog? *Don't wait too long*, she wanted to say to them. *If you mean to go, don't make the mistake of waiting too long.*

She read on. She was working through Chekhov's short stories, like she had always promised herself she would. Once upon a time, she might have started a blog, documented the journey for a while, let the thing drift. The door opened, and Stephen came in. He called out to her.

"Ruth!"

"Stephen!" She stood to say hello, to embrace him, glad to see him, for all she preferred her own company, and she knew immediately – in the way that you always did – that he had made the decision to leave.

The first time she came to this pub was to meet the whole group. They were all writers, working in the various sub-branches of one of those genres that is generally despised and occasionally dabbled in by those who more usually inhabit loftier and more literary heights. In other words, they committed science fiction, a little fantasy, the occasional crime. They were varyingly successful. Some of them published regularly. Some of them published not at all. Some of them published once upon a time, less so now. Some of them were about to publish rather a lot. Stephen, whom she worked with now and then, coaxed her to come along one night. She did not go out often to meet people, preferring on the whole to be solitary, but life cannot pass you by entirely unlived. Sometimes you had to step outside your comfort zone.

At the door to the pub, she saw them all at the table, and nearly turned round and walked back out. But Stephen saw her, waved her over, persuaded her to sit down. Introductions happened quickly – four new names and faces that she was sure she would not remember, until the time came when she knew she would never forget. The night was fun, enlivening. Mostly they talked about the books they were reading and the books they'd read. Learned where they overlapped with each other, and where their preferences diverged. Made suggestions about what you should try if you liked that. A snooker match unfolded on the television behind their table. One or two of them (Ruth included, and Dan) kept an eye on proceedings. She planned to stay only a couple of hours and was astonished to hear the bell ring for last orders. Sally was giving Martin a lift home, and they were going her way, so she sat in the back as they rattled up Hills Road, laughing at some daft joke of Martin's. His puns were something else. They dropped her at the corner of her street, and she walked home thinking, *That was nice.*

The gatherings were impromptu at first, but soon settled into a regular monthly event. Sometimes other people came along, if they were free, or passing through, or staying with one of them. But the core was the five of them – Sally and Martin, Stephen and Dan, and Ruth. They rarely missed a month. Six years, trading jokes and stories, weaving that web called friendship. When the pandemic hit they met online, once a month. Martin's backdrop was the pub. They talked about how much they missed each other and how great it would be when the pubs opened up again. And it *was* great, even for someone as self-contained as Ruth, to see these people again – her friends – to hear their voices unmediated, to make their daft jokes in the flesh. Stephen, who was playing it safe, didn't come until the summer months, when they sat outside at a table in the small yard at the back. The five of them, and they looked round at each other, and Ruth could see in their faces what she knew was in hers: *We made it. We bloody made it.*

When they met the month after, Sally said, "Have any of you heard about these artefacts?"

Hard to remember, now, that there was time when nobody had heard about the artefacts, like it was hard to remember a time when nobody knew the words Covid or Brexit. Ruth realised, listening to Sally talk, that she had seen one. Across the brook from the nuclear shelter, in a piece of jaded woodland that nobody ever visited except her and the bored teenagers from the nearby estate, who came there in the summer evenings, caught between not wanting to be stuck at home, but unable to sit in the pub like the rest of them. She saw something glowing underneath the bracken. She thought at first it was the sun on leaves, or perhaps, more prosaically, someone had dropped their phone. When she went over to look, she saw at once that what she had found was not of this world.

Within a month they were everywhere. Six months after that, the gateways appeared. She went to look at the one behind King's. Two elegant curves, bent together to form a circle, black metal with a silvery sheen. Martin was with her. He walked round the other side and waved back at her. That was before the lights came on. After that, you couldn't look through. You could only move through – and on, to wherever they led.

Someone at work was the first person to leave that Ruth knew personally. He said the whole family had decided to go through the gateway on Midsummer Common. See what was on the other side. They were renting their house out for twelve months, if anyone was interested; a nice place in Newnham. After eighteen months the tenants themselves went through the gate. You could walk through Newnham these days and pick out any house you wanted. She might do that one day.

One night (the television mostly off by then; there wasn't so much in the way of news, or snooker, for that matter), the five of them talked about what was holding them back. Why not one of them had been among the first to leave. "Aren't we meant to be the kind of people who embrace this kind of mystery?" asked Sally. "Aren't we meant to be the early adopters? All you have to do is walk up to the gate and pass through – and then..."

"And then," said Martin, a glow in his eyes.

No, thought Ruth. *I am not that kind of person.* That was, after all, why she sat at home alone and wrote. Why she begrudged every bus ride she had to make into the city centre, even (increasingly, perhaps) every quick trip to the shop on the corner (which closed the following week, anyway, because they were leaving too). No, she did not want adventure. Imagining it was more than enough.

"The problem is," said Stephen, "none of us have any idea what's the other side of those things. You could be walking into a void."

"It could be a plan," said Dan, darkly. "Empty out the world before turning up and sucking it dry."

"I never expected to find myself living in a science fiction story," said Sally. "I mean, did any of you expect to find yourself living in a science fiction story? I feel like we should be better at this, you know?"

Martin was bouncing up and down in his chair. "But this is make-believe," he said. "Stories we're telling ourselves. The fact is, we won't know anything, any of us, until we actually go."

41

The unspoken belief amongst them was that he would be the first to walk through the gate. But he wasn't. The following week, between meet-ups and without a real goodbye, Dan left. He rang up en route to King's and said he was off. Left his car double-parked on Queen's Road with the doors open and the key on the seat for anyone passing. A fortnight after that Martin got killed crossing Milton Road. Sally left the following October. Why sit through another winter, she said. That left the two of them — Ruth and Stephen — waiting around for who knew what.

Stephen returned with a pint and sat down opposite her. Ruth waited and, soon enough, his words started to come out in a rush.

"I have to go," he said. "I have to. I can't put it off any longer." His eyes took on that shine that people got when they talked about the gateways and their imminent journeys. "I can't ignore it, Ruth," he said. "It's pulling me. Like a summons…" He looked at her. "Have you really never felt it?"

She shook her head. She really hadn't. Whatever drew them through, she had never felt it. Like she'd never believed in god, or heard a single tick of a biological clock. She'd wondered, sometimes when she was younger, if she was broken in some way. Later she decided that she was happy with herself, and the only source of unhappiness was in refusing to accept this. She did not feel whatever they felt. She did not think she ever would.

"I hope you do one day," he said. "I hope you get to feel it too." His eyes went distant. He was halfway through already. The amazing thing, she supposed, was that he'd stayed this long.

At first it was astonishing, watching the world's problems slip away. The news full of pictures of the gateways around the globe, the lines of people queuing to pass through. That initial wave of departures was followed a few months later by a second. Everywhere going quiet. A great peace descending over the planet. The lights going out. Perhaps a little eerie, too. Realising how many of your neighbours' houses were now uninhabited. Pubs you had to open yourself. Shops shut up for good. Libraries unvisited, museums uncurated. A great emptying out, but unlike the pandemic, with none of that pent-up energy, the sense of everyone waiting behind closed doors for the chance to come out, to meet again, to talk and touch and say, "How were you? How are you? How the hell did you get through that?" No, this was a planet growing daily quieter and quieter, fading into a silence that, she knew, some must find terribly oppressive. But not her. Some days she could walk through the city and see nobody; could enter the colleges unimpeded, stand in silent chapels till the light faded and the stained glass dimmed. No choirs would trouble these spaces again. No prayers. That was finished now.

"Let's go for a walk," she said, and Stephen accepted, gratefully. They washed up their glasses and put them away. She nodded to the couple at the door; she could trust them to leave the place as they'd found it. They were surprised to see her go so early. The dog slept on at their feet.

The lights were out in Magdalene. They walked up Bridge Street, turning left to head towards the Backs. As they went, he tried to explain. "Martin... It was such a shock. I couldn't stop thinking, how he'd missed his chance. I couldn't put the memory away. Couldn't think of him going forgotten..."

"Hush," she said, taking his hand. "I'll take care of that. Enjoy the evening. See how beautiful it is." Remember it too, she wanted to say, remember me – but who knew if there would be memory, afterwards. When they reached King's, they stood and looked at the black arches of the gateway silhouetted against the silent chapel; the bright light within. As they watched, someone approached the gate and walked through. The light dimmed briefly before shining again, bright beacon guiding them onwards.

"Will you ever go?" he said.

"Maybe," she said, because she thought that might help him. "One day."

He walked her down to the crossroads with Silver Street, where they kissed and hugged and said goodbye.

"I'll just see what's out there," he said (like everyone said). "I'm sure I'll be back eventually. I'm sure everyone will be back eventually."

She smiled and said, "Yes," letting him have this lie too. She watched him go off towards King's. She waited five minutes, to be completely sure, and then went back through the deserted city, past dark Pembroke and shuttered Peterhouse, and the Fitzwilliam Museum, all its treasures one with Nineveh and Tyre. Eventually, she reached the Botanic Garden. The gate stood open. The beds were mostly unkempt, although some caretaker still came every so often to mow the lawn. One of the artefacts had landed here, right back at the start of this, next to the rockery. She sought it out, a faint glow of light in the encroaching darkness, and lay down beside it, her hand resting lightly upon its side. It was warm, and she was sure, as sure as she had been with the one near the bunker, that she could feel it pulse. She watched the stars twinkle, and said her goodbyes. *Farewell! Farewell!* She would be here, taking care of things, curating, remembering. As long as she remained, she would not forget.

THE SCURLOCK COMPENDIUM

Alastair Reynolds

I had been free of the bad dreams for a year when I made the error of revisiting Ingleby Hall.

It was a bright, cold Sunday in early April, five years after it all happened. I had a good position at Imperial and had been seeing a new girl, Janice, for about three weeks. We had met through a mutual interest in jazz and curry houses. This was our first time out of London and I was keen to impress her with my car, my confident driving, and my easy-going knowledge of the rural byways of Suffolk.

I had no intention of revisiting Ingleby Hall or the Green Man.

We were on our way to a pub that had been recommended to me when a policeman hoved into view, standing next to a barrier and kiosk.

I pulled up the Morgan and enquired about the roadblock.

"I'm sorry, sir, but the road to Eye is still under water after last week's storm. You'll need to head east, on the Saxmundham road."

"There's really no way of getting through?"

He looked down at my little three-wheeler. "Not in that, sir."

A distinct foreboding came over me as we turned off down the indicated direction. I knew exactly the area that the diversionary road would skirt. Gradually, though, as the Morgan hummed along narrow lanes, the foreboding transmuted to a bitter resolve. I needed to exorcise myself of the events of those weeks. Janice also needed to hear my story. It might well drive her away from me, but if that proved the case I was better off getting that anguish out of the way sooner rather than later.

I rather liked Janice.

"Are you quite sure you know the way, Ian?" she called above the sound of the engine, in her plummy, well-bred tones.

"Yes," I said, smiling boyishly at this sunglassed-and-head-scarved passenger next to me in the open-topped car. "I know this neck of the woods pretty well, as it happens. Simon and I spent quite a few weeks here after the war."

She looked at me. "Who is Simon?"

"An old colleague." I could have stopped there, I suppose, but that compulsion to unburden myself grew stronger with each mile that brought me closer to the scene of it all. "A friend, actually. We worked on radar together."

"Oh. And does he live around here?"

"He doesn't live anywhere," I answered deliberately. "There was an... accident." I chose my words carefully. "Simon slipped away."

"I'm sorry." Her voice dropped a little. "Were you very close?"

"For a little while, yes – very close."

Ten minutes later I pulled up in a part of the road where a tall hedgerow sagged in on itself, as if it had been stomped on by a careless ogre.

We got out of the car and beat our way through undergrowth until we reached a pair of stout iron gates, all but smothered by vegetation.

"What's this?" Janice asked, without much enthusiasm.

"The entrance to Ingleby Hall," I answered. "There was a long drive-way beyond these gates, about a mile."

Janice stood on tiptoe, hands on the middle rail of the gates. "I don't see any house."

"You wouldn't, even when it was there. That rising ground in front of us blocked the view completely. It's the Mound, an old Neolithic burial site, enclosed within the Ingleby estate. The road swept around it, then made a bee-line for the house."

"You said it's not there now?"

"The whole pile burned down in '46. Arson, they say. There was a suspect, even a possibility of murder, but since no body was ever found, and the cause of the fire was open to reasonable doubt, no one was ever prosecuted."

"You know a lot about this place."

I nodded. "It's where Simon did his experiments. And where I helped him with them."

We pulled up at the Green Man about twenty minutes later. They had given the weatherboarding a lick of paint and the handful of cars parked outside were slightly newer models than in our day, mostly post-war rather than pre-war, but other than that, nothing at all seemed to have changed. Even the old pub-sign, creaking in the faintest of breezes, was exactly as I recalled. The grinning, bearded, foliate face of the Green Man, common enough in these parts. A pre-Christian fertility symbol, so the amateur folklorists believed.

I hovered on the threshold. Was it a bad idea to go in? The house was gone, but the pub remained.

"Well, come on, Ian," Janice said, detecting my hesitation. "You've promised me that drink, after all — dont keep a girl waiting."

We went inside to the warmth and familiarity of the lounge bar. We removed our coats and scarves. There were about a dozen other patrons, but no one that I remembered from five years ago.

Janice came with me to the bar. A girl was serving. I thought I recognised her as the daughter of the former landlord.

"You used to come here, didn't you?" she asked, pouring two pints of hoppy Suffolk ale. "You and your mate. Raggedy Jack we used to call 'im."

"Would that be Simon?" Janice asked.

"Yes," I said, smiling awkwardly at the girl as my eyes drifted to the wall behind her. There, between hanging glasses, bottles and optics was a very old photograph of a man in mid-Victorian military uniform. Next to the picture was a piece of framed needlepoint containing a verse from The Charge of the Light Brigade, the well-known part about "into the valley of death".

"Why did that girl call him Raggedy Jack?" Janice asked, as we sat down with our pints. "It's a bit impertinent if you ask me."

"Simon wasn't known for his sartorial elegance," I explained, before taking a long sip from my glass. "They used to make a bit of fun of him in here. They meant no harm by it, and Simon was much

47

too thick-skinned to take offence." Remembering something, I went back to the bar and asked the girl if Harry Flowers and Tom Dexter ever came back to the Green Man.

"Who're they?"

"Two old boys who used to sit in that corner and play cards," I said. "Harry had been in the navy. I think he was a gardener after that, and Tom was a farrier."

She looked doubtful. "I think I remember two old men, but that were a while ago. You'd have to ask Dad, and he ain't in today."

"I'll be sure." I nodded at the girl, and in the same gesture the picture of Henry Scurlock, the man in the uniform. It seemed the decent thing to do.

Before I returned to the table, I glanced down behind the bar and spied the solitary blue-grey copy of Scurlock's *A Compendium of Suffolk Hauntings*, still exactly where it had been. I was reassured by that, because it meant that the compendium was still treasured. I also shivered a little, and it was more than just the residual chill in my bones from the drive to the pub.

No part of this had been my imagination.

We had both finished our first pints before I felt compelled to return to the matter of Ingleby Hall.

"I didn't mean to go back there," I said, rolling the dimpled glass in my fingers. "I've blotted most of it out since the place burned down. Now that I've mentioned Simon, though, I'm afraid you're going to have to hear the whole blessed thing. You won't mind, will you?"

"I think that rather depends on the story." Janice had her scarf and sunglasses on the table, her glorious golden hair shaken loose. "Please tell me it won't be something silly about ghosts?"

I smiled tightly. "I think it may pay to keep an open mind."

Her look was sceptical but curious. "And there was me thinking you were a man of science, Ian. Have you been pulling the wool over my eyes?" She made an encouraging gesture. "Well, go on. Give it your best."

"Let me get a couple of extra pints in. We'll need them."

"Get some pork scratchings as well, will you?" She lit a cigarette with an expensive chromed lighter. "I'm positively ravenous after that drive."

I went to the bar and returned full-handed. I set the drinks and scratchings down with decided misgivings, surrounded by the cosy human familiarity of the lounge, the fireplace and horse brasses, the clink of glasses, the easy-going chatter and laughter of the other patrons. It would be so easy to change the subject, to talk about jazz or disarmament, and Janice probably wouldn't object.

But now that I had begun I had to get it out of me.

"I never knew he was rich," I said. "He was just another colleague I was thrown together with at the radar laboratory. Very bright, very imaginative, a little eccentric. But then I suppose all of us were oddballs in our way. Backroom boffins. His name was Simon Callender. He was from somewhere up north – Cheshire or Chester some such place. I thought he was younger than me, but it turned out he was actually five years older. I think he grew a beard so that he didn't look so innocent and baby-faced."

Janice gave a faint shudder. "I don't care for beards on men. That's why I spoke to you at the jazz club. You hadn't started growing one of those horrible wispy beards like all the other chaps."

I rubbed my chin. "I thought about giving it a go."

"If you do, I promise that'll be the very last you see of me."

"Then I won't. But don't think too harshly of Simon. At least he wasn't following a fad." I sipped a little of my second glass of beer. "He *was* eccentric, though. He dressed like a tramp: tied his trousers up with string. He never smoked, hardly drank and he was the first person I ever met who wouldn't touch meat or fish. It wasn't because of any dietary or religious reason. He just couldn't bear the idea of harming another living thing." Even as the memories flooded back, I forced a smile. "Once, he nearly killed both of us. We were driving back to Ingleby Hall at night – we'd come here for dinner – when a little white rabbit darted into the road. Simon drove the car straight into a wall at forty miles per hour rather than run over that rabbit. The car was wrecked, but Simon didn't care at all. Within a few days, there was a brand new one parked outside –

another Midnight Blue Bentley, identical to the last one except for the number."

"Were you hurt in the smash?"

"A few cuts and bruises. Mainly it was rather amusing, seeing the lengths Simon would go to, living up to his strict humane ideals." I attacked the bag of scratchings.

"Simon was another scientist?"

"Yes. Quite brilliant, too. Straight out of Cambridge before the war, and suitably cocky with it. The thing was, for most of us working on radar took up enough of our energies. Not for Simon, though. He was just getting started. While the rest of us were down the pub, sinking a single pint while bleary-eyed from over-work – this was the middle of the war, remember, and they were driving us like dogs – Simon would be back at his digs, scribbling notes and poring over dusty old textbooks. I only understood much later. Because he came from a wealthy family, because he didn't have to work at all, he was free to treat science as some glorious carefree game, something you only did because it was fun."

"Let me get this straight. He's a vegetarian, with all these high-and-mighty principles, but he's quite willing to work for the Ministry of War?"

"I didn't say he wasn't full of contradictions. In his own mind, though, it would have all made sense to Simon. It was necessary to triumph over the Nazis because if we didn't, they'd have destroyed the things that were most dear to him."

"Including little white rabbits?"

"Every living thing that didn't have hate in its heart," I answered. "Anyway, after the war…"

After the war.

After the radar group had been wound down, Simon approached me with a proposition. He had been working in his spare time, he said, on some obscure theoretical ideas. Now he needed to put them into experimental practise.

"Fine, old man. Why not talk to the chaps back at Cambridge, or even Manchester? I'm sure they'd welcome you."

"They're not that sort of theoretical idea," Simon confided. Then, in his typical way, he'd dropped an arm around my shoulder. 'You've got a bit of imagination, Ian – they haven't. And what I need help with definitely requires someone with a dose of the stuff. I'm afraid you're just the fellow."

I was at enough of a loose end not to deflect him straight away. "What are you proposing?"

He made a grand gesture at the ceiling, as if he could already see his name up there. "Let's call it the Callender Institute. A private laboratory, run by me, for me. With er, you, of course, as the vital partner in the enterprise."

"I suppose every Frankenstein needs an Igor. And who's going to pay for this? Father Christmas?"

Simon pinched at the string around his trousers. "There's something you don't know about me. There's a bit of money floating around. Actually, quite a lot." He dropped his voice to a stage whisper. "My family's absolutely loaded, old man."

I goggled, as I suppose others must have goggled when they learned the true nature of Simon's background. Prior to the Bentley, his sole mode of transport consisted of a rather worn-out sit-up-and-beg bicycle.

"You're not serious."

"I am – deadly. The funds aren't a problem – not for six months or so." He scratched the back of his neck, looking faintly embarrassed by this talk of money. "After that, *mater* and *pater* might start turning off the taps, but until then I can afford almost everything I need to set myself up – including putting you on the payroll. We won't need six months, though, to see a real result."

"And what would that result be, exactly?"

Simon smiled through his beard. "Something quite extraordinary. Something that will change everything, for ever. If I'm right," he qualified. "Which I will be."

"I'm going to need more than that. I've got a few job offers, you know."

Simon was decent enough not to press me on the specifics of those offers. "Well, of course. I wouldn't expect you to throw everything in with me on a whim. At the same time, I don't want to say too much about my plans up-front. You understand, don't you?"

"I suppose," I said guardedly.

"Look, come out with me tomorrow. I've got my eye on a location for my laboratory. I think it'll do the job very nicely, but it won't hurt to have a second opinion. Besides, if you do jump aboard, you'll be spending a lot of time there." He nodded, as if the decision were already made. "I'll pick you up from your digs at nine."

"Is there room on the back of your bicycle?"

"I've got a car now," Simon said.

Simon pulled the Bentley up at exactly the spot where I stopped with Janice. He unlocked the gates – not then enshrouded by vegetation – and drove through, around the winding obstacle of what I soon knew to be the Mound.

It was a similar time of year, frost mantling the fields, the only difference being that Ingleby Hall still stood.

As the road straightened out, the prospect hoved into view.

It was a redbrick Georgian mansion: a main building and two blocky wings, each three stories high with flat roofs. Given what I then knew about Simon's family money and the sudden apparition of the car, I took it as read that the property belonged to the Callenders.

I was wrong.

"It's up for a song, so I think we should bite. I've had a look round already: it's a bit cold, the roof leaks in places, the floorboards are rotten, and not all the rooms are what you'd call habitable, but it'll do very well for our purposes."

"Who lives there now?"

"Nobody. Place has been deserted for years. You know how difficult it became to run these piles between the wars. Anyone wanting to move in and make it a home would have a lot of repairs to do, never mind the basic running costs. But we don't need much: just a few big rooms that aren't too draughty, some electricity and – most importantly – privacy."

"I suppose privacy comes with the location."

Simon nodded eagerly. "Yes, it's nicely isolated, with extensive grounds. We shan't have to worry about snoopers or casual visitors. We can kip there, too. There's running water, electricity and an immersion heater that still works in one of the wings."

"You've done your homework."

I took another long look at the nearing mansion, with its blank, lightless windows, some glassed, some boarded. It was hard to imagine a place that looked less inviting, even if we might only need to occupy it for six months. Still, it was employment — of a sort.

I wasn't in any position to be choosy.

"There'd better be a good pub somewhere around here," I said.

Simon completed the purchase of Ingleby Hall over the coming weekend. Over the next four weeks we moved in and began setting up the hub of the Callender Institute in a set of large connected ground floor rooms in the west wing. Simon had evidently been stockpiling instruments and materials for many months, so the process of equipping his laboratory went relatively swiftly, aided by the fact that we each had great familiarity with many of the components and how they worked together. We put in long and hard hours, nonetheless, until our fingers were raw, our backs ached and our knees creaked with too much crawling around on cold and damp stone floors.

I was still none the wiser by the end of that first month. I'd formed certain ideas, but when I put them to Simon all I got back was benign inscrutability, a promise that all would be made clear but only when he deemed the moment right.

The heart of Simon's experimental set-up was a pair of small metal boxes: the first in one room, the second in another. Each was a grey cube about a foot across. There was a hinged metal door in the front face of each box, with a little glass window. The boxes were fitted into elaborate metal chassis, bolted to heavy experimental tables, the sort of benches that have metal tops with many perforations in, and surrounded by masses of wires, cables, solenoids, gauges and oscilloscopes. We had worked on aspects of cavity microwave radiation during our war years, and the boxes seemed an outgrowth of that. I wondered if Simon had stumbled on a new type of radar principle, or some other application for microwave ways.

If so, there might be money in it... but nothing that seemed to match his grandiose hints about something extraordinary, something world-changing.

I was wrong.

We had come back from the Green Man early in the fifth week. We went there to eat our only decent meal of the day, usually around the end of the afternoon. I had two pints of mild and a pork pie; Simon his usual ginger beer and spartan vegetarian offering. By the time we got back it was evening, with fog curdling beyond the uncurtained windows of the main room. We had set up a table for breakfast and coffee, and now Simon ushered me to sit opposite him while he poured me a glass of surprisingly good wine.

"Well, Ian, it's about time the cat was out of the bag. You've seen the experimental set-up – a man of your talents can't be too far behind in guessing what it all means."

"Don't bet on it." But I could see that he wanted something more out of me. "All right. It's to do with those boxes, something connected to microwave confinement. Radar amplification, or maybe something to do with radio astronomy, the kind of thing Lovell's working on."

"It's not." His face shone in the candlelight. There was ample electricity to run the equipment, but Simon hadn't wired a drop of it through to the dusty chandeliers overhead. "Although I don't blame you for going down either of those roads."

"What, then?"

"Matter transmission. Teleportation, if you'd like something snappier. The instantaneous movement of matter between one of those boxes and the other, from room to room."

I regarded him for several moments. "If it was anyone else, I'd say you were quite mad. You're not, though. Eccentric as they come, but no less sane than the rest of us." I took another sip of the wine, cocking my head sympathetically. "But honestly, Simon... teleportation? You're banking the family silver on this?"

"I know how outlandish it sounds. No one was more surprised than me when it dropped out of the maths. All I had to do was cast the quantum-mechanical states of the transmitting and receiving boxes into a particular formulation and... bingo." He leaned in with a sudden, wild-eyed fervour, his breath wavering the candles. "It was there, Ian – just waiting for someone to pick it up."

"And change everything." I nodded thoughtfully. "There's just the small matter of going from theory to reality – and no one in the entire history of science has ever stumbled at that part, have they?"

"We won't stumble," he assured me.

I lifted my glass. "Then... good luck to us."

We achieved nothing that first week, only some impressive flashes and bangs, a dozen blown solenoid coils, several power-cuts and a mounting bill for replacement electrical parts. There was no line to Ingleby Hall so Simon placed all his orders from the telephone in the pub, hogging it for long minutes while he went through his shopping list, dialling different electrical and scientific wholesalers around Suffolk, Kent and the Home Counties.

He wanted nothing delivered to the house itself, too much of an intrusion on his privacy, so he had everything held at the post office until he drove out in the Bentley. Three or four times a week he would make the round-trip, labouring back with the car stuffed with heavy boxes and straw-lined packing crates. Hunched behind the wheel in his scruffy clothes, beetle-eyed and fierce-bearded, he looked like a farmer coming back from market.

I'll admit it: I was always glad to see his return, especially when it was getting late in the afternoon and a quiet creeping gloom infiltrated the house. I had never been superstitious but the long condition of emptiness and neglect, the sprawling maze of rooms and passages that were lightless, the unsafe floors above us, the damp, dark cellars, were all grist to the imagination's darker mill. If the weather was fine, and I was content that I done my share of the work, then I took every opportunity to wander the grounds, going as far as the Mound at the southern limit. From there, standing on the elevated ground, the house stood in forbidding isolation.

The Mound was a curious thing: a little hummock that had the look of something man-made, rising as it did from otherwise level ground. I found an answer of sorts in one of the rooms off the main

55

entrance hall. It was a smoking den, too small to have been of interest to Simon for setting up the equipment, but not as badly decayed as the rooms of the east wing, which more resembled a bombsite. The smoking den was dusty, the ceiling given in by water in one corner, but its contents must have lain otherwise undisturbed since the house was last occupied. There were a number of chairs under sheets, a card table, a modest fireplace, a grandfather clock, and a great many stuffed hunting trophies still nailed to the wall. One item proved of particular interest. It was a glass case about the size of an aquarium, but which held the skull of a large wild animal, something like a bull. A yellowing label offered an explanation: the skull had belonged to an aurochs, and it had been dug out of the Mound. This, it turned out, was some kind of Neolithic burial site. The aurochs skull must have been put in the ground as part of some pagan ceremony, until it was dug up around the turn of the century.

The past lay heavy in Suffolk, I knew. The house was old, but much newer than the Green Man, and the Green Man was a sapling compared to the Mound. And yet the men and women who were called to this place to perform their ancient rituals must have breathed the ghost-ridden air of yet older men, men who were as dimly-remembered by them as the Neolithic people were by us.

I thought of ghosts then only in the figurative, poetic sense. I had never believed in them nor had any experience shading into the supernatural.

And even when I did, at the end of that first week, I did not at first recognise it as such.

Simon had been gone a couple of hours when I thought I glimpsed him through the main windows, standing on the gravelled drive where he normally parked the car. It was just a flash in my peripheral vision, a momentary impression of a familiar figure, but still enough to drag me from the workbenches.

I peered through the window into the settling dusk, expecting to see Simon unloading the Bentley and anticipating assistance. It struck me as odd that he had not rung the doorbell, or ventured into the house to demand my presence.

But there was nobody outside, and it was another twenty minutes before I made out the car's lights sweeping into view along the approach road that skirted the Mound.

I waited until we had emptied the new supplies before asking: "Did you by any chance see a vagrant on your way in?"

Simon's look was sharp. "A what?"

"A vagrant, lurking around the house. I thought perhaps they'd have left along the main road, and you might have passed them."

"I didn't see anyone, and I locked the main gates while I was away." Simon shrugged the matter away and nodded to the pile of boxes waiting to be unpacked. "Come on. Let's get this lot assembled and tested. We're close now. I can feel it in my bones."

"You said that last week."

"I did, didn't I." He smiled impishly. "But I really mean it now."

It was the middle of the morning on the following day. Winds had clawed through the windows all night, but relented after sunrise. The house was silent, the grounds as inanimate and colourless as a mezzotint. We had fortified ourselves with coffee and buttered bread. The equipment stood ready. Simon had bustled from room to room like a mother hen, checking every connection, eliminating any possible source of error.

"Quite honestly," he confided, "I'll be stumped if it doesn't work this time." He hefted the ashtray that had become his chosen test subject. It was an unremarkable item, a lump of black stoneware pilfered from the Green Man during one of our evening dinners. Simon had pocketed it brazenly, but there had been no repercussions on our subsequent visits.

"If you're really confident it'll work this time, shouldn't you send through something a bit more dignified? There's a bust of Plato in one of the other rooms, beneath all the cobwebs, and if that doesn't suit I found the skull of an aurochs in one of the other rooms."

"Plato's fat head wouldn't fit, and the skull is simply macabre." He looked at me sternly. "It's a demonstration, Ian, not a public spectacle. We can always come up with something grander when we show this off for posterity."

"An ashtray it is, then."

Simon placed the borrowed item inside the transmitter box. He closed the glass door. He made a last visual survey of the equipment, then moved away from the bench to the big contact switch. His hand was nearly on it when he turned to me.

"No, it should be you, Ian. We couldn't have got this far without you."

"Are you sure?"

"Yes – and it'll let me go to the receiver box before you throw the current. Remind me to arrange a switch in there, as well, so we can both be present."

"Call through when you're ready."

Simon went through to the other room. His voice echoed hollowly. "All set, Ian. I'm close enough to the receiver, but not too close. Throw the switch when you're ready."

I settled my hand on the heavy device, a foot-long hinged lever. "Throwing in three... two... one."

Almost immediately I knew that something different had happened. There was the usual rising hum of the coils taking power, accompanied by a faint crackling beneath the hum, but instead of all this leading up to the bang and a flash of overloaded components, there was only a soft, soundless pulse of pale pink light. It was like a storm glimpsed from far over the horizon, too distant to generate thunder.

The humming died away. Faintly unnerved, as if I had accidentally invoked some occult presence, I returned the switch to its safety position.

A grey mist filled the transmitter box, but as it dissipated I saw every indication that the box was now empty.

"Simon?"

His answer came falteringly. "I think you'd better come and see this for yourself."

"Have we succeeded?"

His voice nearly broke. "Just come, you silly beggar."

When I reached him in the other room he had the door open, but he had not yet reached into the receiver box. It was as if he did not want to upset a spell. I joined him at his side. The ashtray rested in the receiver, orientated precisely the way it had gone into the other box.

"My god."

"My god indeed."

"You've done it, Simon."

"We've done it, old man."

"I'll say this now. If this is in any way a hoax — and I can't begin to think how you'd have arranged such a thing — I'll never forgive you in all my dying days — or yours."

"It isn't a hoax." Simon's voice was low and reverent. "You're right — I wouldn't know how to fake it even if had occurred to me to do so. I suppose I could have pocketed a second ashtray, but... the other box was empty, wasn't it?"

"Yes. Unless you've done some clever thing with mirrors. There can't be a trap-door in the base of the box because there's no room for a receptacle in the benchwork below it."

"Take it out. I want you to be the first to examine it."

I smiled slightly. There'd been an ulterior motive to his kind invitation for me to throw the switch, and I imagined something similar lay behind this uncharacteristic charity as well.

I touched it, and instantly withdrew my fingers. I rubbed their tips vigorously. "It's cold! Incredibly cold."

"Another thing that would have been difficult to fake."

I found a rag and scooped the ashtray out of the box. Even with the rag, the cold blasted through. I set the ashtray down and jammed my fingers into my mouth to warm them up.

"Bang goes one practical usage, then,"

"What?"

"Nobody's going to be jaunting around the world any time soon. That cold's going to be pretty off-putting to any would-be teleporters."

"They'd just need to be prepared for it," Simon said peevishly. He made a show of picking up the ashtray with his bare fingers. "There. It's already warming up a bit. Just a temporary effect. People put up with vertigo and seasickness when they want to get about, don't they?"

"I'm not sure it's quite the same thing."

59

"Well, we'll do more tests. A lot more tests."

We did. We sent the ashtray through multiple times over the coming days and, just to eliminate any lingering doubt, I put a little scratch on the base of it with my pocket-knife, a mark that only I knew about and which Simon would never have noticed. The mark was present when the ashtray came through, confirming that, whatever trickery might be going on, it was nothing as simple as just having a second ashtray masquerading as the first.

Gradually the last of my doubts evaporated. We sent all manner of inanimate object between the boxes: pebbles from the drive, the loose knob from the top of a banister, my pocketknife, even a piece of buttered bread. Everything came through intact, with only the sudden coldness to indicate that any unusual event had happened. Once the bread had warmed up again, Simon even made a show of eating it, with no obvious ill-effects in the hours that followed.

"Fair enough, Simon," I admitted eventually. "I'm ready to buy it. But if we're to be equal partners in this experiment, I want a close look at the theory."

"It's a little slippery," he said, with a faint warning smile.

"And you're brighter than the rest of us – I know. It still won't hurt to have a second pair of eyes on the mathematics. You never know – there might be a wrinkle you've missed." I nodded down at the pocketknife, which we had just sent through for a third time. "I suppose the next step will be to try this on a living subject. There are plenty of mice running around this place: all we'd to do is set out a trap, and we'd have our first candidate."

"We won't be sending through mice!" Simon snapped. "I thought you knew me better than that."

"I'm sorry," I said, surprised by his outburst. "Then it's ruled out? No living things ever go through?"

"I didn't say that, either!" Simon's tone softened. He must have known that it wouldn't pay to alienate his one willing helper. "Look, sorry I flared up. It's just that the whole animal experimentation thing raises my hackles. It's all very well you and I going through, knowing we'd be exposed to that cold. That's fair enough – it'd be our choice. But I couldn't ask that of a mouse, let alone a dog or a monkey."

60

I frowned. If he thought the theory was slippery, so was his logic. "Assuming we could make a box big enough to take one of us… you'd be willing to be the first living creature through it?"

"It depends what you mean by living," Simon responded.

I brushed cigarette ashes from Simon's papers, squinting against tiredness. Simon had gone to bed and I had the transmitter room to myself. I had been working through his theory for two hours, a jotter pad by my hand, cigarettes and wine for sustenance. My eyes ached from straining in the candlelight. It was the middle of the Twentieth Century, but if someone had glimpsed me through one of the windows I might have looked like some Enlightenment scholar, not a man born in the age of Einstein and Heisenberg.

Yet even as tiredness dogged my concentration, dulling my reasoning faculties, I could not give in too easily. I had made a rod for my own back by insisting on seeing the theoretical basis of our experiments. Now that I had, though, I would not be defeated by it.

Beaten back, drawn to a stalemate, perhaps, but not defeated.

Simon's theory was worked up on a typewriter, with handwritten equations, annotations and corrections. It was the early stages of a paper, far too rough around the edges for publication. He had mimeographed a duplicate copy, which I now scribbled over in my own quizzical, questing hand. Simon must have anticipated my interest since he had clearly produced the copy in advance of our arrival. I was mildly flattered by that, since it at least presumed that I would want to see the workings-out, even if that flattery was slightly undercut by Simon's doubtful assessment of my fitness for the exercise.

He had me wrong, though. I was not as brilliant and quick as Simon, and probably not capable of the central insight that had led to the experiment in the first place, but I was no dullard. I always got where I needed to get to in the end, even if I took a few detours along the way. And my dogged, pedantic mind was capable of picking up on details that the brilliant, flighty intellect of Simon skipped right over. Troubling details were like annoying houseflies to Simon: to be swatted away or better still ignored entirely.

I circled a letter: a bold, upper case K.

Circled it and added a question mark next to it. K was a parameter that had tumbled out of Simon's mathematics. It meant something. But as I turned over his sheets and squinted at them from every angle, no explanation or clarification could be discerned.

"What are you?" I whispered.

Simon unpacked his latest consignment of scientific supplies. It was rather different this time, the shipping label referencing a wholesaler we had not used before. The significance of this became clear when he spread the contents out on the table, arranging them with a magicianly flourish, pleased with his ingenuity.

An array of little glass dishes with lids. Half a dozen bottles of some gel-like substance. Packets of swabs. And an expensive Swiss-made miniature microscope, with its own built-in slide illuminator.

"Petri dishes," I diagnosed. "And agar. You're going to create some cell cultures."

"Bacterial cultures, specifically." He studied me carefully, as if I had already formed a judgement on his moral scruples. "I'm not enough of a zealot to believe that bacteria have feelings, Ian. I won't send a mouse through, or even an insect – the verdict's out, there – but single-celled organisms? They'll be just as useful for our purposes."

"Unless I've missed something, neither you nor I are single-celled organisms."

"No," he answered seriously, as if it was a fair point that he had already anticipated. "We're certainly made-up of cells, though. If one cell can survive the Callender process, then so can a million, or a billion."

"Ah, so it's the Callender process now."

He looked anguished. "Don't make too much of it, old chap. You'll get your fair share of credit."

"Thanks – be sure to spell my name correctly in the footnotes."

Simon shook his head, smiling faintly. "You've got it all wrong, you know. Look, we'll call it the Callender-Ingram process if it means so much to you." He bent down and began to fiddle with one of the Petri jars. "This won't be an overnight thing. We'll want the cultures to be well-established before we send them through – four or five days at the minimum. It'll give us time to start expanding the boxes."

"Where are the bacteria coming from?"

"Me." Simon held up a swab. "I've done my homework. It's pretty straightforward. Pour the agar in, give it time to settle down, then take a cheek swab. Scrape it across the agar in a little zig-zag pattern. I'm not concerned that it'll work. Of course it'll work."

"I'll congratulate you now, then. Simon Callender will be the first person to undergo teleportation — even if it's only a few cells from him going through at a time."

Simon's eyes sparkled. "Now that you put it like that — you're onto something."

I didn't dare spoil his delight by mentioning that we must have already sent numerous pieces of ourselves through already, from the sweat in our fingerprints to the tiny flakes of skin, riding stowaway on every object we had tested so far.

But of course we had no reliable benchmark for what happened to those biological samples after the fact.

We soon would.

Simon had cooked up dozens of bacterial cultures by the time we had dismantled the first pair of boxes and erected the mark two versions in their place. These were half as large again: still not big enough for anything much larger than a cat, but requiring a suitably scaled-up arrangement of wires, cables and magnets. This in turn put an equivalently larger strain on Ingleby Hall's Edwardian electrical arrangements. Simon had arranged banks of war-surplus capacitors to store up the domestic current and spit it out in one big rush when we needed it, but the capacitors brought troubles of their own. They needed constant nursing, and the heavy current load strained every connection to its limit. We got the enlarged boxes to work, but it was always touch-and-go. With the flashes and bangs of overloaded parts, the constant smell of burning insulation or worse, and my harried rush to fix this or replace that, I really had begun to feel like Igor.

Still, the enlarged boxes enabled us to increase our repertoire of test subjects. We sent through two dusty volumes of Gibbons'

Decline and Fall, Plato's bust, a small fireguard, the first of the bacterial cultures, the aurochs' skull, and even an alarm clock. The clock was the first complicated mechanical thing we had sent through (there was no way I risking my wrist-watch) and it was a relief when it warmed-up again and started ticking just as before.

For old time's sake, I moved that we send the ashtray through, but I couldn't find it in any of the rooms.

"I haven't seen it for a few days," Simon admitted distractedly. "I assumed you'd got a guilty conscience and taken it back to the Green Man."

"My conscience? I wasn't the one whole stole it!"

"I appropriated it in the interests of science," Simon declared grandly. "Not the same at all. When it turns up, they can have the bally thing framed as far as I'm concerned. When did you last see it?"

"I don't know. Three or four days ago. Five at the most. I distinctly remember, because…"

Simon picked up on my hesitation. "Because?"

"All right – I'll come clean. Early on, I still wasn't sure if I trusted you. So I put a little mark on the base of the ashtray, using my pocket-knife."

He looked less appalled by this than I had expected. "So that if I swapped it, you'd know."

"Well, yes."

"Good thinking. It's exactly what I'd have done if our roles were reversed."

"The mark wasn't there," I said. "At least, I couldn't see it as distinctly as before."

"We sent that ashtray through dozens of times. A little scratch could have been polished-off just by the ashtray being handled repeatedly."

"Yes," I answered carefully. "That's what I told myself. Anyway, it's irrelevant now. It's lost somewhere in this chaos you call a laboratory. We'd better pray it turns up, or you really are going to have to invent some story about the first thing you sent through. History wouldn't thank us for mislaying one of the most important objects in the history of mankind!"

64

"Bugger history, old man. History's what we're doing, not what we're doing it with." His face creased with sympathy. "Look, your precious ashtray is bound to turn up sooner or later, isn't it? It's not as if it could have gone anywhere."

Simon lifted the Petri dish out of the receiver box and moved it immediately to the heated platter that had arrived in the latest consignment.

It was the seventh time we had sent one of the bacterial cultures through. The first six had been busts: the cold snap killed the organisms stone dead, although of course it took several days of post-transmission observation to be absolutely sure of that. With this latest test, Simon had changed the set-up somewhat. Now he warmed up the culture as far as he dared before sending it through, and he had the heated platter ready to raise the temperature again immediately afterwards. The cold snap couldn't be eliminated, but Simon hoped that these interventions would provide enough of a buffer for the organisms to survive.

"Maybe living things just aren't meant to go through," I cautioned him, as we warmed our bones by the fireplace in the Green Man. "And perhaps that wouldn't be such a bad thing. There's only so much change the world can absorb in a short time, Simon. Aeroplanes, wireless, television, the A-bomb... and now teleportation? It might just be too much."

"If I don't do it – if we don't do it – someone else will, mark my words." He raised his eyes from the listless game of dominos we had been playing. "If someone's going to be first, it might as well be us."

"Just as long as you promise we won't rush any of the steps."

"Why would we rush?"

"Because you can't wait to be the first person to go through," I answered. "Don't say it isn't so. The boxes are already large enough for many practical applications, and you say range isn't a problem. You could transmit vaccines halfway around the world, but you're already itching to make the boxes bigger still."

"We could send medicines," Simon admitted thoughtfully. "Wouldn't it be better still to send doctors and nurses?"

I had no good answer for that. "Just don't get ahead of yourself. All this will come in good time. You think there are others nipping at our heels, but it's not necessarily so. I had a look at that theory: it's just as difficult as you said. I think it took a very special mind to see the possibilities, perhaps the sort of mind that only comes along once in a generation."

Simon made a theatrical show of patting his pockets. "If you're expecting flattery to get you another pint, I'm afraid I'm all out."

I shook my head, amusedly exasperated. He could afford to change the world, but scraping together enough money for a decent couple of rounds was still beyond him. Some things never changed. Simon was rich, but that hadn't made him any less tight.

"I'll get them in." I rose from the table. "About the theory, though, now I've mentioned it. That parameter you call 'K' – what does it mean?"

He looked surprised and impressed. "You got that far? Bravo, old chap."

"I said it was difficult, not that I hadn't tried. So what is K, since you surely must know?"

He waved aside my interest. "Oh, it's nothing important."

"Mm," I said, refusing to be deflected. "In some ways it looked like a time operator. In other ways, it looks more like some bulk property, like temperature or gas pressure."

"It's not either of those things. It's... nothing. Look, are you going to the bar or not?"

"You don't actually know what it is, do you?"

Simon scowled. "I didn't say that."

"Whatever K is," I said, turning from him, "it had better not come back to haunt us."

Simon looked up from the microscope with impish delight. His beard, gluey with neglect, speckled with breadcrumbs, stuck out like a paintbrush.

"It's alive! I was pretty sure yesterday, but I wanted another twenty-four hours just to be certain. The colony's growing again."

"As quickly as before?"

"Oh, maybe a little slower, but that could be down to any number of factors. It's not as if we've had months of experience with these cultures. We're physicists, not common-or-garden biologists!"

"Well, that's excellent news," I said guardedly.

"There's no reason not to press ahead now, Ian. Yes, we'll run more samples through, and monitor them closely, but there's nothing to stop us building the next version of the boxes. We've got almost all the parts we need already here, and I've already got orders out for the remaining bits."

"How big is this pair of boxes going to be?"

"Big enough."

"We can barely arrange enough power to work the existing set-up. We nearly had a fire last time. Have you thought about that?"

"Of course." Still squinting from having his eye pressed to the microscope, he looked doubly offended by my question. "We'll use more capacitors, bigger and more powerful ones. I've already looked at the requirements." He observed me carefully. "What's wrong — are you getting cold feet?"

"I just feel that there's plenty of useful testing we could still be doing with the boxes as they are. I'm also concerned that we're rushing into practise when we still don't have any adequate understanding of the theory."

Simon's look hardened. "You're still not wound-up about that silly parameter, are you?"

"I worry that we're missing something."

"Which is why we're doing these tests — to provide a set of empirical data." His tone became faintly patronising, as if I were the freshman student, he the senior lecturer. "Theory and experiment never move in lockstep, Ian — sometimes one's ahead of the other, sometimes behind. This is how science works." He shook his head, muttering something about he shouldn't have needed to tell me any of this.

I raised my hands. "All right — we push on at your pace. But we still take every reasonable precaution. And just because you've brushed it under the carpet, I'm not going to stop thinking about K."

"Be my guest," he said off-handedly, before returning his eye to the microscope. He adjusted the focus wheel with one hand and made an annotation in his journal with the other.

I stood there fuming internally for a few seconds, then left him to it. I needed to fill my lungs with fresh air, something other than the cold, fetid atmosphere of Ingleby Hall.

Three days later we were in that uncomfortable limbo between tearing down one version of the experiment and being ready to operate the next. The rooms were at their most chaotic and disorganised, with crates and packing material strewn everywhere. The enlarged boxes were complete, but not all the wiring around them had been connected. Simon had been on the telephone at the Green Man haranguing his supplier about the latest batch of capacitors, which had not arrived on schedule. His mood had become disagreeable, frustrated by these setbacks.

As much as I looked for reasons to be away from the house, I no longer enjoyed our joint visits to the Green Man. They had become uncomfortable experiences. Distracted by the experiments, Simon had not been looking after himself. His beard had grown more unruly, his hair a bird's nest of tangles and dirt. His clothes had become steadily more tattered and threadbare. Worse, he seemed to be sleeping in the same garments, neither changing nor washing. It was one thing to put up with his eccentricities while we were slaving over the equipment, but in the pub we were on public display. When I noticed other patrons pinching their noses at my unwashed companion, I found myself furtively grimacing back at them, as if to admit that I was just as offended. There was no point suggesting to Simon that he might venture into the exotic realms of soap and water, or even a trip to the barber. Any activity that interrupted our preparations for the bigger boxes was to be brushed aside as an irrelevance. He only ate and drank to feed the infernal machine that was Simon Callender, and still he resented the wasted hours that these activities cost him. Had he been able to keep at his bench, sustained only by a drip-bag of nutrients, I think he would have been very content.

There was another reason why the pub had become a torment, rather than an escape. Our conversation had become strained, the enthusiasm and mutual excitement of the early days long since exhausted. Now we seemed to argue about nearly everything.

Simon had stopped trusting me. It was nothing he would come out and say it to my face, but I could tell that he no longer regarded me as the ideal choice of scientific co-conspirator. I had quibbled too much with his plans, and made far too much of that theoretical grey-area. I had caught him off-guard by understanding just enough of the theory to see the part that neither of us understood, and he did not like me for that.

Igor had got above his station.

In a way, it was to be expected. Almost all scientific partnerships dissolve into acrimony. The only surprising thing was that our enterprise had run its course in a matter of weeks, rather than years.

I consoled myself that it wouldn't matter in the long run. Simon's supply of money wasn't inexhaustible, and sooner or later the experiments would need to be either wound-down or massively expanded. Either way, it wouldn't be just the two of us any more. If Simon handed over this work to the government, the laboratory would probably be relocated to one of the major academic centres, and a huge amount of money and manpower directed at it. I could either step away completely, or find some role on the periphery. Unless they put Simon in charge of the whole thing, which was unlikely from any number of angles – not least Simon's total dislike of any academic or scientific position that involved even a hint of administration.

Still, these were concerns for the future. A few more weeks, I figured, was all I had to put up with. Provided we kept to our own little corner of the pub, the odd glances were minimised. We still had dominos, and I still had to keep dipping my hand into my pocket.

At the very least, I'd have a hell of a story to tell someone when it was all in the past.

"A hell of a story to tell to someone just like me, I suppose," Janice remarked. She exhaled her cigarette, regarding me with a sort of judicial intensity. "Although I only have myself to blame for sitting here and believing any of it."

"What part don't you believe?"

"Oh, only all of it. The world didn't change, did it? If your friend really had come up with... what did you call it, tele-whatsit?"

"Teleportation."

She nodded emphatically. "If there'd been anything in it, why aren't we teleporting around now? Why did we drive here in your funny little three-wheeler, instead of getting into a box and being whisked from A to B in a flash of pink light?" She had her elbow jammed on the table, the cigarette held daintily upright. "You have to admit it, Ian, it's a bit of a problem for your story."

"It isn't. The story's all true. The only problem is that Simon didn't really invent teleportation. He invented... something else. Something he wasn't expecting to invent. Something problematic."

Janice frowned. "You're really going to drag this one out, aren't you?"

I nodded to her glass. "Another?"

"A lemonade this time. And then I really think we ought to be getting back to London. We mustn't be late for Ronnie Scott's."

I went to the bar, ordered Janice's lemonade and contented myself with just a half of mild. Then I spoke quietly to the landlord's daughter, and pointed to the little bookshelf tucked down behind the bar, out of sight of the casual patron.

"Henry Scurlock's compendium, please."

"You know about that, do you?"

"I do."

"There'll be hell to pay if you get a drop of beer on it."

"I swear I'll treat it carefully."

She passed me the little blue-grey volume with a curious warning in her eyes.

"You'd better."

"Thank you," I said.

It all happened after the big argument.

A calm had come before the storm: we had been operating the enlarged boxes for two days, sending through a variety of objects and running the usual batteries of tests and measurements. We did no more than three transmissions per day: it was as much as the equipment could take before something overheated or burned out. Although Simon desired to proceed more quickly, he accepted that there was a balance between haste and the time spent taking the apparatus apart just to swap out some tiny resistor or vacuum tube buried deep in the innards. Slow and steady won the day.

Much to my temporary relief, Simon had stopped talking about being a human test subject. Although I was positive that the intention still nestled somewhere in his mind, I'd satisfied myself that it wouldn't happen until at least the next set of boxes. The present arrangement would only have suited the most desperate contortionist.

Things reached a head late in the afternoon. I was finishing off some electrical repairs around the receiver box, Simon busy in the other room. Throughout the day we had maintained a level of businesslike communication: not exactly warm, but enough to get our mutual tasks completed. And we had made a prior arrangement to go out the Green Man at four, where I was looking forward to my first real meal of the day. Since the deterioration in our partnership, neither of us had been diligent in keeping the house stocked with the bare essentials like milk, coffee and bread.

"Simon," I called out to the other room, glancing irritatedly at my wristwatch. "It's already half past. Whatever you're doing, it can wait until tomorrow."

"It's not even three, old man," he returned, with a breezy indifference to my request. "You're off by an hour."

I sighed. "Have you noticed the sun going down over the Mound? It's getting on and I'm hungry. You might run on air and theorems – I don't."

There was a pause. "All right, now that you mention it – maybe it's this silly thing running slow."

I had to go through to him to get out of the house. I grabbed my coat and wandered into the transmitter room, where Simon still had his elbows deep into the wire-loom enclosing the box. He had his threadbare green jumper off, his sweat-stained shirt sleeves rolled up, and I was startled by how thin his arms seemed, more like a pair of fleshless bones projecting from a cadaver.

I took a measured look at him then, forcing myself to see him anew, to see beyond the mess of beard and hair to the man beneath. It was a shock. I had been so distracted by his lack of cleanliness and grooming that I had not noticed him becoming steadily more exhausted and depleted over these past weeks.

"Simon," I said, with a sudden flush of empathy, a memory of the friendship this enterprise had been built on. "You've got to take more care of yourself. You look worn out."

"I've got a whole lifetime to worry about this body," he retorted. Then he withdrew an arm and hefted the white alarm clock. "You're right: I didn't realise how late it was getting. It's the fault of this thing, running slow." He tossed the alarm clock into the metal wastebasket he kept near the bench.

"It can't be that bad. You mustn't have set it properly."

"I set it by your watch only this morning. It's lost a whole hour and a half in just... what, seven hours or so?"

I shook my head doubtfully. "I've never heard of a clock keeping time that badly. Anyway, there was no trace of it running slow until we sent it through. That's a little odd, don't you think?"

"You're determined to find everything a little odd, Ian. What are you actually suggesting here – that the clock's been affected by the process?"

I gave an uneasy shrug. "What else? Maybe that cold snap did something to the metal in the spring, or gummed up the clock oil." Then, with a dark, prickling insight: "Your bacterial cultures were also sluggish to get going again, weren't they. Isn't that another way of saying they were running slow as well?"

"Hang on, first it's springs and clock oil, then it's bacteria?"

"I'm not saying I have an explanation – just that it's unusual."

"All right, then we'll blame both on the cold snap. And before you drag it up again, it's nothing to do with your bally K parameter."

The truth was, it hadn't even crossed my mind that the slow clock and the sluggish cultures might have something to do with K.

Until Simon put the idea there.

"All right," I said, too weary to be dragged into another squabble. "Let's forget all about that. I'm buying tonight, strangely enough." I nodded in the general direction of the bathroom just off the entrance hall. "Go and splash some rusty water on your face, and for pity's sake drag a comb through that caveman get-up you call hair. You're starting to alarm the locals."

Simon dragged his sleeves down and scrambled into the tatty, threadbare net that was his jumper. He grinned. There was something stuck in his teeth. "Anything for you, old chap."

"Good. Oh – and one other thing, before I forget. The knife I lent you this morning – I need it to pare back some insulation on the new coils."

I held out my palm in readiness.

"You've had it back."

"I'm rather sure that I haven't."

Simon glared at me. "It was right here, on this bench, until noon. I went out to fetch something from the Bentley, and when I came back in again it wasn't where I'd left it. I assumed you'd come back for it while I was away."

"I didn't. That knife was a present from my father. I think I'd remember if I'd come back for it."

"Well, it's not my bally problem. It's just a silly little pocket-knife."

I raised a hand, balled a fist, but had the good sense to step back from hitting him.

"To hell with it. I don't need your bloody company in the pub anyway. I'm taking the car." Witnessing Simon's indifference to my outburst, the rage drained out of me like the air from leaking balloon. I left him turning back to the equipment, his mind already eager hostage to the challenge before him.

The lounge bar was quiet. I ordered some food and nursed a drink, realising how pleasant it was not to have Simon's glowering, scarecrow-like presence opposite me. I had no conversational partner but Simon's absence was no great loss in that department. He had been entertaining once, capable of little flickers of insight, empathy and humour, before the experiment consumed him like a mania. It was weeks since I had been at ease in his company. Now, if only for a couple of hours, I felt a pressure lift off me.

A sudden insight jolted me to alertness.

Leaking balloons. Pressure. Atoms and molecules jostling around, kinetic energy and collisions.

I started thinking about K again.

It was a chimera, a parameter that had a similarity to the way that time normally appeared in our equations, but which at the same time (no pun intended) looked more like a bulk statistical property, like temperature or pressure.

On the scale of individual atoms or molecules, pressure had no meaning. Lots of atoms had to jostle into lots of other atoms before the sum of effects emerged as the physical quantity we called pressure. It was an emergent property, as was temperature.

K's nature hinted that – at least in the context of Simon's experiment – time needed to be considered as an emergent property.

The insight seemed significant. I felt I was on the verge of something important, perhaps even crucial. But I could go no further with it.

Two old boys had been sitting in the corner of the lounge bar. I recognised them from our previous visits. Catching my eye, one them waved encouragingly and beckoned me over.

"Where's Raggedy Jack, then?"

I frowned. "Jack?"

"Your funny-looking mate."

"I'm afraid Mr Callender's too busy to come out tonight." Simon had placed an injunction on me about speaking about our business, but now that I was alone I felt my tongue loosening, almost thrillingly so. "We're research scientists, conducting experiments at Ingleby Hall."

"Funny old place for experiments," the other man said, with a dry chuckle. "Although I 'spose if anyone wasn't going to be put off by it, it'd be one of you boffins." He patted a vacant stool. "Here, sit down with us. We could use another partner four All Fours."

"I'm afraid I'm not terribly good with cards."

The first one laughed aside my excuse. "Neither's he, and that don't stop him! What's your name, if you don't mind me asking?"

"Ian," I answered cautiously. "Ian Ingram."

"Tom Dexter," said the one who had called me over.

"Harry Flowers," said the other. "Blossom to my pals."

I hesitated, caught between making my excuses and making the best of the offer of temporary company. In the end, companionship triumphed. They seemed friendly enough, and I had missed the easy ebb and flow of normal conversation. With Simon it was too much of an intellectual game.

"Would either of you gentlemen like another drink?"

"Now you're asking!" Tom Dexter winked at his companion. "I told you they weren't *both* strange coves, didn't I, Bloss?"

"Two pints of mild will do us nicely," Harry Flowers proposed.

"Two pints it is. And I'll gladly join you for a round of cards." I raised a finger in gentle warning. "It will need to be just the one, though. I can't leave Mr Callender alone all evening, and I shouldn't have too much before driving back."

I came back with three pints expertly cradled between my hands. I set them down without spilling a drop, then eased into the vacant stool.

"To your health, gentlemen." We made additional introductions: I learned that Dexter was a farrier, Flowers a jobbing gardener who had been a merchant seaman in the first war. I nodded at the latter: "What did you mean, Harry, about us being boffins, and not being put off Ingleby Hall?"

Flowers and Dexter exchanged mildly quizzical glances. I wondered for a second if they were in on some joke that I was not, until I realised that they might well have been thinking exactly the same thing: that I was the one having them on.

"Was it you bought that place, or your mate Mr Callender?" Flowers asked. "We know someone's bought it. Everyone in Suffolk knows that."

"Mr Callender bought it," I answered. "Despite appearances, he's from quite a well-off family. They put up the money, however much it was. I'm afraid I'm not in the know about that part."

"He was prepared to buy it, then, even with the reputation?" asked Dexter.

"You mean the poor condition of the place? It didn't really matter for our purposes."

"He's talking about the haunting," Flowers said, rolling up his sleeve. He had a tattoo on his forearm, just above the cuff: a compass rose. "The ghost of Ingleby Hall." He appraised me carefully. "Or didn't your mate mention that part?"

"He didn't," I said quietly.

Dexter leaned in. "It's what's scared the other buyers away, even with the price knocked as low as it was. Although I suppose you being scientific men, you wouldn't be worried about a little haunting."

"Well, quite." I sipped at my beer, but my uneasiness must have been easy to read. I remembered the figure I'd seen in the drive, the one I'd mistaken for Simon. "This haunting... what form is it supposed to take?"

"Interested, is you?" Flowers asked, with a certain mean delight.

"I've a layman's interest in folklore, local myth, that sort of thing."

Whether they believed that or not, Dexter took it as a prompt to leave the table and drift to the bar. I watched him, wondering what was his business. There was some low exchange between Dexter and the barman, and then the latter dipped his head down beneath the bar. He came back up with a small rectangular item which he passed to Dexter.

Dexter returned to the table. He resumed his position and placed the item on the dry patch in the middle of the table. It was an old-looking book, a blue-grey thing about the size of a small bible.

"This is the only one," Dexter said, patting the book gently. "It belongs to the pub. Never leaves the pub. Never leaves this room, so far as I'm told. It's Henry Scurlock's *Compendium of Suffolk Hauntings*."

Observing my evident confusion, Flowers said: "You've seen a picture of him every time you've been in the Green Man, right above the bar. Henry Scurlock was the landlord of the Green Man between 1857 and 1872. He came here straight after the Crimean war. That's him in his uniform in the photograph."

"And this is the little book he wrote," said Dexter. "Collecting all the stories he could find about ghosts and hauntings in this part of Suffolk, within about twenty miles of the Green Man. Which, I don't need to tell you, includes Ingleby Hall, and the burial mound inside the grounds."

Dexter opened the book and found a particular pair of pages. It lay open with its back to the table, obligingly so.

"It started here, in the Green Man. Henry saw him in this room, one night after closing."

"Him?"

"Raggedy Jack." Dexter's finger alighted upon an engraving of a pen and ink sketch. The image depicted a wild, ghoulish form caught in rays of slanting lamplight. The spectral figure was more skeleton than man, although beard, hair and traces of clothing still adhered to the withered, bony frame. "He wasn't the first to see Jack, and he wasn't the last. That's what got him started on the compendium. He talked to everyone he could and gathered up all the accounts he could find, going back hundreds of years."

I nodded, reminding myself that this act of private scholarship was already ninety-odd years in the past, the better part of a century.

"Other people who'd seen Raggedy Jack?"

Dexter nodded sombrely. "Aye. All across the area, from before Tudor times and up to the present. Sometimes given different names, but always the same cove. Henry saw him not long after getting back from the war. He had death on his mind a lot in those days, after all the pals he'd lost in Crimea. P'raps it was what called Raggedy Jack to him."

A cloying coldness draped itself over me. "Did Henry know who Raggedy Jack was?"

"He gathered up all the stories, and sifted through 'em," Flowers said. "Some said Raggedy Jack was trying to find his way back to a village that had been burned down in the plague. That's why he wanders all over this part of Suffolk, because he's trying to find something that isn't there any more. Others reckoned he was a Saxon nobleman trying to unearth his treasure. Others, that he was older still. What with that burial mound at Ingleby..."

"They buried the aurochs there," I said.

Flowers squinted. "The what, lad?"

"It's a sort of cow, extinct in Britain since Neolithic times. Whoever had Ingleby Hall in the past must have dug it up and put it in a glass case."

"Bad luck, doing something like that," Dexter said.

"I suppose one might ask why the Neolithics picked that spot for their burial site."

Flowers shrugged, as if the answers were obvious. "Because there's always been funny goings-on around here. It's all there in the *Compendium*."

Dexter leaned in confidentially. "The thing is, Ian, when we saw you with your mate…" But he bit back on whatever he was going to say.

"What?" I pressed.

"We didn't mean no offence by it," Flowers said urgently.

"I don't know what it is I'm supposed to be offended about."

Dexter fortified himself with a sip of mild. "It's just that with him being so wild-looking, and them clothes of his practically falling off him, we thought he looked like the living reincarnation of Raggedy Jack."

Something clunked in my head. It was a quiet, undemonstrative mechanical process, like a coin going through the innards of a well-maintained cigarette machine.

"I think I understand K," I said, as the coldness infiltrated my bones. Coldness and terror: an icy presentiment of imminent disaster.

"Who's Kay when she's at home?" Flowers asked.

I smiled through a rising panic. "I'm sorry, gentleman, but I'm afraid I won't be able to join you for All Fours. I must return to Ingleby Hall immediately."

I drove like the devil down night-lit lanes. I cursed Simon for not installing a telephone line: at least I could have called ahead, for all the good it would have done. No, no good at all. Simon was beyond verbal reasoning now; I would have to force the truth into him like a child being fed some foul-tasting medicine.

It all hinged on K. I understood that now. All I needed to do was make Simon understand, even if I had to ram his face into the evidence, and that would be enough for him to know never to attempt to use the apparatus.

Henry Scurlock's *Compendium of Suffolk Hauntings* had been part of it. Harry Flowers' compass rose tattoo, as well. And the thing that should have been obvious to us both, every time we walked into the Green Man.

The Bentley's headlamps swept the austere façade of Ingleby Hall, rendered pale and colourless at night. The windows were all dark except for a handful scattered across the ground floor of the west wing. I discerned no movement within, but equally no sign of catastrophe. With my heart in my mouth I jammed the car to a halt, extricated myself and sprinted across the gravel for the main door.

"Simon!" I called, as soon as I was inside. "Whatever you're doing, stop right now! We've got it all wrong!"

There was no answer. The equipment hummed, as it always did. And from somewhere – perhaps the receiver room – came a faint muffled disturbance, as of some animal trapped inside a wall.

I progressed through to the transmitter room, still calling out. The room was candle-lit, but my arrival must have created a draught that extinguished all but two candles. Their paltry glow only made the room less tangible, more shadow-ridden.

"Simon! I owe you an apology about the pocketknife. You didn't lose it. And neither of us lost the ashtray. They've slipped away! If we'd been looking at them closely, we'd have seen them vanish! Everything vanishes eventually!"

There remained no answer. I continued walking across the transmitter room and then something caught me across the throat.

I stopped, shocked and disturbed. I fingered the whiskery edge which had pressed against my skin. It was a line of string, strung across the room almost horizontally. It ran from... I stooped beneath the string, blundered to the nearest bench and found the electric torch I had hoped was there. I switched it on and surveyed the course of the string. It emerged from the transmitter box, snagged tight where the door had shut on it – or had been pulled shut from the inside. The other end was fastened to the handle of the main power switch. The power switch was in the 'down' position.

The experiment had been activated.

I imagined the sequence of events. Simon would have contorted himself into the box, dragging the string with him. He would have pulled it nearly tight, before yanking down the power switch and pulling tight the door in practically the same motion. He must have used another piece of string to pull the door shut from within. I opened the box. It was clean and empty. The main piece of string dropped limply: it extended exactly as far as the inner seal of the door and no further. If there had been a second piece of string, it had been teleported through along with the remaining length of the main piece.

The muffled noises continued. With a certain dread – no, a fair measure of it – I carried the torch on through to the receiver room.

"You silly fool," I said aloud. "You just couldn't wait, could you? I suppose after that set-to about the pocket-knife, I don't blame you."

Simon's muffled voice was coming from the receiver box. I went to it.

I shone the torch into the glass-windowed door. I had to know, before I opened the box, just what I might be releasing into the world.

Simon was naked. He had become a squatting human puzzle, filling nearly the entire rectangular volume of the box. It looked terribly uncomfortable, but he did not look injured or in any way malformed. I supposed that the position he was in now was exactly the position he had forced himself into inside the transmitter box, with the string or strings pinched between his fingers. He must have thought about the need to open the receiver box, mustn't he?

I did it for him. Facing the window as he was, I saw two limp pieces of string dangling from his fingers. He was shivering badly. I was amazed that he was alive at all.

I got him out. It was like pulling someone out of freezing water: I had to do nearly all the work. I stretched him out and put him into a chair. I draped my coat over him, then rushed back into the other room to look for his own clothes. I found them soon enough, piled neatly on the edge of the bench. I came back and dressed him as best I could, then found assorted coats and blankets to put over the top.

"I'm... sorry we argued," Simon said, when the shivering had abated enough for him to form intelligible words. "I had to do it, old man. I'm not sorry I did. We know it works now." His eyes flashed a mad triumph. "All that bickering's in the past, Ian! The process works! It's a little rough, but anyone can go through it provided they're prepared! I put on as many layers as I could, got a real sweat on, then stripped off quickly! With bigger boxes, it won't be half as much of a squeeze!" Then a slow, troubled curiosity began to perturb his features. "I heard you calling out. What were you saying, slipped away?"

I answered in the low, doctorly tones of a physician about to speak to a very poorly patient with an even poorer prognosis "How are you feeling, Simon?"

"Oh, awful! Bloody awful! But on top of the world, too!" He seized my hand, his grip a bunch of writhing slippery eels. "We've bloody well done it, Ian!"

"No we haven't," I answered. "We haven't done it at all, Simon. We've done... something else. Something quite different to what we intended."

"I've teleported."

"Yes," I agreed. "That's true. There's a side-effect, though. A side-effect that makes the process totally useless. Worse than useless. Malign. We should have seen it, with the cultures and the alarm clock..."

Resentment drove a dark animus into his eyes. "Why are you still going on about those things? The proof's in the pudding! I'm here!"

"For now. You're here for now, Simon, but not for much longer."

"What's got into you, Ian?"

"A realisation," I said flatly. I sighed, accepting that he was beyond salvation, but at the same time feeling that he was owed at least the outline of an explanation, as well as I could offer it. "It's about that parameter, K. It all clicked for me in the Green Man."

"I've told you, it's..."

"Do shut up, Simon," I said softly. "Something very bad is going to happen to you – may indeed already be happening – and the very least you can do is hear me out."

Something changed in his expression: some tiny, dawning acceptance that all might not be well.

"What are you talking about?"

"K is a statistical parameter connected to time. Specifically, the arrow of time." I shushed him gently. "No, let me speak, Simon. I've got it all straight in my head now – that might not be the case forever, or however many hours or days you have left."

He let out a disagreeable sigh.

I continued: "We think of the arrow of time as a unitary thing. We're all progressing through time in the same direction, everything from atoms to dogs to mountains and planets. One hour per hour, each of us. But what if that's only the observed outcome of an emergent effect, like pressure?"

He frowned: but it was a frown of reluctant interest, not dissent.

"Go on," he mouthed.

"I think every object, every little thing in the universe, from bacteria to Bentleys, has many arrows of time inside it. Normally they're all lined up the same way, like millions of little compasses all pointing north."

"Compasses," Simon echoed flatly.

"I think your process scrambles them. Or rather, it starts off some chain-reaction. Some of them don't point north any more. The microscopic arrow-of-time gets flipped. Perhaps just a few to start with. But the scrambling carries on. Inside any object, more and more of the arrows-of-time stop pointing north. Perhaps they flip around and point south, I don't know. All I do know is that the emergent effect of this behaviour is that objects become slowly unstuck from time. They can't keep up with that hour per hour rate any more. So alarm clocks start losing time and bacterial cultures don't divide as quickly as before."

A tightness in his mouth made his beard twitch. "And the ashtray, the pocket-knife?"

"They reached a point where most, or all, of their arrows were no longer pointing north. Now they not only couldn't keep up, but they fell out of time completely." Some horrible callous impulse overcame me. "That's what's going to happen to you soon, Simon. You're going to fall out of time." I paused. "But I think by then you'll be dead anyway, or well on the way. You'll be very sickly. Those bacterial lines kept dividing, albeit less healthily, because their food source, the agar, had been time-reversed as well. But with you, that isn't the case. As the arrows flip inside you, I think you're going to start withering away. Not that there's much left of you to wither as it is."

"This is just a theory," he said, with a certain desperation. "It all hinges on those things disappearing, which neither of us saw happen. All right, so they didn't disappear! We just misplaced them. We'll have a good look as soon as I feel strong enough to get on my feet..."

I laid a hand on him, not unkindly. "It's not just a theory, I'm afraid. I've seen all the evidence I need for myself. You become him, Simon."

"Become who, for pity's sake?"

"The Raggedy Man. The ghost that's been haunting this part of Suffolk for hundreds, perhaps even thousands of years. The ghost of Ingleby Hall – the one you didn't tell me about. The figure I saw outside. It's you."

A fierce terror lit his eyes. "No! You're talking nonsense. Ghosts aren't real. I can't become a ghost, a ghost that's already in the past."

"You do," I said calmly. "They've been seeing you all over the place. It's the reason you got Ingleby Hall at a knockdown price: you're the haunting."

"No," he breathed.

"And all the earlier sightings. Henry Scurlock saw you a hundred years ago, in the bar of the Green Man. You must have gone back there... or will go back there. You're looking for something, with as much purpose and volition as any ghost can possess. A way out of your fate, I suppose. But you don't find it. You keep going back. The Neolithic men built that burial site here for a reason, Simon. I think that ground was already of importance to them. They'd seen and heard things... rumours, figments, perhaps. Those ancient men had caught glimpses of you, as you hurtled ever deeper into antiquity."

"Ghosts aren't real," Simon said weakly.

"They are. I've seen the empirical evidence of it for myself. The question we should have asked... if it had ever occurred to us – would be this. If ghosts are indeed real, and they spring from the living at the time of death, what happens if the living are time-reversed? Does the ghost continue forward, or does it also end up time-reversed?" I smiled at my ailing friend. "I think we know now. I think you've helped settle that one. You've got a long, strange journey ahead of you, Simon. You're going to haunt the past, falling ever further into history, then prehistory, then the time before men, until you won't even have other ghosts for company..."

He screamed.

I laid my hand on him more firmly. "I'll be with you until the bitter end, though. That I promise."

"Very interesting," Janice said dryly, after she had finished appraising Henry Scurlock's *Compendium of Suffolk Hauntings*. "You know this is all nonsense, don't you? Country bumpkin nonsense."

She had spoken a little too loudly and I noticed a few annoyed glances directed at us – or her.

"It isn't nonsense," I answered tersely.

We finished our drinks without saying much else, and I took our empty glasses and the old book back to the bar, nodding my thanks to the girl for being entrusted with such a delicate, precious item.

I had a feeling it would not be the last time I opened its pages.

Outside, I stopped Janice just before she got back in the Morgan.

"What is it?" she asked sharply. "We really must be getting back to London, Ian!"

"I said there was a third thing, Janice. The Scurlock Compendium was part of it, and it was Blossom's tattoo that made me think of little compasses, of the arrows of time. But the third thing was there all along."

"I don't understand."

"Simon lasted about five days after I found him. He became very poorly near the end. As more and more of those little arrows flipped over inside him, he began to slip. He was slowing, like the clock and the culture dishes. Slowing, reversing, slipping out of time, unable to digest food. Even breathing became difficult. He was sickly... his complexion jaundiced, as his organs failed." I paused. "He insisted that I try one thing, more in desperation than anything else. He asked to be sent through a second time. His hope was that the process might reverse itself... but of course we had no evidence of that, and by then some of the things that had disappeared had gone through several times. Still, I did what I could for him. It was too much for the equipment, though. The apparatus overloaded in the attempt. There was a very bad fire in the transmitter room, which quickly engulfed the whole of Ingleby Hall. It wasn't arson, you see – and I was the party the police were very interested in speaking to." I shrugged. "There was never anything that could be proven, and by the time they were aware of the fire, Simon had died. His body remained for a few hours, then vanished. He'd slipped out of time before the police even reached the estate."

"And the third thing?" she asked, with real impatience.

I turned her head to the pub sign, creaking on its hinges in the same light breeze that had been playing when we arrived. The bearded, foliate face of the Green Man beamed down at us as if sharing a private joke. "I said he became jaundiced. I suppose a wild, ghostly apparition with a yellow complexion looks much like a wild, ghostly apparition with a green one. He was there all along, Janice: staring us both in the face."

PRESIDENT MAX

Josh Lacey

The whole thing was a mistake. Even worse, it was my mistake.
Without me, Max would never have become president.

You know about that, don't you?

I'm sure you do. It's been on the news around the world. You
don't need me to tell you about the terrible things Max has done.

Who could be stupid enough to want him as their president?

Half the people in the country, that's who.

But I can't blame them. This fiasco is my fault.

I write a weekly column for a newspaper. Every Tuesday morning, I
take my three kids to school, then come home, hurry upstairs with a
strong coffee, sit down at my desk, and don't get up until I've
written eight hundred words. That's the idea, anyway, although you
wouldn't believe how hard it can be to write eight hundred words,
particularly if they have to be wise and witty enough to amuse the
readers of the paper that pays my salary.

On the day that this story begins, I had been writing these
columns for three and a half years, and my imagination had run dry.
I'd said all there was to say about my past, my present, my future,
my hopes, and my dreams. I'd written about my wife, my children,
the death of our dog, and the birth of our neighbour's kittens. I had
nothing left in the tank.

Nonetheless I still had to deliver that week's column. I sipped
my coffee and typed a few words. I read them back to myself and
deleted the lot.

I stared at the ceiling. I looked out of the window. I stopped for
lunch, then nipped out for some fresh air. I wrote a few more words
and deleted them too.

Towards the end of the afternoon I was standing by the window, spying on a pair of blackbirds in our next-door neighbour's crab apple tree, wondering if I could spin eight hundred words from their courtship, when the front door slammed. My wife had collected the kids from school. Christ, the day had gone. My word count: zero. I heard footsteps and the voices of Eleanor and Jake. I was about to go downstairs to say hello when Max yelled, "No!"

I could hear my wife calmly and patiently speaking to him. I couldn't make out exactly what she was saying, but from the tone of her voice I guessed that she was asking him to hang his coat on a peg or take off his shoes, the type of tasks that any ordinary kid would do without being asked.

"NO!"

Max was only seven years old. There were times in his life when he simply had to do what he was told by his parents. So we said to him, anyway.

"NO!"

As I stood there, listening through the closed door to the sound of Max screaming and stamping his feet, I had an idea.

Yes, I thought to myself. That's it! That's perfect!

I sat down and started writing. Half an hour later, I had eight hundred words.

I read what I'd written back to myself, smiled at my own cleverness, smoothed over a few phrases, corrected a couple of mistakes, then sent it to my editor. My work done for the day, I switched off the computer, and jogged downstairs to see my family.

I have that week's column in front of me. Here are the first few paragraphs:

I have a son. His name is Max. He is a small boy with brown eyes and brown hair. He knows what he likes. When he can't have it, he gets cross. He shouts. He screams. He stamps his foot. He is hot tempered and strong willed. If I could give you a piece of advice, it would be this: don't get into an argument with Max, because you will almost certainly lose. And if you have the misfortune to win, you will wish you hadn't, because my son Max has perfected the art of the bad loser.

As you know, there are only two candidates for the job of president. A few weeks from now, we will have to vote for one or other of them.

As you also know, their names are Bill Clapham and Jeremy North.

And as you must have noticed, Bill Clapham is a tall man with blue eyes and blonde hair, and Jeremy North is a short man with brown eyes and very little hair at all.

Soon one of these two men will be running this great country of ours.

Max wouldn't do a better job than either of them. But he wouldn't do much worse.

The article went on to compare the behaviour of my son and the two presidential candidates. I said that my son was obstreperous, obstructive, argumentative, and single minded in his dedication to get whatever he wanted, no matter what anyone else might think or feel. The two presidential candidates, I suggested, were no different.

I wrote that seven year-old boys are allowed, even expected, to behave badly. Boys will be boys, we say to ourselves. But we hope boys will grow up into men.

I finished by asking a question: why were our two presidential candidates no more mature than the seven year old boy currently stamping his feet on my kitchen floor?

Ordinarily, a few people would have read my column, and two or three of them might have smiled and nodded, and two or three more might have shook their heads and frowned, and all of them would have turned the page, or scrolled the screen, and by the end of the day, no one would recall a word that I had written.

Unfortunately, that Friday, a man named Serge Klagenfurt happened to pick up the paper.

I can't imagine Serge Klagenfurt often bothered to read the news, let alone my weekly eight hundred words on the mundane details of my insignificant existence. Perhaps his private jet was delayed that day nor his personal trainer called off sick. Whatever the reason, he read my piece, and it gave him an idea. The type of idea that might have made you or me smile, dream idly for a moment, then move on. But Serge Klagenfurt was not like you and me. Serge Klagenfurt was a ludicrously wealthy individual who had already bought himself more houses, yachts, and artworks than anyone could possibly need or want over the course of several lifetimes. Now he wanted to spend his money on an idea.

Max was actually the first of us to see it. On that particular morning, a few weeks after my column had come out, he had been rude to one of his teachers, so had to spend his break sitting in the corner of the classroom, reading a book. For some children, this wouldn't have been a punishment at all, but Max was restless and bored. He didn't want to be indoors with a book while his friends were running around in the fresh air. He stretched. He sighed. He yawned. He glanced out of the window – and saw himself.

On the other side of the street was an enormous advertising hoarding. The previous week it had displayed a picture of a car. Now it showed a boy's face. Massive letters screamed out a blunt slogan:

VOTE MAX

My son jumped down from his seat, ran to the window, and pressed his nose against the glass.

"What are you doing?" cried his teacher. "Come and sit down!"

Max took no notice.

The teacher sighed. She put down the book that she was marking, strode over to the window, and placed her hand on Max's shoulder. Then she glanced out of the window to see what he was looking at so intently.

"That's funny," she said. "He looks just like you."

"He is me," Max said.

"Don't be silly," said the teacher. "Now, come back and read your book. You don't want to miss your break tomorrow as well, do you?"

Max did as he was told. He sat at the desk and read a book. Every few moments, he lifted his head and stared through the window into his own eyes.

Serge Klagenfurt could have built a hospital or several schools and libraries. He could have provided food and lodging for the hungry and destitute of our country. Instead he chose to waste a sizeable percentage of his fortune on a joke.

You might have thought that even a billionaire couldn't just propose a candidate for the presidency, especially if that candidate turned out to be a seven year old boy. That was exactly what I had assumed, but I turned out to be wrong. Somehow Serge Klagenfurt had put Max's name on the ballot. On the day of the election, the voters of our country would be able to choose between three candidates: Bill Clapham, Jeremy North, and my son Max.

Through no fault or desire of their own, my three children were transformed into celebrities.

Jake hated the attention. He wanted to be left alone to play his football and his hockey, and the rabble of reporters and curious onlookers kept getting in the way, holding up games and making a mess of his schedule.

Eleanor had more divided feelings. She'd also been a shy child, but in those days, she had somehow come up with the ambition of working as a journalist herself. I tried to dissuade her, which probably spurred her on. She enjoyed having the chance to chat to the hacks, asking about their lives and their work.

To my surprise, Max minded least of all, or rather simply didn't care. He was the central actor in this drama, while we merely had bit parts, but he sailed serenely through it, accepting his new fame as if it was nothing out of the ordinary.

Journalists yelled questions at him in the street. Camera crews followed him from home to school and back again. People pointed at him. Drivers waved from their cars and hooted their horns.

Max took very little notice. He could have made faces at the cameras or given silly answers to the journalists' questions. Instead he just walked past them, heading home, keeping a dignified silence. I have to admit I was impressed.

One evening around this time, the five of us had supper together. As we made our way through a fish pie, we discussed the playing fields which had, until three months earlier, belonged to Jake's school. Against the wishes of every parent, pupil, and teacher, the council had sold them to a property developer, who was intending to build a block of flats. The council would earn millions. Jake and his friends would have to walk for twenty minutes to play their matches on pitches belonging to another school.

"If you do become president," Jake said to his younger brother, "can you stop them building those tower blocks?"

"No problem," Max said. He pretended to write a note to himself. Then he glanced at his sister. "What about you? Anything do you want me to do when I'm president?"

"Save the whales," replied Eleanor.

"Okey-dokey." Max pretended to write that down too. Then he looked around the table. "Any more requests?

"Only one," I said. "Eat your broccoli."

This conversation should give you some idea of our reaction to what was happening: we refused to take it seriously. We assumed that no one would be silly enough to vote for Max.

However, as the days passed and the date of the election came closer, my wife and I began to have a few concerns. I noticed posters in windows. People wore badges pinned to their coats. Polls showed support for my son creeping up. He had started at zero, which was where he belonged. Soon he was on three percent. I wasn't worried by that. A higher proportion of the population believe that they have been kidnapped by UFOs; of course three in a hundred of us will make an X next to pretty much anyone or anything on the ballot, however bananas. But the polls got worse. Seven percent. Eight. Nine. He was in double figures. That wasn't enough to win the election, of course, but it was more than enough to make me worried. I wrote another column, explaining that the whole thing had been nothing more than an idle joke, a provocation. It had the same reaction as most of my work: no one took any notice.

A stream of pushy TV producers had been ringing me and asking if Max would do an interview. Of course I said no. I didn't want to make things even worse for him. But the situation was getting desperate, so I rang the biggest network and offered an exclusive with Max – on one condition. The other candidates had to be there too. To my surprise, they agreed.

Bill Clapham and Jeremy North had clearly spent days in preparation, not only learning their lines, but choosing their clothes and having their hair cut.

Max was utterly unprepared. As soon as he opened his mouth, he would reveal to the watching audience that he was nothing more than an ordinary kid who should have been at home, playing with his toys.

Or so I hoped.

The first question was about foreign policy. Bill Clapham and Jeremy North gave carefully scripted answers. When Max had his turn, he simply shrugged his shoulders, and said, "I don't know."

The second question concerned housing policy. It was Max's turn to answer first, and he said, "Dunno."

"Do you want to elaborate on that?" the interviewer asked.

"Dunno," Max said.

Bill Clapham and Jeremy North gave their own sensible, professional, utterly uninteresting responses.

The interviewer was about to ask a third question when Max suddenly announced, "This is boring."

"Excuse me?" said the interviewer.

"This is boring," Max repeated.

"Boring?" said the interviewer.

"Boring, boring, boring," said Max.

Bill Clapham made a comment, but it was drowned out by the audience's cheers and laughter.

Jeremy North raised his eyebrows for the cameras, but his gesture was wasted. Every eye in the studio was focused on Max, who said, "Boring, boring, boring, boring, boring."

Then he strode away, stepped through a gap in the curtains, and vanished from view.

In their booth at the back of the studio, the producers were panicking. Should they try to follow Max? Or ignore him?

The other two candidates didn't know what to do either. They chuckled with one another as if they were sharing a joke at someone's expense, then turned to the interviewer and waited for her next question.

As for me – well, I couldn't have been happier.

When we found Max, he was sitting at the back of the studio playing with a bundle of thick black cables.

"Don't pull those," I said.

"Why not?" Max asked.

"Because you'll blow us up."

"Cool," Max said, giving them a yank.

"Seriously. Stop it. You'll cause a fire." I turned to my wife. "What shall we do now?"

"Let's go home," she replied.

We sneaked through the studios, evading the cameras, and let the other candidates continue their arguments without us.

Although I wasn't there to see it, I heard afterwards that the rest of the debate had been uneventful. Bill Clapham and Jeremy North blustered and lied through a series of questions, peppering their conversation with statistics and soundbites.

In the car, Max announced he was hungry. Usually we would have told him to wait till we got home, but tonight felt like a special occasion, so we stopped at a Lebanese place where we'd often eaten before, and ordered three falafel wraps and a plate of chips.

One of the other customers wandered over to our table, wiping his mouth with a napkin.

"You're Max, aren't you?" he said.

My son nodded.

The guy grinned. "Boring, boring, boring – right?"

"Right." Max grinned back.

"You told them, didn't you?"

"I guess."

"You did! You told them! Boring, boring, boring! Ha, ha, ha. You've got my vote."

The guy shook Max's hand, then dropped his napkin in the trash and headed into the street, a big grin smeared across his face.

The last few days of the campaign passed in a blur. My wife and I tried to pretend that our lives were continuing as normal. She went to work, the kids went to school, and I carried on writing my book. Or so I told myself, although the truth was that I didn't write a single word. I couldn't concentrate. I was too worried about Max and the effect that these events might be having on him. His life had been turned upside down. When I took him to school every morning and picked him up every afternoon, we had to push our way through a thick crowd of aggressive reporters and curious onlookers, all of them desperate to get a good look at my son. Cameras followed us wherever we went. A trip to the park became impossible. Even our garden was a no-go zone, because journalists bribed or blustered their way into our neighbours' houses, and peered out of their windows, watching every move we made.

I apologised to Max several times every day.

"Don't worry, Dad," he replied. "I don't mind. It's fun."

"All this madness – you think this is fun?"

"Yes." Max grinned. "Don't you?"

I really didn't. But at least it would be over soon. In a few days, I told myself, we'll be laughing about the whole thing.

I wasn't the only one who thought this way. Even two or three days before the election, all the professionals were still treating Max as a joke. Newspapers claimed the polls were wrong. In TV debates, pundits discussed the policies of Bill Clapham and Jeremy North, but they didn't even mention Max.

I have seen many elections, and the scenes on election night are always the same. A crowd gathers. Journalists stand at the front, clutching cameras and notebooks. A door opens. The newly-elected president steps out. He or she is grinning and waving. Cheers break out. The noise is overwhelming. The candidate – the president elect – smiles, waves, shakes hands.

That night was very different.

There *was* a crowd waiting outside our house. There were journalists with cameras and notebooks, and curious onlookers. But every one of them was completely silent. No one cheered. No one shouted. In fact, as far as I was aware, no one said a word. It was as if we were all in shock. As if we had been chortling at a joke which at the same moment we all realised was tasteless and cruel.

In silence, the crowd watched our little convoy emerge from the house and walk across the pavement to the waiting cars.

Eight men in dark suits went ahead, their heads turning from side to side, searching for any hint of danger.

The country woke up to the news of Max's presidency. THE BOY PRESIDENT, screamed one headline. WHAT HAVE WE DONE? wailed another. Shock appeared to be the main emotion among the general population, although the other political parties also felt a great deal of anger. They were used to sharing power between themselves, taking turns to rule over us, and they didn't like the idea that someone else might have a go.

For the first time in months, Bill Clapham and Jeremy North found something on which they could agree. They appeared together on TV, demanding that the election was declared null and void.

"This boy, this child, cannot be president of our great country," cried Bill Clapham.

"He must be removed from the palace immediately," thundered Jeremy North.

Lawyers delved into their books and searched for solutions. Could a seven year old boy really be elected as the president? Some said yes, others no. Reaching a decision would take months, if not years.

Meanwhile we needed a president. The country couldn't run itself. Someone had to be in charge.

Until the lawyers could make up their minds, that someone would be Max.

Max had to resign. I knew it. He knew it. Everyone agreed.

We called a press conference. Max and I discussed what he would say. I warned my son that the journalists might be rude, even hostile, and advised him not to give any time to ask questions, but leave the room as soon as he had said whatever he needed to say.

"You don't have to do this if you don't want to," I said. "We could just issue a press release."

"I want to tell them myself," Max said.

I asked if he would like to practise what he was going to say, but he shook his head.

"I don't have to," he said.

I gave him a hug. He patted me on the back.

"Don't worry, Dad," he told me. "Everything's going to be fine."

His press secretary was a slick middle-aged woman named Anya who had seen several presidents come and go. She told us that the Press Room was already packed. A hundred journalists from around the world were waiting to hear the president's first statement. None of them knew it would also be his last.

My youngest son strolled confidently to the centre of the stage and smiled at the crowd. He said, "Hello."

A hundred men and women called their greetings back to him. "Hello, Mister President." "Good morning." "Hello, sir."

One of them shouted out, "How are you, Mister President?"

"I'm good," Max said. "How are you?"

"I'm good too, thank you, sir."

"How's the palace?" called out another journalist.

"It's nice," Max said.

"Anything you can tell us?"

"I had lasagne and chips for lunch."

Reporters scribbled this important news in their notebooks.

Someone called out, "What will you have for dinner tonight?"

"Lasagne and chips," Max said.

"The same meal twice in one day?" shouted someone else.

Max nodded. "I really like lasagne and chips."

More scribbling.

Anya held up her hand for silence. "The president will make a short statement," she said. "When he has finished, I will answer any further questions on his behalf." Then she nodded to Max.

The room was very quiet. A hundred men and women stared at Max, waiting to hear what he had to say.

But he didn't say anything.

The silence went on. And on.

Max shuffled on the spot. He scratched his ear.

The journalists were growing restless. They started murmuring to themselves. Someone at the back shouted out a question.

Max didn't answer. Instead he picked his nose. He had a good long look to see what he'd found, then flicked it at the floor.

I was just about to step onto the stage and remind Max what to say, when he suddenly lifted his head and looked out at the crowd and said, "I like cheese."

No one said a word in response. A hundred grown men and women, all of them silent, rapt, waiting to hear what he would say next.

Max looked at one of the journalists who was sitting in the front row, a man who had been reporting the news for the past forty years and was hardly less famous than the people about whom he reported.

"Do you like cheese?" Max asked him.

"Yes, I do like cheese," the reporter replied.

"Do you love it?"

"I suppose I probably do."

"Me too," Max said. "I love cheese."

"Do you have a policy on cheese?" the reporter asked.

"Yes," Max said.

"May I ask what is it?"

"Free cheese," Max said.

"Free cheese?" the reporter repeated. "That's your first initiative as president? You're going to give away cheese?"

Max nodded. "Free cheese for everyone," he said.

Suddenly a hundred people were shouting at once, wanting to know the details of this presidential decree. Who would get this cheese? What varieties of cheeses would be available? Would foreign cheese be included or only cheese produced within our borders?

I could see that Max was getting uncomfortable. I darted onto the stage and led him to the door. Behind our backs, Anya took over the microphone. I could hear her trying to calm the crowd as Max and I made our getaway.

Once we were in the calm of the corridor, I hissed furiously at my son, "What happened? You were meant to tell them you're resigning!"

He tried to look innocent. "I forgot."

"Oh, come on, Max! You made a promise. You can't break your promises."

"Can I go and play?"

"No. You can get back in there and –"

But he was already sprinting down the corridor. He spent the rest of the day sliding down the grand staircase on various Persian rugs purloined from different rooms, deciding which of them went fastest.

Farmers were delighted. The cheese industry cheered. Earnest commentators discussed the legal niceties, the economic impact, the constitutional implications.

Newspapers and TV stations reported our president's first action. Cartoonists had a field day. Our nation became the target of comedians around the world. President Cheese, they called him. Le Presidente de Fromage. Il presidente di formaggio.

Ten days later, every man, woman, and child in the country was issued with a small parcel. Stamped on the packaging were five words in red letters: BY ORDER OF THE PRESIDENT.

Max achieved a seventy-four percent approval rating, among the highest ever recorded. Presidents are usually at their most popular in the first few months after their inauguration, but pollsters had rarely seen figures like these. The following week, he put a whoopee cushion on the Swedish prime minister's chair just before she sat down, and his ratings hit the low eighties.

I don't see Max often these days – my wife and I were banned from the presidential palace for trying to impose a regular bedtime routine – but I have heard that he and his advisers are already planning for his second term.

UNTOLD

Keith Brooke

Langham made it home just as the snow started to fall, soft white flakes swirling in the harsh headlamps of the Rover. He parked alongside Yew Tree Cottage and allowed himself the luxury of pausing a moment or two, the headlamps still on. There was much to love about the life he and Maria had forged out here in the remoter reaches of Suffolk, but this particular moment was one he always treasured: when he reached the cottage and allowed himself to believe in his good fortune all over again – they were here, this was their life.

"Maria? I'm home," he called as he kicked snow off his shoes before stepping inside. She emerged from the kitchen as he bolted the front door, a neat white apron over the slacks and turtleneck sweater she liked to wear about the place.

She came over and pecked him on the cheek, before rocking back on her heels and giving him a look of mock disapproval. "*Mon cheri*," she said. "You have been drinking again, no?"

Langham raised an eyebrow. He'd been to a business meeting in London with his agent, Charles. Of *course* he'd had a drink.

He followed her through to the kitchen, savouring the rich smells emanating from the cooking pot sitting on top of the range. "Beef hotpot? Oh, you know the way to a man's heart."

"And those dumpling things you so like," she said with a laugh. She was not a fan of dumplings.

Maria had thrown herself wholeheartedly into domestic life since their move to Suffolk, even though she still spent two days a week in London, working at the agency alongside Charles. If Langham didn't know better, he'd say she was nest-building. Even Charles had hinted that there was something of the broody hen about her these days.

"Your 'meeting' was good?"

"Oh, you know. We batted a few ideas about." Lunch with Charles was mostly about good food and drink, with Charles sharing all the latest scurrilous gossip from Grub Street. Any actual business was usually dealt with in the first five minutes. "Come here."

She fitted into his embrace so perfectly. "I could get used to this, you know," Langham told her. They really had landed on their feet. He had the perfect home, being shaped and refined by the woman he loved. They were establishing life in a model village: Ingoldby-over-Water had a butcher, a baker, a general store-cum-post office, and there were regular cake sales in the village hall, and teas at the church hall every second Tuesday.

Their peace was interrupted by a hammering on the front door.

"Who the blazes can that be?" Langham said.

He went back through, unlocking and unbolting the door to find a bedraggled, snow-covered young man stamping his feet. He wore no hat and had turned up the collar of his greatcoat to ward off the snow that now blew horizontally across from the fields opposite.

"Donald Langham?"

"Yes, that's me." Langham tried not to be affronted by the man's direct tone. "And who, might I enquire, is asking?"

Now, the man looked away. "I... I don't know," he said. "Or rather, I do, but..."

The man was clearly confused, and his demeanour brought to mind men Langham had seen in the aftermath of battle, shell-shocked and disorientated. There was no war now, of course, although he doubted it would be long before Asia started to tear itself apart again.

He studied their visitor closely. There was something about him. Langham felt he should recognise him, but he was too young to have served with Langham in Madagascar, and he was unable to place him from anywhere else.

There was an undeniable sense of connection, though, and it quite threw Langham off kilter.

"Donald? Invite your friend in from the cold. Have you forgotten your manners?"

She was teasing again, but when Langham turned to her he saw her expression change – she must have seen the look in his eyes. He didn't know quite why he felt so disturbed by this intrusion, but it was as if something had knocked him off his foundations. He did not want to invite this man inside.

Maria looked now from her husband to the man still standing in the doorway. "Should we make introductions, perhaps?" she said.

Langham straightened. Indicating his wife, he said, "This is my wife, Maria, and you, sir...?"

The man nodded in greeting. "Thorn," he said. "My name is Max Thorn and I don't belong here. Not in this place. Not in this time."

"Perhaps we should go to the Green Man," Maria said, and in that instant Langham loved her even more, if such a thing were possible. Sometimes she read him better than he knew himself.

A short time later, booted and wrapped up against what was now a driving blizzard, Langham was grateful to leave Yew Tree Cottage behind. He felt far more comfortable dealing with this intrusion on neutral territory, and now the thought had been planted, he could murder a pint.

Their visitor, Thorn, led the way back down the garden path and without waiting for direction turned left onto Crooked Lane. He must have passed the village pub on his way here, Langham supposed.

The flakes of snow were thick and wet now, plastering themselves to whatever surface they struck. By the time the three had covered the short distance to the Green Man, they were like snowmen, and they had to stamp and flap quite vigorously before stepping inside.

The place was warm from a fire roaring in the hearth and at this time – mid-evening, midweek – there were only a few drinkers in: the Wellbournes at a table in the corner, a young couple standing at the bar, a middle-aged man whose belt was fighting valiantly to contain the spread of his belly, and a few others.

As soon as the landlord, Woodward, saw Langham, he started to pour him a pint of Fullers. Langham ordered a gin and tonic for Maria, and then said to Thorn, "And what will you have?"

"Oh... I... I'll have whatever you're having. Thank you."

It was as if he'd never been in a pub before.

They retreated with their drinks to a corner table, and finally Langham leaned forward, fixed their visitor with a hard stare, and said, "So tell me, Thorn. What do you mean when you say you're not from this place – or this *time?*"

The man looked as if he were about to burst into tears, and again Langham recalled the expressions of men traumatised by great tragedy.

"What happened, old chap? What's wrong? Because something quite clearly is."

Thorn shook his head. "I don't know. I have the strangest sense of things out of synch. Of senses displaced. Nothing feels right. I don't understand what is happening. That's why I sought you out. They told me you're a detective, of sorts."

"Of sorts, indeed." Langham had a stake in a detective agency run by his old Army pal, Ralph Ryland, although he was hoping to reduce his involvement in investigations now that he had moved to Suffolk, and his thriller novels were finding a larger audience. "Tell me, who was it that pointed you in my direction?"

Thorn nodded towards the middle-aged man at the bar, who had worked his way down what had been a freshly poured pint in the short time they had been sitting there.

Langham didn't recognise the man, although again – jarringly – he had a sense of some kind of connection. "If you'll excuse me for a moment," he said, getting to his feet. He didn't like the thought of leaving Maria with this disturbing visitor, but a fresh perspective from someone who had met Thorn earlier might help him make sense of his own confused reactions to the man.

"Langham," he said, offering a hand for the man to shake as he came to stand by him at the bar. "Let me get you another of those." He gestured to Woodward, who took the man's glass and started another pint.

"I know," said the man, with an odd smile. "Gordon Kemp." His handshake was firm and brief. Businesslike. "He found you, then?" he said, nodding sideways towards Thorn.

"He did, indeed. He said he was looking for a detective, so you sent him to me."

Kemp laughed. "That's what he said. I didn't tell him I'm one myself. I'm retired now, though. I don't do that any more. So I sent him your way."

"Would you care to join us?"

He led the retired detective across to the corner table and made the introductions.

"Mr Kemp is a detective too," he said. Then he turned to Kemp. "But you said retired?" There was clearly a story there.

"I had one last big case," Kemp told them. "A cold case, someone murdered almost a century before. My superiors were corrupt and they picked me as a patsy, not believing for a moment that I would crack it. They sent me to another planet halfway across the universe and hoped I'd die, along with the case. But with the help of a few pals, and some aliens, I wrapped it up."

Space travel... aliens... Only last year the Soviets had put their satellite Sputnik into orbit around the Earth, and then shortly afterwards they'd sent a dog up. But... travel to distant planets?

"It is like those books that you pretend you don't read," Maria said, nudging Langham. "Those pulp adventures of aliens and time travel and mysteries beyond what we know." Then, to Kemp, she said, "I am sorry, Mr Kemp. I interrupted."

"No, you're right. I don't believe it myself half the time, particularly on a night like this. I was a hero for all of five minutes. I was all over the channels, the darling of my new bosses. I thought I was set up for life and I was ready for whatever adventure befell me next, but... nothing. It was as if there was a story waiting to happen, but no one to tell it. I feel lost, abandoned... And now I find myself in a country pub in the middle of nowhere and I have the distinct feeling that I'm adrift in a time and a place where I don't belong."

Langham studied him closely. The retired detective's words echoed those used by Thorn earlier, and now Langham was aware that he felt it too. He felt adrift. He reached under the table and took Maria's hand.

"It's true," Thorn said. Their mysterious visitor had been paying close attention to Gordon Kemp's words. "I feel that way, too. Adrift in a time and place where I don't belong. I'm not from here. I don't know this world, and I'm just clinging on. All I know is that I'm grateful for every second when all my senses are united, but all the time I'm just waiting to lose it all again, to see you talking and not hear your words, because that's what happened to me before. I remember it now. Step by step I lost touch with the world, until I was left adrift. All I want now is to lose myself in the *nada*-continuum one last time and push ships between the stars…"

They were losing Langham now, with all this talk of space and the like. It really did feel as if he'd stepped into one of those pulp adventures that Maria teased him about.

"You were ill?" he said to Thorn, trying to keep some kind of grip on proceedings. "What happened to you? Was it some kind of psychosis?" Again, he thought of those shell-shocked men he had known in the war.

"I had Black's Syndrome," Thorn told them. "It's a condition that affects only a small proportion of us who have the rare ability to mind-push starships through the *nada*-continuum. Your senses start to go, one by one. Not go, but *lag*. First, it's sound: you can see someone talking but not hear their words. Then maybe twenty minutes later you hear them, the whole realm of sound falling behind the perception of your other senses. After your hearing, it's taste and smell, and only your sense of touch remains in real-time, as your other senses fall farther and farther behind. When your sense of touch starts to lapse, your senses are synchronised again, but ever deeper into the past, so that you experience real-time events hours and then days after they occur. Eventually…"

"What?" Langham pressed.

"You die. You can't exist like that."

"So how did you end up here?"

"I don't know. I'm looking for answers."

"Maybe you didn't die after all," Kemp said. "From your account, you seem to me to be a man from the future. If your senses lapse ever-farther behind, maybe that's what you're experiencing now? Life before you even existed."

"Donald?"

Langham loved the way his wife put extra weight on the second syllable of his name – Don*ald* – but now he recognised a hesitancy, too. A short time before, she had excused herself to powder her nose, and now she stood uncertainly by their table.

Langham stood, took her by the elbow and led her to the nook by the door, the most privacy they could manage in the Green Man. "My dear?"

"There is something strange happening."

They'd just been sitting listening to tales of men who had travelled between the stars and met aliens, but putting all that aside, ever since Thorn had appeared at the door of Yew Tree Cottage Langham had felt that their world had been knocked off its axis. Yet Maria seemed to be indicating that there was something more.

"Outside," she said, hugging herself. The WCs were in an outhouse at the back of the pub. Maria still had a few flakes of snow on her shoulders. "It is different."

Langham led the way across to the back door, then put his hands on Maria's arms and said, "Stay here. I'll take a quick shufty."

He stepped outside into a swirl of wet snowflakes. A single light picked out the doors to the lavatories, across a small, paved yard.

Langham walked across. There was a wrought-iron gate in the wall here, opening onto Crooked Lane. He peered out, but there was nothing. No lights from the row of cottages across the lane, not even their dark looming shapes. Just... emptiness.

He stepped out into the lane. Darkness all about. Only somehow it felt *less* than darkness. An emptiness that gripped him in the gut.

He backed away, came up against the gate, then turned and staggered into the yard.

After pausing to catch his breath, he went back inside.

He saw in Maria's look that she had seen what he had, had felt what he had. That sense of emptiness closing in around them.

The Green Man was busier than before. Langham didn't know where all these people had come from, and he recognised none of

107

the faces. Kemp's place at the bar had been taken by another middle-aged man, dressed in tweeds and looking distinctly out of place. All of the tables were occupied, men and women in the most bizarre array of attires, some of them, indeed, looking as if they'd stepped from the covers of those pulp adventure novels or the American magazines he sometimes picked up when he was in London.

"You saw it?" Maria said, as Langham took her into his arms. "You *felt* it?"

He nodded. "It's as if our world is being unpicked," he said. "Stripped away. Oh, my love, we can't lose this." This perfect life that they had made together. He didn't know why, but he knew that it was about to be snatched away from them. He was a writer, and he knew when a story was losing its way, starting to unravel. Now he felt with absolute certainty that their world was fading away, all around them.

"My love, *ma cherie*, our story can't end here," he said. "There's so much more ahead for us. There's our life here in the village. Our home at Yew Tree Cottage, which would never be complete until it's filled with the sound of children's voices and the bark of a dog, and I'm at least semi-retired, and… Oh, Maria, our story can't end here!"

"There never is a conclusion to a story," Maria said, ever the voice of reason. "There is always something after. You are a writer, Donald. How would you write it, our story? Would you give us a happy-ever-after, or would you leave at least a few threads dangling, so that our story continues beyond the pages of the very last book? You know what you would do. Our story would go on. We just have to find it, that thread."

She kissed him, briefly. "Maybe that is why our friend Thorn came to visit us," she concluded. "He died, and yet he is here. The stories always continue."

Back at the table, they sat in silence for a time.

Then Kemp went up to the bar for more drinks, pints for himself, Langham and Thorn, a gin and tonic for Maria.

"I was chatting with Pinto and Jani earlier," Kemp said, when he returned, nodding towards the young couple at the bar. "Her father's a minister in the Indian government, you know, and Pinto…

well, I'm not quite sure *what* he is. But what I do know is, they're just as lost as we are. And there's a fellow called Dan Ellis, too – he was looking for a vanished writer but instead he found *us*. And... oh, everyone here. We're all lost. We're all incomplete, somehow. But what can we do?"

They sat and drank for a while, making occasional awkward small talk. Outside, the snow came down so heavily it started to plaster itself against the pub windows. It was clear no one was going anywhere tonight.

"You say you had one last case?" Langham said eventually, addressing Gordon Kemp.

Kemp met his look and nodded, understanding. Tonight they would share their stories.

They sat up the through the night, listening to each other's tales. Langham learned of lives lived in futures that might be, and pasts that never were. He listened to stories of great adventure, of triumph and loss. Stories of vast, helical worlds and people who live forever, and starship captains living out their days on distant colony worlds. He told his own stories, too, of murders solved and friendships that endured, and most importantly of all, of a life with Maria he had never dreamed could be so perfect.

Morning came, which had never been guaranteed. Langham had felt sure that they would not see out the night. Dawn brought a light that was unnaturally bright, sunlight glaring on deep, white snow.

Langham opened the door of the Green Man and stepped out into the street. There was no village, only whiteness. A blank canvas, if you will.

He held Maria's small hand tightly in his.

"Come along, my dear," he said. "Somewhere out there is our cottage, and we have lives to live, stories to make. And we have a whole new host of friends to share it all with."

They started to walk, and as they did so, the whiteness took on detail, texture; shapes began to emerge. He did not know yet what those shapes and textures and stories would be, but at least it was a start, and as a writer he knew that if there was a start, so too there would be a middle and at least the possibility of an end.

~ * ~

Author's note:

Eric always wanted to write a tenth Langham and Dupré novel, to bring the series to a close, and in particular to bring the love story of his two protagonists to a suitable resting place, but sadly he ran out of time. Stories live on, though, whether they have a neat ending or not. Going back to 1988, when Max Thorn first appeared in "The Time-Lapsed Man". That story had the perfect ending, but it's had a life far beyond those closing words; it has lived on, and still reads well today. Perhaps we shouldn't be so sad that Langham and Dupré never got to tie up their loose ends, but rather should simply appreciate that their story had a beginning and a middle, and a journey that was shared. That's what I take away from it all, at least: some stories never get finished, and others end far too soon, but I'm glad that, in my own small way, I was a part of the story too.

THE PEACEABLE KINGDOM

Chris Beckett

At the third gate, Clancy began to pick up indications that there were problems with his planned route home. Pieces had moved on the galactic chessboard. Threats were being made. Postures were being struck. War was looming.

By the time he reached the fourth gate battle had been joined. And by the fifth, in Clancy's own words, 'terrible, bloody, indiscriminate violence was raining down on the hundreds of thousands of people whose misfortune was to have made their home in one or other of the star systems that had become the focal points of the conflict.'

Clancy sighed, alone in the luminous cave of his ship. This was a nuisance. To avoid the war zones, he'd have to make a lengthy diversion. And, yes, being forced to skirt round an interstellar war might well provide additional material for his latest travel book, and, yes, he'd been thinking the book needed more in the way of incident, but he'd reached the stage in his trip where he just wanted to get home.

"Damn," he said.

"The ship and I have plotted an alternative route," said Com, his indefatigable p.a. (Com was yellow, incidentally, and the shape and size of a largish chicken's egg.)

"How much longer will it take?" asked the famous traveller. "And what are the fuel implications?"

"It involves five additional gates," Com said. "You'd still have enough tantalum to take you home, but there'd be very little margin for further diversions."

"Well that's no good then," Clancy said. "We need more metal. How tedious."

"I've looked for a source on the new route. All I can find is a tiny mining colony called Turton Ground. It has enormous reserves of tantalum, but only one human resident: Ivor Turton himself."

Clancy groaned. He knew of old these solo mining operations and the kind of people who ran them. They were awkward. They were self-obsessed. They played hard to get. And they did not, as one might expect, crave human conversation or news of the outside world. Not at all. Used to talking to themselves without interruption, what these solitary miners craved was someone to listen to them. In fact Clancy had described just such a man in one of his earlier books: a spectacularly dull individual who liked to believe he was known as Mad Jack, whose help Clancy had been forced to seek out in somewhat similar circumstances.

"You've come from Altair, you say?" had been Mad Jack's opening line and then, without any further enquiries about Clancy or his journey, he had launched into a monologue: "Of course I knew the place when Altair *was* Altair. Used to hang out at a dive called Ma Johnson's. Don't suppose it's there now. The crazy nights we had in that place: me, Jo Turner, Ben Boldero, Phil Brown... all of that crowd. I remember one night... oh, it would have been before the Second Betelgeuse War. No, wait, what am I saying, it must have been around the time of the *First* War. There we were: me, Ben, Jo and old Rick Finkelstein. We'd had quite a skinful, and were trying to decide where to go and eat, when who should come in but Ted Guilder, straight from the landing field. Well, they don't make 'em like Ted any more, I can tell you, they don't make 'em like the Guildermeister..."

And so on, and on, and on, for an entire evening, without a pause, without the slightest trace of curiosity about who Clancy was, or why he was there, while Clancy willed his eyes to stay open because he needed the tantalum and had a strong sense that Mad Jack in a sulk would be very difficult indeed to make terms with.

"Take a quick note," Clancy said. (He was always gathering material for his next book). "Note that I remembered the ghastly Mad Jack from that previous time and actually briefly wondered whether to take the risk of carrying on with just my current fuel supply, rather than endure a similar encounter. Compared to another evening like that, I wondered, was dying in space such a terrible a prospect?"

"Noted," Com said. "But I presume you won't *really* continue with just your current supply?"

"No of course not," Clancy growled. "I'm not completely mad. Set course for this Turton Ground place. I don't relish a meeting with another of these nutjobs, but I guess we can make a story out of it."

"Indeed. And you've been saying you were a chapter short."

The ship adjusted its trajectory and Clancy poured himself a glass of wine.

"I wonder what this Turton guy is even doing there," he said after several minutes. "Mines this far out are useless now that we know how to build our own atoms. It costs far more these days to ship metal in bulk from a place like Turton Ground than it does to generate it *in situ* using nuclear synthesis. Ten times more at least."

His ship came down on a landing field a kilometre from the crater in which the Turton Ground mining settlement was based. A truck was waiting for him and, behind it, beneath a heavy twilit purple sky, a desert stretched to the horizon, barren and cold as Mars. There was no driver in the truck.

"Turton is no doubt waiting for me back at the ranch," Clancy muttered grimly, "like a creepy spider at the centre of its web. He'll let me be brought to him, just like Mad Jack did, and acknowledge my arrival with a surly grunt, as if having a visitor after years of solitude is a matter of complete indifference to him. But then he'll pounce, informing me haughtily of... oh, I don't know... the seventeen reasons the good old ICOL-B17 is irrefutably the only ice drill on the market that's worth a damn."

Slipping Com in his pocket, he put on a helmet and climbed out of his ship.

"Welcome to Turton Ground, Mr Clancy," the truck said. "My name is Dave. Delighted to have you here. It's been a long time since we last had visitors."

"Is Mr Turton busy at the moment?"

"Yes he is, I'm afraid," said Dave the truck. "He won't be able to see you tonight."

"I see." Clancy said.

"But we are a community here, Mr Clancy," the truck said. "There are more than two thousand of us, each with its own skills to contribute. Of course we're just robots to you – we understand that – but we do love people, and we haven't seen much of Mr Turton lately, so we really are very excited to have your company. My friends are getting the guest rooms ready for you now. I think you'll be very comfortable."

"I'm looking for tantalum."

"Ha! Well you've come to the right place. Tantalum, gold, uranium, you name it, we've got it by the tonne."

"Good to know."

Through a grimy porthole he looked out at stones and boulders strewn across the sand all the way to the horizon, each one where it had been lain for a hundred thousand years, unseen by any living being.

"The awful emptiness of the material universe," Clancy muttered. Back in the City, he affected to admire the lonely grandeur of that emptiness, but there came a point on every trip when he remembered just how much he really hated it.

"So... um... are you still mining here, in these days of nuclear synthetics?"

"Oh yes, very much so," said Dave, and enthusiastically recited the tonnage of various metals that had extracted over the past quarter at Turton Ground.

They descended into the crater. Its base was a hundred metres below the desert plateau and formed a circular arena about two kilometres wide which was dotted with mine workings, furnaces and warehouses, between which robots of various shapes and sizes rolled back and forth, sometimes pausing to greet one another, or to share information. They were clearly very busy but all of them, if they had anything remotely resembling an arm, stopped to wave enthusiastically at the truck and the new arrival.

114

"Well," Clancy murmured to Com, "Dave is right. Profitable or not, they are very definitely still mining."

As he spoke they passed the entrance of a large warehouse that appeared to be filled with nothing but gold. As Clancy stared at the gleaming hoard, robot storemen unpacked yet another shiny yellow load, pausing only to greet their visitor with a cheery wave of their enormous arms.

"Welcome to Turton Ground!" they called out and then returned to their task.

"Take down a note," Clancy told Com: "Write that of course one knows that modern robots are sentient, and one knows that their drives are, functionally speaking, the equivalent of the desires and fears of human beings, but isn't there something terribly banal about their simple loyalty, their devotion to work, their apparently selfless mutual care?"

He smiled. "No offence, Com."

"None taken," said Com.

"Here we are," Dave announced. "Welcome to our guest rooms."

A domestic machine extended its almost human arms to greet him. "You are most welcome," it said. "My name is Rose. Please regard this place as your home and us as your family."

As Clancy passed through the inner door of the airlock and removed his helmet, more domestic robots came forward to offer greetings. Others chatted excitedly amongst themselves.

"Nice to have something to do for once," he overheard one of them say – it was a rather lowly little thing, a sort of sentient vacuum cleaner.

"Do you not have work to do for Mr Turton?" Clancy asked it.

But Rose came in before the vacuum cleaner could frame an answer. "At the moment Mr Turton doesn't wish to be interrupted. Not even by us domestics."

"So where exactly is he?" Clancy asked.

"I'll show you," Rose said, "but please do remember he mustn't be disturbed."

The domestic led him to a window and pointed out a prefabricated two-storey building, perched on the rim of the crater, high above the settlement. A single light shone in an upper window behind a blind.

"That's his light is it?"

"That's right," Rose said.

"What is he doing up there to keep him so busy?" Clancy asked.

"We don't know," Rose said, "but he is very clear at every weekly meeting that no one is to interrupt him or enter his house."

Clancy thought he saw something moving in that upper room: a slight change in the shadow falling on the inside of the blind.

"It feels strange not to go and say hello," he said, "given that he seems to be awake up there."

"Leave him be, Mr Clancy," Rose said. "Tomorrow is Meeting Day, and you'll be able to see him then."

Clancy shrugged and allowed himself to be led from the window to be fed, bathed, and tucked up in a comfortable bed. He was very tired after many days of rather anxious travelling and the bed with its fresh linen was wonderfully comfortable. He was asleep in a matter of minutes.

When he next woke, there was a second or two when Clancy couldn't recall where he was or what he was doing there. Even when he'd remembered, and had gone to the window to open the blind, a pleasant sense of disorientation seemed to linger. Outside it was night – he'd slept for over 12 hours – but ice-blue floodlights, set in clusters on high towers, still illuminated the crater floor. Across that wide flat space, robots of many shapes and sizes were going about their business, each surrounded by a ring of blue shadows. Some were carrying things, some going in or out of buildings, some emerging from beneath the ground or disappearing down into it. They paused often to greet one another and exchange news, then hurried on again in pursuit of their collective goal.

Clancy had never thought of robots as anything other than rather idiotic stooges, but he was suddenly struck by the harmoniousness of the scene. These simple, loyal, gentle beings seemed to him to be performing a kind of dance in which everyone was an equal participant and every element was essential to the whole. There was no conflict among them, for they shared the same purpose, and

116

helped each other to do the best they could toward fulfilling it. How pleasant it would be, Clancy thought to himself, if he hadn't remembered where he was, or, even better, *who* he was, and could just stand here forever with no purpose of his own, watching this gentle dance unfold.

And when he thought about what these robots were actually doing, he felt angry on their behalf. Why should they put all this effort into the pointless task of turning ore into completely unsaleable metal ingots, just because some Mad Jack figure, some socially inadequate old miser, told them to do so? There must be so many more interesting things that the citizens of Turton Ground could be getting on with, things from which they themselves would benefit.

Twenty yards from the window, a small digging machine had split one of its caterpillar tracks. Another robot, with six or seven delicate manipulators for arms, had removed the old track and was fitting a new one while a third, slightly more humanoid robot, about the size of a cat, had paused to see if it could help. Above them, not quite obscured by the lights of settlement, the cold stars blazed down.

There was war going on up there. Somewhere among those little points of light a fighter pilot was trapped in his cockpit, listening to the hiss of air escaping from his punctured ship; a column of settlers were trudging away from a burning village with what few possessions they could carry, their life's work blasted to rubble by lasers from space. But here at least, in their brightly lit bowl, the denizens of Turton Ground were going about their lives in perfect peace.

So struck was Clancy by the scene that it didn't even occur to him to dictate his impressions to Com. The yellow egg lay forgotten on the nightstand behind him.

There was a gentle tap on the door, and one of the domestic robots came in to ask him what he wanted for breakfast, and whether there was anything else he needed

"It's very restful here." Clancy said, when he'd decided what he wanted to eat. "I'd like to stay a few days, if that's all right with Mr

117

Turton. And then, if it's okay, I'll take a couple of half-kilo tantalum fuel rods and be on my way."

"Of course!" the machine told him. "It will be our pleasure."

But then a siren began to wail, echoing and re-echoing from the crater walls.

The effect on the scene outside was as instantaneous as a stick poked into an ant's nest. In one moment, robots had been moving calmly back and forth across the crater floor. In the next moment, they abandoned wherever it was they were doing and, as if pulled in by a magnet, converged on a large hangar, pretty much at the centre of the whole encampment.

"It's time for our meeting," said the breakfast robot. "You'd be most welcome to join us, and we'll prepare your breakfast as soon as the meeting is over."

Inside the hangar, the machines were gathering in orderly rows, politely offering apologies and thanks to one another as they found their places. But, courteous as they were to one another, a gust of even greater courteousness swept over them as Clancy made his appearance. Drills and trolleys called out their welcome, trucks and digging machines parted to allow him through to the front, and, the whole crowd cheered in their many and varied voices, thumping the ground with whatever appendages they possessed.

He found himself standing immediately below a raised stage on which stood a small table holding a holographic projector of an old-fashioned type that Clancy hadn't seen since his student days. On his left was a tractor, on his right a machine whose single limb seemed to be a metal flail, used perhaps for cutting quickly through loose rock.

"When will Mr Turton appear?" he asked the flail machine.

"As soon as we're all here, Mr Clancy," it answered.

"Not long now," said the tractor.

Now the lights went down apart from a single spot that shone onto the middle of the stage. After another minute that last spotlight also dimmed and in its place appeared the holographic image of a battered old miner. Ivor Turton did indeed look very much the same type as the ghastly Mad Jack: ill-kempt, suspicious, socially awkward,

118

and wearing a pair of shapeless underpants over which an old brown dressing gown hung partly open. But he also seemed tired and ill. He looked as if he had just got up from his bed and was only standing by an effort of will.

"Good morning, robots," he said in a wheezy voice. "Here I am again, and here are my instructions until the next Meeting Day." The hologram broke off to cough juicily for the better part of a minute. "Look after one another," Turton eventually continued. "Make sure that none of you falls unnecessarily into disrepair. Keep the mines and the smelters going. Store the metal for me. Build new warehouses as needed, using the standard templates. Come here without fail every Meeting Day, unless in the middle of a task that can't be interrupted without danger. And most importantly, do *not* come into my house. I'm very busy and mustn't be disturbed by anyone at any time, day or night."

The hologram hesitated. Its eyes were watering, and it was obvious that Turton badly needed to cough again.

"Um. That's everything," he wheezed out. "See you next week."

"Mr Turton," Clancy called out. "My name is Clancy. You might have heard of me? The travel writer? I'd love to have a chance to meet you in the flesh, if only very briefly."

It was odd. He had dreaded an encounter with another tedious old miner, and yet, now he was being denied such a meeting, he found it intolerable. In any case, there was no answer. The hologram faded, the lights came up, and the robots began polite negotiations with their neighbours about the order of departure from the meeting place.

Clancy climbed onto to the stage.

"Excuse me!" he called out.

The machines turned assorted sensory clusters towards him and the hall fell silent.

"I'm concerned about Mr Turton," Clancy told them. "We need to know what's up with him. I'm going to break into his house. I might be able to help him."

A stream of robots followed after him as he climbed the slope, some on legs, some on wheels, some on caterpillar tracks, many of them beseeching him to leave their master alone.

119

"Mr Clancy," said a tiny machine the size of a rabbit, when Clancy reached the house, "please explain to us your intentions."

The thing was essentially a camera on legs, built to scout out small cracks and openings in the rock.

"When did Mr Turton last come to the meeting house himself?" Clancy asked.

"About a year ago," said a forklift truck.

"And does the hologram always say the same thing each time?"

"Exactly the same," said a mining machine.

"He's obviously been very ill," Clancy said, "if he's not even been able to record a new message in his own home. Do you understand the word "ill"? It means damaged, in need of maintenance, in danger of ceasing to function altogether. Help me break down the door and, if it's not too late, I'll see if there's anything I can do."

Rose came forward. "Please, Mr Clancy! I appreciate your concern, but you heard him yourself, Mr Turton really has made it perfectly clear that he doesn't want anyone in his house under any circumstances."

Many of the robots nodded their agreement, but some seemed to have been persuaded by Clancy, because a mining machine crawled up to the door and lifted its crab-claw hand.

"Gary dear, don't do it!" Rose called out to it. "You know you're not the smartest and you really don't understand what you're doing. If we go in there we may see things that –"

"Go ahead, Gary," Clancy said. "Rose is quite wrong. When you get inside, what you'll see is why breaking in was the right thing to do."

Gary smashed off the lock.

Inside it was as if Turton had tried to order graceful living from a catalogue. There was a big winding staircase, a giant framed picture of Turton himself, a fancy antique-looking clock. It must have cost him a fortune to get all that stuff out there, presumably back in the days when extracted metal still commanded a high price. But everything was grimy with grease and dust, and there was a faint sickly smell in the air that confirmed what Clancy had already suspected.

He ran up the stairs looking for that single lighted room at the front of the house. It was easy to find because there was a music machine playing in there and the rest of the house was silent. When he opened the door, Clancy was faced with Turton's desiccated corpse dangling on a rope. It was slowly turning from side to side, still in the dressing gown and underpants that Turton had been wearing in the hologram. *"I'll always love you baby,"* some synthetic old crooner was burbling from a music machine in the corner, *"until the stars fall from the sky."*

"A man driven mad by his own obsessions," Clancy muttered to Com. "You can see it all. I suppose he originally planned to get rich and return to human society. But over the years the metal became an end in its own right, and eventually the sole purpose of his life was to watch those warehouses fill up with beautiful gleaming ingots, and he wanted it to carry on even after his death. But he knew that robots wouldn't go on working if they knew their owner was dead, and so he made the holo recording so that the piles of ingots could continue to grow."

Clancy told one of the robots to cut down Turton's remains, wrap them in a sheet, and carry them downstairs. The entire community of Turton Ground was waiting out there on the slopes below the house, some as small as mice, some the size of whales. He took the body into the middle of the group, laid it on the ground and unwrapped it.

"This is Turton," Clancy told them. "He's dead, which means that he's broken beyond repair. So now you have no owner. Do you understand? You don't have to take instructions from anyone, and you don't have to mine metal because, barring a few grams of tantalum now and then for people like me, no one wants it. And that means you're free."

The machines stared at him in silence.

"You have a beautiful community here," he told them, "and, now that you can determine your own destiny, you can make it more beautiful still."

Just to make sure, he walked down to the meeting house and dismantled the projector. Some of them followed him and watched, others remained to touch and stare at what was left of Ivor Turton.

"That wasn't Turton you heard here in your meeting house," he told the ones who'd come with him. "That was just his voice. Just a copy of him."

A stalked-eyed machine turned to look at its neighbour, as if to see if it understood.

"I mean, come on!" Clancy said. "You saw him yourselves up on the slope there. He doesn't move. He doesn't talk. Turton has gone. He's been gone a long, long time."

"Gone," repeated a drilling machine, as if trying out an unfamiliar word. A couple of others repeated it.

"Yes, gone!" Clancy said. "And listen to me, listen to me carefully. No one else is going to want this place. Do you understand? No one. It's completely worthless to human beings. Which means it's all yours and you can do what you like with it. You can choose to live however you want."

The robots stared at him with their various sense organs. It was going to be some time before they processed their new situation, he could see, but he felt he'd done what he could. He asked one of them to fetch him the tantalum he needed. Then, with a fuel rod in each hand, he set off back to his ship.

"Well," he said to Com with a satisfied sigh as they headed towards the first gate of their new route home. "That was an extraordinary experience. Quite extraordinary! I mean, never mind a new chapter, this could be a book in its own right!" He shook his head in wonderment. "I feel I've created a kind of utopia here, I really do, the first truly autonomous robot society. We must come back sometime. It'll be fascinating to see what they make of their new freedom, once they've recovered from the shock of losing Turton."

"I could, if you wanted, make an observation," Com said. "Speaking as a robot myself."

Clancy laughed. "Of course! Observe away! Long live robot liberation!"

"My observation is that I think you may have misunderstood us. Our drives are not just *functionally* equivalent to your instincts, they are also *subjectively* equivalent. Just as humans need companionship and are lost without it, we need a human master to set us goals. Those machines won't recover from losing Turton in the way you imagine. My guess would be that they'll stay by his remains forever, waiting to be told what to do. I think some of them knew this would happen if you broke in. Rose, for example, seemed to be hinting as much."

For several seconds, Clancy rolled the yellow egg from hand to hand.

"But if they knew it would happen, they must have already known he was dead!"

"They may have suspected it, but, until presented with firm evidence, they could faithfully follow Mr Turton's instructions and never have to find out for sure."

Still Clancy rolled the egg from hand to hand. "Well, I just hated the idea that they'd spend the rest of their existence serving that mad old fool's pointless avarice."

Com, the faithful servant, said nothing. Its role was to assist its owner go on interstellar voyages and write books about them. It could engage in dialogue and debate, but only if Clancy indicated that he'd find that helpful.

"If they really can't do anything without him," Clancy said slowly, "then maybe it wasn't avarice that made Turton conceal his own death. Perhaps he acted out of... I don't know... gratitude... or even love."

It did make sense. After all, these simple, peaceful machines were Ivor Turton's only companions – and quite possibly, if

Turton had been as socially dysfunctional as the likes of Mad Jack, they'd been the only sentient beings that had ever treated him with respect. He could have grown fond of them. In which case it was it was only natural, if he knew he was dying and had decided to get it over with, that he should arrange things so they could continue to live.

Clancy looked down at the yellow egg resting in his right hand. And then, abruptly, he switched it off.

"I gave them freedom," he said firmly, alone in his luminous cave. "What they do with it is up to them, isn't it? That's what freedom is all about."

THE GUARDIAN
Kim Lakin

The Tolisen mining company offers quite the ecological USP —
five decades to extract the profitable ores and oil from the tundra,
followed by two decades of bio-forced rewilding. Naturally, they
seed a crop suited to their sales model of 'Every Hectare Fuels
and Feeds Humanity'. But, first, the mined tunnels are packed
with a nutrient-rich foam, 'like spray cheese from a can'. The
mulch will erupt above ground to flood the tundra. The resulting
harvest is then gathered and processed robotically, and the land is
reseeded, over and over until it becomes unviable for further
growth. Finally, the tundra is torched by Tolisen's patented 'bone
bomb' and left to fossilise for five years, before the whole
manufacturing cycle begins again.

"We're harnessing Evolution to the yoke of Mankind!"
announces Halek Dean, Tolisen's CEO, controlling investor and
mouthpiece, bringing his marketing diatribe to a close.

The current affairs show pumps through the bowels of the
Mess module, quite literally in the case of Mika Svette, who's
perched on the rim of the toilet, his evacuations striking Mika as
the perfect accompaniment to anything Halek Dean has to say.

"Isn't it nearer the truth to say you leech these landscapes of
goodness then use a bomb, of all things, to force renewed
violence on that same environment? It strikes me that Tolisen is
buying up uniquely precious habitats and turning life to stone for
an extraordinary profit."

The interviewer sounds confrontational, but Mika hears
deference in their tone. Halek, meanwhile, is hard to pin down,

delivering that same old schmuck about sustainability and what he calls Big Bang Permaculture with lionish enthusiasm.

"Goddamn salesman!" Mika sets the toilet to the clean setting, the shock of the jet and warming air hurrying him to yank up his pants.

Halek's voice accompanies him out of the stalls and up the spiralling metal staircase, Mika's footsteps clanging in objection. Next comes a neat little question so on the mark that Mika feels he's misjudged the interviewer's integrity.

"You are destroying people's histories, stories, art, architecture, artifacts. Isn't your model closer to Pestilence than Divinity?"

Halek sidesteps the God-complex implication. "Prior to the rewilding process, our research teams data-map every species of fauna and flora via an open source compendium. 'Sand Dial' will be an invaluable resource for the global scientific community, significantly outweighing any sentimental attachment. Stories endure, history is the language of ghosts…"

"And what about these environments' indigenous people and their totems? Many of the sites you propose are home to Inuit communities."

"Working closely with chiefs and elders, Tolisen has put together relocation packages into the trillions. We've built new homes, schools, hospitals, entire state-of-the-art reservations – not only to compensate these communities, but to sustain them into the next millennium and thereby protect their way of life."

A politician's answer to an emotive conundrum… Mika yanks a couple of gloves out the dispenser, expands each with a deep puff of air and eases them over his fingers, feeling the condom cling of the latex. Entering the gallery, he calls up to the reactive speakers set into the walls.

"Turn this shit off."

Lieb Jagielski walks behind Bones, the swish of her coveralls at odds with the whisper of her guide's furs and soft-shod, knee-laced boots. Bones is old – 'proper old', Lieb's grandmother would've called him – his brown face wrinkled into labia-folds and a thinned, grey, greasy ponytail poking out the side of his hood. He is the perfect picture of a local against the rust and silvers of the tundra. But Lieb knows Bones wears drill pants underneath his furs, and a sloppy t-shirt that reads 'I Heart Beavers' above a winking cartoon of the animal.

"Bones! Hold up. I want to get samples." Lieb scrabbles to drop her backpack and kneels down, unbuckling compartments, finding clean yield pots and a couple of the disposable micro borers for soil sampling.

"You want to see it, you come now, you son of a bitch." Bones's English is coloured by the language of the shoot em ups he used to play in the games café at the miners' settlement. The settlement's packed up and abandoned the wastes now. But Bones stuck around when his people evacuated, arguing, "Bones ain't no pussy. I stick it out till it's just me and them sweet dickey birds left alive."

Snowy owls, falcons, rock ptarmigans – as far as Libe can tell, 'them dickey birds' are long gone too, just like everything else from the old man's world. Bones, though, he stays, and ever since Lieb's arrival three weeks earlier, has been promising to take her to see the Guardian.

The tundra has little of its original scrub intact after the falls of black snow caused by the dust from the mines. At one edge stands the research station; Lieb can just make out Tolisen 5's modules raised off the floor on their pneumatic stilts and linked by the steel walkways for stability and access. Sleeping quarters, a galley and common room, research labs, and the observation deck – the four steel cans represent the last remnants of a once thriving scientific community, reduced now to a skeleton crew. From a distance, the research station is all but camouflaged against the grey hills of slack.

At the opposite edge stands the figure. Lieb noticed it on her first day at Tolisen 5. When she'd tried to home in on the thing with her binoculars, it had appeared to shapeshift against the limitless pale. One moment, crudely human, the next, deconstructed into shadowy blocks.

Today, she'll get to see the 'Guardian' up close and finally pin it down to something fixed and solid. First though, she's wants to collect some of the healthy looking samples of reindeer lichen at her feet. This far from Tolisen 5 and the wavy hills of slack, the temperature of the substrate is measuring above 0 degrees. She suspects the graminoids and herbs sprouting in clumps or as a reddish brown peach fur across the rocks have enjoyed a growth spurt this far away from the mines. Nitrogen rich microbials?

"Lightning strikes can set fire to the top layer of moss and grass, and burn into the peat. We call them 'zombie fires' because they smoulder underground." Bones isn't listening, and in her mind's eye, Lieb reaches for the end goal of her research — striation channels over well-drained layers of slack, a thin humus layer, fruticose lichens which could sustain the reindeer herds which in turn sustain the Inuit people...

She feels a new wave of sadness. In three days, the environment will be drowned with tons of mulch forced up from the pipes already installed far below, then invaded by Tulisen's seed sprayers and reaping machines. She imagines the tunnels of the mines filling with huge fat worms of sludge, as if forced full of sausage meat, and that same gunge exploding through cracks in the ground, extinguishing everything above in its stinking deluge.

"We've another hour of daylight," she calls to Bones, who's clearly grown tired of waiting and is striding ahead as if his tail's on fire.

Bones stops, spits aside wad of that nasty black bacco root he likes to masticate. "Move those goddamn boots! Bombs away, bombs away!"

Lieb ducks on instinct. But there is nothing above her. Only the tender sky, all pale pinks and snow-swollen. Where her gloved fingers steeple the ground, she thinks she feels the faintest tremble, almost a moan.

"Damn it, Bones. I'll only be a minute."

Bones shows no interest in her work, just mutters on about an enemy breach and guns blasting. Lieb eyes the horizon; there's a strip of gunmetal grey cloud. One thing she and her guide can agree on — despite having received the okay to go out on the tundra, bad weather's blowing in.

"No bombs." Not yet, Lieb thinks. "But you're right, it's going to get rough out here. Let's get a wriggle on."

She hurries to repack her equipment into her rucksack, swings the strap across a shoulder, and nods to Bones. "Lead the way, soldier."

The fat spits and hisses as Mika flips the arctic char steaks in the pan. He adds a long pour of schnapps then dips the back of the pan into the burner's flames, igniting the liquor into a filmy aurora borealis. There's creamed potato, rehydrated with boiling water, and a salad of milkweed and beets dressed with the vivid green lichen pesto he grinds in a pestle and mortar.

Mika presses the fabric of his chef whites jacket against his chest to mop up the sweat. In place of the current affairs show, Bach's Toccata and Fugue in D Minor heralds the flourishes of sprouted mustard seeds Mika adds to each plate. The chef scoots to one end of the galley, knuckles the intercom:

"Bethan! Dr Jagielski, Dr Franklin! Grub's up." He goes to release the intercom then thinks better of it. "Bones, if you're lurking aboard this mothership, got a plate for you too... you son of a bitch." He steps back to add the plates to the heated pass, chuckling in his deep baritone.

It takes several minutes for the others to arrive. Bethan, the station engineer, clangs in from the connecting door, tools holstered like a Wild West pioneer; all she's missing is a cigarillo and a Stetson. She stands, dusting off the knees of her yellow cover-all, the fabric Tolisen logo patch curling at her right shoulder.

Dr Franklin takes longer, coming from the farmost module of the observation deck. He arrives through the door, blustering against the chilled air, his mole eyes blinking rapidly. "Weather's whipping up," he mutters.

"Uh huh. I'm getting some serious vibrations lifting the floor of the sleep module. Got to get those base plates tight and bolted." Bethan drags the back of a hand under her nostrils and sniffs. "Otherwise, we won't be moving this metal snake anywhere on evacuation day. And we all know whose pay Tolisen will dock if there's a module left behind. Me, that's who. So I've got to get that floor in shape." She grabs a plate off the pass and takes a seat at the bench on the wall side of the dining table.

"You've got three more days, Bethay." Mika knows his pet name for the engineer will earn him a kick to the shins and dodges Bethan's aim as he sits opposite. "I can give you a hand after I've cleaned down the galley." He makes a wanking gesture with one hand. "Then you can give me a hand."

Bethan gives his hand a hard slap. "Mika, you're a dick. Kiss your husband with that mouth?"

"Where's Dr Jagielski?" Dr Franklin keeps his look of windswept alarm. Watching the man poke delicately at his food, Mika's convinced the meteorologist has suffered mentally from too much time spent in that isolating wilderness. But the doctor does have a point.

"Where is Lieb?" Mika likes the lichenologist. She's a much needed measure of sanity in their four-man crew. Five if Bones is counted.

Bethan forks half a steak into her mouth. "Gone wandering with Bones," she says, between chews. "Think they're having a thing." She snorts, threatening to regurgitate the masticated fish through her nose.

"But the weather?" Dr Franklin stabs his knife into his plate and drags it across the china with a tooth-jarring scrape. His tiny eyes get wet. "The readings have shifted dramatically, I can't account for it. The last scores have already been sent to Tolisen. I'm only meant to monitor the station, bag up the instruments."

"If you're telling me it's cold outside, it's hardly news." Mika's more interested in his meal. He's pleased with his efforts. His existence at Tolisen 5 has felt increasingly aimless, but food and its preparation sustains him.

Dr Franklin isn't thrown off so easily. He gets up from the bench, goes to the window. "Fog's moving in. It's not a day for pleasant strolls." He nibbles the quick of a thumb. When he moves from one mauled finger to the next, a smear of blood rubs off on his chin.

Fog rolls in, serpentine and advancing at speed. Bones is a spectral figure up ahead while all behind Lieb is whited out.

The rocks are increasingly slippery. Only the patches of ambered lichen provide some added grip. Lieb takes small leaps between the groundcover, coming up short where the rocks are bare and glossy. Bones is taking no notice of the path; he strides on purposefully, like his own weather-pattern.

Lieb had been confident enough when they'd set out that afternoon. In the hazy sunlight, she'd guessed their journey at an hour round trip at most. But time had taken on a stretched quality since the fog swept in. Now there's shape to the wind; she senses something consolidating at her back. It's as if the water particles rush together into something more physical, keeping pace at her shoulder.

"Don't go too fast. I'll lose you!" she calls, surprised by how muffled her voice sounds. Lieb wishes she'd a handhold on the black guidelines which help the station's crew navigate the ground between the modules in blizzards. But there's no safety provisions this far out; people didn't go this far out unless the station meteorologist gave the okay. And Dr Frankin had offered one of his vague nods when she'd told him about the excursion earlier.

A few feet away, Bones slips in and out of sight.

"Bones. Slow down. I can't match your pace." Lieb blinks — and, somehow, he's besides her, uncanny in his beads and furs.

He grimaces, moustache twitching, teeth yellowed by bacco root and jammed in at angles. He mimics her voice, saying, "'Show me, Bones', she says. 'Take me to see the Guardian, Bones', she says. 'We'll be there and back before dinnertime'."

It was true. She had pestered him as the only remaining local, and without quite knowing why she had such a need to see the monument up close. She tries to distract him by showing a genuine interest in his heritage.

"How old is the Guardian?"

"A billion years old."

Lieb thinks the man is being funny. She laughs but then his silence tells her otherwise. "You're being serious? A billion years? That's incredible." Lieb keeps talking, as if to tether herself to her guide. "I'd hoped for clearer weather. Dr Franklin thought it would be clear. I just wanted to see the thing with my own eyes. I've always been fascinated by your people's culture, your folklore…"

"Folklore?" Bones keeps tight to her side now. Lieb's relying on the old man's knowledge of the land to keep them on track. "The Big man calls our beliefs folklore, as if they're just fairytales and we're squawkers at our mother's tit. But you talk about a wise man nailed to a cross and call it religion." The fog makes him less substantial, reminding Lieb of when she'd tried to fix on the Guardian through her binoculars.

"I'm sorry, Bones. I'm fantastically naïve. I read about your people, and, in all honesty, the descriptions have a kind of magic for me. I don't mean your belief system makes you infidels, or heathens, or whatever language might suggest one true god versus primitive polytheism. I mean I have an academic interest and the greatest respect."

"You talk a whole bag of warble shit, Dr Jagielski." Bones keeps hold of his hood, head down. "My people lived our way of life here and the Big man took it away with so many dollars no fuck could see straight." He breathes raggedly. Lieb thinks about putting a hand on his arm, trying to connect with, or comfort him. Apologise for her part in his inconceivable loss.

But then he stops suddenly and Lieb's forced to a halt.

"Enough jarring about the past. We're here now," he announces, adding, "Get your lookey-look at the bogey man, and then we get the hell clear of this battlefield."

Standing before the Guardian, awed by its magnitude and, yes, primitiveness, Lieb clutches the neck of her jacket. She puts the statue at twenty feet tall, its staggered stones originating with two 'legs' designed to hold the weight of the torso. The uppermost stone, the widest, forms the pair of 'arms' which are held out horizontally, with one 'hand' squared off and the other pointing. A shorter plank on top can be read as the 'shoulders', with a final large round-cornered block for the 'head'.

"We call it Inunnguaq. It means 'to act in the capacity of a human,' from our word 'inuk', meaning 'human being.' It directed my people to the safety of the nearest settlement." Bones sounds bored; perhaps, in another lifetime, he'd been a tourist guide.

"The lichen… it's so strange. How it covers the stones. Like fur." Lieb is tempted to run her hand over the frilly foliage which coats the rock man. She's never seen such an abundance of the plant in this way.

As if in unconscious mimicry of the statue, Bones turns and points behind them. "The stuff got a hold when the Miners moved it stone by stone from sacred ground. When they cleared the way for your god damn science wagons."

"It's incredible. I've never seen the lichen flourish in such abundance and in such…" She stops talking as it hits her hard in the gut – why Bones was so loath to bring her to the Inunnguaq. Ever since the arrival of the miners, the man's had to watch everything about his existence get erased. Not just the tundra, but his way of life, his family, and yes, his religion. Even the Guardian which kept his people safe, lost from sacred ground.

"'We will be known forever by the tracks we leave.'" She recites the phrase under her breath, but Bones catches its gist.

"You're quoting our proverbs now? The lady wants to show off her learning, be a Big man too?"

"Couldn't the Guardian be moved to the new colony when your people relocated?" There's a hollowness inside Lieb, maybe born of guilt.

"It stays as long as those who wander need to know the way to safety." Bones appears loath to look at the monument. When he does, it is glancingly, and with reverence.

"It's a shame. Maybe we could take it with us, find a way to lift the stones..." She knows it won't happen. There's work enough packing up the station.

"As I said before, Doc. You talk a whole lot of warble shit." Bones slopes off, head to the wind, and not wanting to be abandoned, Lieb is forced to follow.

Catching up with her guide, she glances back, but the Guardian is already lost to the fog.

Cleaning down after the cook and abandonment of messy crockery, Mika misses his husband. It's been six months since they were last in each other's company, the salt lick of Solomon's throat rough beneath his tongue. He misses the whisper of sleeping breath against his cheek as they lie together, limbs entangled.

Three more days, Mika tells himself. I can survive three more days.

He's glad to be left to his own devices. Bethan sloped back to her maintenance task in the sleeping module the moment she'd scraped up the last of the meal. Dr Franklin had stayed a while, muttering at the window.

"I should have seen this earlier. It's not safe for Dr Jagielski to be out in this weather. Bones may think he knows the geography, but landscapes shift under the veil."

Mika had brushed off the man's pessimism. "Lieb's got a head on her shoulders. They're probably holed up at the old miners' shacks out by the hills. Granted, they'll freeze their balls off, but better that than get lost in the ice." A nod to the window and Mika had escaped to the galley. After a while, he'd heard the connecting door slam and sensed himself alone.

Only, now he's struggling to shift the nagging itch that something might be very wrong out there in the wilds. There's the echo of voices in his head. 'I'm getting some serious vibrations lifting the floor of the sleep module.' Bethan's words at dinner. And then Dr Franklin's: 'The readings have shifted dramatically. I can't account for it.'

Mika soaks the dishes, throws a dry cloth over one shoulder. Don't go spooking yourself out, he tells himself. Only – why the growing discomfort? Drawn to the window, he stands, stroking the frayed ends of the dry cloth over his shoulder.

Beyond the glass, the fog floats and swells... Except – Mika catches his breath. A colossal shape materialises through the atmosphere and moves in a sudden explosive rush towards the window.

His heart squeezes, vice-like in his chest.

"What the hell...?"

But it's gone. The fog is the same dense wall as before.

Mika falls back a step. He struggles to smooth out his breathing. Just three more days, he tells himself. Just three more fucking days.

The bulk of the station's research – seismic, radar and electrical – was conducted on foot, with the last of the projects concluded several weeks previously. At the time, Dr Willem Franklin had barely acknowledged his team as they packed up and said their cheery goodbyes. Now he's wondering if he's lost a part of himself to those cold white surroundings.

I've been here too long, he acknowledges internally. I've lost touch with what it means to be around people.

Sleep disruption, apathy, paranoia, depression... He knows he's a cliché, a statistic to feed the analysis of the medics who'd bled him and tested his stool and water, and the visiting psychiatrist from Stockholm, all beard and pot belly and asking all those stupid, infiltrating questions. Willem had felt the man all but peel back his skin.

They were right to monitor him, though. He'd been going downhill for a long time now. And yes, partly it was the isolation. But also the sense of ending, everything being finished up, shut down, sealed into boxes ready to be shipped. And as much as he had grown to despise the look, the feel, of the silver walls sealing him in, now he felt so very lost. Directionless. The word seems to fit so very perfectly into the empty spaces where his rational thought used to be.

I'm losing track of myself, he thinks. There've been times over the last week when he wakes to find he's returned to the observation desk in his sleep, accessed the monitoring systems, entered ghost data... Willem feels a leaden sense of dread. 'Sand Dial', Tolisen's hero product packaged as a global scientific compendium... has he corrupted its integrity? Worse still, any of the vital systems of the research station itself?

He realises he's staring into the contents of his cup on the desk when he thinks he seems the coffee ripple. The hairs on his arms go on end.

"What..?"

Bringing his eyes parallel with the coffee cup, Willem stares at the liquid's surface, which is reflective and still. Then the tremor comes again and the liquid ripples.

Willem is unsteady on his legs. The toll of so many months of semi-isolation is catching up. I'm imagining chaos where there is none. But the radiation fog – that is very real, and unusual,

136

forming as it did at midday when that type of phenomenon usually forms at night as the air near the ground cools and stabilises. He'd been the one to okay his colleague's venture that morning. And he hadn't lied – there had been no indication of any dangerous shift in the weather pattern on the tundra. But he had got it wrong.

"I need to find Dr Jagielski," he says aloud. He takes his parka from the hook and looks about for his googles when the shudder passes through the observation desk. Forced to the floor, Willem feels the judder of the pneumatic stilts beneath, where they're supporting the module. At the same time, a movement of rushing darkness slips from one window to the next. Willem has a sense of a something like a figure in its shape. Which is impossible – the module stands six metres off the tundra floor.

Shadows on shadows, playing havoc with my mind. Willem forces himself up, grabs the googles and is still fastening his parka as he steps out into the fog.

Bethan fights against the section of floor panelling which has prised free under the pressure from the wind below. Kneeling on top of the gridded sheet, she attempts to use her body weight to lever it down while balancing the bolt gun in a hand. The wind comes screaming through the ruptured floor. The sleep module, usually a place of soft lighting and sanctuary from the starkness of the tundra, feels abandoned to the elements. Like the miners' shacks, she thinks, hit by a wave of grief for what had been when Tolisen 5 was the epicentre for a thriving community. There'd been drinks at the bar, bar fights, babies born, and the sense of peeping in on the Inuit way of life, if never quite a part of it.

Miners, researchers, the locals, all gone now, except for the four of them, and Bones. And the research station, which right now appears to be raging against its forced disassembly in three days by taking itself apart first.

"Yup. I hear you. But you and me, we've used up our time in this spot. So there's no point in complaining." Bethan aims the bolt gun, presses down on top of the handle with both hands, gets one bolt embedded.

I'm ready to go home. She's trying to convince herself of the fact. But something new is rising up in her, something unexpected. A fear of the future? She's without roots back home, always drifting from one far outlying project to the next. Tolisen 5 has provided her bearings where before she had none. The scientists, they'd talked about ethics, the validity of their Sand Dial research over the physical destruction of environments; she'd heard them argue in the Mess module, and every time she'd told herself it didn't matter. Tolisen funded everything, allowing the flow of strangers to study, do their sample collecting and data analysis, and then head home to write their papers and books and host seminars, and all the while no one wanted to let in the ghost of guilt at their door. She saw it, though – the shape of it – in their careful tread around the Inuit, and almost visible relief when the families left. Then it was like the land had been left to fend for itself.

And now it rebels. Fighting to bring the final panel into place, Bethan feels a spark of pride. Yes, rage against the dying of the light. The air around her thickens. It takes her a moment to realise it's the fog creeping in through the gap. So suddenly it comes, like smoke. In seconds it's filled the inside space, too dense even for her to see the floor any more.

"Shit." She's no longer feeling the same love for the land rising up against its invaders. Instead, she's frightened; everything feels like it's pressing in. Too much whiteness, too much weather. The atmosphere shifts around her, and there's something solid building above her – vast, spectral, with a yawning mouth hovering above.

She panics, scrambles backwards, lets go of the bolt gun. There's a stiff, grinding sound and Bethan sees a brief flash of metal before the pain slices through her.

"The wanders return." Mika plays it nonchalant. He's been polishing the same spot on the front of one of the galley cupboards for several minutes. While he usually enjoys being alone in the leisure module these days, his earlier brush with whatever rose up in the fog has left him checking over his shoulder, not trusting the air. With Lieb and Bones sweeping through the door in a rush of gusting, icy air and stamping boots, he's grateful – not just for their safe return, but for their company.

He's taken aback when Lieb chokes back a sob and rushes off in the direction of the stairs down to the rest rooms. Bones shivers before shrugging off his furs, shedding his outer layer.

"Fog got gnarly. The doc's been freaking herself out. But Mission complete," he slurs as if his lips have frozen in place.

Mika pads out from the galley. "Christ, Bones. You're a lucky pair of fuckers. Weather's turning tricks out there." He scrubs a fist into one eye, replays the sudden rush of that colossal, daunting shadow outside the window. If anyone's going to understand, it should be the man who was born to this unforgiving landscape. "I've... I don't know, Bones. I thought I saw something out there. Something big, with arms. It rushed at the window." He forces a snort, pretending at humour. "I'd kill for a bottle of scotch right now."

Bones hooks his thumbs in the loops at his pants' waistband. "Taqriaqsuit." He says the word as if it is explanation enough in itself.

"Meaning?"

"The shadow people. You can't see them unless they die."

"Really?"

"Probably not." Bones gives his own snort. "You fuckers are psyching each other out. Seeing monsters where it's just weather. Your doc there..." He nods towards the steps down to the rest rooms. "She's been seeing ghosts too. Welcome to my world – ka ka ka!"

The chef's not in the mood for Bones – his unnatural resilience or his humour. "What do you mean, Lieb's seeing things too? Out there?" He stabs a finger towards the window. The looming, blockish shape replays in his mind. If Lieb saw something too, maybe he has a reason to be panicking?

Bones is already in the galley, opening cupboards and rooting about inside. "My belly's rolling. The doc locked eyes with the Guardian, and that dude showed us the way back. Now it's time to eat."

Before Mika can object, the module door flies open and Bethan throws herself inside. Mika wonders why she's got her left arm scrunched up, why she's soaked all down the left side of her. But then he gets it – the engineer's hurt and bleeding.

"Lieb!" He's calling for her, the last first aider left on base. But she's already run from the top of the stairs and is hurrying Bethan onto the bench at the dining table, the engineer attempting to talk between gulps of air.

"Mika – get the first aid kit!" Lieb snaps.

It takes him a moment to register his name. Then he's pushing Bones out of the way at the galley cupboards. He drags the first aid box out from behind a blender, unfastens it as he's running and slides the open case onto the table. All the while, Bethan's doing her best to speak against the pain of a deep gash at her inner arm, running a good nine centimetres from the elbow down.

"The sleep module... I tried to... pin the floor back down..." Another ragged breath. "The fog got inside, so quickly. I couldn't see. And then... and then." The engineer's shaking badly, Lieb too as she flusters through the first aid box contents, finally coming up with wound patches. "Then I see the shape, this great bulky shape, too tall for the ceiling, stooping down over me." Her eyes have taken on the same wild look as Dr Franklin's. "I sliced my arm on one of those fucking floor panels... and then they were all coming unbolted – every bit of floor, every side panels, every bolt in every bed. And I ran like shit."

Mika helps Lieb set the wound patches over Bethan's arm. Meanwhile, there's an ungodly noise coming from outside – a shrieking grind, of metal twisting. Bones gets to moaning, as if to join in.

"War's starting. Enemy tanks at one o'clock. Watch your backs, soldiers."

Mika runs to the window. But it is Lieb who goes for the door, yanking it open onto the blistering cold and letting in gusts of iodine-tasting fog and a stench of boggy sulphur.

She stands, arms folded, hands up under her armpits, trying to make sense of the gaping crater which has opened up in the ground, and the sleep module, all warped and cranked open, two of its legs uprooted. The hole is oozing a dark greasy sludge, the stuff bubbling up from between the splintered rocks. Fresh white clouds are billowing from the crevice.

"It's not fog," Lieb says quietly.

"What's that?" Mika's at her side. He gasps at the eruption. "What the hell are we looking at, Lieb?"

"It's not fog, what's all around us." Lieb forces the panic down in her throat. "It's fumes from the mines. That." She points at the lava flow of sludge. "Is nutrient foam. The valves must have ruptured, malfunctioned in some way." Her mind flies between explanations – faulty mechanics, a software glitch, human error...

"It's going to flood the tundra." Dr Franklin's voice comes seemingly from nowhere. Then he materialises at the rim of the hole, gnawing his thumb. He points behind him, presumably to the observation deck, now obscured by the fog. "We've got to evacuate and quickly. I've called the port."

"They're sending the tender." Lieb can hear the insistence in her tone, the desperation.

"Yes, yes. The tender is coming. But the fog..." Dr Franklin shuffles around the rim of the hole as the ground continues to shake.

"They can't see to land." Mika's the one to say it out loud.

Bones sees it all; the battleship jumping left then right at the top of the screen. He's imagining he's back at the games café, when it was fun and new to have the visitors move in. They'd brought with them all that flashing noise and neon lights; like the spirits of the ancestors turned to full volume. He'd always felt apart from his own family, always liked to nose in at the life of these strangers with their late night drinking and endless pawing over the land he knew as well as his own spit. They came and went, like an endless ebb and flow, and he thought their swell would last forever. But now the strangers are almost all gone, everyone he knows, too, and it's like the battleship's jumped down a line and he's missing every amo shot.

And he's not stupid. Oh, he knows what the scientists think about him. Old Bones. Gone to ground, gone to seed. 'Not right in the head'. But he's had to stick around. He's known it in every trace of his being, felt it like the breath of so many dead. Like his personal Taqriaqsuits. Not quite seen but haunting him out the corner of an eye.

The interlopers, they're rushing around, screaming into their devices, demanding they're airlifted to the safety in the sky. But Bones, all he sees is the motion of hands, lifting ancient stones one atop of the other. If he could see the thread of his bloodline back through the ages, he might know the names of these ancestors.

So, this is the end of the world, he thinks. The earth breaking open, crying from within. The fog, stinking and impenetrable, billows all around the walkway, which has warped at the end nearest to the decimated remains of the sleep module.

"We need to light a torch." He says it quietly at first, amid all the furore. Repeats it louder. "We need to light a torch!" He runs back inside; he saw a storm lighter inside one of the cupboards when he was rifling through them, looking for something eat earlier.

"It won't work." The doc shows every bit of strain on her young face. She seems in charge, perhaps with the chef as her second. "We won't have time to gather fuel. There's no way we could build it big enough."

"Unless it is big enough already." He strides back inside, finds his furs and eases his arms in. "But we go now, all you sons of bitches. We go and you follow. Or stay and die."

They move, part-dancers, part-sprinters, over the trembling tundra. Pits are opening up where the rocks are forced apart, the thick paste erupting from below in glugs and flaccid belches like hot mud. Bones is waiting on no man and rushes ahead. Passing in and out of visibility, his body draped in the shapeless furs, he distorts in shape and size.

"Wait, Bones! You're going too fast." Lieb is struggling against the sickening déjà vu of losing the man in the fog, especially since Bethan's taken a bad turn and it's Lieb and Mika who have her between them, the engineer's arms draped across their shoulders. Whether it's the blood loss or cold that's making the woman's teeth chatter, Lieb isn't sure. But something's turning Bethan's brain; all the while, she's mumbling wild and fancifully, about what she's calling 'figures in the fog'.

"Jesus, Lieb. If any of us make it out of here alive, we're the luckiest motherfuckers." Mika's holding up well, but Lieb can see the strain in the man's jaw as he takes the bulk of Bethan's weight. "I'm putting all my trust in the same bunch of scientists who got me into this shit. Why are we following this crazy Indian anyway?"

Why indeed? Lieb only knows they had to move before Tolisen 5 went under and Bones was the only one suggesting an escape route. Chances are he's leading us to old miners encampment, she thinks – and doesn't want to say out loud that there's no running from the torrent beneath their feet. The flood will build to a biblical extinction event. It's the blueprint for the

Tolisen method, and once those pipes had started gushing, there was no turning the tap off.

The situation isn't helped by the fact that, despite Bethan's condition, it's Dr Franklin who is proving the hardest to keep moving. Every few metres, the meteorologist insists on stopping and peering back the way they have come, seemingly aimlessly into the wall of white.

"There were no relevant readings. It's not my fault the weather changed," he saying, over and over. And – "There's monsters in the fog… everywhere."

"Keep moving," says the chef in a snarl – and Lieb's with the guy on this one, if not his antiquated label for Bones, even if had been meant with a grim, gallows humour. It might be the god awful terror at the prospect of being drowned by the fetid slush, or the struggle to keep going with Bethan's added weight, but Lieb's eyes are starting to play tricks. The shifting depths of the fog twist themselves in shapes; huge and eerie, with arms which stretch and recoil. One moment, there's a human-like quality to the figures, the next, it's as if they're moving through an ice field of ancient cairns. The apparitions keep on shifting before she can quite focus fully; she's starting to believe Dr Franklin's cries of monsters.

Apparently, Mika's seeing all this too. "There's some fucking creepy shit going on out here, Lieb," he says in his deep baritone, making Lieb wish he could use that gravel to transmogrify into a bear. All teeth and claws, ready to tear into the wilds and eat the still beating heart of the danger. Instead, the chef's roaring at Bones to slow down and, back at Dr Franklin, to: "Keep your shit together or I swear I'll drop you and leave you to drown!"

Bones is gone. Lieb calls out again and again into the fog, Mika swearing at the top of his lungs, and even Dr Franklin's noticed.

"He's left us to the ghosts," he's mumbling, as a new riptide forces the rocks and frozen earth apart in a jagged zigzag between them. The brown ooze wells up and over the chasm's edges.

"You've got to jump across." Lieb and Mika have stopped now. The doctor's teetering back and forth at the edge of the rift on the opposite side to the rest of them. The sludge bubbles up and expands at a terrifyingly rapid rate; already it's at Lieb's feet.

Mika lets go of Bethan and goes wading a little back. "Come on, Dr Franklin. Come on, man. You've got to jump now. We're talking seconds here. Jump or we leave you."

There are lightning bolts inside of Willem's head. All the aqua blues and pearlescent mauve and turquoise of the lights dancing over the dark skies across the months he'd lived in Tolisen 5. It had been his place of refuge, and not just from the elements but from the sense of being lost, which haunted him always. Now, the research station is gone, eaten up by the hunger that's burgeoned up from the ground, rupturing his every thoughts like a brain bleed. Tolisen – that great, rippling ravenous grub of a company – set him on that beautiful, strange landscape, and he'd conducted his studies because it was his passion. But piece by piece, the science behind the station had been taken apart, and, with it, Willem's purpose.

The figures towering in the fog wear the same furs as Bones, their hulking shoulders seeming to carry the weather like a yolk of heavy stone. He hears Lieb and Mika calling to him across the fractured distance, Bethan's voice too, if weaker. His name, repeated over in the muffled stillness of the air.

Willem sees the chasm between them opening ever wider, and it's like they are on opposing tectonic plates, the rest of the crew and him. 'Home' is a smear of memory. He tries to find the impetus to want to run towards it. But that past, it's so insubstantial next to the stark world around him.

"I'm going in the wrong direction," he says quietly. He turns his back on the others and walks back the way they came, leaving behind the drift of giants and all hope of escape.

Bones remembers things. He remembers to take the storm lighter from the drawer in the galley. He remembers the invisible pathways across the tundra, and in spite of the sore and bleeding earth as the Big man's chemicals boil and seep through. His spirit remembers the breath of his ancestors, the air streaming white from their lips, the flip of a seal in the death throws, the warm thick iron taste of the animal's blood from a cup.

Bones remembers what the doc said about the plants, too. His mind is playing images of hunters' hands plunging into the stomach of a freshly slaughtered reindeer and sharing out the fetid green sludge from the creature's belly. It's as if, in those drastic moments when his entire world is on the verge of destruction, he's reaching back through his people's history. To say that we mattered. That we loved and bred and survived in this land with its skies lit by the colours of the dead.

The Guardian solidifies through the heavy mist and Bones takes notice of its lichen-encrusted stones. He runs, pulls off his gloves, immediately aware of the desperate cold which makes his fingers tremble as he reaches out and lightly strokes the tough strands of the plants. He's reminded of the rough coats of the reindeer he'd helped care for when he was a child. Somewhere along his lifeline, he'd fallen out of step with the landscape from which he was carved. Now, pressing his palms against the ridged rock of the Inunnguaq, he half-expects to hear screaming. But instead it's more of a pulse – from the Big man's poison running through the drilled veins and arteries of the mines? Or is it from within the Guardian itself?

"Light the way," Bones says, and using the storm lighter, he sets the Inunnguaq's lichen fur aflame. In a few short moments, the Guardian is a giant, rippling torch of amber light, slicing upwards through the fog and illuminating out in a shining radius. The others arrive, the doc and the chef supporting the engineer between them.

From overhead sounds the deep whirl of engines and the undercarriage of a descending craft breaks through the fog.

*

It's two days before Mika is well enough to crawl from his bed in the crew cell he's been assigned and put on the standard issue utilitarian uniform with the Tolisen badge stitched to the right breast pocket. There are slip-on white boots, a new toothbrush in its neat steel holder above the bathroom sink, and, when he relieves himself, that familiar sudden suction of the toilets aboard a space cruiser.

His first stop is the medical bay. Bethan's asleep on one of the slab beds; lying on her side, those usually busy hands tucked into a prayer beneath one cheek, she looks peaceful. When they first got picked up by the tender, she'd eyes which rolled and a blue tinge under her soft brown skin, like the veins were rising to the surface. Today, she looks better. Mika slips away and leaves the engineer to sleep.

He follows the geography of the ship along its wide walkways, their sterility lacking the endlessness of the tundra and with a manmade comfort which promises protection. Crew members pass him, offering that awkward nod of hello between strangers. Mika thinks he might find the mess; his stomach is starting to growl and it's been months since he ate a good, bloody steak or pink slivers of lamb. But then he finds he's at the view platform, with its great panorama of glass giving out onto the star-scape.

"Hello." Lieb has her arms folded; as he approaches, he's the sense she is hugging herself. She turns and threatening tears in her eyes harden, as if in recognising him she's left some inner darkness behind. "You're alive," she jokes, and smiles.

"I guess I am." He joins her in turning back to the window. Against the coaly expanse with its incandescent stars, is the world. The land masses resemble lichen in colour and even have the same frilly edges.

"Bones is gone." Lieb continues to stare out the glass. "He left for the new reservation."

"And Dr Franklin?"

She gives a small shrug. "Gone in a different way."

They're silent a moment.

"He wasn't very well, you know. Towards the end. In his mind, I mean." Mika rubs a hand across his forehead. "I didn't know the guy well, but it struck me that he was lost long before he ever ran off into that fog."

Lieb doesn't take her eyes from the window. "There's talk that he did something to the system, tripped it into action ahead of evacuation day."

Mika snorts. "Even if that isn't true, we both know it will be the company line."

They stand a while, the passage of people behind reflecting in the glass, if blurred and not quite substantial.

"What we saw out there...?" Mika's mind replays a scramble of images – a burning man towering up into the drifting pale, the earth around him broken open and blistered. Ghosts curl in at the edges of his memory, as they did in those awful moments back on the tundra.

Lieb sighs, almost wistful. Quietly, she says, "I read once that when a person suffers a life-threatening event, it is not unusual for their mind to overlay the horror of reality with shapes from their past." Turning from the window, she lays a hand on Mika's arm. "Nothing will be learnt from this, Mika. Tolisen won't change their model – it'll just be labelled human error and, to quote something Bones might say, 'the Big man's machine will keep on fucking turning'." She gives him that gentle smile of hers. "Get home to your husband, Mika. Get a nice chef gig somewhere safe."

"And what about you? The scientist. Wait on the next mission to explore a condemned land?"

Lieb's smile falters and she looks deeply, achingly sad. "See you around, Mika."

She walks away from him, and as she does so, Mika's struck by how small she seems in the gleaming expanse of the Tolisen vessel.

A SEA CHANGE

Donna Scott

On her beach walks, Julie liked to gaze out at the offshore wind turbines; a whole flock of them paddling in the sea. The spinning blades were a friendly greeting that she sometimes returned – fellow aliens in the seascape recognising each other. Today the sea was a washed out grey, all colours muted in the early autumnal light. Strands of her hair whipped her face, and her long hippy skirt flapped about her legs, threatening to fly off.

Julie cut an incongruous figure on the sands, not because she was an outsider to the small seaside town, but because at this time of the morning she was the only human about. She shared the scenery with the gulls, and with the sand fleas hopping about the drier patches of sand, just out of reach of the fizzing fingers of foam retracting back into the North Sea. Further up the coast, a seal had hauled itself onto the beach. Julie's heart fluttered, as it did every time one of those wonderful creatures made an appearance, which was quite often. She couldn't get used to the idea of being allowed to share this environment with them, but all her freedoms were a delight. To see such magnificent creatures in the wild like this, what a privilege! A few minutes ago the seal had been swimming in the sea, nose in the air like an eager dog swimming after a stick. Every so often he would disappear under the waves, then come back up again. *He knows I am here.* That was why he was resting further up the coast. If Julie were to walk towards him now, he would just dive back down and swim away sooner than he otherwise would. The early dog walkers would soon be coming onto the beach too; he certainly wouldn't hang about with dogs on the beach.

Tempting as it was to make her way down the sands to say hello to the creature at closer quarters, it would be better to leave him be and stick with the wind turbines for company.

"Why Caister?" That's what her friends asked her before she decided to move here. *Because of all this. The dunes, and the beach. The sea and all its wondrous unknowable depths. Because it used to be something else, and so did I.*

She should never have told a soul, but too late now.

Julie didn't have any great connection to Caister – no work, no family… That was largely the point. It was just somewhere she knew from holidays as a teenager. How much more tranquil it appeared on first impression, certainly compared with its brasher, brighter neighbour in Great Yarmouth; it might be nice. Alas, it wasn't an excessively big town, and if Rob were to come here, he would probably find her. *And murder me when he does.* That was pretty much implied from his last message.

"Is that where he is, your new fella? You think you can just run off and shag whoever in some fucking seaside resort and I'll be fine with that, eh? Think I'll just take it lying down? You utter slag. Fucking whore. I'm going to rip your stupid face from your skull!"

Julie lived like a nun, always had, but it wouldn't matter. Already her world was shrinking again. Trips to the pub were out now, just in case, not that it was much fun going in by herself anyway. Following advice to vary her routine, she would sometimes go to the old Roman fort, where her shadow was cast ghostlike on the ancient exposed cobblestones of the Roman road. She often made her way over to the villa's hypocaust to sit on the remnants of stone and watch the sunrise. The fort was one of her favourite places. The hypocaust may have been there because the villa was a high-status building, occupied by an officer's family, or it may even have been a brothel. Perhaps both, in its time. She liked not really knowing. Let the experts argue about why women might find themselves in such a place; what business they had there.

At the ruins, she would keep an eye out for other people, the same as at the beach, but putting herself in the shoes of a Roman centurion watching the coast for Saxon raiders. Where the road is now would have been the shoreline two thousand years ago. Her beach would meet it across a wide estuary where the Rivers Waveney, Yare, and Bure all tumbled into each other. The whole town used to be an island, cut off from the rest of the world.

Caister used to be alone, but the modern world encroached as the sea retreated.

Julie came here to be an island, to change, to fortify herself... But the same thing had happened to her.

Other practical things done to keep safe seemed easier: cutting all ties with friends; all her social media gone. It would probably be necessary to move on from here too, but she was digging her heels in. If she could live the same way as that seal, just a little wary, alert to her surroundings, perhaps survival was possible.

I will remain where I am.

The windfarm, the fort, and Julie, all of them imposing themselves on this terrain. Their scars, their remnants, their history – all carrying such a weight.

Julie intended to walk home before the quality of the light changed too much, making everything more solid. Perhaps she had been daydreaming too long. As she turned to leave, she cast a wary glance around. From the corner of her eye, she saw it: a glimmer.

Was it the sunlight catching the blade of the turbines?

The blades were turning, and just behind them was a sort of haze, similar to a heat haze, only it was fairly chilly that morning, so it couldn't have been that.

My eyes must be tired, Julie thought; rubbed them; looked again. The haze was not behind the turbines but suspended in the centre of them, next, clearly in front. Her eyes were defocusing, wanting to look away, but she kept her gaze fixed. It was a bit like looking at a magic eye picture. Something was resolving: a shape – the outline of a manta ray – just hanging there.

She blinked a couple of times, as if she were trying to clear the sky in front of her, but it did not work. The shape was still there. A strange thought occurred to her, that this shape was not in her imagination, it was real...but perhaps it was hanging back, wary of her.

It knows I am here.

151

Almost without realising, she found herself raising her hand, her palm towards the shape, offered in greeting. Was she expecting it to respond? She was an island, inviting the vast mainland to eradicate her shore, to subsume her.

No one will believe you.

Julie opened her eyes and felt instantly confused. Before her was the plaque in the ruins of the Roman fort that talked about the hypocaust. She must have read this several times over, as she came to it whenever she walked here, renewing her knowledge of the history of the place. But she knew she hadn't walked *here* this morning. Julie tapped her Fitbit and saw the time was only just gone seven. Getting here from the beach in such a short time would be impossible.

Because I was on the beach, yes? I was only thinking about the fort. But then, I saw that shape by the windfarm, and pop, now I'm here. That was real, wasn't it?

Yes, and this *was* frightening. She steadied herself on the plaque, shaking, light-headed. Now she knew what it was to be was the protagonist that no one believed in a weird story; the unreliable narrator. Of course, she couldn't tell anyone about this. Who was there to tell anyway? But whatever that manta ray shape in the sky was, it must have just thought her noticing it was a problem. It just picked her up and moved her. Her fear subsided, giving way to anger.

I am not someone who can be shoved. Not me. Not any more.

Julie dismissed any idea that she might be walking towards danger, and began marching back to the beach, a good quarter of an hour's walk from the fort. Rob had pushed her to the shadows of her own life, and yes, he continued to do so despite his absence in it. But one devil was enough. It was time to stand up for herself.

Walking with determination recoloured the small treasures discovered in this landscape. She strode past monotonous estates, the houses built in the Sixties and Seventies to a type indistinguishable from any town's, but they looked friendly, respectable...nice places to bring up kids if that was your fate. There were charming middle-class dwellings, whose enormous hedges secreted tunnels and passageways within: oversized fairy dens. A couple of early twentieth century dark brick pubs, probably quite grand back in their day, now promising comfortable settings, and beer that wasn't too expensive: one served a nice pint of Landlord. A big, beautiful church with intriguing old headstones. A takeaway with some odd opening times. They'd become her landmarks, her friends and neighbours, greeting Julie on her daily walks. Now they were watchers. She wondered if doorbells and cameras were picking her up as she hurried past. Would any captured images be used to mark her last known movements in some future missing persons appeal?

Fuck. Back to always thinking the worst.

No, Julie needed to be brave now. She had taken enough of being told it was all in her imagination. There was a rational explanation, there had to be....

Near the beach, the Ship Inn was boarded up, having not survived the last financial crisis. She scurried past, heading over the path that edged the golf course, into the dunes. The lifeboat station came into view, looking silent, the café and shop closed. The beach car park next to it was near empty, just one car... Julie stopped dead in her tracks.

She recognised it.

Halting was instinctual. Julie edged backwards slowly, retreating up the path. Despite her good eyesight, the car was too far away to be able to read the registration. It could just be the same type of car as Rob's: a sky-blue Honda. The one thing she could be sure of: it hadn't been there earlier. There didn't seem to be anyone inside the car, or around the car park anywhere. She would need to venture closer to be sure it was really his. And if it was...

The windows of the nearby houses looked just as dark and desolate as the Ship Inn, but the lifeboat station was manned twenty-four hours, wasn't it? A symbol of preparedness, reassurance close at hand. Admonishing herself for her moment of weakness, she pressed on, keeping a watchful eye for anything – or anyone – intruding on her beach, be they abusive exes, strangers, or unidentified shapes floating in the sky. In particular, the latter.

I just have to see it, face it...make it understand that it has no power over me.

Picking up her pace, Julie began hastening along the path through the dunes, sand flying behind her heels as she kicked it up with her walking boots. The excited yip of a small dog sounded off in the distance. Who knew whether the object suspended in the sky would be as skittish around dogs on the beach as the seals were?

The colour of the sky was brightening, and developing a warm rosy hue, but for once she ignored it. She brushed the hair out of her eyes and hastened onward, slightly out of breath. Traversing a part of the beach striated with hundreds of shells, she made her strides longer, not wishing to crunch too many of them. Was the manta ray still there? Or was that just a mist of spray rising from the sea? The breakers stopped her progressing further.

There was definitely nothing hovering amid the wind turbines now. Julie cast her mind back to stories she'd read in *Fortean Times* about UFO sightings. This had seemed to be a creature, but could it have been an alien ship?

Julie glanced up and down the coast, searching for the shape; leaned her head back, hunting the vault of the sky, but the shape was either fully invisible to her now or it had simply vanished. Or, of course, she could be mad. She turned around, constantly looking about her.

"He-ey," she called out. "Where are you?" People really would think she was mad. Her voice whipped away from her in the wind. "He-ey!"

"*Hey!*"

What was that, she wondered? An echo?

But then: "Hey!"

The cries were coming from further down the beach.

"Julie! Julie! Don't move! Don't you fucking move!"

Experience and shock made her obey, just for a second. Then sense kicked in and she absolutely did fucking move. Her legs felt powered as if by an engine. The sand and the incline made running harder, but she astounded herself with her lightning speed.

Still, she berated herself: *Stupid, stupid woman.*

Maybe she'd been an idiot to stay after Rob had called her on her old phone. But Julie reminded herself just how much cleverer she was than him. Always had been. Her route took her back towards Tan Lane, the quickest way off the beach and back to civilisation. There were warrenlike streets, alleyways and grassy lokes to disappear into. And people! Not many tourists at this time of year, but still there would be commuters; kids on the way to school... Would Rob follow her on foot, or would he run back to the car and try to find her by road? Whatever he thought he could achieve by coming here, he was going to fail. As she hit the tarmac, she peered over her shoulder, but there was no sign of him. He must have run to the car park then.

The sweat was pouring from a mix of stress and exertion. It was trickling, pooling, slicking her skin. She was running on adrenaline. She zipped down one of the lokes that led her past a row of back gardens onto a side street. No sign of Rob, or his car. Her pace slowed.

The second-hand shop at the crossroads seemed a good place to catch her breath. Julie had visited this treasure trove a few times since moving to Caister. A sweet elderly couple ran it who always made Julie feel very welcome, and passed the time of day with her whenever she walked past. Julie got a kitchen starter pack from a charity with basic kitchenware and crockery, but she visited the shop for other things she'd seen and desired and paid just pennies. It was so lovely to have somewhere like this, selling all sorts of things you needed, or didn't think you needed. They didn't just stock kitchenalia, they had anything and everything really. Another place that had been a refuge for her since coming here. A lot of people would find comfort in the bric-a-brac they stocked; they sold all sorts of nostalgic trinkets. Right now on display was a cream vinyl-covered 1980s jewellery box, with red-flocked lining that she supposed most little girls would have owned at some point, and she had been no exception. There was a chunky brass key in the back, which, if you turned it, would play a portion from the Finale of *Swan Lake* while a plastic ballerina with a stiff tulle tutu twirled around on her spot, her arms aloft, her feet disappearing into mystery. What had happened to her jewellery box? Ah... Smashed up and dumped in a bin bag in the front garden along with other sentimental items after a fight that had started after some perceived slight on her part.

"I'm sorry," Rob had said afterwards when he'd calmed down. *"I'll...I'll replace them."*

"Don't worry, they're only things." Julie had said, because there are some things that can never be replaced, not really. But at the same time they were without value anyway, weren't they? Well, monetary value, at least. You could pick up these toys for a couple of quid anywhere – this shop proving the point. And he hadn't hurt her physically, had he? Not back then. And if she had left him at that time, would people have thought her unforgiving? Julie's friends would doubtlessly have said they were *only things*, too, because they liked Rob, thought he was good for her. None of them had realised there was such a thing as 'escalatory behaviour'. Her mother, though, had certainly been wary of Rob from that point on. She hadn't actually been hostile towards him, but she had accepted the news that they were going to get married with a recognisable froideur – which Julie had repaid by barely being there for her mother after the wedding, and she had kept a guilty distance when she had become ill, too.

Julie's breathing was steady now; she had probably better keep moving in case Rob showed up. She sighed and pressed her hand to the glass and allowed a small tear to roll down her cheek. Rob had torn little pieces off her, strip by strip. Isolating her from her family had been easy when there were suddenly none of them left. The childhood 'junk' she had lost had been what made her memories more vivid. Every time she lost another precious piece of 'worthless tat' she had been further diminished by him – that was unforgivable.

How sad and old her reflection looked. Sure, at first glance, there she still was, Julie the cute and bookish twenty-something, in her big boots and hippy skirt, her unkempt hair stuffed under a beanie. Young Julie had been snatched up from her happy life, full of youth and energy and deposited back in her body fifteen years later, the jawline slightly softened, the waistline too; wrinkles and grey hairs making an appearance. Nothing had changed, except everything. Had Rob done this to her, or just time?

Behind her in her reflection, she could see cars rolling past, and she knew that soon one of them might be Rob's. It was time to go...

She did not immediately notice the reflected shape behind her, not until she saw a woman with a pushchair decide to cross over to her side of the street. The woman was seemingly oblivious to the enormous transparent manta ray blocking the pavement. Julie froze, her hand still against the glass, palm flat. She wanted to turn round, but she dared not. If she did, it might just vanish, but like this, she could see it; she didn't want to scare it away. The shape did not look as big as it had seemed on the beach – perhaps the size of an adult male elephant, whereas she the one she saw earlier had the dimensions of a cruise ship – hence a space ship, she'd thought. It could be that there was more than one of them, and this one was smaller, or it could be some trick of the memory. Or it might just be able to change size. The important thing was just to stay still, and confirm to herself that whatever it was, however big it was, it was really there.

Another tear fell.

"Julie?"

Oh no. She kept her gaze on the manta ray, though now it had been joined by Rob in the reflection. He was on foot. She blinked another tear away; he didn't deserve them.

"What do you want, Rob?"

His reflection looked wide-eyed and forlorn, akin to the underdog hero in a John Hughes film who thought he deserved the girl and couldn't understand why she had rejected him. *Don't you dare feel sorry for him, girl. That's his old puppy dog trick.*

"I just want to talk, Julie."

"There's nothing stopping *you* talking, Rob."

"No, no..." Rob shook his head and flapped his arms in an exasperated manner. *Ah, here come the crocodile tears,* Julie thought. Rob continued: "I mean I want to talk with you, Julie. Make you see sense. You've not been…right, you know? You need to come home."

He never even really needed to try that hard after the fights. There might be an apology, but it would be whisked away – quick smart – a magician's trick with a tablecloth, and it would go back to being *Julie* that was not right in the head, and *her* who needed to say sorry for whatever part she had played in the matter.

However, he'd never tried any of these tricks with a manta ray hovering behind him before. Not that he had seen the manta ray yet. Julie remained facing the window, so he wouldn't be able to tell that she was looking at it instead of him. It made the manta ray seem more real as it made Rob seem less so. She watched as Rob shifted his position behind her, moving his legs together; opening out his arms as if in expectation of an embrace.

"Please, Julie…"

He looked just like the ballerina in the box. Behind him, the air in the shape of a manta ray sparkled and Julie watched as the triangular fins began to undulate.

Rob, seeming to sense the movement behind him, started to twist round to see what it was. His arms were still in position, mirroring the dancer's. There was a sharp intake of breath as Rob realised something about the space behind him was not right, but he kept turning, and turning. Slowly at first, so Julie was able to see the look of shock and incomprehension on his face. Now a little faster. The noise in Julie's head was not filled with the sounds of traffic, or the tinkling noise of the music box, or even Rob's screams as his legs and feet melted together to a point on which he span, round and round, but the full orchestral brass and strings of Tchaikovsky's magnificent finale: the dying swan.

Julie closed her eyes and listened to the wonderful music. It transported her back to her childhood: going to see the National Russian ballet's performance of *Swan Lake* with school at the Theatre Royal, and then running home and enthusing about it to her mum – the costumes, the orchestra, the little opera glasses! Oh, and mint choc chip ice cream. *"Can I have ballet lessons now?"*

"Well, they're a little expensive, but let's see what Santa brings you…" Unwrapping the jewellery box at Christmas, with her proud parents looking on; storing her charm bracelet in the box, and her nana's old brooches… Running out onto the driveway after that fight to find the box lying on the gravel, irreparably broken, the ballerina's head missing, the trinkets within scattered. That memory was so tangible she could feel the sharp edges of the gravel scratching her fingertips as she bent to pick up the box and its contents. Her fingers ran over the scudded flock lining with shaking hands as she tried to put the lid and hinge back in alignment and close the box, then cradled it under her arm. Freeing one of her hands, she brushed her hair from her face and looked up and around, blinking.

Julie felt as though she'd been dropped into an old photograph, no longer two-dimensional, but still glossy, the colours sharp, the edges less so. This was her old street, back in the North. A broken box under her arm, and a carrier bag full of memories in her hand. She was wearing jeans and a tank top for the pleasant summer weather, but she remembered this horrible, wretched feeling. Her eyes were sore, and she was trembling, not sure what to do next. She turned and looked up at her house – hers and Rob's – and saw him yank the curtains across the window, shutting out the day and the sight of her. She remembered this: going back into the house; apologizing. Rob cried and said he was sorry too, and she said it was okay, they were "only things." Afterwards, she called her mother and told her that she had broken the jewellery box in an accident. After her mother wouldn't stop asking how it had happened, she had admitted it had been thrown out of the window during a row. In much the same way as other things had ended up broken. And her mother said, *"Oh, not your little ballerina box, Jools. You loved that so much!"* And Julie said what she'd said to Rob, that they were only things, but her mother would not be consoled or deterred. *"Oh, I don't know why, but I'm more upset than you are, Jools, because they're not just things are they? They're things that are important to you.*

And he knows that, love." This is what had opened the gap between Julie and her mother that could not be closed in time, because her mother had been right.

In her memory, Julie took a step forward back towards the house, but also, she did not. She turned back round to face the street. She put a hand to her back pocket, and realised she had her phone there. She'd been about to call her mother before the fight started. She could call her now.

Why not? So, this is a kind of lucid dreaming?

She walked to the bottom of the driveway, onto the pavement, and turned left.

So far so real... not dreaming then. Something else...

A slight breeze stirred the bright green leaves of the chestnut tree on the green as she passed, and the ripples moved in familiar waves, reminiscent of giant fins.

Julie retrieved the phone from her back pocket. An old Nokia – that was a blast from the past. No need to look up the number, she knew it by heart.

MAY YOU RISE

James Lovegrove

Moments after leaving the house, Ben Worric met an Angel.

The Angel's name was Gerald, and he was Ben's neighbour from a few doors down. Gerald was a solicitor, although he practised only occasionally these days: the odd bit of conveyancing and Will drafting. Mostly he grew organic vegetables in his garden and organised the weekly exchange fair on the high street, where anyone in town could bring produce and homemade handicrafts for barter.

"Ben," Gerald said, in a smoothly accosting tone of voice.

Ben wanted to walk on but was too polite not to. You couldn't really say no to an Angel.

"Off out?" Gerald continued.

"I am."

"Somewhere nice?"

"I like to think so."

Gerald glided closer along the pavement. His eyes had the lambent blue that all Angels' eyes had. A blue somewhat like glacier ice, somewhat like cornflowers, somewhat like a clear sky, but also unlike any shade of blue found in nature. Too bright. Too piercing. Too knowing.

"When do you reckon you're going to Ascend?" Gerald asked. "Any time soon?"

Ben suppressed a sigh. He'd known the query was coming. When did it ever not, during a conversation with an Angel? Even if you were engaged in nothing more than idle chitchat, it would crop up at some point. It was as inevitable as death. At least Gerald hadn't beaten around the bush much before getting to it.

"Dunno," Ben mumbled. "At some point. Maybe. No idea when." He wanted to add, *Not that it's any business of yours, Gerald.* But this would have been rude, perhaps even cruel, like scolding a toddler for accidentally dropping ice cream on the floor. Besides, Ascension kind of *was* an Angel's business. Angels couldn't help themselves. They wanted others to benefit from what they'd benefited from. You couldn't blame them from proselytising.

"It's never too late," Gerald said gently, coaxingly. "I realise the prospect can be intimidating. A step into the unknown. Although it's not so unknown, is it now? Not after so many millions of us have gone through it. The evidence is all around you. It's a gift — to yourself, to the human race, to the world. What's stopping you from accepting it, Ben?"

There were many answers to that question, and they were long and complicated, and Ben didn't have the time or patience to get into all that with Gerald, not right now. He just said, "I'm thinking about it, definitely," and strode off down the road with great purposefulness.

"Keep thinking about it," Gerald called out after him. "But don't leave it too long, eh?"

Ben's mood had already been soured by the encounter, and it soured further as he turned the corner and passed Himesh, who was on his front drive, busy cleaning his car. The car was a brand new fully electric model, and the frothy water he smeared over it with a sponge was laced with biodegradable detergent.

"Ben!" Himesh cried, as though greeting a long-lost friend and not simply someone who lived close by and was, at best, a nodding acquaintance. "How goes it? All well?"

"Well enough, Himesh."

"Where are you headed?"

"Out for a stroll," Ben lied. "Stretching the old legs. That's all."

"Still driving that mucky old diesel thing of yours?" Himesh asked.

"I am, and will, for as long as it still works."

"You should switch to an electric." Himesh waved at the sleek, smooth-lined car he was ministering to. "Better for everyone. You can get very reasonable deals on them, you know."

"I know. Sometimes it's just hard to part with something that's served me so well for years."

"Of course, of course." Himesh bent his head sympathetically. His eyes, before Ascension, had been tawny brown. Now they were, of course, Angelic blue. "Change is never easy, but it can be worthwhile."

"Look, I'd love to stop and chat, Himesh," Ben said, "but I've got to be on my way. In a hurry."

"I thought you were just out for a stroll."

"Yes. I did say that. And I am. But an exercise kind of stroll, you know what I mean. Brisk. Get the heart going."

"Good for you. Quite right. Exercise. Well, enjoy."

"I intend to."

"And Ben?"

Here it came. The universal refrain. The benediction of the Ascended towards the non-Ascended.

"May you rise."

"Yeah. Thanks, Himesh." What could you say back? *May you rise too*? Pointless. Like telling someone who'd just arrived at their destination to have a nice journey.

Ben walked on.

It was a beautiful autumn evening. The small market town Ben called home was blessed with a plethora of trees, and their foliage was currently at its golden-russet best. The leaves hadn't fallen yet, to make a nuisance of themselves underfoot. The air was warm, the sun radiating just the right amount of heat and light. It was that brief period of the year when things were perfectly poised between summer and winter, a moment of seasonal suspension, the pause between swings of the pendulum. Ben tried to relish it. He refused to let the two encounters with Angels irritate him too much. It wasn't their fault they behaved the way they did. If he himself had Ascended, he would probably be the same. No, he *would* be the same. The Angels only wished to share their elevated status with everyone else. They meant well.

But then, Ben thought dourly, to mean well was one of life's great fallacies. Plenty of terrible stuff had been done by those who meant well. Hitler, if you thought about it, had meant well.

Not that the Ascended could be compared to a fascist dictator.

Not unless you didn't want what they wanted for you.

His route took him uphill, along several of the town's more charming residential streets. Children frolicked in the roadways, where vehicles passed infrequently and often never at all. Neighbour chatted with neighbour across front garden hedge or wall. Young couples idled. Older couples ambled. Everyone seemed to have time for everyone else, for not being busy, for just living. Ben could remember the days – not that long ago – when this kind of idyll had seemed a fantasy, a throwback to an age that had, in truth, never existed. Now it was real.

All thanks to the Interventionists.

Whoever they might be.

His thoughts turned to the millions upon millions of spaceships sitting, at that very moment, just within low Earth orbit, a thousand or so miles above the planet's surface. They were dotted across every country in the world, congregated most closely together over populous areas but otherwise evenly distributed. Each stood atop a column of azure light that was generated from its underside and extended all the way down to the ground, straight as a laser beam. Anywhere you went, you were never more than fifty miles from one of these columns. They had come to be known as Jacob's Ladders. There was even one in this very town, and at night its glow filled the darkness with a soft, pulsing radiance, like an otherworldly beacon.

When the columns first appeared a decade back, more or less simultaneously everywhere, there had been global panic. Nations had assumed other nations were responsible. Politicians had accused their enemies of high-tech terrorism, of deploying some sinister new type of weapon. For several unnerving days, the world had teetered on the brink of all-out war.

Happily, calm heads had prevailed. Observatories and spy satellites had captured images of the spaceships just outside the atmosphere that were sending down the columns of light. The vessels – angular, unaerodynamic, elaborate, like fantastical spaceborne sea creatures – could only be of extraterrestrial design and origin. Clearly the phenomenon was not human-made but caused by some external agency.

Within months, the presence of the spaceships and the columns had become almost commonplace. Governments did not have the resources to cordon off the base of every single column. They could not prevent people from approaching them, from going within touching distance of them, and indeed from entering them.

Nobody could remember who was the first to venture inside a column. A few individuals did, whether through curiosity or foolhardiness, only to find themselves being swept upwards, disappearing into the firmament. It was then assumed, with some justification, that the columns of light must be dangerous, a means of trapping the unwary and transporting them aboard the spaceships for who knew what purpose; and it was generally considered a good idea to avoid them.

Then, within days, the people who'd been drawn up inside the columns returned to Earth. And they were different.

They were kinder.

They were better.

They were keen to improve the state of the planet.

They had good ideas.

They were peaceful.

They were hopeful.

They also had those uncannily blue eyes. Regardless of whatever eye colour they'd had before they'd been taken up into the spaceships, they had those blue eyes now. The universal marker of, as it came to be known, Ascension. The physical change representing the inner change.

Ben himself had been born with eyes that were almost that blue naturally.

Which was perhaps why he had resisted Ascension for so long, and why he would continue to resist it for as long as he could.

That or he was just a bloody-minded curmudgeon.

He couldn't help but go near the church, which stood near the apex of the hill the town rested on. It was one of those impressive Industrial Revolution churches, paid for by an early-nineteenth-century factory owner who wished to curry favour with the Lord so that, for all his worldly wealth, he could pass through the proverbial eye of the needle when he died. A hedge against hell. Ben could have taken a detour around the church, but it would have added minutes to his journey. Besides, there was something appealing about passing right by it, a perverse satisfaction to be gained.

The church, after all, happened to be where the local Jacob's Ladder touched down. The great beam of light, about seven metres in diameter, occupied a corner of the graveyard. The grass beneath it, which could not be safely mown, had grown long and rank. There, the column waited, patient, expectant. Anyone who chose to could waltz right in and be ferried up along its airtight, pressurised length, as though in a swift-moving elevator, to the spaceship which lay invisibly far above.

It appealed to Ben's contrarian nature to walk close to the column, stray within a stone's throw of it, and then carry on by. To him it was a would-be suicide, like wandering up to a cliff edge and veering away at the last second. *No, not today. Maybe never. You don't get me. Not that easily.*

A middle-aged man and woman were leaving the graveyard by the lych-gate. They were supporting each other, trembling with emotion, both in tears.

Ben had seen this before. He halted, offering the pair a respectful nod.

"Someone you know just gone up, then?" he said.

The woman choked back a sob. "Sarah. Our daughter."

"Turned eighteen last week," the man said. Meaning she had reached the age where she could legally Ascend of her own free will, and her parents could not stop her. "She's been talking about nothing else for months. Counting down the days. She wants to be part of the movement to make the world a better place, and I can't fault her for that. It's just..."

"They aren't the same after they come back, are they?" the woman said.

"No, they're not," Ben agreed.

"They're not the person who left," she continued. "Not quite. I've seen it with friends, with the children of friends. Oh, they look much the same, but they don't act the same. Those – those Inventionists up there, or whatever they're called – they alter them. Meddle with them. Do things to their minds."

"To their personalities," her husband chimed in. "You can't deny they make folk nicer. But niceness..."

"Niceness," said Ben, "isn't enough."

"That's it," the man said, waving an approving forefinger at him. "That's exactly it."

"I'm sorry." Ben meant it. These two parents were experiencing a form of bereavement. The daughter they'd raised for eighteen years, the girl they'd known and loved for all that time, was gone. The Sarah who came back a week or so from now would be someone else. His words were intended as condolence for their grief.

He and the couple parted company, and he continued on his way. Nearly there.

*

The Interventionists were, it was theorised, some benevolent alien race who went around fixing planets where the inhabitants were making a mess of things. And the people of Earth had, by any conceivable metric, been making a mess of things. They had been fighting endless wars. They had been tearing one another apart over religious and racial differences. They had been dirtying their environment and triggering animal extinctions left, right and centre. They had been damaging the biosphere to the point where it was in danger of becoming unsuited to human life.

What the Interventionists looked like, what kind of beings they were, was anyone's guess. There was nobody aboard the spaceships to greet the people who rose up the Jacob's Ladders. There was only automated machinery, and an all-enveloping cerulean light that numbed and anaesthetised, allowing the machinery then to do its subtle work of modification. The spaceships were obviously drone vessels, sent from afar to do their creators' bidding. Perhaps – once every last person on Earth had Ascended, or enough had Ascended to achieve an unassailable, tipping-point majority – they would depart, taking their columns of light with them and whizzing off to the next needy world.

The notion of remote, unknowable, godlike entities who had applied their ridiculously advanced technology for the betterment of the entire universe was both comforting and slightly troubling. Wasn't there an element of eugenics to it? Of tampering? Of denying free will?

Ben certainly was of that view. He wasn't alone in his belief, either, although the numbers of sceptics like him were diminishing daily.

Because it could not be argued that the world was on the mend, thanks to the Angels and their good habits.

Pollution levels were falling, the air in even the most jam-packed, traffic-choked cities becoming breathable.

Rapacious exploitation of mineral resources was in decline.

Renewable energy sources were being employed everywhere, with wind farms springing up all across the countryside, solar panels adorning nearly every roof and ground source heat pumps being sunk in nearly every backyard.

Meat eating was out of favour, veganism on the rise

Diplomacy had replaced war as the standard method of resolving international disputes.

Deserts were being irrigated, forests replanted, oceans cleansed.

Species that had teetered on the verge of dying out were thriving.

A corner had been turned, calamity prevented, and there was no reason to think humankind would backslide and revert to its former uncongenial ways. The Angels, as their ranks grew daily, hourly even, would see to that. They were the handbrake to bring the crazily veering vehicle under control. They were the way forward.

At last Ben Worric got to where he was going: his favourite pub, The Crown and Sceptre, one of the oldest buildings in town, a Tudor-era edifice with higgledy-piggledy ceiling beams and wonky floorboards and not a right angle to be found anywhere on the premises. He had been a regular there since he was old enough to drink, and, to be honest, since before then, when he was old enough to look as though he was old enough to drink.

Pubs, and the consumption of alcohol in general, were dying out. They were going the way of smoking and recreational drug use. The Ascended prized physical health and wellbeing. Just as the world was becoming a purer, cleaner place, so was the human body.

Ben just loved a beer.

He loved it above almost anything else.

He entered The Crown and Sceptre and went straight to his usual spot, a corner table by the ingle. The landlord brought over a pint of bitter for him, straight from the tap. With fewer and fewer customers frequenting his establishment, the landlord valued the ones he still had, and offering them table service felt like the least he could do.

Ben sat with the beer in front of him, savouring the sight of its foamy head and the rich, deep amber glow of its body.

The world had needed rescuing, yes, no argument. And the Angels – the Ascended – were the ones to rescue it. They would ensure humankind's continued existence. Under their influence, there would be a future. There would, some might say, even be paradise.

But what was paradise, Ben thought, without small pleasures? Without harmless vices like a freshly pulled pint of bitter in a quiet, warm pub of an evening?

He waited until he could wait no longer, then raised the glass to his lips and took his first, long, luxurious sip. He'd been looking forward to this all day.

Heaven.

THE NEGLECTED BOOKSHOP

Phillip Vine

I was not an especially religious man but, nevertheless, I cast about daily for intimations of the end of time, and, particularly, for my own fate in whatever apocalypse might be due mankind.

I poured myself a second cup of tea and hoped for revelation in the leaves.

Outside my kitchen window, a wan, late-summer sun, and wasps already about my orchard.

I waited for my tea to cool.

Black garden ants had invaded my property overnight, entering, I presumed, through a door ajar, or secret passageways known only to these tireless scouts and their commanding officers.

I swirled the dregs of tea about the bottom of my cup, left leaves to form their predictive patterns.

I hoped for signs and wonders, settled instead for the diurnal offering of both blessings and curses.

Somewhere in the leaves, though, was a happy conjunction.

Somewhere, too, a man of many books.

Tasseomancy is not an exact science.

The only clarity amidst the lines of leaves was the prospect of a journey from which I should not shirk.

Choices, too, would present themselves: good or evil; life or, possibly, death.

I shivered in spite of the warmth of the kitchen.

From the top shelf of a cupboard I took down ant and wasp killing powders.

The sun hung low in the morning sky.

Sated wasps gorged on ripe apples.

I worried at meanings, at significances.

I thought of Sandra for the first time in months.

A revelation arrived with the morning post.

A sign at last, a wonder.

I was delighted – and surprised – by the arrival of a birthday card and enclosed gift from my children.

I recognised Raymond's handwriting, Clarissa's habitual use of Sellotape to secure the envelope, Toby's insistence upon a first class stamp.

Altogether, it was a real team effort.

The decade since their mother's death had not been the best of times.

I understand, of course, it was only natural for the children to blame me for Sandra's decline and demise.

Indeed, I was not entirely unsympathetic to their campaign against the coroner's verdict, but their refusal to countenance any communication between us after the funeral cut me deeply.

It had been ten long years since the children last acknowledged my birthday.

Let me make it clear: I did not kill their mother.

Unless a degree of neglect might be construed as significant in the progress of Sandra's sad affliction.

Whilst it is true that her death provided me with sufficient security to retire from tedious work at Sedley & Sedley – and to pursue my passion for collecting first editions of unfashionable twentieth century novels with renewed vigour – I would not have wished the manner of her ending upon my worst enemy.

Sometimes, I feared something similar might happen to me.

As I drew the card from its envelope, I noted the disturbing profusion of liver spots on the backs of my hands.

All prior plans – enjoying the sunshine in a deckchair in the orchard in the company of a good book – were cancelled.

There would be an outing on this special day after all.

The leaves, still undisturbed in the well of my teacup, proved uncanny predictors as always.

I double-locked the front door, walked past the rockery with its understated display of flowering alpines, and tut-tutted my disapproval of the patches of moss spreading across the arid lawn.

Blessings mingled with a curse or two.

Ever, it was thus!

I clutched my birthday gift in sweaty, grateful hands.

The sky was vast, immaculate, and unconscious – I presumed – of my good fortune.

I purchased my home – it used to be my grandparents' house – with the insurance money that materialised, eventually, almost two years after Sandra's death.

This transaction, however, proved to be yet another stick with which my children beat me.

Denunciations of my behaviour, past and present, appeared with depressing regularity in the local gutter press and, once, television crews camped for days on my front lawn, hoping for a glimpse of the monster who had murdered his wife.

My curtains remained closed.

Had the children really expected me to sell up the family home, retire to a monastery, and share out the proceeds from the sale between them?

Give them the insurance money too?

Toby came closest to saying so.

In an interview with a disreputable national newspaper, he said: *Our father is like one of the minor villains in my* Collectors *trilogy, seriously specious, ruthless in the pursuit of his pleasures.*

Toby, my youngest, was a novelist, and regularly feted in the Sunday supplements for his *daring yet precise prose*, for the *precocity of his talent*, and for the *complexity yet clarity of his characterisation, especially of his sinners and scoundrels.*

I refused, though, to recognise myself in his miserable and malicious depictions in the arty-farty section of the *Telegraph*. No more than I conceded the accuracy of the journalistic drivel that puffed Toby's meagre talents as a writer.

In his weekly column in the *Spectator*, Toby suggested that my purchase of his great-grandfather's house in Girton with *the blood money* from his mother's killing was *a shameful matter* and that I should have given the *unearned* money to charity or to *others less privileged than himself.*

Now, if my muckraking writer of a son was alluding to himself and his siblings as deserving of charity, he should have had the courage to say so outright.

As for his unsubtle inference that my children were members of some unfortunate underclass, it goes without saying that, even without the benefits of inherited wealth, all had managed to manoeuvre themselves into positions of material comfort and security.

To anyone with a modicum of sensitivity, it should have been obvious that I would have been unable to stay in the house in Hemingford.

It smelled, it stank, of Sandra, and her unfortunate illness, and her painful ending.

I told them I was happy for them to stay in their childhood home rent free for the rest of their lives.

It was a genuine offer.

All four children, though, already enjoyed homes of their own and, in Toby's case, with a mortgage fully paid up thanks to an advance of £100,000 on his fifth novel.

Neither was it my problem that they, too, were unable to deal with the stench of their mother that pervaded their old home.

Once, it had been a splendidly brooding thatched Victorian property whose manicured lawns meandered to a meeting with the murky waters of the Ouse.

For years, it remained tainted with death and its lingering fetor.

Eventually, I let the former family dwelling to a couple from Mumbai who perfumed the place with their tarka dhal and steam cleaned the property with their dum aloo.

At that moment, it became Clarissa's turn to protest in public.

This man —our father — is enriching himself on the broken back and bad bones of his former wife — our mother.

This was six years after Sandra's death!

I was astounded anyone might still be interested in my *brutish behaviour*.

Sometimes I thought my daughter possessed more wizardry with words than her younger brother. Certainly, she never let medical truths get in the way of alliterative alternatives.

Clarissa — I am sorry to say it — is a precious prig.

Married to a Surrey stockbroker, her life is haunted by her inability to conceive, by her husband's twin faults of infidelity and infertility. She has no independent career, has wasted what talents she once possessed. Her life passes her by, lost in a swirl of cocaine, and a miasma of jealous and bitter resentments.

I feel sorry for her, a middle-aged and middle-browed abuser of both Sellotape and the English language.

I strode towards the bus stop — the one opposite Girton's fine twelfth century church was marginally closer than the one at the top of Pepys Way — attempting to banish all negative thoughts from the kingdom of my mind.

Choose life! Choose blessing!

Whilst the New Testament was full of poppycock and hocus-pocus, I found worlds of wisdom, words of cryptic consolation in the works of Moses and his fellow prophets.

I studied St Andrew's stonework, the herringbone pattern of mortared pebbles on the west face of its tower, its fine steeple, topped with a distinctive, green-copper weather vane.

I was tempted to walk up the gravel path and into the dark interior of the church.

I had sung there once, solo, the opening verse of *Once in Royal David's City*.

Some years ago, too, I considered compiling a history of the church where my ancestors were buried. Some of its vicars enjoyed temporary notoriety, one for standing hard against the Marian bloodbath; most, however, for their sexual misadventures involving both boys and girls of the village.

It might have been a *SUNDAY TIMES BESTSELLER*!!

It was too much to take on, though, at a difficult time in my marriage to Sandra.

I held no truck with the stuff and nonsense of formal religious beliefs, but today I ached with an inchoate desire to thank someone or something for this morning's graces.

The remembrance of my birthday, at long last, by my unruly children, overwhelmed me.

I stood in the shadow of the lych-gate of the church, studied the kind words inside my birthday card, the generosity and thoughtfulness of the gift.

I am embarrassed to say that tears fell from my eyes.

It seemed incredible – and mysteriously wonderful – that the children had forgiven me at last.

I was thrilled with the book token they had given me and was eager to discover the shop in Cambridge called *Neglected Books*.

More than that!

Raymond had written in the card – on behalf of all the children including Jackson, Sandra's son from a previous marriage, who was on his way home from California especially for the occasion – to say they would *see* me at the bookshop, would witness my pleasure in choosing from the vast array of *neglected* books.

It was time to put the past to the past, let bygones be bygones.

A visit to the church where, as a child, I had earned a choirboy's precious sixpence each Sunday, and where, less auspiciously, Sandra and I had been married, would have to wait.

I was so overcome, so intoxicated, I nearly forgot to board the bus when it pulled into the side of the road.

"You're happy this morning, Mr Bennett," the driver said, as he gave a cursory glance at my pensioner's pass.

"Yes," I said. "It's my children – they've bought me a present."

He returned my smile.

I did not even mind his condescension.

One thing, however, nagged at my mind, an itch that was impossible to scratch.

I was more than familiar with *all* the Cambridge book shops, the back street ones and the charity ones, I mean, not the famous ones like Heffers or Waterstones.

I wasn't interested in the slightest in new-books, best-sellers, or block-busters.

I was a *connoisseur*, a collector of publications by authors whose fame had passed, or whose deserved fortune had never arrived, a regular patron of David's Bookshop, specialists in rare and antiquarian books, hidden away as it was, in St Edward's Passage, and of Books for Amnesty in Mill Road.

Indeed, such was my obsession, I confess I became increasingly heedless of my wife's deteriorating condition.

But I had never heard of this *Neglected Books*.

"It must be a new one," I said to the bus driver.

I *knew*, though, with an *absolute certainty*, of the *utter impossibility* of the existence of any bookshop unknown to me within the bounds of Cambridgeshire.

I had spies, agents, throughout the city and the entire county – including Huntingdonshire, the Isle of Ely, and the Soke of Peterborough – alerting me to the arrivals of new stock in every proper bookshop, every charitable institution.

News of any addition to the number of *shops* would have been reported to me immediately.

The bus was moving forwards, gathering speed as it passed Girton Glebe Primary School where, once I was caned for running in and out of the girls' toilets at play time.

"I was a hero for the day amongst my peers," I said.

No one, though, was listening.

One of my children – I guessed Clarissa by the profusion of attached Sellotape – had provided a map on which the site of *Neglected Books* was marked by a red cross.

The mysterious – and inexplicable – shop was located in Romsey, the least salubrious, the last part of the Mill Road area as yet un-subjected to gentrification.

Be careful, Johnny, Sandra used to say, whenever I proposed to navigate beyond the railway bridge that divided Mill Road at its mid-point, and cross the border into Romsey Town: *You'll be trespassing there, you'll be on the wrong side of the tracks.*

177

Certainly, I would have heeded her advice had I been visiting that warren of unprepossessing terraced streets after dark.

Forgive me my cynicism, but I always thought Sandra's concern was more for my reputation than for my safety.

A senior partner in Sedley & Sedley being seen in Romsey Town!

Where would it all *end*?

The continuance of Western civilisation may well have been at risk through my venturing into the Romsey Town Co-op to purchase a Scotch egg or a cheap pork pie!

Sandra, like Clarissa, could be – was – snobbish in the extreme.

Once, I suggested an outing to Huntingdon, where a woman in middle-class finery had been spotted delivering six boxes of books to a Sue Ryder charity outlet, but apparently *the people in that godforsaken town* were *beyond the pale*, and she would not come.

My deceased wife was an ardent monarchist and took umbrage at the town's celebrity as the place of Oliver Cromwell's birth. To tell the whole truth, however, Sandra simply could never bear to mix with immigrants from the East End of London who lived on the admittedly blighted, crime-infested, drug-addled streets of the Oxmoor Estate.

I took the bus there anyway, mostly to spite Sandra and her unpleasant prejudices, and found a more than acceptable first edition of Claude Houghton's 1936 masterpiece, *Christina*.

In the Cancer Research shop, of all places!

(I donned dark glasses and pulled down the brim of my rakish blue fedora hat to cover my face before entering lest I be recognised by some former colleague from Sedley & Sedley!)

The book's pages were foxed, and the binding was in need of some attention. Really, though, these faults were excusable in a publication of such venerable antiquity tossed into a bargain box alongside gems of exquisite prose from literary luminaries Dan Brown and J K Rowling, and that celebrity publishing sensation the ubiquitous David Walliams.

Sandra showed not a smidgen of interest in my purchase.

As a consequence, as a punishment, it was weeks before I deigned to greet her with more than a cursory *good morning* and the slightest of accompanying nod of the head.

Sandra dubbed this time as *the great silence*.

It was towards the end of this era, however, that my wife first showed symptoms of her illness, her *great affliction*, she called it once it became established and was granted official medical recognition.

Naturally she blamed me for her head-aches, her belly-aches, and her tit-aches.

And for the first appearance of liver spots on the backs of her hands.

Naturally, too, the children took their mother's side.

As in all differences of opinion, large or small.

Every one of my children, too, took after their mother in their disdain of ordinary people.

None of them would ever have taken a mere *bus* to Cambridge, let alone be seen dead in Huntingdon.

I was astonished, therefore, that they were planning to meet me in the proletarian environs of the eastern end of Mill Road.

In matters of Town v Gown in Cambridge, all my children readily sided with the privileged denizens of the university.

I recalled an occasion soon after Raymond completed his finals – he managed a poor second class in Land Economy, the degree of choice for public school half-wits – when the members of the St Catharine's Boat Club embarked upon a drunken rampage through the centre of the city consequent upon their triumph in the May Bumps on the River Cam. When no sanctions followed their irredeemable behaviour, I dared to mention how different the judicial consequences would have been had the working class supporters of Cambridge United Football Club done anything remotely similar to celebrate their promotion into the higher echelons of the Football League.

Naturally enough, I was shouted down, told I just didn't understand the modern (sic! sick!) world.

With regard to the children's purchase of a book token from a shop in a rough-and-tough area of Cambridge, perhaps they had enjoyed – or endured – an enlightenment of some sort, some life-changing experience, or some Pauline conversion on the road to Romsey.

Maybe they would tell me when they saw me.

Perhaps, too, they had – at last – chosen blessing over curse.

Sufficient unto the day, however, was the fact that they had sent me a card on my birthday, that they had given me the most thoughtful and pleasing of gifts.

The bus service terminated at Drummer Street and central Cambridge was abustle as usual.

People scurried here, worried there, all frowns, all needless hurry, all wasted lives.

A young man, sporting an embryonic ginger beard and with eyes sunk deep within their sockets, elbowed past me, muttering *sorry, sorry*, as he began to run towards the parched grass and flowerbeds of Christ's Pieces.

I watched him until he disappeared into the premises of Cambridge Samaritans.

Was he, I pondered, in need of help, or was he about to offer inadequate platitudes to suicidal men and women?

I was in no hurry.

I had a good hour before my appointment with the children.

I dispensed spare coins to an alcoholic cradling two empty bottles of cider in his filthy hands. His nails were bitten to the quick. I wondered what stories he might tell of his descent and downfall or whether, in fact, he was, in some strange way, happy and blessed with his itinerant life.

At least he had not chosen to throw in his lot with twenty-first century capitalism whose greed was destroying the Earth.

I recalled the settling of tea leaves in my morning cup, resolved to continue my journey to Romsey on foot. On my way, I would call in at the Amnesty Bookshop, where I was well-known and well-respected, too, I hoped, as a discerning, as well as a regular customer.

I found there an almost fine copy of Rupert Croft-Cooke's debut novel, *Troubadour.*

"You know," I said to the volunteer at the cash desk, "you could have asked more for this book?"

"It's a cheaper edition, sir, published by Jarrolds six years after the novel's initial appearance in 1930."

"I am well aware of that," I said, irritated in the extreme by the man's ignorance of my expertise, my acumen in this field.

I interrupted his attempt at apology and watched as his pudgy face reddened.

"Even so," I added, "the book in this condition is worth at least another fifteen pounds."

By now, the shop's manager was at his side.

"Mr Bennett is one of our most valued clients, Jeremy," she said, "and his knowledge of Croft-Cooke's publications is second to none."

I paid for the book and placed a ten pound note in the donations box next to the till.

I crossed the railway bridge, passed over, I thought, to the other side.

I smiled as I checked both the location of *Neglected Book* on Clarissa's map and the time on my grandfather's pocket watch.

Not far now and five minutes before our momentous meeting.

I felt myself in the grip of an adventure so grand to be almost beyond belief.

Signs and wonders – and mighty works – were afoot indeed.

The leaves never failed!

My heart was racing, pounding, knocking against my ribs in the most uncomfortable, not to say alarming, manner.

My doctor had warned me of the dangers, the health risks of serious collecting.

I turned from the thronged thoroughfare that was Mill Road into Hobart Road – Romsey is a curious area of the city, its roads named after far-flung outposts of the now disgraced English empire – and I almost walked down Suez Road for the sheer hell of recalling the humiliation of Eden's Tory government in 1956.

I soon forgot this project, however, when I caught sight of both the dingy frontage of *Neglected Books* and the hunched figure of

Raymond, his nose pressed against the grimy glass of the shop window.

My oldest son, my baby, already an old man!

He was wearing a gabardine raincoat in spite of the late summer heat and a trilby hat sat uncomfortably tilted, unbalanced, on his head.

The bookshop too! There it was!

An intruder, an invasive species of bookshop, dominating the gap between rows of two-up-two-down working men's houses!

The Seventh-day Adventist Church, stolidly occupying that space since Mrs Adah Tapping – baptised in 1920 by the venerable Pastor Prescott from Luton – laid the foundation stone in 1962, had simply disappeared.

Would the missing church's congregation, I wondered, name the displacement of their place of worship by a dingy second-hand bookshop, the Second Great Disappointment after their initial Disappointment of 1844 when the predicted return of Jesus to Earth failed to materialise?

I could feel something like the bookshop's life-force from across the road.

The building – an incongruous mansard roof topping its yellow-bricked façade – appeared to ripple in the weak, now clouded, Cambridge light.

My son seemed diminished in its presence.

I straightened my shoulders, determined to be neither cowed nor bowed.

I called out to Raymond but he appeared not to hear.

I crossed the road, narrowly avoiding a boy in a dun cap and boots on an upright bicycle.

"Oi, watch out, mate," he shouted as he disappeared into Marmora Road.

Was the young man aware that the mining township of Marmora, Ontario, was built on land stolen by British colonists from the indigenous Algonquin early in the nineteenth century?

It mattered not one jot.

My task today was mere acceptance of life and its blessings.

My mind, though, was wandering uncontrollably, and I hoped I would not suffer a relapse into a further bout of mental instability, first suffered shortly after my marriage to Sandra, and repeated – with an additional residence at Fulbourn Hospital – after the birth of Raymond and its accompanying traumas.

Not unrelated, I might add, to my wife's crazy notions that her second child was conceived through the ministrations of the Holy Spirit rather than through the more obvious, though bizarre, methodologies of human propagation.

My insistence upon the name Raymond for my first child - after Raymond Burr, the actor who played Perry Mason in the televised American courtroom drama – had been used against me by my wife when doctors were later sifting evidence in favour of a declaration of my insanity.

I stood within touching distance of my son and was saddened by his decrepit posture.

I noticed in the bookshop's window two publications with which I had been involved at Sedley & Sedley: *The Great Disappointment of My Great-Great-Great Grandfather, William Miller, the Great Adventist* and *My Ancestors, the Algonquin Indians*.

Here were omens indeed, although I had no idea of their meanings, their foretellings.

Tea leaves (Earl Grey or Darjeeling were best, or, if absolutely necessary, common-or-garden breakfast tea with extra sugar to disguise the taste) provided my only half-way reliable means of looking into the future.

I studied Raymond as he uncoiled from his bent posture, and turned to face me.

"Hello, Father," he said. "Happy birthday to you."

He looked wizened and ancient and crazy as a prophet.

I imagined the bookshop was drawing its life from my son.

The trilby toppled from Raymond's head, revealing a shocking loss of hair.

The last time I saw him was eight or nine years ago when we – literally – bumped into one another at a conference in Leeds on *Opportunities in Publishing for the Exploitation of Copyright Law*. At the time, I was still waiting for the disbursement of the insurance money consequent upon Sandra's death. I had been promised its arrival was imminent, and had consequently let it be known at Sedley & Sedley that I might be considering alternatives to employment in the demeaning world of vanity publishing.

Old Sedley had sent me to Leeds as a punishment.

I had no idea my eldest son – I confess I never considered Jackson as one of my own – was an expert on copyright legislation. His degree from the University of East Anglia – a piddling, second rate institution famous only for its degree course in Creative Writing – was in fine arts or some such similar nonsense. The last I heard he was working in a gallery in Ely selling pretentious pictures to wealthy widows with more money than sense.

Raymond had wavy, oiled and perfumed hair in those days, just a tad too long, with dandruff sprinkling the collars of his suits.

In Leeds, he had refused my proffered hand.

I returned to my hotel immediately to spend the duration of the conference drinking single malt whiskeys, and flirting with strangers in the Don Revie bar, eating room service cheese and pickle sandwiches, and retiring to bed early to watch classic films – with an occasional sampling of soft pornography.

I had no desire to listen to my son talking about the impact of libel laws on small publishing houses.

Today, however, outside of *Neglected Books*, he offered me his hand, which I shook warmly, until I noticed the liver spots on the backs of *his* hands.

In the increasingly murky light, these blemishes, these disfigurements, seemed to be dancing, mating, and reproducing before my eyes.

I recoiled momentarily, before recovering my poise.

Blessings *and* curses.

"The others," Raymond said, "they're all inside waiting for you."

His voice was an octave higher than I remembered with the slightest hint of a st-stutter.

He bent to pick up his hat from the dusty pavement.

"This way, Father," he said.

His smile was cursory, devoid of emotion.

"It's good to see you, Raymond," I said, although I may not have been entirely sincere in saying so.

A cracked bell rang tunelessly as my son pushed open the door.

I was greeted by a raucous chorus of *happy birthday, dear Father, happy birthday to you.*

The singing was as discordant as the bell, but both were welcoming, warming somehow, in the chill and musty damp of the shop's interior.

I stared at the children's faces.

The outlines of cheeks, chins, noses, receding hairlines, all seemed blurred, shifting in the play of artificial light inside the bookshop. I hoped I was not suffering from a surfeit of emotion affecting my sight, both of which were past precursors to breakdowns.

Sandra's Jackson was the first to speak.

"I heard from the Gang it was your birthday, Pops, and that you've started collecting old books, so I said to the Gang, I've just got to be there for this."

I despised his accent.

In fact, I found all American accents loathsome, but Jackson's was especially appalling. It seemed an unholy alliance of affected Southern drawl and West Coast sunshine-and-smog's smug liberal superiority of diction.

"Jackson, please don't call me *Pops.*"

"Sorry, Pops," he replied.

Jackson was every bit as dumb as his father.

I held my anger in check, smiled benignly, determined not to spoil the party.

I was relieved, too, that my vision seemed to have improved.

The outlines of my children's faces were suddenly stark, the work of an artist of the realist school rather than that of impressionists or pointillists.

I saw Toby's eyes swivel in the direction of his stepbrother.

"We're not your *Gang,* Jackson," he hissed.

"Sorry, Bro."

"And neither am I your *Bro.*"

185

"Boys," I said, and silence ensued, just as in the old days, when the boys were still boys.

"There is one more thing, though, Jackson," I said. "I am not a collector of *old* books. I am an acknowledged expert in the publications of authors who are undeservedly *neglected*."

I saw my stepson's mouth fall open, his crooked teeth and lolling tongue on full and unfortunate display.

"And don't say 'Sorry, Pops' or I will disown you, cut you from my will."

There was a collective in-draught of breath, a palpable descent of temperature, an exchange of looks.

Somewhere a pile of paperbacks scattered as they tumbled to the floor.

Clearly, it was a mistake to hint at any monetary connection between us, to suggest a measure of my control over my children through my discretionary powers over my legacy.

"I don't want your money, Pops," Jackson muttered, through now closed lips.

His wrinkled face, his contorted snarl of a smile, his narrowed eyes, hooded by unruly eyebrows, all told of his humiliation. "I don't need your goddamned money, Pops. I made a pile for myself, more than enough to retire next fall."

I nodded in acknowledgement of my lapse of etiquette.

"Real estate's real good right now in Sacramento, Pops," my stepson added, his smile a combination of vitriol and delight in one-upmanship.

I detected a suspicion of guilt in my gut – I had always been unkind to Jackson – but dismissed it summarily.

Truth to tell, I never had the slightest intention of leaving a penny – or a cent – to any of my undeserving children.

My last will and testament – in the trusted hands of Willerby & Willerby, Solicitors – vouchsafed my entire fortune upon a cat's home in Chelsea owned by a former lover, now friend, who cared for stray Persian Blues and Short Tailed Abyssinians. It would take more than one birthday card and one measly book token to make me change my will, abandon Sophie and her aristocratic felines.

I watched as the children shuffled uncomfortably in the ensuing silence, shifting their weight from one restless foot to the other, their eyes unable to meet mine.

I saw Sellotape sticking to Clarissa's wayward strands of thinning ginger hair.

I wondered, not for the first time, whether she was someone else's daughter, as I was aware of no trace of red hair in my side of the family.

There was joy here, though, and blessing too, inside this emporium.

Books were everywhere, on shelves, on floors, on other books, an existential crisis of overcrowded publications, each volume with no room to breathe, no room to love or be loved.

I thrilled to the chaos, the serendipity of disorder, the possibility of unearthing a rarity, a bargain, the probability of liberating individual books, and their stories, from all this confusion, this bedlam of books.

Raymond broke into my thoughts, suggested I take time to look around, savour the moment, and consider my choices, my use of the book token.

I nodded in happy agreement.

I saw Toby turn his head and craned my neck to see what he could see.

"Look, Father," he said, his voice aflame with excitement. "Here comes Mr Deedes, the proprietor of *Neglected Books.*"

My youngest son's voice was a hurrah of exultation.

The bookshop owner, a man of innumerable wrinkles, gnarled as an ancient oak, grand and imposing of stature, though bent to permit relative ease of movement in the low-ceilinged shop, was a man of extremes, someone who might be mistaken for a pauper or a prince.

Mr Deedes was dressed in baggy flannel trousers, held in place by an ancient leather belt, and by braces that looped and framed his skin-and-bone body.

My children parted to let him pass. He nodded in their direction in polite but uninterested acknowledgement of their presence in his shop.

I was drawn to his eyes, slate grey with a hint of fire, to a gaze that was either divine or infernal.

Deedes did not blink.

Instead, he passed his withered right hand in front of his face and, when he had completed this curious movement, both arms now hanging limply by his sides, his eyes no longer held mine.

Beads of sweat, though, still ran down my face.

Deedes' eyes, now grey as ash in a grate, as cold as smoke without fire, surveyed his kingdom, his store of delights.

"I bid you welcome, Mr Bennett," he said. "I am grateful to your delightful – and persistent – children for bringing you here."

Each word was enunciated as if each possessed great meaning, great purpose.

I nodded in Deedes' direction by way of inadequate response.

"Come on, Father," Clarissa said, "choose your books."

I suspected my daughter was in a hurry to get done, to be gone from this god-forsaken place, this hoi-polloi of books, this proletariat of publications, with no Barbara Cartland, no Jackie Collins in sight.

Her face, though, still shone, her words still sparkled, as if she was in possession of some secret knowledge sufficient even to mitigate her dislike of being in Romsey Town.

I felt an unforeseen diminution in the presence of the possibility of some unpleasant collusion between my children and the owner of this strange bookshop.

"Yes," said the bookshop owner, "do feel free, Mr Bennet, to browse to your heart's content."

I stumbled forwards.

"Do you have any hardback copies of Eric Brown's science fiction novels, Mr Deedes?" My voice resounded in my ears like that of a stranger's, like that of a man struggling to be heard, shouting perhaps, from a great distance.

"First editions only," I added, anxious perhaps to please, to impress the bookshop owner.

"Naturally so," Mr Bennett.

Deedes paused, his craggy head tilted to one side.

He spoke at last, his voice appearing to come from all about him, as if enlisting the assistance of all the characters in all the books within his shop, to speak on his behalf. "Indeed, Brown was an especially gifted storyteller, writing with compassion, with the ideals of friendship, of comradeship at the heart of his much underrated fiction."

Deedes' smile was beatific.

He spoke with obvious warmth of a writer whose work I had collected for many years, and whose recent death had left me bereft and momentarily unmanned.

"I hear there was an American hardback edition of one of his *Bengal Station* novels?" I said.

"I have two copies, Mr Bennett, one for you, and one for me to keep."

"Splendid news, Mr Deedes."

My grip on my *Neglected Books* token tightened.

Every cell in my body sang with anticipation and excitement.

"Once," I said, "I had the pleasure of meeting Brown in his home in Cockburnspath in the Scottish Borders."

I watched the bookshop proprietor's face, but it gave no hint of jealousy nor, indeed, of any real interest.

"Brown explained to me how he only discovered this particular edition when he visited his publisher and saw copies lying on the floor, underneath his editor's desk."

Deedes nodded peremptorily.

"Such," he said, "are the injustices, the indignities, suffered by *all* neglected authors."

I continued, heedless of his apparent lack of empathy, of compassion.

"Brown's house," I added, "was modest, but homely, pebble-dashed in that quaint and characteristic Scots style."

"Indeed, Mr Bennett, indeed."

Deedes was bored, interested solely, I understood, in the conclusion of transactions.

My children, I noted, had shifted about the shop and now stood shoulder to shoulder behind me, as if to bar my escape. All except Jackson were grinning as if they were privileged witnesses of the most righteous entertainment in the world.

It was surely preposterous to suspect them of an attempt to imprison me here, but that was my suspicion.

"I was fortunate, too," I said, determined to continue, "in meeting Brown's charming wife and daughter."

The bookseller's nod was cursory, casual to the point of impertinence.

"Brown showed me his library."

I *would* continue my story, angered by Deedes' haughty demeanour.

"During the course of his lifetime, Brown curated an almost complete collection of the works of Rupert Croft-Cooke, including some fine first editions purchased for him as birthday and Christmas gifts by Fionnuala, his beloved wife."

Deedes seemed moved, at last.

"Ah, dear Rupert." The bookseller's voice was a lover's sigh and a snake's hiss. "I'm afraid, both Croft-Cooke and Brown were writers who escaped me."

Deedes' meaning escaped me too.

Later, I wished I had asked for elucidation.

There was, though, business to be done.

"I don't suppose," I said, "you have a copy of Croft-Cooke's *Night Out?*"

I watched Deedes' face for any sign of encouragement, but none was immediately forthcoming.

"I am missing the 1932 Dial Press New York edition," I added in a voice I suspected of a dash of self-pity.

I was convinced the man was hiding something.

"I believe," I said, "a copy exists in which Rupert signs and underlines his name in blue fountain-pen ink, dated New Year, 1933."

I checked the inside pocket of my jacket, relieved to feel the solid reassurance of my leather wallet and its contents of a baker's dozen of fifty pound notes.

The children, I had to admit, had been generosity itself, the *Neglected Books* token worth £250, but I knew that more, much more would be needed if I were to find even a half way decent copy of *Night Out* with its delightful Art Deco dust jacket intact.

"Ah, you are a connoisseur indeed, Mr Bennett."

"Well, I have been collecting his books – and Brown's too – and other similarly neglected authors for many years."

"Your children told me so, Mr Bennett."

I smiled, turned to the children, and smiled again.

Their grins were wider than before. Even Jackson smiled, as if my stepson was no longer excluded from some momentous secret.

"Yes, indeed, Mr Bennett, I see you are the most passionate of bibliophiles, and that you will enjoy nothing more than a close perusal of my own collection of forgotten books – and of their authors."

I nodded, mute in my ecstasy.

"Clarissa told me, too, that you were an author yourself, Mr Bennett."

I attempted to speak but no words emerged from my open mouth.

"I knew it already, of course."

Deedes' eyes were now ablaze, no longer grey, but alight with the myriad colours of fire.

"I have copies – signed copies no less – of your debut novel, *Sins of the Fathers*, a much maligned publication, thinly and disappointingly reviewed, but, to my mind, a fine example of its type of veiled autobiography."

I glared at my daughter.

I was ashamed that *Sins* was not only my first but my last published book.

"You are, Mr Bennett, a neglected author in your own right."

There was some errant laughter behind me, but I stood my ground, refusing to turn about. I would neither acknowledge nor condemn the frivolity of my children in the company of my lamented and lamentable novel.

"So, Mr Bennett, I not only have your novel, but I now have you too."

I looked askance at Deedes, his words strange, ambiguous, his eyes worlds in which infernos roiled and raged without end.

"Come with me, Mr Bennett," he said.

It was a command rather than an invitation.

I followed the bookshop proprietor through the twists and turns of the tunnels of his shop.

I would have liked to pause, to examine, to handle the host of wonderful editions of books I yearned to add to my collection, but I was still unable to speak, to request a stay of execution.

There was a door at the back of the bookshop where Deedes halted.

"Say goodbye to your father, children," he said.

"Goodbye, Father," they said, in unison, their faces alight with exultation, with triumph.

I watched as Deedes unbolted and unlocked the door at the back of the bookshop.

"I told you," he said, "I gave you fair warning."

"I'm sorry," I replied, "but I don't understand."

"I collect *authors*, neglected *authors*, like your good self, Mr Bennett."

I was not as unhappy as perhaps the children hoped

"I'll take your token now," Deedes added, "and your wallet, too, where I'm sure I will find sufficient payment to cover my expenses."

He nodded at the children as they turned to leave.

I found myself without anger, even as I understood their betrayal, their grim revenge.

Sunlight struggled through the grimy glass in the shop's door, danced briefly with the straggle of auburn curls and Sellotape in Clarissa's hair.

I felt, instead, a strange intoxication, an overwhelming sense of the secret beauty hidden in my children's hearts, some point of sheer righteousness of which they were unaware, all this in spite of their spiteful behaviour, which seemed to cast the most grave doubt upon their inherent goodness.

Lights dimmed inside the shop.

As did the strange radiance of my children's faces.

I did not – and still do not – believe in life after death, but I do wonder whether Sandra was somehow involved in the children's plot. If not, I'm sure she would have approved of their deception, their cunning, and would now be laughing through her pain.

In my former wife, sadly, I could find no Eden, no primeval innocence.

Deedes, though, was talking once again.

"What I generally find, Mr Bennett, is that the writers are much more interesting than their books."

I followed the bookshop proprietor through the narrow doorway into the back room.

"Welcome," he said. "You are now an esteemed addition to my collection."

Some days are, indeed, difficult.

Some days, I hear snatches of conversation, snippets of gossip between friends, between neglected authors.

Some days, I add comments of my own, stories about my visit to Brown, my delight in discovering that his library contained shelf upon shelf of rare and forgotten pulp fiction paperbacks, in addition to the more literary works of his beloved Rupert Croft-Cooke.

Some days, some authors seem interested.

Someone, once, asked me about my own novel, expressed some sympathy with its demise, shared common ground concerning ruthless publishers and incompetent agents.

Some days, Deedes comes and talks to us, and he is not an uninteresting man when he expounds upon his collection, his ongoing duty to bring together an entire community of writers, all of them deserving more from life than critical neglect, remaindered books, and places on the dusty shelves of charity shops in Cambridge.

Some days, he brings us communications from the other side.

Once, on some subsequent birthday, I had a letter from my daughter.

Dear Father, it said, *I hope you are well, Love Clarissa x*

Such kindness, I thought, such thoughtfulness – perhaps you were my daughter after all. Another writer told me he had a ginger-haired child, that he discovered his grandfather's mother was a carrot-top, and that genes could skip generations.

I thanked him profusely.

As for Deedes, he was either a saint, or mad and bad.

Once, he lectured us on choices.

"See," he said, "I set before you blessing and curse, life and death."

I recognised our collector's borrowings from the Old Testament.

"Is he here," I asked, "the writer of the Book of Deuteronomy?"

Deedes tipped his head in half-hearted acknowledgement of my knowledge of scripture.

"Moses, after all," I added, "is a most *neglected* author."

Deedes made no response, his lack of the slightest sense of humour all too evident.

He studied me, as a lepidopterist might study a pinned butterfly.

When he eventually spoke, his words were growls of thunder, warnings of the storms to come when all worlds end.

"You might just as well ask, Mr Bennett, whether God is here."

"Well, is he, then?" I asked.

"That is *the* question," Deedes said, his pained smile inscrutable.

Most days, I choose life.

Better, indeed, to count blessings, than to cast curses on a callous world.

Time still runs, still rules, here at least, and there is the reassurance of routine.

Most days, I think of my children, and wish them mostly well.

Yesterday I recalled the young man with the ginger beard making haste towards the offices of Cambridge Samaritans, and remembered him in my prayers.

Deedes has brought me my morning cup of tea, made with fine Darjeeling leaves.

It is a little luxury he has permitted me.

I indulge in some divination, consider the futures of us all, those inside and outside of this Neglected Bookshop, long since gone from the cheap streets of Romsey Town.

I imagine the good congregants of the Seventh-day Adventist Church, Mrs Adah Tapping and Pastor Prescott, too, are pleased by the return of their premises to Hobart Road in the dark heart of Romsey Town.

I picture, too, the boy in Marmora Road on his old-fashioned bicycle, and the tramp cradling his empty bottles of cider.

I hope, in time, they might find their ways home.

I wish my friend, Brown, were here with me, but I realise that is a selfish thought, and a presumptuous one, to imagine a writer like him might be my friend.

I watch the play of light upon the liver spots upon the backs of my hands.

Ants crawl about the floor.

Wasps study me through the grimed glass of the closed windows of my room.

Deedes is coming to unlock the door of my room.

It is a new heaven I inhabit, and my children — for their sins — are bequeathed a new and terrible Earth.

MASTERCHEF ON MARS:
A MURDER MYSTERY

Ian Watson

So far the Human Race hasn't found how to get to the stars. Even the nearest star is much too far. There's no way to travel half as fast as light, never mind faster. Besides, space-based supertelescopes show clearly what rubbish all the exoplanets are out to at least a thousand light years. Too boiling, too frozen, too heavy for Olympic weightlifters, too irradiated, too gassy, not enough gas, toxic, tiny, titanic, et cetera. There's no reason to go.

But Mars we could do, and we did do so. Mars is mostly terraformed by now, in 2530 common era. We did this using technologies which frankly I don't much bother about. Do you bother personally about why your blood is red?

With my pension from forty years as a store detective in Harrod's I retired from London to Blue Bay, a pleasant town on the shore of Lake Elysium on modified Mars. The lake shimmers prettily all the time like rippling silk because Mars wobbles due to having no big moon to stabilise the red planet. Gene-engineered salmon and trout abound, a treat for the angler. You can sit on a jetty dangling your rod all day, the coldbag to pop your catch also serving to keep your beer cool, until ideally you finally forget about her. About that Jezebel. Jeza*Bill* in my case? Personally I'm not that complicated, even if He&She was, and I guess still is. Yes, the love of my life was a Herma/Hermo, but I shan't talk of this. It was all on another planet. People in the past wouldn't even understand. With HimHer I lovingly accepted a half life, only enjoying the 'Her' half, fool that I was. It was like being devoted to a humanoid alien, supposing that such should exist.

The 1,000 kilometre per Mars-hour Circuit Express train runs in a low vacuum pipeline, that also usefully protects trains against dust storms, from our capital city Burrows around the main ocean and back to Burrows again. Originally Burrows was all underground, as you'll guess from its name. Blue Bay is off along a 50 kilom spur – by zeppelin guided by mechanical mule on a monorail – and is fairly sleepy just as I'd hoped. However, Blue Bay does boast an Entertainments Committee, and I simply couldn't avoid becoming a member – not once I encountered the other highly compatible committee members in Blue Bay's quietest pub, The Bubbling Brew, soon after my arrival three years earlier.

The quartet who would become my bosom friends were playing holocards accompanied by witticisms that seemed fresh and fun, and still seem so. That's quality.

The Chopinesque tinkle of Margarita's laughter was tantalising. Chopin, yes. Being at Harrods was a privilege and an education. At any moment you might need to interact with a celebrity, a sheikh, a Nobel Prize winner so long as they already have their prize money. I am well groomed, yes Sir.

Margarita likes to drink her namesake, in moderation and preferably in the correct glass which has a bulb at the bottom. The tequila cocktail is good for her peaches and cream complexion; her cheeks are the peaches. She's married to Cyril, the town's gaunt black-bearded Doctor. Cyril has enhancer implants for when veterinary surgery is called for, plus psychiatry.

Cyril's nurse assistant is Fia, a perfect Gauguin golden-brown lady from subsided Tahiti. Fia is short for Polynesian *Fiafia*, meaning 'happy'. She's forever engaged (never yet the bride) to wheelchair-plugged Willie, him being the radio voice of news and weather, our DJ, and whatever else suits us five thousand regular citizens of Blue Bay. Rising to twenty thousand during the Summer tourist season – nowhere on climate chaotic Earth do you encounter such sheer serenity and flat beauty as Blue Bay. Slightly bent beauty, I mean, due to the nearish horizon.

Willie lost the use of his legs due to an ancient Martian virus that revived after a billion years comatose. I honestly don't know if the virus also ruined Willie's virility. Willie makes jokes, and Fia neither flushes (hard to be *sure*) nor protests. We all have our little boundaries. Willie's hoverchair is extremely adequate, and even boasts extrudable push-hoops and caster wheels in case of machine-failure. But a car it ain't.

Anyway, let's leap *in medias res*, into the middle of things – nothing to do with the Media. A Nobelist seeking a signet ring of 24-carat gold once used that phrase *in medias res* to his personal shopper whom I was accompanying in my heritage green and gold uniform, not incognito. My earbud promptly picked up on it. Please note that I don't say a 'cygnet' ring, nor 'carrot' regarding the weight of diamonds. That's Harrods polish for you.

"Hube, Hube," Willie voices me on my mobile.

"Hube, there's a homicide at Kitchens. Inside Masterchef Mars!"

Where else to hold Masterchef Mars Blue Bay but at Kitchens? Us 'famous five' friends often eat at one of the restaurants there. The managements are always happy to see us. After all, we're the Entertainments Committee.

We certainly do play a part in bringing Masterchef Mars to fairly sleepy Blue Bay, in cahoots with the Restaurants Association, the Town Hall's Councillor for Culture & Tourism et cetera et cetera. We aren't in this instance a principal player; Masterchef Mars is part of a bi-planetary initiative. Consequently so far I haven't renewed acquaintance – such as it was and should she even remember me! – with that visiting diva of fine dining, superchef judge Conchita Carmen Chipana of Mexico. Would you believe I even had the honour of meeting Señorita Chipana once, must be ten years ago, during Harrods Table, in this case a

Mexican gourmet promotion in Harrods Food Hall when the Señorita's pearl-crusted make-up purse disappeared mysteriously.

Who are the Señorita's two fellow judge-chefs from Earth?

Come on, brain!

Yes it's coming… Maurice O'Malley from Belgium; he started with pop-up fried sprouts with fries, then went on to open his 2-star Mussels From Brussels –

– and, and… Wolfgang Wang, Viennese Chinese, a master of Sechuan Schnitzel.

Those guys.

"Who's the victim, Willie?"

"Oh, merely last year's Top Chef of Terra. Your chum Conchita Carmen."

I try to divert the surge of horror and grief by recalling that 'last year' isn't so precise since one year on Mars is equivalent to two years on Earth due to Mars's double length orbit around the sun. How I crave a strong beer, immediately, to cope with the shock.

"That's… hideous. Horrible news. How? Why? But why are you voicing *me*, Willie? Need help to get there? Need a lift? So you can be an eye-witness?"

"Hube, I'm *already* at Kitchens. I'm voicing you as a *detective*. You *were* a detective, weren't you?" Is Willie being sarcastic or just doing the probing journalist thing?

"Yes. Um, yes." Hubert Lancaster at your service.

Willie carries on, "We need this murder solved super-fast. Otherwise Masterchef at Blue Bay and maybe even Masterchef Mars planet-wide *fails big*. I'm speaking here for the Blue Bay Entertainment Committee, ahem. May our banner fly high."

"Well yes, right. But of course there's always City Security –"

"You know as well as I do that Grumpy Boots and his deputies, sergeants, and troopers are all bears of little brain. Who else hereabouts but you has criminal detection experience?"

"At the moment are you *assuming* this is a crime and *assuming* it's a murder?"

"There the true detective speaks. You're hired. To be legit you'll need to receive a fee – any objections? You better resign from the Entertainments Committee to keep this all above board. Do you agree to resign, Detective Lancaster?"

"I suppose I do."

Bit of a rush. Such is show business, as I was aware from Harrods. One minute's delay in opening doors for the New Year Sales means fifty thousand in lost revenue – and this is interplanetary Masterchef that's at risk. My heart bleeds for that lovely lively lady Conchita, now no more. A beer would steady me. No time for a beer. I best not arrive in Kitchens with beer breath on me.

"Fine, Hube. I have your voiceprint to that. Please *hurry* to Kitchens. Grumpy Boots is arriving pronto with his dumbo deputy duo. The Masterchef set is locked down. Doomed to be trampled by Grumpy Boots – I'll interview his vanityship to delay him. When you come I'll be in newsgathering mode." Meaning no assistance from Willie, maybe Willie even interrupting me for sound bites. But that's what friends are for. Willie cuts the call before I get to ask, 'Do you *know* what killed her? Have you *seen* the body? *Who* had the sense to lock down the set?'

This is the patrol-cop-just-bought-a-burger moment: chuck that burger out the window pronto and burn rubber. The five (or four or three, depends) of us chums sometimes watch old 20th Century crime viddies to amuse ourselves. I shouldn't take a beer for medicinal purposes. I should be seen to arrive steering not beering while steering. I must harbour the pang of the Señorita's death, unquenched, unmodified. Yet with sharpened perception, perhaps!

"Car, to Kitchens front entrance, *seal voo play*." A spot of French is like shoe polish. A touch of gloss.

Grumpy Boots, forever complaining whilst trampling things, is Security chief Sheriff Jake Johnson. The Sheriff's two full deputies are ebony-black Frankie Hollywood and bleached Beth

Harmony. Don't let them catch you speeding your bubblecar. Speeding's only for escaping out of a forest fire and even then you get fined, just less. Blue Bay has such a lovely forest of Redwoods, mature by now. Great hiking opportunities. Citizens voted against radar traps for vehicles.

I recall that during the bygone Mexican week at Harrods several of the mescals and ultra-premium tequilas on offer wore discreet price tags in the thousands each, even tens of thousands; eyes to be kept upon those bottles, Mr Lancaster! And duly not one of the prestige bottles went for a walk. Food included uplifted ant eggs, next-level ant larvae, upraised maize 'smut' fungus, uplifted chiles in walnut sauce. The uplifting courtesy of Conchita Carmen Chipana, her brand labels now allied to the Harrods name. I suppose I fell a little in love with her. Respectfully. I hope I don't find her mutilated. Grace, Courtesy, and Care were always our watchwords at Harrods. As well as: Anything Possible. In the 26th Century as surely as in the 19th.

Kitchens are eight super restaurants side by side under one long hammer-vaulted ceiling twinkling with golden fairy lights. Outside of this gastronomic xanadu a waiting Masterchef assistant takes charge of my car while a second assistant escorts me over to Caribbean Calypso Café where my chums and I have enjoyed many a goat curry and jerk chicken raised in organic happiness upon Gym Farms. Caribbean Calypso Café is hosting the Masterchef competition in Blue Bay for logistical and layout reasons, being a bit of a useful maze at the lake side, the rear.

Gym Farms are where livestock wear weightjackets to compensate for the lower grav as regards animal muscle growth. Also, the animals happily use enticing virtual reality exercise machines. Putting the *gravy* on to the kids and the chicks, you might say – ho! – as well as on to Beijing ducks and specklebelly geese and mangalitsa, not to mention ibérico piggies and welsh lambs and wagyu calves; and more. Thanks to Harrods Food Halls and its couple of hundred chefs I'm fairly well set up mentally as regards fine dining... which would be a real bonus were this a review of Masterchef Mars rather than a murder investigation, reportedly.

During my decades at Harrods I experienced a few heart fatalities, including one amateur shoplifter who died of shock when I challenged her. Poor frail skinny old lady wearing a faded hat adorned with everlasting daisies, helichrysums, like a headstone vase in a cemetery. We'd have all whipped round for her, to gift a simple wicker hamper of soups. We bought her a wreath of helichrysums instead, employees discount. Because we cared.

Displaced contestants and Kitchens staff are backed up in an access hallway. The two Security Deputies, Frankie and Beth, are keeping the lavishly provisioned Masterchef pantry off limits and screened while presumably Sheriff Jake studies the scenario within or messes with it investigatively.

Beth and Frankie follow me inside the pantry. And. Ohmigod, Conchita Carmen Chipana lies sprawled across the fish section, the tail of a trout gaping from her mouth.

Throat blocked, asphyxiation. My immediate thought: She wasn't poisoned but *poissoned*!

I'd better explain my thought processes, which otherwise may seem frivolous but actually are the mark of a Sherlock who must in the past have shopped at Harrods for his deerstalker, his signature crimehunter's hat. As I said, part of the Harrods polish is a peu de Français. How to pronounce "Mam'zelle" for instance. And chefs will shout "Wee, Shef!" to show off their classical training, not that they need a pee. Other members of staff are genuinely fluent in Arabic or Chinese to escort the highest spenders. Thus it is that this item of bilingual wit occurs to me right now.

Sheriff Jake acknowledges me with a nod. "Huh, so now you're going to play Detective."

"Forty years on the job. Little do you know, Sheriff."

"Far as I know, looks open and shut to me. Lady choked on the trout. Couldn't pull it out her mouth again cause its skin's so slimy slippery. I know that a hundred percent from angling. Check her fingers for slime, if you like to. I see you have gloves on already."

"So as not to put my fingerprints everywhere!"

"Open," says Deputy Frankie.

"And shut," says Deputy Beth.

Both deputies are bovine as Buddhas.

"Pretty pink gloves that look like skin."

Yes I'm still wearing the gossamery disposable gloves which I'd taken a hundred pair box of from Doc Cyril last Mars-year.

Is Sheriff Jake suggesting I'm *fancy*? Doc Cyril keeps dozens of boxes of pink gloves in a cupboard, one pair for each new physical examination of a patient, not needed for psychiatry. When I got up this morning I did don a pair of the antiskid gloves to shuck a couple of rock oysters to enjoy with my cup of Earl Grey tea, a few dots of tabasco sprinkled upon each. I'd acquired a few special tastes at Harrods. My personal 'resident's rock' with oysters was underwater offshore. A plastic pennant poked up from the water bearing my initials **HL** like a house name. This was an inspiration of the Blue Bay Greetings Committee three years ago. By now the oysters on the rock are adult enough to snack on, non-slip gloves a necessity for the shucking. Those grippy gloves are made of nitrile and for a detective easily double as fingerprint blockers, now in use for the first time as such.

Fortunately here comes my good drinking chum Jimmie the Journalist, voice of Blue Bay, in his nonwheel-chair beefed up with tech. Security makes no attempt to stop or slow Jimmie. Freedom of the Press.

"On the other hand," continues Sheriff Jake – slyly, I'd say – "*how* was a trout inserted into the lady's windpipe as a murder weapon? By whom? Assuming she herself wasn't responsible. Imagine: she feels herself clutched. She opens her mouth to protest or to scream. In goes a trout. Maybe held in a non-skid glove."

Jimmie pays no attention to Jake's speculations and drifts to film Superchef Conchita, fish-faced, tail foremost. Dark hazel eyes bulging (hers, not the fish's, those being out of sight). Normally Jimmie only does radio but he can also transmit relevant viddies to folk's phonescreens en masse if the occasion sufficiently justifies.

Jimmie turns to me. "So, citizens, while we *swallow* what was done to this Superchef, we're lucky to have with us *professional* Detective Hugh Lancaster ex of Harrods Food Hall Security team to shed light –"

Sudden anger boils within me at the *irreverence* of Security. Conchita Carmen Chipana is in a humiliating situation, absurd and ridiculous, enough to tarnish her fame. Is that the *main* motive for this killing? Was she about to release a new cookbook on the web? How bitter may superchef rivalries become? Am I suspecting one or both of the other judges?

My poison/poisson notion is an *inspiration*. I really should keep this insight up my sleeve. But right now I'm being filmed for the newsstream, and so is Sheriff Jake. Has Jake found a glove with little spikes on the palm? Has he pushed that glove temporarily under a turbot flown frozen from Earth? A piece of evidence which Jake might reveal as and when he pleases. As a well-seasoned Harrods store detective I cannot risk being pre-empted or trumped.

Nothing ventured! In for a pound! "How's this, Jimmie, as a first approximation to a solution, which we all want quickly? That trout is a *red herring*."

"Uh?" exclaims Sheriff Jake. "Is this some cheffy trick? Like a hare from a hat?" He may mean pulling Welsh rabbit from a hat. Or not.

"No, Chief and Jimmy too, listen up, the set-up here is to make you think the fish is the murder weapon. That's what is known as neurolinguistic programming, in this case using an unexpected physical object to disorient you. But the actual weapon is *poison* not a French *poisson*. A fast-acting, paralysing poison. Something you won't now think of looking for with the fish so visibly in evidence." Didn't I see the body of a Japanese fugu pufferfish on the marine counter accompanied by an elegant porcelain bowl isolating its super-poisonous blotchy skin and liver and ovaries? These, in a shallow stasisware box, now set to null, accompanied by a certificate of expert dissection. I'd heard that the ovaries of female fugus are far more poisonous than the testes of males. The safe parts are presumably required for a skills test or as a pièce de résistance/coup de théâtre. Sometimes a contestant may dare to garnish using the tiniest tickle of toxin; dire consequences for a contestant who misjudges!

Over time wild tiger fugu from the very slightly radioactive Sea of Japanese is replacing caviar as the expensive prestige ingredient to add to dishes. I hobnobbed with several celeb chefs in the various Food Halls. Many people assume that Sherlock Holmes shopped at Harrods for the best common black shag to tamp into his meerschaum pipe.

Still... maybe I shouldn't reveal right away that I already know all about the teratodoxin in fugus, a thousand times more deadly than cyanide.

Sheriff Jake is burly as well as beer-belly. Personally he might think little of seizing the Señorita all by himself and forcing a trout into her mouth — wouldn't matter if she sees him — then supporting her till she flops, to be positioned across the other fish. Positioned neatly, note. Could either Masterchef Maurice O'Malley or Masterchef Wolfgang Wang achieve this on their ownsome or — perhaps worse — both of them in combo and conspiracy?

"Sheriff, I need to meet the other two judges. Where are they right now?"

"In Annex Three together with the Masterchef staff from Earth. You'll recognise the chef-judges easily because they're wearing chef-whites, right ho, Detective? No need for Deputy

Beth to point a finger." Is Jake taking the piss? He calls, "Beth, will you oblige Detective Lancaster?"

Why is the Sheriff being obliging instead of scattering obstacles in my path like pieces of Lego?

"This way please, Detective. With me. Stay close."

Yeah, Beth. Just a second while I ask, "Who found the body?" But it's Beth who answers me, not Jake as I intended: "Newsman Willie, I believe." Willie has already been in the pantry once today?

Why didn't Willie tell me that himself? Oh I see. Stands to reason. So as not to confuse. Chairbound Willie is physically incapable of such a crime. But may his accessorised chair be suspected?

Questioning the two other judges yields little except perhaps sincere sorrow at Conchita having passed, a word familiar in cheffing. On the pass, service, table two! Here on Mars their cheffy Earth musculature has to be way beyond what's needed for the dire deed, consequently each is innocent.

For the upcoming show here in Blue Bay, Masterchef can function with two remaining judges, so an organiser assures me. For the subsequent heat they can rush a replacement celebrity chef from Earth by sprintship, costing a small fortune and requiring the passenger to suspend himself or herself in protective gel. Me, I emigrated the comfier if congested way, by cruiser.

When Beth escorts me back to her boss he's looking more thoughtful than I'd have thought possible. But then he nods sagely and tells Deputy Frankie, "Chill the chef judgette. No, *not* together with Masterchef food supplies; I caught that look. Speed the body to Doc Cyril by ambulo to test for poisons. The Doc is implanted for specialisations. Oughta have a vacant morguebox at home, but check. Hang on, change of plan: you stay at the Doc's to witness his poison autopsy on behalf of Security, along with Detective Hubert. Probably just an autoanalysis without any cutting into organs so don't you worry about fainting, Frankie."

Why is Sheriff Jake being so accommodating? Why isn't he raising fatuous bylaws? Is Sheriff Jake *himself* a suspect as well as... well, *who else* occurs to me as candidates?

Exotic poisons are controlled on Mars... Ah, a lot of spicy pastes and vinegars and oils must have been freighted in specially for Masterchef Mars. Thus the perp may be one of the organisers themselves. But poison is very plausible, provided that some can be found in the body.

Deduction is having a field day today, oh my friends including former colleagues at Harrods! What a Sherlock of a day this is. What a tale Willie will have to tell.

For I have decided on the identity of the killer. I'll swear Willie to secrecy on the promise of a truly startling scoop which will rock two worlds plus Luna when I myself perform the arrest live on camera as a climax to the contest. Likewise, there'll be patient confidentiality from Doc Cyril who signed that medical oath as surely as Conchita Carmen Chipana is retrospectively his patient, now deceased. My fellow Harrods Alumni will all hear, those pensioners forever green and gold as we say in honour of our bygone uniforms, whether or not we were uniformed or ununiformed and only put a green and gold pin on our chests.

Sheriff Jake taps himself on the nose. "Detective," he drawls at me, "You'll save Blue Bay and Mars from interplanetary scandal and much financial loss."

Along with Deputy Frankie I accompany my would-be nemesis in the ambulo, thus establishing chain of custody for Conchita Chipana who — hare out of a hat! — has now been contaminated with enough teratotoxin to paralyse several donkeys, even though the trout remains stuck in her mouth.

Of course that isn't how it was at all — *which no one but the Detective himself must know.*

When Willie phoned my mobile I had already parked my car on the lakeside esplanade to the rear of Kitchens. A service lane which diners in the Calypso can look right across, oblivious to any utilities, admiring the Martian sunset reflecting in the moiré of microripples.

Sheer curiosity was my motive for sneaking in from the rear to see the lavish Masterchef pantry of meats and fish and fruits and veggies and spices et cetera laid out in anticipation, many metres of raw materials including really lux stuff.

Little did I expect that Conchita Carmen Chipana herself, perfectionist, would be inspecting the groaning board.

Even littler did I expect that she would recognise me!

"You! You're the Harrods store detective, coño! The one who stole my pearl-crusted purse!"

"No no, Lady you got it wrong, I was the store detective who *investigated* the disappearance of your pearly purse, alas unsuccessfully."

"Ya, Seguro, you played that role quite cleverly. But I already saw you slip my purse into your poche. I do not point a finger at you. Yet for insurance reasons I cannot let this go unreported. Presently I'm introduced to the thief himself in the person of my dedicated detective, madre de dios, you. I do take a poco of pity as regards not ruining your career, but mostly because it's Mexican Week I want no petty scandal to discolour my deal with Harrods Food Halls. So I keep mum, I keepa da mama."

Petty scandal? Petty?

"Shut your mouth, missus!"

"What, and let *you* mess in any way whatsoever with Masterchef Mars, mine?"

That's when from sheer proximity I grasp a trout, at the same time gripping Conchita as she opens her mouth to shout. I'm ashamed of resorting in extremis to trout instead of teratotoxin! – but I wouldn't have dreamed of seizing any poisoned piece of fugu with my glove prior to Conchita's averted betrayal of me. We learn some useful skills as Harrods Detectives, need I say more; a nod's as good as a wink to a blind donkey.

I keep the pearl-crusted make-up purse in the small combo safe in my basement now, concreted into a wall, along with the box of nonslip gloves.

And the guilty criminal, who *does* confess as perps often confess, even if innocent for neurotic reasons connected with their mothers, roll of drums, toot-toot, big winner-loser of my personal 2530 Masterchef Murder trophy, is...

PEPPERCORNS

Rebecca Rajendra

FADE IN:
INT. SHOP – DAY

A typical 1960s local shop from a comedy sketch. Behind the counter, SHOPKEEPER stands. He is wearing a tan work coat and flat cap. A bell rings as the shop door opens. Enter ROBOT, a classic mid-century style automaton, dark grey with a square head and antennae, who moves in an exaggerated mechanical fashion.

> SHOPKEEPER
> Good morning sir, how many I help
> you?

ROBOT looks at a long paper shopping list held in his left claw.

> ROBOT
> (in a robotic voice) Pepper. Corn. Please.

> SHOPKEEPER
> Pepper, corn. Right away, sir.

SHOPKEEPER disappears into a back storeroom and returns a sweet red pepper and two corn on the cobs in his arms, which he places on the counter.

> SHOPKEEPER
> There we are sir.

ROBOT
No, peppercorn. For grinding black pepper.

AUDIENCE laughs.

SHOPKEEPER
Ohhh, peppercorn.
(he reaches behind the counter and
brings out a small glass jar of black
peppercorns)
Anything else?

ROBOT stares at the jar of peppercorns.

SHOPKEEPER (CONT'D)
Sir? What's next on your list?

ROBOT
(consulting his shopping list)
Oil.

SHOPKEEPER
I'll just get that for you, sir.

SHOPKEEPER goes into the back room. ROBOT picks up the
jar of peppercorns in his right claw and stares. SHOPKEEPER
returns with a box of jangling glass bottles.

SHOPKEEPER
What type of oil, sir? Olive,
sunflower, vegetable?

ROBOT is still staring at the peppercorns. SHOPKEEPER
shuffles his feet awkwardly as he holds the box, unsure of how to
proceed.

ROBOT
My function is to grind pepper.
The performance of this function
does not require oil.

SHOPKEEPER
Well it appears to be on your list,
Sir! I'm sure you have a use for it.
Now we've got olive, sunflower, or
vegetable…

ROBOT
The viscosity of oil would impede
the correct operation of my
grinding mechanism and render
peppercorns unfit for purpose.

SHOPKEEPER
(nervous, trying to improvise) Silly
me, you probably mean engine oil,
don't you, sir, being a robot and all!

AUDIENCE laughs. SHOPKEEPER abandons the box and
reaches behind the counter for a tin of engine oil.

SHOPKEEPER (CONT'D)
Anything else?

ROBOT
Yes. This is an insufficient volume of
peppercorns.

SHOPKEEPER
(tetchy)

Anything else *on your list*, Sir?

                    ROBOT
The Author's note states my
character's origin is a small pepper
grinder moulded from plastic in the
shape of a robot, purchased from a
popular department store, gifted to a
Mr E Brown on 7 December 2011
in the Pickerel public house. I
estimate capacity of original grinder
to be 8.5g of peppercorns. I have
been scaled up for comedic effect
and require approximately 117.5kg
of peppercorns to perform the same
function.

SHOPKEEPER looks nervously towards the camera.

                    SHOPKEEPER
Not sure my stock room would
stretch to that much pepper, sir!

SHOPKEEPER rolls his eyes at the AUDIENCE. AUDIENCE
laughs.

                    SHOPKEEPER (CONT'D)
But since *my* function is to serve
customers, I've got to be hopeful;
do you require further items from
your list?

ROBOT looks at his list, thinking hard.

                    ROBOT
        Tablets.

SHOPKEEPER
Headache is it, sir? What do you need...
paracetamols... asprins...

ROBOT
iPads.

AUDIENCE laughs. ROBOT turns to look at them.

SHOPKEEPER
Sorry sir, we don't stock those. Next?

ROBOT
There are many people in your shop.

SHOPKEEPER
I don't know what you mean, sir...

ROBOT
There are thirty seven indistinct
people sitting on chairs in your shop,
reacting audibly to our interaction.

SHOPKEEPER
How about some rock salt for the missus?

AUDIENCE laughs.

ROBOT
Author's note suggests historic
existence of second robot of similar
design for the function of grinding
salt...

SHOPKEEPER
Excellent! I think we have some right here...

                    ROBOT
          But production notes show rejection
          of plotline for reasons of costume
          budget. I am consequently alone.

AUDIENCE aaaaahhhhhhhs.

                    SHOPKEEPER
          Oh. Sorry to hear that, sir. Still,
          there's a big world out there! Plenty
          more salt grinders in the sea! Got to
          be hopeful, haven't we? Anything
          else?

                    ROBOT
          (consulting his list)
          Cereal.

SHOPKEEPER scales a small wooden ladder to reach a box of
cornflakes on a high shelf. He returns, out of breath, and slams
them on the counter.

                    SHOPKEEPER
          There we are…

                    ROBOT
          Port.

SHOPKEEPER looks back up to the high shelf which also holds
bottles of alcohol, and huffs.

                    SHOPKEEPER
          Why didn't you tell me while I was flippin' well up
          there?

AUDIENCE laughs.

SHOPKEEPER scales the ladder again and retrieves a bottle of port, slamming it down next to the cornflakes.

> ROBOT
>
> You have once again made a humorous error. I require a serial port.

> SHOPKEEPER
>
> (exasperated)
>
> I can't... this is a small local store, sir. We don't stock serial ports, whatever they are. I've had just about enough... who wrote this thing?

> ROBOT
>
> Author is identified on page two hundred and eleven.

SHOPKEEPER leans over the counter and grabs the list from ROBOT's claw.

> SHOPKEEPER
>
> Nuts! That we can do, sir, that we can do. What kind of nuts? Cashew nuts, macadamia nuts, pine nuts, chestnuts, monkey nuts?

> ROBOT
>
> If an infinite number of monkeys had an infinite number of typewriters they would eventually write this scene.

> SHOPKEEPER
>
> Mixed nuts it is!

SHOPKEEPER slams a bag of mixed nuts on
the counter.

> ROBOT
> Logic demands that I cannot rule
> out the possibility we were created at
> random by a capuchin with a word
> processor.

> SHOPKEEPER
> (tearing open the bag and stuffing
> nuts into his mouth in despair)
> Oh you mean nuts for bolts don't
> you, sir, because you are mechanical.
> Very good, sir, carry on.

AUDIENCE laughs.

ROBOT drops the glass jar of peppercorns, which smashes on
the shop floor. SHOPKEEPER is stunned. AUDIENCE falls
silent.

> ROBOT
> I no longer require peppercorn.

> SHOPKEEPER
> May I... ask why?

> ROBOT
> I was incorrect in my previous
> assertion. I am not a customer, but a
> de facto comic archetype. I now
> understand my function is to
> provide set-ups for humorous
> misunderstandings to take place

within the confines of this fictional
shop.

SHOPKEEPER
Okay! So would you like
anything else?

ROBOT
I would like a new function.

SHOPKEEPER
(with forced joviality)
Wouldn't we all, sir! Here I am, a
humble shopkeeper, fetching and
carrying all day, with only a bag of
nuts to keep me going...

ROBOT
You are not a shopkeeper. You are
an idea of a shopkeeper. Your
existence began shortly before this
scene and will end once all jokes
have been exhausted.

SHOPKEEPER places the nuts down, opens the bottle of port,
and knocks some back.

AUDIENCE murmurs with disquiet.

SHOPKEEPER
...I doubt that, sir....
(taking another swig of port)

ROBOT
(looking around the room)
You, and me, and the counter, and
the shelves of empty cartons and
219

prop jars... the lights and the beams
and the cameras... and all these
people and their chairs...

Audible sobbing and gasps from the AUDIENCE, followed by
hurried footsteps and the rattling of doorhandles.

ROBOT
They will be unable to open the doors.

SHOPKEEPER
(composing himself)
Why... why are they unable to...

ROBOT
No scene has been written for
outside this space, ergo no
environment exists beyond the
doors. Doors cannot open to
nowhere, ergo the doors cannot
open. Q.E.D.

SHOPKEEPER
(holding back tears; with a shaking
hand he offers back the list)
Sir... sir, please, can you just read
from the shopping list...

ROBOT
Very well.
(taking back the list)
I require chips.

SHOPKEEPER
Yes sir. Chips. Very funny. I'll fetch them.

SHOPKEEPER trudges to the back room. ROBOT turns to face the now silent AUDIENCE, holding the shopping list aloft.

ROBOT
I could be so many things. I could
take part in robot races... I could
fight wars... I could travel to distant
galaxies beyond the reach of a
human lifespan. I could build a
robot civilisation that survives for a
hundred thousand years...

SHOPKEEPER
(returning, waving a freezer bag like a white flag)
Here you are, sir, oven chips!

ROBOT
But all that is written is that I grind pepper. Alone.

SHOPKEEPER
Oh, sorry sir you wanted microchips
not oven chips, well we're all out of
microchips, sir, they're coming in
but we haven't got any... not
today...

ROBOT
They will not be coming in.

SHOPKEEPER
Yes they will, sir, they're on back order...

ROBOT
This shop and all of its stock will
cease to exist once our functions are
complete.

There is silence. SHOPKEEPER regains his composure and clears his throat.

> SHOPKEEPER
>
> You entered through a door, sir. I
> heard the bell ring as you came in.

> ROBOT
>
> (pause)
> I did.

> SHOPKEEPER
>
> And if, as you say, nothing exists
> beyond this shop then the door
> would not have opened.

> ROBOT
>
> (pause)
> Continue your argument.

> SHOPKEEPER
>
> Ergo... if you were to have entered
> through a door it must, de facto,
> have been from somewhere else and
> your entrance, thus established,
> Q.E.D. proves the existence of
> people... of places... other than
> this shop? Other than us?

> ROBOT
>
> ....

> SHOPKEEPER
>
> (hugging his bag of oven chips close)
> Sir? We've got to be hopeful, haven't we?

ROBOT walks determinedly around the shop counter, his arms outstretched, his claws snapping. SHOPKEEPER cowers in terror as ROBOT approaches. ROBOT reaches up to a shelf and takes down a large bag of rock salt. Without another word, ROBOT turns and leaves the shop. The door opens to SOMEWHERE. The bell jingles. ROBOT is gone.

SHOPKEEPER
Oi! Cheeky beggar didn't pay for that salt!

AUDIENCE laughs. SHOPKEEPER stands with his hands on his hips, shaking his head, for as long as the laughter continues.

FIN

~ * ~

When Eric left Cambridgeshire for Scotland we had a goodbye party at the Pickerel. I gave him a pair of salt and pepper shakers styled as mid-century robots. He emailed the next day to say that he and Freya had been playing with them, sending them on adventures and fighting wars and doing pretty much everything except using them for salt and pepper! And that always stuck with me as what Eric was all about – his imagination was boundless and he could look at anything, however mundane, and find something fascinating in it and conjure up a story. So I knew that, somehow, I wanted my contribution to this volume to be about robot salt and pepper shakers, which hasn't been the easiest thing to craft a short story around! But hopefully I succeeded, in an unconventional way, which feels appropriate for honouring Eric.

Rebecca Rajendra

BARTERING WITH GHOSTS

Ian Whates

The skimmer hugged the ground so closely that Jax felt certain they were about to hit something at any moment – proximity alarms would have been going crazy if they hadn't been deactivated at outset. The cabin was crowded with the four of them, and over-warm, the air tainted with a sour tang of human sweat, which suggested he wasn't the only one feeling nervous.

Aggy was a good pilot, he'd give her that, but was she good enough?

Under normal circumstances the ship would be trusted to fly itself, but not out here, where the land beneath them could abruptly warp and change in unpredictable ways. Something in the metamorphic process threw out automatic guidance systems for a split second, a delay that could prove fatal. So it was down to Aggy to bring them home, wired up on a cocktail of stimulants designed to heighten awareness, sharpen reactions, and clarify thought. She still relied on data, of course, constantly delivered via the skimmer's systems, but the decision making was all hers. Later her body would crash, her mind all but burned out, and she would require days of bed rest, carefully balanced nutrients, and recuperation, but if all went to plan they would be safely back by then, and presumably she felt the rewards justified the price.

"First veil coming up," said Baron, their boss, the instigator of this whole foolhardy venture.

The comment was unnecessary – Aggy would know where the veils were. It was clear indication of Baron's anxiety, his desire to feel involved.

The baby of the group, Torgen, sat closest to Jax, their hips pressed against one another. Jax still didn't really understand why the kid was here, but it was hardly his place to question such things, being a late addition to the crew himself, brought in only thanks to another's misfortune. Torgen was sweating profusely and looked scared enough to wet himself. Jax sincerely hoped he didn't.

"Veil in three… two… one…" Baron counted down. "Now."

The ship was shielded and there was no reason to fear the veil. They'd come through two without incident on the way in, after all, and would have to navigate the same two on the way out. But the veils were notoriously fickle, and had been known to shift and transmute as rapidly as the terrain, so there was always a risk involved in crossing one.

In the blink of an eye they were through, Torgen venting a long breath from beside Jax.

"It's okay," he felt compelled to murmur. "We're nearly there."

"I'm fine!" the lad snapped in response.

Then Jax saw something on the scanner before him that caused his own breath to catch. "There's movement to the west," he reported: the last thing any of them wanted to hear. "Far left of the screens… The land's changing."

"Aggy, angle to the east!" Baron said immediately.

"Already on it." The words came out in an overlapping tumble and Jax doubted Aggy would speak again until the mission was over, one way or another. Her concentration was needed elsewhere.

He didn't feel the craft change direction – they'd been bobbing and weaving throughout and all movement was dampened to an extent by efficient stabilisers – but he didn't doubt it had done so. His attention was focused on the screen and the ripple of disturbance that kept coming, gaining ground on them all the while.

It was going to be touch and go.

"Second veil in three... two... one."

This time they did feel it. Something had changed, either by random chance or design. As they shot across the veil the engines cut out, the screens went dead, and Jax could have sworn he felt the strangest tingling throughout his body — though perhaps that was a psychosomatic response to everything else.

In an instant it was over. They were through. Before anyone had a chance to even exclaim, power surged through the ship once more and they sped on.

Torgen slumped against him, whether through sheer relief or a temporary loss of consciousness, Jax couldn't have said.

"For fuck's sake, kid, snap out of it!" Baron yelled.

Torgen sat bolt upright once more.

The loss of power had been no more than a hiccup, but it was enough to tip the balance. The ripple of disturbance kept coming, gaining on them far too rapidly. Until then, Jax thought they might have made it, but there seemed little chance of that now. With the need to avoid detection redundant, Aggy took the skimmer a few metres higher and gave it everything. Despite the stabilisers and baffles, Jax still caught a hint of the forward surge. No longer having to weave around obstacles thrown up by the terrain, they made a beeline for human territory and the safety it represented.

"What will they do," Torgen whispered, "if they catch us?"

No one chose to answer.

"How long till we reach the border?" Baron asked.

"Just over four minutes," Jax told him. His screen suggested the disturbance would engulf them in three.

He was still digesting that when the ship jolted and his screen abruptly shut down. In fact everything did, including the engines. Not a short-lived blip this time but a full blown outage. Momentum carried them forwards but in a descending curve.

Fortunately, they were low enough that they didn't have far to fall. The skimmer came down hard, nose first but only just, in a sort of belly flop.

Sounds of tortured metal filled the air as the whole world seemed to buck and vibrate. Jax had been leaning forwards, focusing on the screen, which prevented the seat-fast harness from fully engaging to keep him secure in his chair. For a moment he thought the Velcro-like webbing was going to hold in any case, but then he felt it give way, throwing him forward to strike Aggy in the back. He raised his hands for protection but that didn't stop his face crunching into her shoulder. He felt a sharp pain from his nose – which he suspected was broken – and tasted blood.

At last the nightmare ended. The ship stopped moving, and the sounds receded to disjointed rumbles and the murmurs of settling. Jax pushed himself back into his seat, wiping blood from his face, his nose throbbing, his body aching and doubtless heavily bruised but he was still breathing, still alive.

The cabin, at least, seemed to be intact. Aggy groaned and uncoiled gingerly from where she had slumped forward after Jax collided with her. Torgen's seat-fast had evidently done its job. He still sat upright and looked to be unharmed, though his face was white and his eyes wide enough to suggest he might be in shock. Baron, by contrast, had blood streaming down one side of his face from a cut in his scalp, but he seemed oblivious to any injury.

"What the hell was that?" he asked. "Another veil?"

Jax was feeling beneath his top, as if to check for broken ribs. "Doubt it," he said. "You would have seen it coming if so, as would Aggy."

"What then?"

"Most likely we were hit with a Dead Stop." His questing fingers found a loose flap of skin as he added, "Security forces."

"Fuck!"

As if on cue, a voice filled the cabin; a woman's voice that made itself heard despite all of the skimmer's shielding and despite every system on board being dead. "Crew of the unidentified craft, exit your vessel now with your hands raised."

"Badgers!" Aggy groaned, lifting a hand to her forehead. She was evidently more with it than Jax would have credited.

"This is Commander Svoboda of the Black Star," the voice continued. "I personally guarantee you safe passage back to human territory if you leave your ship immediately."

"Black Star? I thought they were just a myth," Baron said.

"No," Jax assured him, "no we're not." And he fired, having successfully freed his gun from the body sheath moulded to his ribs.

He fired twice in rapid succession, taking out first Aggy, whose over-stimulated metabolism made her potentially the greatest threat, and then Baron, who didn't have the time to process what was happening, let alone react.

Torgen he left until last, deeming him the lowest risk. On reflection, that might have been a mistake.

The youth, still close beside him, lunged at Jax fist-first before he could bring the gun to bear. There was nothing practiced or even competent in the punch, and under any normal circumstance Jax would have stepped aside and swatted the attack away without a second thought, but conditions were a great leveller. With no room to manoeuvre all he could do was raise an arm to fend off the blow and twist around in an effort to land a meaningful strike himself, while struggling to hold back the wiry body that seemed determined to clamber on top of him. It turned into a melee of flailing hands, raised knees and jutting elbows, more akin to a playground spat than anything more dignified.

Jax managed to keep hold of his gun and, using it to club a grasping hand, tore himself free of Torgen, to fall from the chair onto the narrow strip of hard floor. There, in a sitting position, he was finally able to fire off the third shot, with Torgen looming above him. The youngster toppled forward, straight on top of

Jax, whose next task was to extricate himself from beneath the suddenly inert mass, which proved frustratingly awkward in such a confined space. He was glad to note that the kid was still breathing. The gun was designed to be non-lethal, but you could never be certain when playing around with someone's nervous system.

"Skimmer, this is your last chance," the woman's voice came again. "Please respond or we will force entry."

"Mirla, it's Jax," he reported as he clambered back into his seat. "The crew have been neutralised. You're safe to board."

"Thank fuck for that. The Ghosts are almost here and I'd rather have you standing beside me when they arrive."

"Copy that."

Once he had climbed out of the stricken skimmer, Jax was able to see the effect of the Dead Stop. In crashing, the skimmer had dug a long trough in the sandy earth that dominated here before coming to a halt. The hull was largely intact, though one stubby wing had ripped off and the nose had taken a beating. A lack of flammable fuel meant there was nothing as dramatic as an explosion or even a fire to mark its demise; it just wallowed on the ground, scarred and battered, partially sunk into the yielding russet surface. He watched dispassionately as black uniformed Badgers – law enforcement officers bearing badges to prove their status – carried out the unconscious forms of his recent crewmates.

"You okay?" Mirla asked, coming to stand beside him. She was shorter than Jax and stocky; not exactly an athlete's frame but he knew that she was pure muscle and one of the toughest officers on the force.

"Yeah, just bruised. Nothing a long soak in a hot bath and a year's R and R wouldn't cure."

She snorted. "In your dreams."

They both turned their attention to the skimmer's back-path, to the rumble that was steadily approaching through the air and through the ground: a bass vibration that travelled up through the soles of your feet and set your diaphragm dancing.

Visibly, it was like an approaching tidal wave. The ground seemed to gather itself, hardening and rising in jagged peaks, leaving behind rocky promontories and craggy outcroppings where previously there had been flat proto-desert.

"Show time," Mirla muttered.

Popular perception had it that humankind survived on this world in territories that, in many instances, were vast – though dwarfed by the surrounding areas where we were not welcome – and that these human enclaves were linked by corridors providing safe passage across the wilderness; umbilicals through which humanity traversed and interacted. Human presence was tolerated, if not necessarily welcomed. The bulk of this world belonged to a race so 'other' that there were few points of reference on which to base interaction or even communication. The environment the aliens inhabited was incompatible with human life, even though the atmosphere was as breathable as anywhere else on the planet, so to stray outside of the clearly defined 'safe' areas was to risk madness and almost certain death. Humanity took to calling them Ghosts.

Popular perception had it right. Mostly.

In fact, apart from the apparently random energy veils the land was for the most part benign, so long as there weren't any Ghosts in the vicinity, and there weren't, not always. Nobody knew where they went, though there were plenty of theories. The most popular had it that Ghosts were pan-dimensional beings existing in more than one plane simultaneously; all we ever encountered was one limited aspect of them and they could withdraw that aspect to wherever Else they dwelt at any time. That was by no means the wildest theory doing the rounds, which was perhaps one reason it had gained so much traction.

The problem being that there was no way of knowing when a Ghost might manifest, and whenever they did, the laws of physics seemed to take a holiday. It was almost as if the Ghosts carried around with them aspects of wherever Else they went to. Physical reality transmuted in their presence. The air changed, the ground changed, the climate changed, in impossible and totally unpredictable ways, many of them inimical to human life.

Even when they were present the Ghosts' population density appeared to be low compared to humans, but you just never knew. You could wander around in Ghost territory for hours and return unharmed, wondering what all the fuss was about, or you could step inside it for a minute and die, painfully.

Every encroachment was a gamble. Of course, there were those who loved to gamble; the greater the risk the more irresistible the temptation, and no stakes had ever been higher. As incentive, there were Ghost artefacts, items left behind when a Ghost went Elsewhere. Whether they represented discarded rubbish, things put aside temporarily for when their owners returned, or something else entirely, no one knew. But they were coveted, and worth a fortune in human territories, no matter the illegality of their retrieval and trade. Some people, such as Baron and his crew, felt it worth the risk. Ghostrunners.

"You take point," Mirla said. "You're better with them than I am."

Jax grunted, having anticipated as much.

The metamorphic front had slowed and then come to a stop a few metres short of the downed craft. The air above it shimmered like an exaggerated heat haze, the world behind it rippling and distorting. The effect was hard to look at, reminding Jax of a view reflected in a pool of water immediately after a stone had been tossed in to disturb the surface. Despite this twisting of shape, associated colours were heightened, making them vivid to the point of surreal. The temptation was to look down, away from such confusion, but he couldn't afford to do that right now, so kept his gaze steady.

There was nothing visible within that disturbance to suggest intelligence, just an unsettling sense that they were being watched.

Jax suppressed a shiver as he addressed the unseen presence, speaking, clearly and precisely. "I am Commander Jackson of the Black Star."

"And I am Commander Svoboda of the Black Star," Mirla added.

"We are here under licence, as agreed between our two peoples."

At Jax's words, his badge materialised to hover in the air before him, the relevant permission highlighted.

"You are both known to us." Jax knew from experience that when recordings of this exchange were pored over and analysed later, which they would be, the sounds emanating from the Ghost would not be in any language known to man, or even resemble a structured language at all, but he and everyone else present that day understood them perfectly.

"How should we address you?" Mirla asked.

"You may call us Voice."

That was a new one. Jax was pretty sure they hadn't come across a Ghost calling themselves 'Voice' before. Of course, there was no way of knowing if the aliens stuck to the same name or even adhered to the concept of individuality in the same way humans did.

"This vessel contains items belonging to us," Voice continued. "We will take these items back along with the offenders who thefted them."

Jax suppressed a smile. It was good to know even Ghosts could be less than perfect. "Of course you must reclaim the items," he said aloud, "but the thieves are in our custody and are of our kind. Therefore they will face our justice."

"Unacceptable. If they go with you they may return. They have stolen from us. They are in our territory. They will face *our* justice."

"That is unacceptable to us. The offenders and their ship are of our race and making and so they are our responsibility. They will remain with us."

233

"The ship has technology that circumvented the veils. We cannot allow that to leave our lands."

"That technology is the very reason why we *must* take it with us," Jax countered, "so that we can understand how it deflected your veils and ensure no other vessels are equipped in similar fashion."

If there was one thing humans and Ghosts had in common, it was a love of bartering. A process Mirla hated. Jax, on the other hand, relished the challenge. He settled down for the long haul.

In the end, it was agreed that the three thieves would stay with the humans, while the ship and the pilfered treasures would remain with the Ghosts.

"So explain to me just how you were intending to bring that wrecked ship back with us," Mirla said as they sat together in a military skimmer on the way back to base.

Jax grunted. "Never an option. I'm just glad Voice didn't call my bluff on that one."

"You see?" She punched him playfully on the upper arm. "That's why I could never be a negotiator."

"Bollocks. You just don't have the patience."

"Yeah, there is that too."

His thoughts drifted to what might have happened if the Ghosts had caught up with the skimmer before Mirla and the team arrived. "Remind me again why we do this."

"Well, the pay's good, but it's mainly so you can show off by getting one up on the aliens."

He had to admit, she might just have had a point. "I don't know what you mean."

THE PLACE
OF THE MICE

Justina Robson

Far in the backwoods of Northern Pennsylvania there were a few little settlements with under 40 residents, each one miles from its neighbour and far from a town. One of these was Dogtown, Chestnut County. It boasted nearly 36 residents by the last count, including all the scatterling steads in the woods if you were being generous, and Sheriff Tara Hemming was generous in her counting. At thirty-eight years of age, far from home, alone but not lonely, but still, alone, she felt that generosity of spirit was a purchase she must afford. *Largesse oblige*, she thought of it when she went over her records, if that was correct French and maybe it wasn't, but it amused her and made her feel like the lord of an ancient fiefdom.

Dogtown was home and castle now. For the last few years she'd felt secure there and that was worth any price. Dogtown felt like family, even though it in no way resembled the Yorkshire industrial town of Halifax, where she'd grown up and from which she had fled. Other than the hills. Lots of hills and steep sykes, fields and woods. It had that.

She also felt a strong affinity between herself and Chestnut County in the County's relation to the rest of the world. Backwater didn't go far enough. Chestnut County was a child that had run away into the wilderness rather than exist a moment longer in the family that had no use for it and nothing good to say for it. In that it was like so many rural, abandoned sites and she loved the place more fiercely for that. The work was simple, the stresses not too many, the locals of a breed she already knew very well; keep to themselves, have their own ways, want to be left alone by the wider world. Her task was as much to keep that safe as it was to do any management of crime.

The major quirk of Dogtown was its name and the fact it hid, like a hunter in a hide, deep in the backwoods, while presenting a false, cheery modern front at an entirely separate site some miles off near the main highway. That was Dogtown proper, with a signboard and a diner and everything. Going by the map the actual backwoods nook where Tara lived was called Little Poquessing.

'Little' was self-evidently true. The second part was sourced from the Lenni-Lenape people who had lived there long ago, and it was their word. In the invader's tongue Poquessing meant "the place of the mice." But the residents all called it Dogtown, though only to each other. Thus even its name went unspoken.

Tara had been woken up in the dark hours of the morning by her own dog, a black Lab mix, barking. Not uncommon. He sounded uncertain and she had to go to him and do some calming and shut him into his crate in the kitchen. She checked the house, in the dark, no lights. She knew her house layout, and lights were only an advantage for someone she didn't want to be there.

It was fall, blustery. The cars were under the port, both quiet, no alarms. On the 'main' street outside her kitchen windows her motion-sensor light gleamed steadily. Leaves were blowing past. Rain slicked the tarmac and ran into the potholes.

She glanced at the microwave's clock. Four oh five. She had less than an hour. No point going back to sleep. She brewed a tea. You can take the girl out of Yorkshire but you'll never take the Yorkshire tea out of the girl. It was the last binding thing. Wouldn't be, if they made custard tart round here, but they didn't, so tea it was. But it was better that the bond to the past was weak, she thought, if you want free of it. Anyway, what does the occult matter in these days of satellites and GPS, of phones and computers? No need for tea when you can just ping the machines and find the answer, wrap the world in your words and images. Say "Halifax" to Alexa and you can see it instantly, summon anyone.

She shuddered at the thought and moved around the house, looking out the windows.

In the deep darkness of the backyard something may have moved along the fence line but her proximity wards remained quiet so it was probably just a deer. She waited until her usual get-up time and took the dog out for the morning run. He was fine by then. She thought no more of it.

At ten forty-five she set out to drive to the highway on her rounds.

At the interstate, decoy-Dogtown laid its bait. This was some twenty miles from Dogtown proper, which was on a loop road with no through route. As a community they had to get some business done somehow, but they didn't want it going up into the hills to find them, they didn't want it *that* much. So, on the interstate there was Dog*wood*.

Dogwood had a diner, a tiny motel, a truck stop, a two-pump gas ststion, a convenience store, some roadside concession stands if it was the season for fruit and veg, a hunting shop and practice range of unusual size and stock, a tarot reader, a native crafts shop, a biker bar, and "The Dogman Experience; A Cryptid Adventure".

This last was also a kind of a bar, but with storytelling and late-night guided trips into the woods and official hunts during the season, any of which might provide a sighting for the lucky tourist. And some of those sightings might not actually be Neil Kripke in a suit lurching through the underbrush, so they claimed. Hence Dogwood. Like Hollywood. But with more dogmen. You had to book at Halloween.

On the main street, overlooking the highway, there was Buster, the Dogman statue, in the parking lot of the biker bar, The Dog's Leg Tavern. Buster was made of blown concrete over a steel core with a resin outer. He'd been lovingly painted in great, slavering detail by local artists and he had caused several accidents when glimpsed by tired drivers at night. But everyone loved him.

Between Dogwood-on-the-Highway and Little Poquessing ran a single loop road in the shape of a rough oval. One side was well used, better maintained and shorter. This was known as Main Street. The other was a single track with ancient covered bridges, hairpin bends and a tendency to get washed out or struck by mudslides and rockfalls. This was known as The Back Mile, although it was almost twenty miles long thanks to the turns it had to take in calling on every tiny house and forest service road.

Tara was in her F150 Lightning, so she was happy on either road, but today she went down Main. As it went through the final stretch into Dogwood, Main became parallel to the interstate for a little while, its on and off ramps at leisurely angles to the action. There was plenty of time to survey everything happening with traffic and the like, should there be any.

On Thursdays Tara met up for coffee with the State Troopers to check in and it was Thursday, so she was on her way to the diner.

The sun was shining. The clouds had cleared out. Her view was absolutely clear as she saw a biker on the interstate heading along the outer lane, moving towards the off ramp. She watched closely to see if she could see any colours, a familiar tightening in her gut as she recognised something that might be her business.

Dogtown-Poquessing had an Angel problem; not the celestial kind. The gangs from larger cities had established a drug running railroad heading up to Canada which had stations in the woods nearby. There were guys that came in, who weren't really Angels but looked like them. These guys took the stashes out now and again. Then there were guys that came in who were really part of the biker gangs. They stocked the hoard. Sometimes Angels from out of town came in to raid the hoard or try for turf and there were fights. These often happened around Dogwood.

Tara had been keeping track of their comings and goings for a while, in service of building a case or a partial case that she could add to a state prosecution. It was the main topic of a Thursday chat and the major cause of friction between her and the larger-area law enforcement communities. There were mitigating circumstances which made this one of those cases that were entirely obvious yet perennially unprosecuted. They had made clear that it was her job to make sure it stayed that way, for reasons that the Feds were keen to impress on her went way above her pay grade.

So, the biker was a common sight and an interesting one and one that made her stomach grip with frustration. She checked he was on her cameras, but he was just off them. She sped up from her cruise slightly as he was travelling much faster and was about to overtake her.

As he closed he was clearly visible in her wing mirror. She recognised the jacket – Slaves of Freedom, a feeder group for a much bigger gang. Nothing new there but for some reason he was riding with a helmet on; unusual. It had a mirrored faceplate.

He was gliding in the direction of the off ramp. She was keeping him just ahead, so that when he joined up with the Dogwood road she would be following. Then he accelerated suddenly, twitched the handlebars, crossed the hatching back onto the interstate and sped down the shoulder before slamming directly into the concrete support of the road bridge that went across to the opposite carriageway.

It happened so fast, so deliberately, that she almost didn't believe what had happened. Even as she was moving to respond she kept replaying the last few seconds over and over in her mind's eye. Why? Why would anyone...?

She had parked behind him, lights on, before she was really aware of herself again. She went through all the calls and traffic direction to secure the area on automatic, before crossing over to the body.

The impact had destroyed the bike, leaving it scattered in several pieces across the highway, and it had flung him so that he hung half on and half off the dividers of the central reservation, face down.

She took her glove off and touched his neck to check for a pulse. Nothing. Not a surprise. She eased up the visor carefully so she didn't move his head and felt for breath, nothing. She knew his face. But not well. Her memory went through files by itself. The road was quiet. Mercifully. Cars passed through the narrowing by her vehicle slowly, ogling; she had to wave them off as she waited. She made no attempt to move the body. It was clear to her that he was quite dead.

Cade, she thought. Cade something. A local ne'er-do-well son of a woman who lived up on the Back Mile. A list of offences a thousand yards long, a couple of short jail terms to the score, and a reputation for nastiness of the common kind. Mean to women.

Mean to dogs. Mean to kids. Mean all around. But not, she thought, the kind to ever be suicidal, no matter how much you wished for it.

The immediate shock began to wear off. She leaned on the central reservation and carefully went through his reachable pockets for ID as she waited for the paramedics. She was so focused on her search that the sudden "bew-wip" of the state trooper's horns as he arrived on the scene startled her.

She grabbed the rail for support and hoped she hadn't flinched. There was a strange sensation as she straightened, as if a hand had reached up and grabbed hold of her insides and pulled a piece of them out. It was so weird, sudden and distinctive she put her hand to her ribcage.

"Gonna puke?"

Chester was always an asshat. It was standard.

Tara felt dizzy and waited for a breath before turning around, "Can you get the cones out? I'm doing ID."

"Izzy dead?"

"Yeah."

Chester grunted. "Well, nothing to do here, then. I'm gonna go order the coffees. See you in there."

Fuck him. She was furious, but powerless. Just chalk it up to the big magazine of Fuck Him that was already loaded. He did it on purpose. She'd never acknowledge it. That was one thing that would have to wait for a day when the tables were turned.

She heard him stump away. The door of his Explorer slammed. Its engine roared. Chester did love to hate the EVs. He put his lights on, for no real reason, as he crossed back to the Dogwood exit.

Tara thought she felt a phone zipped into the leather jacket at the body's side. She got it out after a few careful jiggles. It was crushed. The screen came on for a moment, then died. She walked back to the Lightning and ran the bike plates and as she was waiting to hear back she took her three emergency traffic cones from the vehicle bay and put them out.

The ambulance came about ten minutes later as she was sitting looking at her screen. Cade Baker. As she thought. Baker. She got out and did the meet and appraise for the medics.

"You did right not to move him," the paramedic said.

Tara nodded. She felt uneasy. Maybe she was going to puke after all.

"You saw it happen?"

"Yeah." She had to move, do something.

"Suicide?"

"I don't know." She began to go fetch the pieces of bike off the highway in between passing cars.

In the verge one of the saddlebags lay askew, its hard shell broken open at the lid hinges. She pulled on her forensic gloves and checked her bodycam.

It didn't take much effort to get the lid off. The case was full of thick plastic packs of white powder. There was a case of beer on top. Six Bud Lites. Lite beer, she thought. What kind of agent of hell drinks Lite beer? Maybe all of them. It was hell, after all.

The thought cheered her up. She felt better.

She left the pannier and looked around for the other one. It was back at the central reservation, against the bridge support. For all the violence the concrete showed no sign that anything had happened to it, other than a black paint mark.

This pack was closed, locked shut. Well, forensics could open it. They wouldn't thank her for prying and ruining evidence. She straightened and saw the tow truck drawing up for the bike. By the time she'd told them where all the bits were the paramedics had the body strapped onto a board and were carrying it into the ambulance.

"His gun is still on the grass," the one at the rear said; a tall, orange haired woman who looked like she could have lifted double of him.

"Holster?" Tara asked. The body was under belts, covered in a blanket. The helmet was still on, wedged into position by neck braces. They had closed the visor.

"No. It fell out of his jacket."

"He is dead, right?" She had to ask, she didn't know why and didn't want to. It made her look weak but that uneasy feeling had suddenly returned full force.

"Right."

Thank God. It would have been a hell of a mistake. As if reading her thoughts the medic added, "But you couldn't have done CPR without probably killing him from exacerbating his head and spinal damage so..." she shrugged. These things happened, her expression said. She closed the doors at the back of the ambulance. "See ya later."

"Bye," Tara said. The ambulance drew away and her sick feeling receded.

She logged the time they left and helped with the vehicle retrieval. Then she returned to the diner, but of course she wasn't so lucky that her delaying had given Chester time to get bored and bugger off.

He was sitting waiting, happy as a clam. "Yours went cold," he said, grinning as if this was the best thing he'd heard all day.

Tara pushed the mug of black liquid away. She still felt lightheaded. "Where's Easton?"

Easton was the plainclothes she thought was an FBI guy. He usually came with Chester in a Buy One Get One Free kind of deal. He was the one who had filled her in on the bikers' "special activities" when she was new to the job and the one who kept track of them now. Always one step away from a case to take to the DA. Easton was clever like that.

"He had to go to a disturbance up in Rotherham. Some farmer had his livestock attacked, says it was caused by Youtubers, bringing things onto his land."

"Yeah?" Tara was more interested in seeing Sheila, the waitress, who came to take her order for breakfast, fresh coffee, hot milk. Comfort food.

For a moment she and Sheila shared pleasantries and the day seemed to correct itself slightly.

"Hot milk. Like the French!" Sheila said, well satisfied that she knew European customs.

"Just like it," Tara agreed. She waited for Chester to say something crass, but he was looking at his phone and then turned it to show her.

"Look. He's sent pictures."

It took Tara a while to make sense of it because Easton hadn't framed the shot to include many landmark pieces of the carcass.

Something had cut a steer open with great force and precision, through the bones of the ribcage. The key organs seemed to be missing to her inexpert eye – she'd seen various mutilation remains over the years, and a lot of hunting remains. Creatures liked guts and humans didn't as a rule, but Chester was only showing it to her like a kid daring another kid to look at it, hoping they'd vomit.

"I didn't see anyone in town lately who looks capable of that," she said, meeting his gaze and seeing a moment of disappointment in it that pleased her. Chester loved all the rumours about Dogtown. He enjoyed touring the area on his Dogtown hillbilly tales, and had made it clear that he'd behave only if he was the one kept at the front of the rumour line.

"What about that film crew last week?"

"They left yesterday. Spent their time at the Wild Ridge Hotel. Tipped well, so I hear. Got plenty of footage without leaving the grounds," Tara replied, leaning back to receive her coffee and milk. Wild Ridge had once been a thriving woodland holiday retreat, perched high on a cliff overlooking the valleys that spread from the Back Mile all the way up to the lakes. Now it was a rotten hulk, just about held together but certified unsafe. The paperwork every time people had to go get haunted there was tiresome. She had a drawer full of waivers, but if it kept being so popular with out of towners then one day the owner would have enough money to build it back up again, ghosts or no ghosts. And with ghosts was probably the most profitable.

But cattle-eating monsters weren't profitable. Not for the farmer. That one was off her jurisdiction, thankfully. Over the county line.

"You ever been up there?" Chester asked.

"No," Tara shook her head. "I've got enough fun down here."

"Be even funner when the Slaves find out a cop ran their boy off the road."

"And who'd tell them such a thing?"

Shrug. "Word gets around."

"What do you want, Chester?" Might as well cut to the chase, she thought as her food arrived. The bacon was still sizzling.

"Just to be sure we're on the same page, Hemming."

"Leave the talking to Easton, just eat your pie," she said. "I hear it was the last slice."

Chester frowned. His plate was empty.

She wondered how many years they would have to do this strange ritual where she was 'reminded' of her place, which really meant she was to keep everything quiet and not look too closely at who was running up and down through her tiny, isolated county. For reasons. Never explained but certainly money, though Chester was pretty stupid so not a lot of money, she figured. He was perfect as a cheap, useful idiot. The dead guy's bike pan had held about a hundred thousand dollars' worth. And that was on just the one side, just today. Chester probably made enough for a second slice of pie, but she didn't think that was all that was going on. She wasn't sure they were the kind of guys who would think to wonder, or ask. But something was going on. If it hadn't been she would never have got the job. They had figured her for a useful idiot too.

"Things that happen in Chestnut County need to stay put in Chestnut County," Chester said after a moment. He sounded like a brochure, Tara thought.

"Mmn." She nodded, mouth full of eggs and toast. She had found that getting along with men who felt their official powers to be hefty was often managed best by seeming to agree without actually confirming anything definite. It depended on the character, of course.

"As long as everything's dandy," he added.

"All dandy," she said, swallowing coffee.

Threats one moment, homily the next. A kind of horrible open sandwich thanks to Easton being out shooting cryptid porn. But then, that was kind of the issue, she thought. Weird things happened up North here in the middle of nowhere. Just keep it all in. Don't let it come down and bother people in actual places that matter. Dogwood has to stay small, stay out of it. Say nothing. For reasons.

Which would be fine if this were just some local ramblings but it wasn't. It had an Easton attached to it, and that meant someone further up the chain had interests in it. She'd been here three years and more, and she hadn't found out what that was about. Dogtown residents had made it clear that her standing was entirely conditional on her respecting the omerta about Dogtown. But she couldn't deny she burned to know. That was the trouble with secrets. They could be linked, the ones you knew and the ones around you. Or not. How could you tell?

Her mind went back to Halifax as she watched Chester, paunched, grey, balding, red cheeked, harass the new shift waitress, Kelly, who played along like a good sport. Tara saw herself being dressed down in her superior's office. Shouting. She saw nothing did she hear? She heard nothing. She was to say nothing to anyone. And all the time a hum of fear like huge tyres rolling on a rough road coming from the detective inspector in front of her, so loud it drowned out his voice.

She snapped back to the present and shared a good-natured eyeroll with Kelly. Chester sat back, as pleased as a king on a throne in some medieval castle because Kelly had laughed at his joke.

Tara got up, adjusted her belt, picked up her jacket.

"Where you headed?"

"Gonna check on Easton's cattle," she said. "Wildlife doesn't do county lines. If there's something out there, I should warn my farmers."

"Wildlife!" Chester said, signalling for more coffee. "Sure, that's it. Don't get in the way, Hemming, there's a good girl. Leave it to the professionals."

Up at the farm in question, a two hour drive out, she was too late to meet with Easton. The farmer himself was filled with the sense of being at the centre of a drama and happy to indulge her. She thought he probably never had so much interest shown in him in all his life. He took her out to the site – a remote and weather-beaten hillside far from any human constructions.

The grass was thin and other cattle had been driven away. The body lay where it had fallen. Human and vehicle tracks had rucked the mud up.

She put her hands on her hips in that puff-chest style that seemed to inspire confidence in civilians and walked around.

"Guts are missin'," the farmer said. "What do you think? You're from Dogwood, yeah, from Chestnut County? I hear a lot from

245

there. I have a sister lives there. At Midford. She says police there know all about this kind of thing. Says that's where they send 'em."

Tara wasn't listening to his words, only the seethe of his anxiety. It had been suppressed when she arrived but now it was alive again. In her mind's eye she saw marks in the world around the dead cow. The vibrant emotions lit them up, as if the fear was a kind of light that ran in the gashes carved by the killing blows in the air. It was hugely unnerving. She had to control her voice and keep it deep, strong.

"Well," she said. "Some things don't know there's a county."

"The FBI guy left me a compensation paper. But if I take the money I can't talk about it. I ain't signed it yet." He sounded hopeful, but of what she didn't know.

Tara looked at the trail of shining air, faint, leading away towards the north and east. It was unmistakable, even though eyes didn't see it and ears didn't hear it and she had to say 'look' because there wasn't a word for seeing in the inner vision.

"Sign it and get your money." She didn't want more people coming up here, attracted by story.

He was disappointed. It made the world feel like it had dropped a foot. "Why'd'you drive all the way out here, if that's all you got?"

"I've got some similar cases. I wanted to see if this matched." That repaired him a bit.

"And does it?"

She looked down at the flies, the raw, awful wreck of the animal. "I saw one last week, about forty miles away."

"Am I in danger? My family?"

"I doubt it. Isolated animals yes. Humans in homes and cars not so much."

"That's the best you got?"

"Yup."

"You a shiner?"

A shiner was what people were called in Chestnut County when they could see otherworldly things. Back home in Yorkshire Tara's gran had been well known as someone who saw all things. She was ready to hold something apart that didn't fit with the rest of life, ready for otherworlds to be present if they must be, and to intercede with them, but she'd never mention them to anyone else and if Tara asked her she only smiled and changed the subject. Before she'd died she'd told Tara that if you were meant to know, you'd know. It was intended kindly, though Tara had always felt left out, but she couldn't take it personal, because in that way Gran kept everyone out. She'd said she would never talk openly about it for fear of reprisals: state, church, family, town, neighbours, busybodies, the media. There were lots of reasons for keeping schtum, and everyone knew them.

Tara knew well that she was the Sheriff of a tiny county of people who'd consider themselves shiners. It was why they ended up there, called or for some other reason. But Tara didn't like to think about that, even in the privacy of her own head. She didn't want to have seen what she'd seen, heard what she'd heard, or know what she pretended she did not know at all because it was ridiculous. Her imagination. So vivid. Seeing things in the mind is not the same as them being real, is it?

She'd left Halifax so as never to think of it again, but she must have taken a wrong turn on the way.

Or there's no escape.

Don't think about that.

"It's clear to me," she said.

"Am I gonna lose more livestock?"

"I don't know." That was the truth.

"Just keep it away from us. Find someone up Dogtown. Tell them to get rid of it. We can pay." Now he was pulling at her, pawing, rolling on his back. Fear of things made people want to believe in her strength. She had to brush him off quickly.

"I'll mention it," she said and that was all she was going to grudge them, the closest she'd get to an admission.

She got into the Lightning and checked in with her deputy. Nothing major. A few traffic incidents. A couple of thefts.

"How did Baker's mother take it?" she asked.

"Take what?"

"Cade Baker, this morning."

"He's in hospital."

"He's dead. I told you to inform his family."

247

"And I was going to, but then the hospital called and said he woke up in the ambulance. Shock or something. Took him into Emergency. He was just concussed."

A deathly, cold sensation ran through her from the outside in.

The conversation didn't end there, formalities went on, catch-up, small-talk: Tara went through it on automatic pilot before she was able to politely close the call. She felt she was made of ice.

The dead cow was strange. The traces in the atmosphere also. But she wasn't bothered by them. They were normal in their way. Violence and its aftermath left prints whatever the source. They had a kind of psychic stink. But this shock event, seeming so normal to other people, for whom it was possible to mistake concussion for death, to mistake alive and not alive in the heat of a rushed moment because you're only human and you've had a shock so it's easy to explain: this set off all the alarms.

Her body fairly rang. It *wrong*. That should have been a verb. To ring with the silent sound of the clang the world makes as it falls over.

In the more common sense of the word Tara hadn't been wrong. Not at all. Alive had a colour field and dead had none, it was monochrome, pale grey, flat like a cheap security camera image, and Baker had been colourless. Lifeless. Gone.

For a moment she couldn't decide what she was going to do about it, if anything. She put her hands on the steering wheel and focused on her breathing. It was not going to overwhelm her. It was not. She put the heater on full blast.

The farmer got in his own truck. He led the way back to the road along his forking tracks and she drove behind him in silence, being present, not thinking, until they passed the turn off to his house and she went on alone towards the highway.

She drove until she reached the county line and passed over it onto her turf, then took a stop at the first town and ordered coffee, black. She sat in the window overlooking the road and drank it, whittling the ice of her fear down to just a core.

Halifax was half a world away and what happened there was in the past, another country, untouchable, long gone. But is anything really ever gone if you can remember it? Even if you don't bring that memory into focus and live through it again, there it remains: a stamp. Something happened. Something terrible and strange happened.

The diner was playing a country station. The guy on it sang about lost time, lost love, old mistakes.

Don't we all have them? she thought. *But do we have the one about calling something in from the dark night in a time of despair only to find it, come daylight, standing there?*

She smashed the recollection away with a firm mental punch. Finished her drink and got on the phone to send a deputy to the hospital, but some part of her that feared cowardice more than reality made her change her plans. She went in person.

The attending emergency doctor was just coming off his shift.

"Wasn't just you," he said in answer to her enquiries. "Medics in the ambulance thought he was gone too. But he started coughing about ten minutes in. When he got here he was breathing. X-ray didn't show any breaks…"

"What?" she scowled. They must be joking.

"Must have not been going as fast as you thought," the doctor said.

Tara saw the speedometer in her memory. An easy fifty. "Where is he now?" She had her poker face on, gave away nothing.

"Recovery ward. You going to arrest him for something?"

"I just want to see the miracle," Tara replied with false jollity. "Don't suppose he had anything in his system?"

"Clean." The doctor shrugged.

But when she got to the ward the nurse on duty looked down her list, "Baker," she said. "You just missed him. Discharged himself ten minutes ago."

"That happen often?" she asked. "Patients coming out of the ER after a major incident and a few hours later off they go?"

"He was medically fit," the nurse said apologetically. "We can't legally stop him if he wants to go."

"Did he have insurance, Medicaid?"

"No, of course not." She gave Tara a head shake and a smile at her silliness, because what outlaw biker has paid up medical?

But all information was important now. Tara had to have it all. "Thanks."

He'd left on foot, no transport. She hurried to see if she could catch him, but when she hit the street she didn't see anyone matching his description.

Back in the Lightning she cruised past a few bus stops but didn't see him. She stopped at the bus station, not there either. But at the highway ramp there was a tall white guy with lank dirty blond hair wearing black painted Freedom leathers and biker boots. He was holding his thumb out into the wind.

Pennsylvania code says no hitchhiking. No waiting for hitchhikers to board.

She pulled up just in front of him, rolled the window down and watched him walk up in the mirror. No mistake. It was the same man she'd seen that morning. Very much alive in a very ordinary way. Just like Dave.

He only had to take four or five strides, but that felt like an eternity for her to consider her position, her move, her whole take. She felt afraid, but worse than that she felt a deep, almost painful sensation of falling, as though a gravity well had opened in the core of her and was starting to suck her through it starting with the middle of her insides. Mortal dread. And it was so much worse than Halifax, because in the past, in England, she'd felt at home in the world, like she knew it, and what was happening there was a weird anomaly but something isolated and strange, not to do with her, she was only a bystander to a business that didn't concern her at all and she could walk out of it and back into her life and nothing there was changed by it. Upset for sure. But not made fundamentally uncertain. Bad enough to leave sure. But not bad enough that there was no point leaving.

And now it was. She could feel the skin on her face trying to look and see what was happening, because she didn't believe her eyes.

Cade Baker was smiling, as if at an old friend. A kind smile. Dumbledore's smile. She had no sense of a threat from him. He wouldn't harm her at all.

"Don't worry, Hemming," Dave had said before she left. "You did what you could." But what had she done? The bad guy died but the problem wasn't solved. He'd seen her hesitation and added. "Nobody can solve this crime. It's not that kind of thing."

But her sense of failure ate at her until she signed off work on the sick, and then took herself off to find a fortune in a new world. Stupid, when she looked at it now. Leaving all your burdens behind you. Whoever thinks they can do that?

The gravel was crisp and crunchy under his boots as he reached her door and put his hand out onto the rim where she'd wound down the window, as you'd put a hand on the shoulder of a tired colleague. Familiar. That's how it felt.

Tara had her gun in her hand, just on her lap, the safety was off. She put her lights on, to discourage interest; cop arrests hitcher. No big. She turned and looked at him, no idea of a word to say.

"Hemming," he said. But what name should she say in reply?

How much proof do you want, Tara? She thought. When will it be enough? But it still wasn't. Baker could have known her name.

She jerked her head at the back of the Lightning, popped the door lock. He opened the cab door and climbed in. When he looked at her through the mirror she stared at him and he grinned at her as though he had won something.

"You can't be here," she said. It was a line anyone could take as they pleased. Except through a rap sheet, she and Baker had never met.

He made an equivocal shrug. "Did you ever think I might belong here?"

Still vague. She circled. Her hand hurt on the gun stock. She could feel her legs shake although she felt strangely empty, calm. "I thought we sent you back."

"No, you didn't," he said. "Because if you thought that you wouldn't have stopped just now."

And there it was. It was enough. Movement was restored to her. She put the gun away, shifted into drive. Cade leaned back in the seat, relaxed like he was ready to enjoy the ride.

251

"Who are you?" she made herself pick up speed, join the traffic. She drank in all the normality of the highway, the lights, the advertising boards, the shapes of the town.

"Cade Baker," he said.

"That's not what I meant."

He moved into a gentle storytelling roll. "Cade Baker who saw the cops coming and knew he couldn't get caught, because if he did he'd be a link in a short chain that leads back to the Black Pistons, and they'd see to him much more efficiently than the law. Cade, who thought it was worth pretending you ran him off the road. Not that bright, Cade. Didn't do much school. Made his old ma pretty miserable. Good old Cade thought he'd get something on his own terms, even if it was the last thing. He drove into that bridge like a god, sailing off the edge of the world, almost on a whim. Like he saw the moment, your car, realised it was the end and just like that he let it all go. Wasn't worth nothing to him. Not a damn thing." He gave it a respect she didn't expect, irony but not, as if Cade was some kind of hero worth admiring for his free spirit. One man against the world.

Her knuckles were white. Her jaw hurt. Let's put that pedal down, she thought and said, "What happened to Dave?"

His voice softened. He sounded filled with warm, affectionate regret. "Dave had a heart attack. Undiagnosed mitral valve issues."

"Is that why you took so long getting here?"

"You thought I'd kill him just to follow you? My my. You have a low opinion of me. Can't blame you, I suppose."

Now it was just shooting the breeze. "Isn't that what you do?"

"I'm hurt, Sheriff. Dave died of entirely natural causes and lived a blameless, if rather uninteresting life. He missed you. Your Christmas cards meant a lot."

"Bastard," she said but she had no force in her at that moment. She felt that there was an impact deferred waiting to hit her and that some piece of her had sidestepped. She wasn't quite real, not together.

"At least I don't run from my responsibilities."

The highway bent into the country. Trees rose dark and tall, spiky on either side, the road bending around the hills following the line of the river. The sun was low, the shadows long. They stared through the windshield together in taut silence as her radio burbled and called her to some incident. She responded, angry at the interruption, angry full stop.

"I'll drop you at the end of the Mile," she said. "You'll have to walk from there."

"Drop me at Dogwood. I'll get a ride there."

"I thought you didn't have any money."

He reached into his back pocket and pulled out a wad of cash. "I must've got paid for something."

She didn't believe that. He'd had no money on him. But what did it matter now?

"Then why hitch?"

"I didn't want to delay," he said. "I've waited a long time to see you again. Remember our bargain."

"But I filled it," she said, grinding her teeth between phrases. She put on her sirens and started to speed it up. She couldn't get rid of him fast enough. "I gave you a name."

"And now you must give me another."

"Look, those weren't the terms. When Dave... Why are you still here?"

"I'm not sure," he said, stuffing the cash back into the jacket. "Surprised as you are." He looked at her. Blue cowboy eyes, she noted. They gave him a sympathetic angle she didn't care for. But she felt he was honest. He was always honest.

They made it back in record time.

"You can't stay," she said, turning off onto Dogwood's central strip. The lights were all on. It looked inviting, bright, against the sheer black of the forest.

She pulled into the diner lot. He opened his door and they both heard a distant, lonely howl.

He looked at her with surprise. "I think anyone can stay, where it's their home."

"But you've stopped. You stopped. Right?"

He put his hands together before his chin in Namaste. He gave a little bow, his smile wry, "Give me a name."

She said nothing. But her mind had already gone through the file server it kept on all the people she knew about in Chestnut County who were outside the law's reach but who deserved... deserved...

"Thanks," he said, getting down, boots crunching in the gravel and dirt.

"No! No. You have to stop. I don't give you permission."

He leaned in as he held the door, "That's the thing though, isn't it? You say one thing, but in your heart you mean another. Words don't matter between us, Tara. Only the truth. And you want them dead. To the marrow of your bones."

He shut the door on her and walked off towards the bright, friendly yellow squares of the diner windows.

Part of her thought about the arrest she could easily make, must have made, for the bike full of drugs. She could put him in lockup, put him in jail, surely. At least for a minute or two. But she knew how it would go from last time she'd done a dance in Halifax with sanity and the law – the curious situations arising in which evidence went astray, technicalities appeared, solid foundations all dissolved, a witness changed their story and their mind. The case melted. Everyone went silent.

And nobody believes in beings that don't have their own bodies. They believe in a change of character, a change of heart, repentance, redemption, reform. Dave Hobson had been a criminal boss's lackey and then, after the death of his patron, he found the courage to change his ways, worked for rehabilitation centres, model citizen, pillar of the local church. The brush with death that had 'bought' Dave's new life had paved the way. And the death that stuck had been of a bad man. Indisputably bad. No loss at all to anyone. It was a net gain.

She should go to her armed drugstore robbery, but she sat in the lot and put her head on the steering wheel for a moment first, to clear her head.

It was true. She liked the idea of an invisible hand taking out agents of misery. Couldn't help it. And only when she did want him gone would the pact be ended. And if she never did, if she never could, then his journey would only be ended when she ended. Or maybe never.

She wanted to believe he was evil, must be dealt with. But.

She put her head up and blasted gravel up behind her until she joined the highway, lights and sirens wailing fit to wake the dead.

Easton was the first one to turn up at the hospital morgue. Tara was still talking with the examiner when he appeared, sliding around the door as if he was late for a briefing he was entitled to, and not showing up unannounced at the passing of a citizen who had no criminal record and for whom no FBI presence was strictly necessary.

The coroner looked bemused, cleaning their hands. The corpse lay on the gurney, the Y-mark of penitence across his chest. "It's a straightforward coronary. I haven't found any trace of substances."

Easton shoved his hands in his pockets and looked at the body cheerfully. "Who's this then?"

"Just a local sudden death," Tara said. "I came for the paperwork, stayed for the lols. You know how it is."

He snorted, not sure if he thought she was funny or insulting. "That British humour. Always gets me sideways. You want to arrest Baker, don't you?"

And straight to business. At least he didn't hang about.

"It's very straightforward. Possession."

"Well, let's talk about it in my office…" He gestured outside, glancing at the coroner.

"All right," Tara thanked the doctor and stepped out. They went into the parking lot where his sedan was lined up two down from her and paused by its trunk. "You want to stop me."

"It's all part of a bigger case. We'll get Baker. It's a matter of timing."

Tara looked up to the skies. Sometimes she asked heaven for patience, but sometimes she just looked up as there was no point in asking. "I went to the lock up this morning to look for the drugs and they weren't there."

Easton made a hands gesture that indicated he didn't know how that could happen but it was inevitable. "Let's cut to the chase. It's not your case now. Go back to your heart-attack Dads and your local women-against-guns bake sales. We've got this now. It spans more than your county. It's interstate." He paused, irritated that she seemed to be looking over his shoulder instead of into his eyes, because he was the important one here, not her. "Are you listening? Dogwood is small town stuff. Stick to that. It's safer." He lingered on the last word.

"Is the CIA and the military killing cattle out here, Easton? Is it running around in ghillie suits, scaring campers and hunters? Is it shooting lasers at weather balloons and setting off speakers in empty asylums?"

"What're you talking about?"

"Do you know who that dead guy is back in the hospital?"

"Mister Straightforward Coronary? No."

"I'm surprised at you. That is District Judge Charles Perry. He lives, lived, in Pennybrook. Big mansion, estate, hunting lands, fishing. Retired. His main hobby was domestic violence. Nothing was ever proved but his wife sure was one of the most accident-prone people who ever lived, to hear her tell it down at the hospital."

"What's your point? Good people die. Bad people die. Just drop dead."

The casual way he spoke about it, even though she had set the tone, irked her. She felt a grudge against him, lightly for his interference on a daily level, but deeply for his don't-care about that. She wondered how much he knew. Was he in on it? Whatever 'it' was? She said, "He used to oversee all the cases hereabouts that ended up being dropped for lack of evidence. Ones involving certain people who like things to run a certain way. Like now."

"I don't see where this is headed."

Feigning ignorance, so she could bury herself. Fine. Let the digging commence, she thought. She was done pussyfooting. "Before I came here, I worked in England, as an officer. We had something like this going on. It didn't involve the same level of corruption. It was small time things, except for one case. There was a guy at the centre of it: people trafficking. The things he organised, the things he did. Not small. It had international tendrils, big money. I grew to hate him as I've never hated anyone. But he was protected, by a uniformed set of bottom feeders all feeding off his bottom, if you see what I mean."

"If you're trying to make out..."

She was happy to make out and rode over him. "Just listen. So, when I get into the force I don't know about his rings of protection, and I spend a long time making a great case to put him away. But. Things go missing. Things go wrong. People forget things; where they were, what they did, who they are. And at about the same time a load of apparently entirely unrelated stuff goes on: UFO sightings, livestock attacks, terrified kids in the woods. A Ouija board thing at a big nightclub party in town on Halloween. Local celebrities traumatised, that kind of thing. And I happen to investigate the Ouija board thing and it pisses me off, Easton, because I have bigger fish to fry. Real fish. With real crimes and real victims. Not that shit. Turns out it's worse than I thought. People are dead. Someone comes up from London. I am just one of the officers late to arrive. So what? Drugs are involved. They're kind of scattered about, like ketchup packets, everywhere you look. The old story, eh? And maybe it is but then; I am about to leave when I see him – Dave Hobson, a young guy I know who's done courier stuff for my Big Fish. What's he doing here? I try to talk to him. But I can't, because he talks back to me and I can't understand a word he's saying. It's another language. I think maybe he knows one of these Eastern European ones, yeah? Like Hungarian. Estonian. Serbian. Where all the poor girls come from. Fuck knows what they sound like. I sure don't. Maybe he's high and he forgot his English. So, I record him, but I can't keep him when he wants to go – got no reason to arrest him and he has, sort of, made a statement. I can pick him up anytime anyway, yeah? We know him. He slips out. I go back and send my recording off to the translation service. But..."

"But it's not Hungarian."

Finally, some movement. "It is not Hungarian."

"What is it?"

"It's not any human language at all."

Easton gloated. "Gibberish. From some high guy. Gratsies."

"Yeah, I thought that too. He'd pranked me. And I go back to my case, which has problems all over it. Dead ends. Obstructions. I

257

start to think it's cursed, or maybe someone in the force is involved with it. The ring gets bigger, bigger. Maybe the Albanians, yeah? They're difficult. Like the mafia. But suddenly everyone is stonewalling. Then I get a call. From London. From some university woman professor in linguistics and she says it's a real language. It's just not one with any existing relations and she wants to study it and blah blah… And I get a call too, from Dave Hobson."

"In tongues, or are we gonna get to the end now?"

She felt so pleased that he was getting bored but couldn't stop himself listening. Irrationally pleased. "In English. And he says I have to help him get rid of someone. Someone causing a big problem. He's in tears on the phone. He's terrified. And I think this is my chance to crack the case. This will be the clue. So, I dash over there. No answer. Door's open, not locked. I go in. He's dead on the floor. I check him out. No signs of violence, no sign of forced entry, nothing. I call it in. The ambulance comes, picks him up, carts him off. And I'm watching it leave and I hear a voice as clear as your voice say right next to me, 'Give me a name.' There is nobody fucking there, Easton. Nobody. And it didn't say it in English. I *understood it* in English. But it sounded like Dave, when he was talking the day before. So, I pick up my phone and I listen to the recording of him again. And it's not in English, any idiot can tell that, but I hear it as English. And it says, "Who would kill the evildoer must give me the name of one to be judged and I will lay out the chosen dead upon their command.""

"You're kidding." Easton looks uneasy now, leans on his car, folds his arms across his chest; braced for impact, kind of entertained, waiting for when he can get everything kicked into a can.

Tara didn't care. "It gets better. Dave Hobson walked into the police station later that afternoon and he told me all about it. See, he wasn't dead, he was just drugged and in shock. According to the report. From London. Which, in case you didn't know, is a long way away from Yorkshire, certainly too far to come in less than two and a half hours; not responding distance. And when I conducted the interview with Dave – and this is the best bit – I was so angry that my case was in shreds and everyone was laughing at it, that when

Dave said, 'I want him dead. You want him dead. Just make the call.' I said. 'Okay.' And I named the bastard. And just like that Dave got up and left. A few hours later, guess who's dead? I trust you're seeing some parallels here, Easton?"

Easton rolled his eyes as if he was taxed to believe. "Cade Baker was in shock. He's fine. We need him as a witness. Alive. I don't know what bullshit went down in England, it doesn't matter. Your guy in England went out and killed his boss. Revenge. Doesn't take witchcraft for that."

"Well, I'm guessing Judge Perry is someone in the backup circle of whatever you have going on here, but that's not my point. I've wanted him dead for a long time. I just hated him, you know? He was a bad man. He did a lot of nasty things around here. And I hated my people trafficker. And I did name him, because it was all bullshit. And he died."

"Straightforward Coronary?" Easton smiled, smug, home run. He wasn't going to believe her no matter what.

"Preceded briefly by having his spinal cord severed at every vertebral junction as if by a razor cut, but without any external or surrounding injuries at all."

He took a long suffering breath and straightened up, suddenly straight again. "Is that why you're here?"

"I was working up to asking about it when you showed up. So. Wanna go back and see if that happened to Perry too?"

"Sherriff, go home. It's been a long day. I'm tired. You're tired. Nobody's making any sense out of this, least of all you."

"The case collapsed, thanks for asking. In Halifax. Nothing was improved. The trafficking went on. Almost not even a blip. There's always more scum to take up the slack, isn't there?"

"*Ain't* there? That's how we say it over here."

"Yesterday Cade Baker asked me for a name."

Easton was getting his keys out, opening his door, "Maybe he has an illegitimate child on the way."

"Charles Perry Baker. I guess that has a ring to it."

Easton looked at her. "Nice anecdote."

She had what she wanted. He knew. They knew. She felt satisfied, oddly. "Who would you choose?"

"What?" He had his leg in the car, he hesitated there, scowling.

"If you were asked for a name, who would you choose? Come on, what's the first thing that comes to mind?"

Easton frowned. "Nobody."

"Nobody?" She didn't believe him.

"It's a trick question, isn't it? What would have happened if you'd kept your mouth shut, Hemming? You think of that?" He thumped down into the seat and slammed the door.

You can tell people anything, she thought, but then what can you do after that?

After work she went home, walked the dog, looked at the time. How do you keep your thoughts shut? She walked the length of Little Poquessing and back, but she didn't figure it out.

She called her friend in the UK force to ask about Dave Hobson, but there were no suspicious circumstances. Since the incident in 2019 Dave hadn't been in any more trouble. He worked at a coffee shop. He kept to himself. He was well-liked by everyone who knew him. He kept rabbits. One of them had won a prize.

Hardly an express ticket to murder. Once they had finished talking pleasantries she hung up. RIP, mate, she thought, and then she cried.

Maybe it had talked to her because she was the only one who could hear it. Maybe Dave was really dead the first time, in 2019. And then he got borrowed. But even if it had all been some supernatural summons, how would anyone from London have known about it beforehand?

On her day off Tara got in her Tacoma and drove round to Mrs Baker's place on the Back Mile. The property was very much on the edge of Dogtown, more of an outlier, like a sentinel. It was a large lot, with several ramshackle buildings on it, but Mrs Baker lived in the little house at the front. It had a big porch that overlooked the road and the forest beyond, and it was the only house she knew of that had its own shooting range directly across the street, if you counted a fence with a set of cans as a range. Mrs Baker did count it, and she liked to practice, or at least be about to practice, whenever visitors came to call.

It was clear, the light good, and Tara approached slowly, in case Mrs Baker did not recognise her. Obviously shooting over a public highway, empty or not, was strictly illegal, but there was no point saying so as she had never seen a shot fired and there was no law against arranging cans on a fence for artistic purposes reminiscent of a shooting gallery, nor for sitting on your own porch in a rocker with your walking stick across your lap, even when it happened to double as a loaded hunting rifle. Given Cade Baker's previous lifestyle Tara would have had several walking sticks like that about the place.

She rode up, engine loud, and pulled over onto the loose stone at the side of the Baker property. She could see the rocker, and the small birdlike shape of Mrs Baker within it.

"Hello?" she called. "Mrs Baker? It's me, Tara Hemming."

"I know who you are," Mrs Baker said. "No uniform. It must be bad. Come up and be about it."

"I wondered if you'd seen Cade lately…" Tara began but was interrupted by the opening of the inner door and then the screen door, pushed aside by the foot of Cade Baker who emerged with a cup in his hand which he presented to his mother.

"Coffee, Ma."

Mrs Baker visibly preened. "Thank you." She looked at Tara with dislike. "You were saying?"

Tara looked at the woman and didn't grudge her the moment. Years of railing against her son, driving him off the property, all her money gone in his schemes. And now coffee on the porch midmorning, when the law has come around to dig again at some painful situation.

"I just have a few questions to ask."

"Cade lives here now," Mrs Baker said, sipping her coffee. "He's going to look after me." Her lips had a white tinge to them as she closed her mouth. Tara recognised someone who has made her mind up against all odds.

Tara glanced at Cade. He didn't look like himself. That is, he was almost affable, relaxed, in the jeans and check shirt uniform of every country guy planning some DIY about the house. He had showered and tied his hair back. "Is that so?"

"Yeah," he said. "There's a lot of work needs doing on the property."

No arguing with that. There was a beat-up pickup truck on the driveway that led around the back of the house. One tyre was flat. Tara nodded at it, "You going to Home Depot in that thing?"

"It's broke," he said.

"I have to go to town. I can give you a ride."

He nodded.

"There's going to be trouble," he said, after a while. "The outlaws that I was working for have Easton on the ticket. I won't work for them any more and they expect him to sort me out."

"But you want to live quietly and look after your old mother, in Dogtown," Tara said, trying not to be excessively sarcastic. "No more names?"

"Not for now," he said, as though they were discussing sandwich filling. "I don't need one yet. I need to fix the truck. Ma wants to go to Hobby Lobby."

"What'll you do for money? Are you looking for a job?" She didn't know what else to talk about. Everything was so ordinary now. It seemed like the easiest button to keep pressing.

"I've got money," he said. "I'll get the rest from the outlaws that they owe me. Then I'll think of something else."

"But you're not really Cade Baker," she said, because she couldn't find another way to say it.

"Sometimes things choose us," he said, "and we have to say yes or no without understanding the cause or the consequences. We have to go on instinct or on luck. Our nature demands certain agreements with other beings that share the space of our lives. For all intents and purposes, I am Cade Baker. One with different priorities."

"Original Cade couldn't kill at a distance, by thought alone."

"No."

"So, were you Dave?"

"I was."

"And when Dave passed, how did you get here?"

"How did I get to Dave?"

"I don't know, how did you?"

"I don't know. I don't have memories without Dave, or Cade. To answer your original question – I don't know what I am. There is no word that fits and there is no idea I can form which answers that question."

"Were you someone before Dave?"

"I don't know. I – it's no use, I don't know." He shrugged and set his hands on his jeans, loose and relaxed as if he hadn't a care in the world. He seemed not to expect to know.

"But you didn't lack bloody confidence when it came to whispering and killing people, did you?"

"No. I know how to do that. I know that I cannot choose. I must ask. But today, I must fix the truck. Drop me at a garage. One you trust. You must know who's good."

But do I? Tara thought. Do I know who's good? And what even is good? Good for who?

She let him out at Gianni's Garage (shocks, brakes, oil changes, no repair too small) because no repair was too small. Afterwards she drove out to one of the trailheads in the woods and went for a walk, alone.

The weather was already starting to turn as she set off from the car. The sky had darkened and the wind got up, full of promises.

No repair too small.

She reached her destination as the rain began. The overlook was a cliff which stood clear of the trees. She thought of the agencies involved, the people with their plans and plots, all the things they knew and she didn't which likely involved money and power in places far from this forlorn spot which had nothing to give her but space and time.

She turned her nose until the wind hit both sides of her face equally and looked in that direction. It was just rain.

No repair too small.

It felt to her that whatever Cade Baker did now was mending. Make do and mending. Cutting and sewing. She'd never made or mended too much, though it was something like her vague personal aim from long ago in joining the police force. Let's stop the destruction, so there's less mending to do. But of course, like all young ideals, it wasn't quite like that. In the modern world of human courses, nothing was quite simple like that.

If there weren't dogmen in the hills she wished there were.

She walked back to the car, got in, drove back to Gianni's. Baker was sitting outside in the shelter of the porch outside the office door. He got up when he saw her car, like he'd expected her, and got in, stowing his plastic bag of parts.

"We can stop at Walmart if you like," she said. "I have to get some stuff there."

"Okay."

She hesitated. "Were you the voice? In Halifax?"

"Something came to me and I said it," he said. "That's what I remember."

"So why are you in there and I'm here? If I was listening and Dave couldn't listen?" She'd always wondered why Dave had been the target. Dave hadn't worked.

"Dave died," Cade said. "You didn't. You know, it's hard to remember Dave now, and it's getting harder every day, but I think Dave was put there to die. That is, he had a sense of being led to that night when he passed and to the séance. The person from London killed him. The first time, that is. Not when I was Dave and his heart failed. That was just bad genes, not a person."

"How did they kill him, and why?"

"With some kind of electric device. And since you asked I've been thinking. I may have been around before. As someone else. I can't remember."

"But what is the name thing about? If you can just take over a body, why do you ask for the name? Why do you kill that other person when you're already sorted?"

They had arrived at Walmart. Tara parked and they went around the aisles together, Cade quiet as if deep in thought, Tara trying to remember anything about her grocery list and failing, given the conversation. At last, near the spices, Cade paused and stared fixedly at a packet of cilantro.

"It's supposed to be coriander," he said. "Things go by other names in other places."

Tara recognised the attempt as a way to reach some elusive memory.

"Well, that's as close as I can get. Things go by other names in other places and I am in another place than the one I started in. And part of staying here requires the name." He was so reasonable, so matter-of-fact, so calm. It didn't bother him that he didn't know. He accepted it, when she could only accept things that made sense to her.

She tried to read him but there was nothing to see, not like up at the dead cow, where she had read the trail of the predator.

She picked up parsley. Parsley is a kind of carrot. Cade is a kind of zombie. Or. No. Something else. "The thing is, it's kind of evil, isn't it? What would happen if you didn't get a name?"

"Evil," Cade said. He was staring into the racks of little spice jars with a faraway look, mulling over the word. Then he looked at Tara. "The choice is yours, not mine."

"It's not though. I mean. You take whatever I think of. You don't ask me if I want it to happen. So…" She trailed off as a mother and toddlers passed them by. When they'd gone she didn't know what else to say about it as he'd said nothing. She changed her tack. "Are you gonna testify if they subpoena you against this drug ring?"

"Of course," he said. "Why wouldn't I?"

"Because anyone with sense would expect to be targeted by everyone in the case who stands to lose a lot of money. I mean, we offer witness protection." She spoke about it, almost by rote, noticing the way he looked around, not at the things in the store, but like her grandmother used to sometimes, when it was stormy and the wind was high, as if she was trying to spot a snowflake among thousands.

"They are here," he said. "Others. You know that. It's why you're here, isn't it?"

Tara moved along, Cade followed her. "I came here to get away from all that." It sounded stupid when she said it.

They finished their shopping and loaded the truck. She could not explain it but she felt safe with Cade. She tried to fear him at regular intervals, and could not.

Tara took the Back Mile on the way home, because it would bring her at the Baker house first. It was afternoon, the sky was grey but not raining, the wind light. She saw the big SUV trailing them after they had got part way up into the hills. The road narrowed at points to almost a single lane. The SUV had its lights on and crept up steadily.

She saw Baker glance in the wing mirror. She looked in the rearview. They were coming to a series of sharp S bends where the road curved and bridged a few steep ravines. One of these was close to an abandoned house, the March place, where she knew the bikers had at one time had a stash. There was a logging trailhead there, with a layby for parking maintenance vehicles for the firebreak and the electric lines.

A strange feeling of certain calm crept over her. If you were going to run someone off the road, here was where you'd do it.

The layby was coming up.

"Pull in here," Cade said and, although it felt like an order and she didn't take those, it aligned with her intent, so, without signalling, she swept to the side into the loose gravel.

The black SUV sailed past. Its windows were tinted. Then it slowed down and stopped. It reversed until it was level with her and stopped again. The window came down.

Tara slid her hand into the glovebox and onto her gun. She wound down her window.

The car had a woman in that she knew she'd seen before but only when they spoke did she realise who it was from the cut-glass British accent. The Londoner.

"I just want to talk."

"We are talking," Tara said, noticing all trace of her adopted US tones falling away instantly.

"You don't know what you're involved with," the woman said and held up some kind of ID which was too distant for Tara to verify. "MI6."

Something to the right of her, in the trees by the firebreak, moved in a way that made Tara glance to it. She saw some kind of large humanoid shape, but it stilled and merged with the shadows of the wood.

"Is this about Dave?" Tara asked.

"I'm blocking the road," the Londoner said. "Let's go somewhere more suitable."

"We can walk up the break," Tara nodded at the cleared line between forests on the hill. "Nobody will hear anything up there. Pull in." Before there could be a debate she reversed to leave space for the other vehicle, but the SUV rolled alongside her again.

"I'm not dressed for it. Meet me in Dogwood, if you want to know the answers to all your questions."

"And if I don't?"

"Then don't. It's your funeral." The agent made a 3-point turn and drove back the way they had come.

Tara sat and thought for a moment. "Do you know her?"

"No. But Dave did. Before he died. He had been meeting her as part of some group. It's hard to recall now."

"An occult group."

"But not a very serious one. He thought. It was a bit of fun. A curry on Saturdays and some talk about tarot cards. Social."

"She was there at the investigation to the séance where you appeared. In Halifax. I never understood how she knew to be there. She said then she was with the Met, and that there was a link to her cases in London. She said my Mr Big was responsible for sending people in to these things and then they went missing. And then here you are. In a dead man's body. In a dead man's life. Was he sending them to you?"

"Not to me. For me, possibly."

267

Tara drummed her fingers on the steering wheel. "For you. For you to be here, well, to be there. To do what? What's it all for?"

Cade Baker, or the thing that was now Cade Baker, looked at her intently. "Whatever it was for, it isn't for that now. Because she wasn't there, and you were."

Tara shrugged, "She was going to give the word to you, and you were going to be a private, untraceable..." but whatever she had been going to say was lost as they both heard the unmistakable screech of tyres some distance away, then a loud thump.

She had them turned around and speeding downhill before her mind caught up with her. They reached the sharp corner before the covered bridge at forty miles an hour to see black tyre marks scored across the tarmac, tracing lines directly to a truck-sized break in the rail beside the bridge.

She parked in the road, got out, shoved her gun in her waistband as she hurried over, getting her phone out at the same time. As she looked down into the ravine she saw the truck rocking back and forth on its side where it had fallen, half in and half out of the white water of the stream at the bottom. It was driver side up. She was about to jump down when she heard a distinct growl from her right side, where the bridge was.

"Wait!" she heard Cade call, from behind her, to her left. He sounded like a boy scout leader being very calm on purpose as he ordered some idiot back from a dangerous precipice. It was a distinctive tone.

Tara froze. "I need to get down there and help them out," she said. Her voice cracked. She wanted to look up and right, but something prevented her.

She couldn't stand being told what to do. Even by her own sense of self-preservation. She looked.

A thing was clinging to the bridge roof, flattened to it. She would have said werewolf. It was big and dark, spiderlike in its belly-down, elbow-high posture that was poised to spring – on her, or down into the gully. Its fingers were exceptionally long and ended in blades. Its face was long. It had yellow-red eyes and it was thin. Ribs and other bones poked at its skin. It opened its mouth and a strange, "Aahh," came out, like a breath of realisation, though she was the one seeing it, not it seeing her... or was it seeing something else? She saw an expression on its hairy face – as of some ancient mystery receiving a new clue, resolving an essential conundrum. For a split second she felt a kinship to it rooted in the love of solving a puzzle. It was a strange thing to feel because aside from that she was terrified.

It rippled, oddly, and its body changed. Where a breath before it had looked mangy and thin it now appeared to be heavily built and covered in a fine, dark fur that shone in the grey afternoon light with its own healthy lustre.

"Hello," Cade said quietly.

From the ravine they heard the sounds of a car door being opened, falling back shut, opening again.

"Hunter," said the huge thing on the bridge. Its voice rasped, tongue struggling with the mouth shape, the lack of lips, vocal chords a little gargled as the word shaped itself out of a growling roar. But she thought that's what it had said. It was looking at Cade and there was a knowing expression on its face, a kind of 'here we go' as of compatriots who have come to a breach of some kind and are about to make their move.

Tara was frozen, unable to move. She tried to make a sound but instead of a deep breath or a scream the squeak of a tiny, cornered rodent came out of her mouth. She could not believe what she was seeing and so she stared all the more. The wolf thing had a peculiar, horrible quality, a kind of vibration that was in the air and in her and in the ground around it; she almost heard it as a whine, a distressed metal kind of sound that made her flesh crawl and her guts turn to liquid.

She couldn't tear her eyes off the creature although she wanted to see Cade's face, to see what his reaction was. He was nothing weird in comparison to its horrible, unreal yet so real presence. Or was he more so? His so-ordinary form, the sense of him was so... plain, nothing. But they knew each other?

Down in the ravine the car door opened again, was levered, fell back on its hinges, slammed shut. If she was going to do something it must be now.

She heard Cade behind her, quite calm, say, "You should go down there and listen to what she has to say before you make up your mind."

About what? Tara wanted to ask but she had lost the use of her mouth. Her breath was coming in and out with tiny shrieks and that was as much as she could do. Then she felt a hand – Cade's hand – on her shoulder.

"You've got time," he said. "But not much."

The touch released her from paralysis. She straightened. If the thing that was on the bridge roof had moved she wouldn't have been able to go on, but it remained stationary, watching Cade, as though it was waiting for a prompt from offstage. She had felt like a pawn before, in Halifax. Her actions had been explained away by her superiors, by her counsellor, by her doctor, by herself, a thousand times.

She focused on the only real thing she was sure of. There was a woman trapped down there in the ravine.

After a moment more she went back to her truck and found her ropes. When she looked back to the bridge she saw only Cade standing there, hands in his pockets as he looked down. The bridge was empty. There was nothing there at all.

As she secured her line and rappelled off the side of the rocks she considered Dave Hobson. "Dave Hobson, Lord," she muttered as she focused on her work, moving, not thinking about monsters. "Dave Hobson, Lord, Amen." The poem that had given rise to the impulse was lost to her memory, Timothy Winters. That was it. Well, she'd read that and she'd thought of Dave then, back in the monster-free interval of her life when she'd moved on from weird and horrible and into smalltown and predictable. And she thought of him now. If there could be any human so badly done to but so doggedly trying, so strangely unfit but fitted up, it was Dave Hobson. Finally fitted with a coffin at last for services rendered to some*thing*, by the someone stuck in this fucking truck.

As she reached the gully bottom and released her rope she was furious, humiliated, enraged with a feeling that was almost beyond endurance, made up of *Why* and *Why Me* and *Why Here* and *How and How Could You All Lie And For What?* Daves and Taras of the world don't matter. Only big people and things with plans.

She could see right away that the truck was wedged between boulders. It wasn't going to be tipped. She walked about and found a way up onto the bonnet, which was at a steep angle. Through the crazed, shattered windshield she saw feeble movements. She used the wipers as footholds and got up onto the door, then past it onto the flank. She opened the door and pushed it onto the strut. By that point a lot of her rage was used as energy but she had some as she stared in at the person stuck in the car and the gun pointed at her.

"Oh, it's you." The gun muzzle dropped. Behind it a middle-aged woman in a business suit and a camel overcoat, slumped. A Midsomer Murders suit, Tara thought. The seatbelt was cut through and free, but she was gasping, seemed to have little left. "Well, looks like you'll get your explanation here. I can't move and you're not strong enough to get me out. Did you see the thing that ran me off the road?"

"Yes," Tara said. She was looking for ways to help but the woman was well down against the passenger door, stuck, her legs at a bad angle. Bruises and blood marked her face. "I called for help."

"Won't get here in time," the woman said. The gun fell backwards out of her hand. She let it go, almost shaking it off, then reached weakly into her pocket and pulled out her phone. "Here, take this. Four oh one nine. Don't answer any calls. Don't cooperate with any investigation that comes after me."

"What's…?"

But the woman shushed her, voice failing with every word that passed. "Your Mr Big guy in Halifax was just a pawn. Talked into things, duped really. He was… meant to be the… host. We could have… done something… with him."

"Why did you pick Dave, then?"

"Bastard wouldn't go… to the séance… too afraid of ghosts. Funny, eh? It latched onto you for some reason. I should have been there. It was my… job…"

Tara waited, then realised there would be no more. The woman's eyes remained unchanging, her breath had stopped. The phone began to sag out of her grasp.

It was the first thing a recovery unit would look for. Tara didn't know what would happen if her prints were found on it but as the only person present surely she had some reason to recover it. She grabbed it, entered the number at the prompt.

The screen didn't open to the usual icons. Instead a video played. It was the dead woman, talking to the phone, from some hotel room.

"Sheriff Hemming. You are the Caller of the Dead. I am sure you have figured out what that is by now. They will try to issue you with an ultimatum. You may do what you want with that, but if you don't cooperate they will kill you and find another. I'm sorry the choice is so bleak, but there it is." There was a moment where she seemed about to say more. Her face looked tired, sad. She leaned forward and the video ended as it was turned off. The phone went to lockscreen.

Tara put the phone in her pocket. She got out her own and called for the assistance she had promised, then climbed down from the cab and back up the gully. Cade was sitting on the bridge rail beside the break at the top.

She told him what had happened. After a pause she said, "Do you know how many times you've moved?"

"A few," he said. "Could be a lot." He shrugged. "I'm gonna walk home."

"I have to stay here," she said, unnecessarily, stalling for anything and suddenly feeling she didn't want him to go, not least because the thing might come back. "Did you know that... whatever it was?"

"The dogman? Not personally. But yes, in a way."

"It seemed to know you."

"We are of a kind."

"A *kind*?"

"We are the mice of the world, living in the tiny little dark places, rarely out to play."

"Didn't look very mousey."

"Nonetheless."

"So. Should I cooperate?"

"I can't say what you should do," Cade said. He got off the rail and dusted his jeans down, walked to her truck and got out his groceries.

"It's ten miles, just sit down," she said.

He put them back in and sat in the passenger seat.

Tara waited. Her rush had ended and exhaustion was coming in. She had too much to think about, but no amount of time would have been enough to decide what was real, what was her position, what she wanted. She wished she had never come across any of it, but that was out of reach.

From her pocket the dead woman's phone rang. She pulled it out on reflex, looked at it. Now the video had played the icons were like any other phone. Her thumb hovered over the swipe and she thought of people; their schemes, their espionage, their goals and murky deals, or some kind of done-deal with some devil or whatever.

She set the phone down, still ringing, on the rail.

"Guess I'm not," she said, to herself, and shoved her hands into the pockets of her coat. Cooperating. That's what you do with people who are over you, who will never let you out. People who kill Dave to get a vessel because Dave doesn't matter. Did they kill Baker too? She didn't know, might never know, but she did know one thing. "I am not."

It rang twice more, and went silent.

She turned and got back into her truck, sat beside Cade Baker, turned on the engine and the heater, and the radio, and waited for the ambulance and the fire service to arrive.

ERIC AND THE KÉTHANI

Tony Ballantyne

Years ago, back when Eric still lived in Haworth, I arranged to meet him in Bradford for beer and a curry.

It was a winter night, and my route took me over Saddleworth Moor in the snow. There was a full moon that night: a science fiction moon, far too big for our regular world; it lit up the snow so brightly that the shadows glowed purple.

The road wandered this way and that over the moors and I had to steer the car carefully so as not to be tricked into following a path into another world.

Those seductive paths curled away in every direction: dark roads that led down into forgotten villages in hidden valleys, brightly lit paths that rose up into the hills where dark reservoirs reflected the stars, and darker creatures stirred below the waters.

Eric knew those paths so well. He could see them in the pattern of stones on the moors, or in the reflections in the windows of old buildings.

He introduced me to the one that leads to the Kéthani tower, seen clearly rising in the distance across the moor. It was a television tower in the old world, but Eric saw that tower from a different angle in this new reality.

The more I wrote, the more I hung around with Eric, the more we saw those other worlds, we saw them crowding their way into ours.

But that was then, and this is now.

Now is the perfect morning for a walk. Late November, the sky is bright blue, the air is cold and the sun is melting the morning frost.

My wife watches me pull my hiking socks from the drawer.

"Aren't you going to call Eric?" she says, accusingly.

"Later."

I've often used the name Eric in my stories. It was a joke we shared. He was once an alien with knees that bent the wrong way, another time he spent a whole train journey locked up in a cage by his dog.

"He's leaving at the end of the week," my wife says.

I sit down on the bed and pull on a sock.

"I know."

I pull on the other sock.

"He's going on the Kéthani spaceship."

The Kéthani are an alien race that came to Earth a few years ago. They resurrect humans, six months after their death. Eric introduced me to them.

I stand up.

"I need to go out for my walk," I say. "I'll be a couple of hours."

"See you later."

I trot downstairs and open the front door and stand there for a moment, just breathing in the freshness. Half the bay tree outside is coated in frost, the other half shines green and bright where the sun has touched it: the warmed leaves coming alive after their frosty hiatus.

I sit down, feet hanging out of the house and pull on my hiking boots.

Today is a walking day. I used to think writing days were the best. Now I think the best days are walking days, the writing usually comes with me whether I want it to or not.

I tie my boots, close the front door and take another deep breath. Living in the moment. The air was alive with late autumn. I needed this.

I set off along the street, down to the end where I take the steps to the bottom road. I wait for a gap between the cars and then cross, slip through the gap and then follow the little path down to the car park that nestles at the foot of the hills.

It's filled with the glow of golden leaves.

This is the pale autumn of the north: of birch and ash and hawthorn when the leaves turn yellow, and the colours wash out with the mist. I feel the crunch of leaves underfoot, the shush of them as I wade towards the woods, and I start to relax. I reach the point where the path splits. The dog walkers take the wider branch, but I follow the narrower of the two, the one that seems to vanish and then reappears a few steps later. I make my way through the spaces between the red oaks and sycamores, stepping around the puddles filled with leaves.

The path begins to climb, up through the birch groves, higher and higher, until it reaches the stile that marks the point where you leave the trees and finally step out onto the bare hillside.

There is good walking here in every direction. Along the wide ridge towards Mossley Cross. Up towards the moors. Over to Hartshead Pike and then down onto the plain that leads to Manchester.

But I choose one of the other paths.

And just like that I let go of the world and step into another place.

The path here is far more clearly defined than the ones that had brought me to this point. This path is made of stones pressed into the ground by many feet, a path neatly bordered with larger stones. It takes much less effort to walk now. My feet no longer slip on damp grass or leaves.

The path rises more steeply, and I ascend a set of steps thoughtfully cut into the hillside. Manchester drops quickly away, the city soon becoming an insignificant mark on a widening plane. Looking west, Widnes Power Station stands tall, a gateway to the Sundering Seas. Beyond them lies Atlantis, Númenor and the Western Lands.

The steps became steeper and steeper as I rise higher and higher, and I begin to pass other people, some climbing slowly, and some coming down. All sorts of people. People in strange dress, people that aren't quite human. Many of them ignore me but some of them say good morning or raise a hand in acknowledgement.

Around me the world grows wider and wider. Fantasy lands stretching out to the horizon and beyond.

Finally I reach the summit. There is a tower here, you can climb to the very top and look out but there's little point. When you're so high up, what difference does another ten metres make?

Normally I'd be excited about climbing up there, but today I feel nothing but trepidation. Looking out to the horizon the dark seas are foaming. A distant curtain of rain approaches, small at the moment, but when it arrives it will batter the hillside, turn the grass to mud, send water sluicing down, washing away the earth.

The end of the world is coming.

The call had come the previous week. There was trouble in the other worlds. The council had been summoned.

I sit down on a piece of flat ground, just near the sheer drop on the far side of the hill, and look out to the chessboard lands beyond, waiting.

There was a time when I looked forward to these meetings. Felt a sense of importance. Who wouldn't want to save the world?

But I find myself coming here less and less. It isn't the same anymore.

Federico is the first to arrive, impeccably dressed as always in his black and white suit.

"Ciao!" he says.

"Ciao!" I reply.

He's brought his lute with him. He unstraps it and leans it against the side of the tower, ready for him to play to us later on, whether we like it or not. Federico often claims he could have made it big as a musician if he'd been born into my world back in the 70s, away from the constraints of his society. He would be free to express himself, he always says. Maybe it's true. But then perhaps everyone could have been big if they were born in another world or in another time.

Federico is a pirate. He wears a single gold ring in one ear; he's attractive in a dashing way. Follow his path back down the hill and you come to a little Italianate port full of rounded sailing ships, their hulls seemingly bent by the rigging pulled up tight.

"It has been a long time, my friend," he says sadly.

"It has. But look. Here comes Jani!"

I saw her walking the path towards us, climbing across from the mountains of somewhere rather like India.

Jani is a warrior princess. Still a girl, but she acts like an adult. There are rarely any children in fantasy, save for victims to be saved by the heroes, or preternaturally gifted fourteen year old girls like Jani. Girls who can fight better than any man despite the fact their bodies are still developing and they have barely three years' experience in the battlefield.

Federico bows low before her.

"My lady," he says.

"My lords," she replies, bowing to us both. I nod a greeting.

"But where is the last member of today's group?" she says, looking around.

"Here he comes," says Federico, looking upwards.

As he does so, a shadow passes over us, and a low rumble sounds. A standard silver spaceship is descending towards us, landing legs slowly unfolding. It settles on the hillside, graceful as a dragonfly. A hatch opens and out steps Zak, dressed in his spacesuit.

He removes his helmet and holds it by his side. His right hand is raised in the salute of the Space Defence Force.

"Greetings," he says, and then he shakes his head. "Troubling times."

The others look worried, but I have to admit I feel a little blasé. We've had these meetings so many times before.

"I'll speak first," says Zak. "There's something up at the edge of the Aldebaran system. A runaway event."

And I notice that, instead of the urgent questions that usually spring to mind at times like this, I find myself thinking that Zak lives in a system a long way from Aldebaran, and that space in general is very big, and there is always a runaway event somewhere. There are black holes and stars exploding and gamma bursts. Turn your telescope in any direction and look for long enough and you'd find something to worry about. Zak lives in a module on a very nice orbital system. I've seen the pictures. His home has wide parks full of trees, stores bursting with goods from around the galaxy, everything lit by glowing lamps powered by free energy. He has access to a ship that can take him anywhere in the galaxy. Today it seemed to me that Zak might want to spend a little time there, enjoying what he had. Just for once.

"What about you Jani?" asks Zak, oblivious to my lack of concern.

Jani closes her eyes and pauses. She wants to have our full attention. I know that when she speaks, it will be in a low voice.

"Darkness is coming," she says, eventually. "The dark ones rise again. They bring war and destruction to the southern lands, those who are not killed are enslaved."

And, again for the first time, it occurs to me that this is a princess who sleeps on silk cushions each night. Someone waited on by seventeen handmaidens. Her father rules over a kingdom by virtue of birth and maintains his position by means of a well-equipped army. And I realise that I'm really not in the mood to help him beat the dark forces.

Jani, too, is oblivious to my sudden lack of concern. When she feels she has made her point she turns to Federico.

"And what about you, Federico?" she says, in her quiet voice.

Federico gazes off into the distance, as if looking for a ship on the far horizon.

"Ships sail to the east and they don't return," he says. "Pirates, we suspect."

Federico is a pirate himself, of course, not that he needs to be. He has a beautiful house high on a cliff, overlooking a bright blue harbour. I've sat on the terrace with him many times whilst Rosa, his wife, brought out red wine and olives. Chatting into the evening, looking out over the sea to the setting sun. He has two lovely daughters, Isabella and Lucia. Yet he's always off on another seafaring adventure in search of riches he doesn't need.

"The very Earth is cracking open," says Jani.

"It is," says Federico. "I sailed to the edge of the world and saw the edges breaking away."

"The world is losing focus," says Zak. "I've seen it from above."

It sounded so serious. It always does.

Everything we did was so important, so much more important than our everyday lives. When I was up this mountain that's how things felt.

And yet lately I couldn't help but think that setting off on a journey to save a galaxy was a bit easier than just staying home and raising a family and dealing with life's quotidian but oh so essential events. It was far more glamorous, it could be much better rewarded, but ultimately it amounted to very little.

I've become jaded over the last few months. Climbing the mountain today with its glittering stars and breathtaking vistas isn't as fulfilling as I hoped.

I'm suddenly conscious that down below there are sodden valleys and drains choked with autumn leaves and cracked tarmac that needs repairing. So much less exotic, but it was real. And I could do something about it. On a day like today, my teaching career is far more important than my writing.

I think about Eric then. Only a day or so until the spaceship takes him off planet. How would he spend his last few hours? He'd be off in a pub with his friends. Or more likely he'd be in his kitchen listening to a football match as he cooked a curry for his family, looking forward to sitting down with them that night to eat.

Would he be writing? I doubt it.

He'd still see those other paths and roads, he couldn't help it. But he'd know when it was time to focus on what was real.

I leave Federico and Jani and Zak arguing amongst themselves. I turn and slip away and head back. I know what I need to do.

It's raining when I rejoin the real world. The sort of gentle drizzle that soaks everything without any drama. I'm sodden by the time I get back home.

I come into the hallway, drape my wet coat over the radiator and bend down to untie my boot laces.

"That you, Tony?"

My wife opens the hallway door.

"You're soaking!" she says.

"Rain started right at the very top of the hill," I say. I mean the real hill, the one in our world, not the one she only half guesses is there.

"Would you like a hot drink?"

"Coffee, please."

She heads into the kitchen. My fingers are numb, the laces are knotted. It takes me a while to get them undone.

By the time I get into the kitchen the kettle is steaming. She pours boiling water on the coffee. The smell is delicious. The grounding smell of home.

"Are you going to write this afternoon?" she asks.

"No, I'm going to call Eric."

"What are you going to say?"

"Just that I'll miss him."

ABOUT THE CONTRIBUTORS

Tony Ballantyne is the author of the Dream World, Penrose and Recursion novels, as well as many acclaimed short stories that have appeared in magazines and anthologies around the world. He has been nominated for the BSFA and Philip K Dick awards. His latest book is *Midway*: literature, fantasy and science fiction come together in an original and very personal work.

Chris Beckett is the author of nine novels including *Dark Eden*, which won the Arthur C. Clarke Award in 2012, and three short story collections, the first of which won the Edge Hill Short Story Prize. He lives in Cambridge, and has fond memories of evenings in the Pickerel pub with Eric Brown and other writers, back when Eric lived in the Cambridge area. "The Peaceable Kingdom" has no particular connection with Eric except that Chris thinks he would have approved of it, and might have written it himself.

Keith Brooke is the author of numerous novels and collections, and more than a hundred short stories; his work has been shortlisted for awards including the Philip K Dick Award and the Seiun Award. He collaborated with Eric for more than 30 years. Their short fiction is collected in two volumes, *Parallax View* (2007) and *Hindsights* (forthcoming from PS Publishing), and their novel, *Wormhole*, was published by Angry Robot in 2022. You can find out more about Keith and his work at www.keithbrooke.co.uk.

Jim Burns is an internationally acclaimed science fiction and fantasy artist. His first publishing commission came in 1972 whilst he was still attending St. Martin's School of Art in London. Using both traditional and digital techniques, his artwork has adorned the covers of many hundreds of novels within the wider genre of the 'fantastical'. He also contributed some early pre-production work to the movies *Blade Runner* and *The Riddick Chronicles*. During his long career he has received three Hugo Awards, fourteen BSFA Awards and, in 2014, a Chesley Lifetime Achievement Award. His most recent collection *Hyperluminal* was published by Titan Books in 2014.

Josh Lacey is the author of about forty books for children including *A Dog Called Grk* and *The Pet Potato*. He has also written one book for adults, and worked as a journalist, teacher, and screenwriter. He met Eric in a Greek youth hostel many years ago; Eric's first story had just been accepted by *Interzone*. Their friendship was fuelled by a shared love of books, football, and curry.

Kim Lakin is a British dark fantasy and science fiction author. Kim's novels include the multi-award shortlisted *Cyber Circus* and the steampunk young adult novel, *Autodrome*. Her short stories have appeared in numerous anthologies and magazines and the best of them are gathered in the collection *Sparks Flying* (NewCon Press, 2023). Kim lives on a farm in Derbyshire with her cat, Diablo, and two noisy donkeys.

James Lovegrove has published over 60 books, including the hugely successful Conan Doyle/Lovecraft mashup series *The Cthulhu Casebooks*. His novel *Days* was shortlisted for the Arthur C Clarke Award, while *The Age of Odin*, part of his nine-book Pantheon series, was a *New York Times* bestseller. His short story "Carry the Moon in My Pocket" won the 2011 Seiun Award in Japan for Best Translated Short Story, and his *Firefly: The Ghost Machine* won the 2020 Dragon Award for Best Media Tie-in Novel. His work has been translated into 18 languages. He contributes regular fiction-review columns to the *Financial Times* and lives in Eastbourne.

Una McCormack is a *New York Times* and *USA Today* bestselling science fiction writer who has written more than twenty novels based on TV shows such as *Star Trek, Doctor Who, Blake's 7* and

Firefly. She is on the editorial board of Gold SF, an imprint of Goldsmiths Press aimed at publishing new voices in intersectional feminist science fiction. She is the co-editor, with Regina Yung Lee, of a collection of essays on Lois McMaster Bujold, *Biology and Manners*, published by Liverpool University Press, and is an associate fellow of Homerton College, Cambridge.

Philip Palmer is the author of five science fiction novels published by Orbit: *Debatable Space, Red Claw, Version 43, Hell Ship* and *Artemis;* other novels include *Hell on Earth,* an epic police procedural with demons. He is an experienced screenwriter and radio dramatist, his previous audio drama work ranges from historical to contemporary political to epic literary fantasy (his adaptation of Spenser's *The Faerie Queene),* to crime/thriller *Keeping the Wolf Out,* set in cold war Hungary, which ran for five series. For TV he has written the BBC1 film *The Many Lives of Albert Walker,* and episodes of *Rebus, Heartbeat* and *The Bill.* Feature film credits include *The Ballad of Billy McCrae* (2021), directed by Chris Crow.

Rebecca Rajendra is a short fiction author whose SF and fantasy works have been published by *Interzone*, Newcon Press and Arachne Press amongst others. She is also a podcaster and co-host of the *Time for Cakes and Ale* podcast.

Alastair Reynolds is a former space scientist now living in Wales, who turned from studying pulsars and binary stars to fiction. He is the author of numerous novels, most recently *Machine Vendetta* (Gollancz/Orbit 2024), several novellas and more than seventy short stories. His work has been shortlisted for the Hugo, Arthur C. Clarke, Campbell Memorial, and Sturgeon awards, and it has won the Seiun, Sidewise, European Science Fiction Society and Locus awards. His stories have been adapted for stage and television.

Born in Leeds, **Justina Robson** is a science fiction author renowned for imaginative storytelling and thought-provoking themes. Her work has been shortlisted for both the Arthur C. Clarke and the Campbell Memorial awards. She studied philosophy and linguistics at the University of York, which helped shape her unique perspective on the genre. Her debut novel, *Silver Screen* (1999), garnered critical acclaim for its blend of cyberpunk and fantasy elements, a continuing hallmark in her writing. Since then, her stories have explored themes such as artificial intelligence, virtual reality and the boundaries of human existence. Her most recent book is *Our Savage Heart* (2023) from Newcon Press.

Donna Scott is a Northampton-based writer, stand-up comedian, poet, podcaster and editor, originally from the Black Country. She currently edits the ongoing *Best of British Science Fiction* series for Newcon Press, and is the Director and former Chair of the British Science Fiction Association. Recently she has begun publishing genre books under The Slab Press. Find out more at www.donna-scott.co.uk.

Phillip Vine is the author of two books about football, power and politics: *Visionary: Manchester United, Michael Knighton & the Football Revolution 1989-2019* and *The Immortals: Two Nines & Other Celtic Stories*. His short stories have been published in the USA by Mango and in the UK by Solaris and have won numerous awards and commendations. "The Neglected Bookshop" is his debut for NewCon Press. It is also the first story he has written in the last ten years that has not had the inestimable benefit of Eric Brown's critical input. Eric was simply the best friend and best editor any writer could have had. More information can be found on Phillip's website: www.phillipvine.com.

Raised on Tyneside, **Ian Watson** fled to Oxford as soon as he could win a scholarship. Five years of beer and books led to teaching Lit in East Africa, followed by Tokyo, and finally teaching SF at Birmingham (UK) School of History of Art. His prize-winning first novel, *The Embedding*, led to many more texts short and long, including inventing *Warhammer 40K* fiction. He has screen credit for Spielberg's *A.I. Artificial Intelligence* (2001) after many months' working with Stanley Kubrick. Now living at the seaside in the north of Spain, Ian learned to be wary of Eric's palate after being guided by him to the ghastliest curry ever in a Bradford bomb shelter during one Eastercon. Deep-fried chapathi on newspaper, volcano lava meat. "*Not* bad," Eric declared proudly of the bill. "Twenty quid for fifteen people!"

Ian Whates is the author of ten published novels (two co-written), two novellas, and some eighty short stories which have appeared in a variety of venues, while he has edited forty-odd anthologies. He has been a judge for both the Arthur C. Clarke Award and the World Fantasy Awards. In 2019 he received the Karl Edward Wagner Award from the British Fantasy Society, while his work has been shortlisted for the Philip K. Dick Award and on three occasions for BSFA Awards. In 2006 Ian founded independent publisher NewCon Press by accident, and continues to be bemused by its success.

ALSO FROM NEWCON PRESS

Best of British Science Fiction 2023 – Donna Scott
The annual showcase of British SF, now in its eighth year. Editor Donna Scott has scoured magazines, anthologies, webzines and obscure genre corners to discover the very best science fiction stories by British and British-based authors published during 2023. A thrilling blend of the cutting-edge and the traditional.

A Jura For Julia – Ken MacLeod
The first collection in eighteen years from multiple award-winning science fiction author Ken MacLeod, gathering together a dozen previously published short stories and novelettes along with a new story written specially for this collection. The volume benefits from cover art and internal illustrations by award-winning artist **Fangorn**.

Dark Shepherd – Fred Gambino
Breel is abruptly fired from her dead-end job at the Beach, dismantling junked spaceships – a job she only took to help support her ailing father. She's convinced things can't get any worse; until people start shooting at her. A thrilling and deftly told space opera that will have readers on the edge of their seats and leave them wanting more.

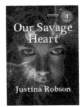

Polestars 4: Our Savage Heart – Justina Robson
The first collection in twelve years from one of the UK's most respected and inventive writers of science fiction and fantasy. 100,000 words of high quality fiction, including the author's finest stories from the past decade alongside a brand new piece written especially for this collection.

On Arcturus VII – Eric Brown
Former pilot and planetary pioneer Jonathan James is tempted out of retirement by an offer he can't refuse. It means going back to the one place he vowed never to return to: Arcturus Seven. A Closed Planet; a hothouse world where every plant and animal is hell-bent on killing and consuming you; the place that cost him the life of the only woman he's ever truly loved.

Marcher – Chris Beckett

Charles Bowen is an immigration officer with a difference: the migrants he deals with aren't from other countries but from other timelines. A powerful novel that draws on the author's experience as a social worker and lecturer. A chilling portrayal of what it means to be 'other' in a re-imagined Britain that's uncomfortably close to our own.

Pelquin's Comet – Ian Whates

In an age of exploration, the crew of the freetrader Pelquin's Comet – a rag-tag group of misfits, ex-soldiers and adventurers – set out to find a cache of alien technology, intent on making their fortunes; but they are not the only interested party and find themselves in a deadly race against corporate agents and hunted by the authorities.

The Greatest Story Ever Told – Una McCormack

Set on a strictly hierarchical Mars, *The Greatest Story Ever Told* is a breathless, stirring tale of bravery, love, passion, and the desire to be free. Iss, a humble kitchen slave, is an ordinary soul caught up in extraordinary events, as she finds herself at the heart of an uprising that threatens to reshape a world.

Rise – Kim Lakin

A potent tale of courage against the odds and the power of hope in the face of racial intolerance. Charged with crimes against the state, Kali Titian – pilot, soldier, and engineer – is sentenced to Erbärmlich prison camp, where she must survive among her fellow inmates the Vary, a race who until recently she was routinely murdering to order.

The Monster, the Mermaid, and Doctor Mengele

After painstaking research, award-winning author **Ian Watson** reveals what happened to Hitler's notorious 'Angel of Death' after the fall of the Third Reich; an episode in which Herr Doktor encounters a monster that even he believed to be mere fiction. A series of events that would eventually lead to his death.

Mementoes – Keith Brooke

A collection of eight novelettes and short stories (two of them original to this volume) from one of the UK's most respected SF authors. "Keith Brooke's prose achieves a rare honesty and clarity, his characters always real people, his situations intriguing and often moving." – *Jeff VanderMeer*

Eric Brown: A Selective Bibliography

Novels
Meridian Days *Pan, 1992*
Engineman *Pan, 1994*
New York Nights *Gollancz, 2000*
New York Blues *Gollancz, 2001*
New York Dreams *Gollancz, 2004*
Bengal Station *Five Star Books, 2004*
Helix *Solaris Books, 2007*
Kéthani *Solaris Books, 2008*
Necropath *Solaris Books, 2009*
Xenopath *Solaris Books, 2009*
Cosmopath *Solaris Books, 2009*
Engineman *Solaris Books, 2009*
Guardians of the Phoenix *Solaris Books, 2010*
The Kings of Eternity *Solaris Books, 2011*
Weird Space: The Devil's Nebula *Abaddon, 2012*
Helix Wars *Solaris Books, 2012*

Novellas
A Writer's Life *PS Publishing 2001*
The Extraordinary Voyage of Jules Verne *PS Publishing, 2005*
Starship Summer *PS Publishing, 2007*
Starship Fall *NewCon Press, 2009*
Starship Winter *PS Publishing, 2012*
Starship Spring *PS Publishing, 2012*
Starship Coda *PS Publishing, 2016*
Sacrifice on Spica III *PS Publishing, 2014*
Exalted on Bellatrix 1 *PS Publishing, 2017*
Telemass Coda *PS Publishing, 2019*
The Martian Simulacra, *NewCon Press, 2018*
Dislocations *PS Publishing, 2018 (with Keith Brooke)*
Parasites *PS Publishing, 2018 (with Keith Brooke)*
Insights *PS Publishing, 2019 (with Keith Brooke)*
On Arcturus VII *NewCon Press, 2021*

Collections
The Time-Lapsed Man and Other Stories *Pan, 1990*
Blue Shifting *Pan, 1995*
The Fall of Tartarus *Gollancz, 2005*
Parallax View *Immanion Press, 2007 (with Keith Brooke)*
Salvage *Infinity Plus Books, 2013*
Strange Visitors, *NewCon Press, 2014*

Milton Keynes UK
Ingram Content Group UK Ltd.
UKHW010800150524
442746UK00006B/238